DEEP-SEA PLUNDERINGS

They met in full career, rolling each over each.

(See page 6.)

DEEP-SEA PLUNDERINGS

BY

FRANK THOMAS BULLEN

With Eight Illustrations

Short Story Index Reprint Series

BOOKS FOR LIBRARIES PRESS
FREEPORT, NEW YORK

First Published 1901
Reprinted 1970

STANDARD BOOK NUMBER:
8369-3288-9

LIBRARY OF CONGRESS CATALOG CARD NUMBER:
75-106251

PRINTED IN THE UNITED STATES OF AMERICA

TO

DR. ROBERTSON NICOLL

A SMALL BUT SINCERE
TRIBUTE OF AFFECTION AND ESTEEM

F. T. B.

PREFATORY NOTE

Warned by previous experience, I do not propose to make any apology for the publication of these stories in book form, but I hope my generous critics will at least pardon me for expressing my gratitude for the way in which they have received all my previous efforts. Naturally, I sincerely hope they will be equally kind in the present instance.

F. T. Bullen.

New Bedford, Mass., *September, 1901.*

CONTENTS

LIST OF ILLUSTRATIONS

DEEP-SEA PLUNDERINGS

THROUGH FIRE AND WATER

"WHAT a clumsy, barrel-bellied old hooker she is, Field!"

Thus, closing his telescope with a bang, the elegant chief officer of the Mirzapore, steel four-masted clipper ship of 5000 tons burden, presently devouring the degrees of longitude that lay between her and Melbourne on the arc of a composite great circle, at the rate of some 360 miles per day. As he spoke he cast his eyes proudly aloft at the splendid spread of square sail that towered upward to a height of nearly 200 feet. Twenty-eight squares of straining canvas, from the courses, stretched along yards 100 feet or so in length, to the far-away skysails of 35 feet head, that might easily be handled by a pair of boys.

Truly she made a gallant show—the graceful ship, that in spite of her enormous size was so perfectly modelled on yacht-like lines that, overshadowed as she was by the mighty pyramid of sail, the eye refused to convey a due sense of her great capacity. And the way in which she answered the challenge of the west wind, leaping lightsomely over the league-long ridges of true-rolling sea, heightened the illusion by destroying all appearance of burden-bearing or cumbrousness. But the vessel which had given rise to Mr. Curzon's contemptuous remark was in truth the antipodes of the Mirzapore. There was scarcely any difference noticeable, as far as the contour of the hull went, between her bow and stern. Only, at the bows a complicated structure of massive timbers leaned far forward of the hull, and was terminated by a huge "fiddle-head." This ornament was carved out of a great balk of timber, and in its general outlines it bore some faint resemblance to a human form, its broad breast lined out with rude carving into some device long ago made illegible by the weather; and at its summit, instead of a head, a piece of scroll-work resembling the top of a fiddle-neck, and giving the whole thing its distinctive name.

The top-hamper of this stubby craft was quite in keeping with her hull. It had none of that rakish, carefully aligned set so characteristic of clipper ships. The three masts, looking as if they were so huddled together that no room was left to swing the yards, had as many kinks in them as a blackthorn stick; and this general trend, in defiance of modern nautical ideas, was forward instead of aft. The bow-sprit and jib-boom looked as if purposely designed by their upward sheer to make her appear shorter than she really was, and also to place her as a connecting link between the long-vanished galleasses of Elizabethan days and the snaky ships of the end of the nineteenth century. In one respect, however, she had the advantage of her graceful neighbour. Her sails were of dazzling whiteness, and when, reflecting the rays of the sun, they glistened against the deep blue sky, the effect was so fairy-like as to make the beholder forget for a moment the ungainliness of the old hull beneath.

The wind now dropped, in one of its wayward moods, until the rapid rush past of the Mirzapore faltered almost to a standstill, and the two vessels, scarcely a mile apart, rolled easily on the following sea, as if in leisurely contemplation of each other. All the Mirzapore's passengers, a hundred and twenty of them, clustered along the starboard poop-rail, unfeignedly glad of this break in what they considered the long monotony of a sailing passage from London to the colonies. And these sea-farers of fifty-five days, eagerly catching their cues from the officers, discussed, in all the hauteur of amateur criticism, the various short-comings of the homely old tub abeam. Gradually the two vessels drew nearer by that mysterious impulse common to idly-floating things. As the different details of the old ship's deck became more clearly definable, the chorus of criticism increased, until one sprightly young thing of about forty, who was going out husband-seeking, said—

"Oh, please, Captain James, *do* tell me what they use a funny ship like that for."

"Well, Miss Williams," he replied gravely, "yonder vessel is one of the fast-disappearing fleet of Yankee whalers—'spouters,' as they love to term themselves. As to her use, if I don't mistake, you will soon have an object-lesson in that which will give you something to talk about all the rest of your life."

And as he spoke an unusual bustle was noticeable on board of the stranger. Four boats dropped from her davits with such rapidity that they seemed to fall into the sea, and as each struck the water she shot away from the side as if she had been a living thing. An involuntary murmur of admiration ran through the crew of the clipper. It was a tribute they could scarcely withhold, knowing as they did the bungling, clumsy way in which a merchant seaman performs a like manœuvre. Even the contemptuous Curzon was hushed; and the passengers, interested beyond measure, yet unable to appreciate what they saw, looked blankly at one another and at the officers as if imploring enlightenment.

With an easy gliding motion, now resting in the long green hollow between two mighty waves, and again poised, bird-like, upon a foaming crest, with bow and stern a-dry, those lovely boats sped away to the southward under the impulse of five oars each. Now the excitement on board the Mirzapore rose to fever-heat. The crew, unheeded, by the officers, gathered on the forecastle-head, and gazed after the departing boats with an intensity of interest far beyond that of the passengers. For it was interest born of intelligent knowledge of the conditions under which those wonderful boatmen were working, and also tempered by a feeling of compunction for the ignorant depreciation they had often manifested of a "greasy spouter." Presently the boats disappeared from ordinary vision, although some of the more adventurous passengers mounted the rigging, and, fixing themselves in secure positions, glued their eyes to their glasses trained upon the vanishing boats. But none of them saw the object of those eager oarsmen. Of course, the sailors knew that they were after whales; but not even a seaman's eye, unless he be long-accustomed to watching for whales, possesses the necessary discernment for picking up a vapoury spout five or six miles away, as it lifts and exhales like a jet of steam against the broken blue surface. Neither could any comprehend the original signals made by the ship. Just a trifling manipulation of an upper sail, the dipping or hoisting of a dark flag at the main-mast head, or the disappearance of another at the gaff-end sufficed to guide the hunters in their chase, giving them the advantage of that lofty eye far behind them.

More than an hour passed thus tantalizingly on board the Mirzapore, and even the most eager watchers had tired of their fruitless gazing over the sea and at the sphinx-like old ship so near them. Then some one suddenly raised a shout, "Here they come!" It was time. They were coming—a-zoonin', as Uncle Remus would say. It was a sight to fire the most sluggish blood. About five hundred yards apart two massive bodies occasionally broke the bright surface up into a welter of white, then disappeared for two or three minutes, to reappear at the same furious rush. Behind each of them, spreading out about twenty fathoms apart, came two of the boats, leaping like dolphins from crest to crest of the big waves, and occasionally hidden altogether by a curtain of spray. Thus they passed the Mirzapore, their gigantic steeds in full view of that awe-stricken ship's company, privileged for once in their lives to see at close quarters one of the most heart-lifting sights under heaven—the Yankee whale-fisher at hand-grips with the mightiest, as well as one of the fiercest, of all created things. No one spoke as that great chase swept by, but every face told eloquently of the pent-up emotion within.

Then a strange thing happened. The two whales, as they passed the Mirzapore, swerved each from his direct course until they met in full career, and in a moment were rolling each over each in a horrible entanglement of whale-line amid a smother of bloody foam. The buoyant craft danced around, one stern figure erect in each bow poising a long slender lance; while in the stern of each boat stood another man, who manipulated a giant oar as if it had been a feather, to swing his craft around as occasion served. The lookers-on scarcely breathed. Was it possible that men—just homely, unkempt figures like these—could dare thrust themselves into such a vortex amongst those wallowing, maddened Titans. Indeed it was. The boats drew nearer, became involved; lances flew, oars bent, and blood—torrents of blood—befouled the glorious azure of the waves. Suddenly the watchers gasped in terror, and little cries of pain and sympathy escaped them: a boat had disappeared. Specks floated, just visible in the tumult—fragments of oars, tubs, and heads of men. But there was no sound, which made the scene all the more impressive.

Still the fight went on, while the spectators forgot all else—the time, the place; all senses merged in wonder at the deeds of these, their fellow-men, just following, in the ordinary way, their avocation. And the thought would come that but for an accident this drama being enacted before their eyes would have had no audience but the screaming sea-birds hovering expectantly in the unheeding blue.

The conflict ceased. The distained waters became placid, and upon them floated quietly two vast corpses, but recently so terrible in their potentialities of destruction. By their sides lay the surviving boats—two of them, that is; the third was busy picking up the wrecked hunters. And the old ship, with an easy adaptation of her needs to the light air that hardly made itself felt, was gradually approaching the scene. The passengers implored Captain James to lower a boat and allow them a nearer view of those recently rushing monsters, and he, very unwillingly, granted the request. So slow was the operation that by the time the port lifeboat was in the water the whaler was alongside of her prizes, and all her crew were toiling slavishly to free them from the entanglement of whale-line in which they had involved themselves. But when the passengers saw how the lifeboat tumbled about alongside in the fast-sinking swell, the number of those eager for a nearer view dwindled to half a dozen—and they were repentant of their rashness when they saw how unhandily the sailors manipulated their oars. However, they persisted for very shame's sake, their respect for the " spouters' " prowess, and, through them, for their previously despised old ship, growing deeper every moment. They hovered about the old tub as they saw the labour that was necessary to get those two enormous carcases alongside, nor dared to go on board until the skipper of her, mounting the rail, said cheerily, "Wunt ye kem aboard, sir, 'n' hev a peek roun'?"

Thus cordially invited, they went, their wonder increasing until all their conceit was effectually taken out of them, especially when they saw the wonderful handiness and cleanliness of everything on board. The men, too, clothed in nondescript patches, with faces and arms almost blackened by exposure, and wearing an air of detachment from the world of civilized life that was full of pathos; these specially appealed to them, and they wished with all their hearts that they might do something to atone for the injustice done to these unblazoned warriors by their thoughtless, ignorant remark of so short a time before.

But time pressed, and they felt in the way besides; so, bidding a humble farewell to the grim-looking skipper, who answered the inquiry as to whether they could supply him with anything by a nonchalant "No, I guess not; we aint a-ben eout o' port hardly six month yet," they returned on board, having learned a corner of that valuable lesson continually being taught: that to judge by appearances is but superficial and dangerous, especially at sea.

Night fell, shutting out from the gaze of those wearied watchers the dumpy outlines of the old whaleship. Her crew were still toiling, a blazing basket of whale-scrap swinging at a davit and making a lurid smear on the gloomy background of the night. One by one the excited passengers sauntered below, still eagerly discussing the stirring events they had witnessed, and making a thousand fantastic additions to the facts. Gradually the conversation dwindled to a close, and the great ship was left to the watch on deck. Fitful airs rose and fell, sharp little breaths of keen-edged wind that but just lifted the huge sails lazily, and let them slat against the masts again as if in disgust at the inadequacy of cat's-paws. So the night wore on, till the middle watch had been in charge about half an hour. Then, with a vengeful hiss, the treacherous wind burst upon them from the north-east, catching that enormous sail-area on the fore side, and defying the efforts of the scanty crew to reduce it. All hands were called, and manfully did they respond; Briton and Finn, German and negro toiled side by side in the almost impossible effort to shorten down, while the huge hull, driven stern foremost, told in unmistakable sea-language of the peril she was in. Hideous was the uproar of snapping, running gear, rending canvas, breaking spars, and howling wind; while through it all, like a thread of human life, ran the wailing minor of the seamen's cries as they strove to do what was required of them.

Slowly, oh, so slowly! the great ship paid off; while the heavier sails boomed out their complaint like an aerial cannonade, when up from the fore-hatch leapt a tongue of quivering flame. Every man who saw it felt a clutch at his heart. For fire at sea is always terrible beyond the power of mere words to describe; but fire under such conditions was calculated to paralyze the energies of the bravest. There seemed to be an actual hush, as if wind and waves were also aghast at this sudden appearance of a fiercer element than they. Then rang out clear and distinct the voice of Captain James—

"Drop everything else, men, and pass along the hose! Smartly, now! 'Way down from aloft!" He was obeyed, but human nature had something to say about the smartness. Men who have been taxing their energies, as these had done, find that even the spur actuated by fear of imminent death will fail to drive the exhausted body beyond a certain point. Moreover, all of them knew that stowed in the square of the main-hatch were fifty tons of gunpowder, which knowledge was of itself sufficient to render flaccid every muscle they possessed. Still, they did what they could, while the stewards went round to prepare the passengers for a hurried departure. All was done quietly. In truth, although the storm was now raging overhead, and the sails were being rent with infernal clamour from the yards, a sense of the far greater danger beneath their feet made the weather but a secondary consideration.

Then out of a cowering group of passengers came a feeble voice. It belonged to the lady querist of the afternoon, and it said, "Oh, if those brave sailors from that wonderful old ship were only near, we might be saved!"

Simple words, yet they sent a thrill of returning hope through those trembling hearts. Poor souls! None of them knew how far the ships might have drifted apart in that wild night, nor thought of the drag upon that old ship by those two tremendous bodies alongside of her. So every eye was strained into the surrounding blackness, as if they could pierce its impenetrable veil and bring back some answering ray of hope. The same idea, of succour from the old whale-ship, had occurred to the captain, and presently that waiting cluster of men and women saw with hungry eyes a bright trail of fire soaring upward as a rocket was discharged. Another and another followed, but without response. The darkness around was like that of the tomb. Another signal, however, now made itself manifest, and a much more effective one. Defying all the puny efforts made to subdue it, the fire in the fore-hatch burst upward with a roar, shedding a crimson glare over the whole surrounding sea, and being wafted away to leeward in a glowing trail of sparks.

"All hands lay aft!" roared the captain, and as they came, he shouted again, "Clear away the boats!"

Then might be seen the effect of that awful neglect of boats so common to merchant ships. Davits rusted in their sockets, falls so swollen as hardly to render over the sheaves, gear missing, water-breakers leaky—all the various disastrous consequences that have given sea-tragedies their grim completeness. But while the almost worn-out crew worked with the energy of despair, there arose from the darkness without the cheery hail of "Ship ahoy!"

Could any one give an idea in cold print of the revulsion of feeling wrought by those two simple words? For one intense moment there was silence. Then from every throat came the joyful response, a note like the breaking of a mighty string overstrained by an outburst of praise.

Naturally, the crew first recovered their balance from the stupefaction of sudden relief, and with coils of rope in their hands they thronged the side, peering out into the dark for a glimpse of their deliverers.

"Hurrah!" And the boatswain hurled the main-brace far out-board at some dim object. A few seconds later there arrived on board a grim figure, quaint of speech as an Elizabethan Englishman, perfectly cool and laconic, as if the service he had come to render was in the nature of a polite morning call.

"Guess you've consid'ble of a muss put up hyar, gents all," said he; and, after a brief pause, "Don't know ez we've enny gre't amount er spare time on han', so ef you've nawthin' else very pressin' t' tend ter, we mout so well see 'bout transhipment, don't ye think?"

He had been addressing no one in particular, but the captain answered him.

"You are right, sir; and thank you with all our hearts! Men, see the ladies and children over-side!"

No one seemed to require telling that this angel of deliverance had arrived from the whale-ship; any other avenue of escape seemed beyond all imagination out of the question. Swiftly yet carefully the helpless ones were handed over-side; with a gentleness most sweet to see those piratical-looking exiles bestowed them in the boat. As soon as she was safely laden, another moved up out of the mirk behind and took her place. And it was done so cannily. No roaring, agitation, or confusion, as the glorious work proceeded. It was the very acme of good boatmanship. The light grew apace, and upon the tall tongues of flame, in all gorgeous hues that now cleft the night, huge masses of yellow smoke rolled far to leeward, making up a truly infernal picture.

Meanwhile, at the earliest opportunity, Captain James had called the first-comer (chief mate of the whaler) apart, and quietly informed him of the true state of affairs. The "down-easter" received this appalling news with the same taciturnity that he had already manifested, merely remarking as he shifted his chaw into a more comfortable position—

"Wall, cap', ef she lets go 'fore we've all gut clear, some ov us 'll take th' short cut t' glory, anyhaow."

But, for all his apparent nonchalance, he had kept a wary eye upon the work a-doing, to see that no moment was wasted.

And so it came to pass that the last of the crew gained the boats, and there remained on board the Mirzapore but Captain James and his American deliverer. According to immemorial precedent, the Englishman expressed his intention of being last on board. And upon his inviting his friend to get into the waiting boat straining at her painter astern, the latter said—

"Sir, I 'low no dog-goned matter ov etiquette t' spile my work, 'n' I must say t' I don' quite like th' idee ov leavin' yew behine; so ef yew'll excuse me——"

And with a movement sudden and lithe as a leopard's he had seized the astonished captain and dropped him over the taff-rail into the boat as she rose upon a sea-crest. Before the indignant Englishman had quite realized what had befallen him, his assailant was standing by his side manipulating the steer-oar and shouting—

" Naow then, m' sons, pull two, starn three; so, altogether. Up with her, lift her, m' hearties, lift her, 'r by th' gre't bull whale it'll be a job spiled after all."

And those silent men did indeed " give way." The long supple blades of their oars flashed crimson in the awful glare behind, as the heavily-laden but still buoyant craft climbed the watery hills or plunged into the hissing valleys. Suddenly there was one deep voice that rent the heavens. The whole expanse of the sky was lit up by crimson flame, in the midst of which hurtled fragments of that once magnificent ship. The sea rose in heaps, so that all the boatmen's skill was needed to keep their craft from being overwhelmed. But the danger passed, and they reached the ship—the humble, clumsy old " spouter " that had proved to them a veritable ark of safety in time of their utmost need.

Captain James had barely recovered his outraged dignity when he was met by a quaint figure advancing out of the thickly-packed crowd on the whaler's quarter-deck. " I'm Cap'n Fish, at yew're service, sir. We haint over 'n' above spacious in eour 'commodation, but yew're all welcome t' the best we hev'; 'n'

I'll try 'n' beat up f'r th' Cape 'n' lan' ye's quick 's it kin be did."

The Englishman had hardly voice to reply; but, recollecting himself, he said, " I'm afraid, Captain Fish, that we shall be sadly in your way for dealing with those whales we saw you secure yesterday."

" Not much yew wunt," was the unexpected reply. " We hed t' make eour ch'ice mighty sudden between them fish 'n' yew, 'n', of course, though we're noways extravagant, they hed t' go."

The simple nobility of that homely man, in thus for self and crew passing over the loss of from eight to ten thousand dollars at the first call from his kind, was almost too much for Captain James, who answered unsteadily—

" If I have any voice in the matter, there will be no possibility of the men, who dared the terrors of fire and sea to save me and my charges, being heavily fined for their humanity."

" Oh, *thet's* all right," said Captain Silas Fish.

THE OLD HOUSE ON THE HILL

CHAPTER I

THERE is something in the stress and struggle of tumultuous life in a vast city like London that to me is almost unbearable. Accustomed from a very early age to the illimitable peace of the ocean, to the untainted air of its changeless circle of waves and roofless dome of sky, I have never been able to endure satisfactorily the unceasing roar of traffic in crowded streets, the relentless rush of mankind in the race for life which is the normal condition of our great centres of civilization. Yet, for many years, being condemned by circumstances to abide in the midst of urban strife and noise without a break from one weary year to another, I lived to mourn departed peace, and feed my longing for it on memory alone, without a hope that its enjoyments would ever again be mine. Then came unexpected relief, an opportunity to visit a secluded corner of Wiltshire, that inland division of England which is richer, perhaps, in memorials of our wonderful history than any other part of these little islands, crowded as they are with reminiscences of bygone glorious days.

I took up my quarters in a hamlet on the banks of

the Wylye, a delightful little river, taking its rise near the Somersetshire border, and wandering with innumerable windings through the heart of Wiltshire, associating itself with the Bourne and the Nadder, until at Salisbury it is lost in that most puzzling of all streams, the Avon. I said puzzling, for I believe there are but a handful of people out of the great host to whom the Avon is one of the best-known streams in the world from its associations, who know that there is one Avon feeding the Severn near Tewkesbury, which is Shakespeare's Avon; there is another, upon which Bristol has founded her prosperity, and there is yet another, the Avon of my first mention, which, accumulated from numberless rivulets in the Vale of Pewsey, floweth through Salisbury, and loses itself finally in the waters of the English Channel at Christchurch in Hampshire. But I must ask forgiveness for allowing the wily Avon to lure me away thus far.

One of the chief charms of Wiltshire is its rolling downs rising upon either side of the valley, which in the course of ages the busy little Wylye has scooped out between them in gentle undulations, a short, sweet herbage for the most part covering their masses of solid chalk, coming to within a foot or two of those emerald surfaces. This is the place to come and ponder over the rubbish that is talked about the overcrowding of England. Here you shall wander for a whole day if you will, neither meeting or seeing a human being unless you follow the road that winds through the Deverills, five villages of the valley, all, alas, in swift process of decay. Even there the simple folk will stare long and earnestly at a stranger as he passes, before turning to resume their leisurely tasks, the uneventful, slumberous round of English village life. To me it was idyllic. A great peace came over me, and I felt that it was a sinful waste of nature to shut myself within four walls even at night. Long after the thirty souls peopling our hamlet had gone to bed I would sit out on the hillside behind the cottage, steeping my heart in the warm silence, only manifested —not broken—by the queer wailing cry of an uneasy plover as it fluttered overhead. And when, reluctantly, I did go to bed, I was careful to prop the windows wide open, even though I was occasionally awakened by the soft "flip-flip" of bats flying across my chamber, dazzled by the small light of my reading lamp.

The grey of the dawn, no matter how few had been my hours of sleep, never failed to awaken me, and, hurrying through my bath and dressing, I gat me out into the sweet breath of morning twilight while Nature was taking her beauty sleep and the dewdrops were waiting to welcome with their myriad smiles the first peep of the sun. And so it came to pass that one morning, just as the eastern horizon was being flooded with a marvellous series of colour-blends in mysterious and ever-changing sequence, that I mounted the swell of the down opposite to the village of Brixton Deverill, with every sense quickened to fullest appreciation of the lovely scene. Hosts of rabbits, quaint wee bunches of grey fur, each with a white blaze in the centre, scuttled from beneath my feet, and every little while, their curiosity overpowering natural fear, sat up with long ears erect and big black eyes devouring the uncouth intruder on their happy feeding grounds. Great flocks of partridges, almost as tame as domestic fowls (for it was July), ran merrily in and out among the furze clumps, or rose with a noisy whir of many wings when I came too close; aristocratic cock pheasants strolled by superciliously with a sidelong glance to see that the erect biped carried no gun, and an occasional lark gyrated to the swell of his own heart-lifting song as he rose in successive leaps to his proper sphere. I felt like singing myself, but Nature's music was too sweet to be disturbed by my quavering voice, so I climbed on, all eyes and ears, and nerves a-tingle with receptivity of keenest enjoyment. Reaching the summit, I paused and surveyed the peaceful scene. Far to the left lay Longleat, its dense woods shimmering in a blue haze; to the right, Heytesbury Wood, in sombre shadow; and behind, the forest-like ridge of Chicklade. But near me, just peeping over the bare crest of an adjoining down, were the tops of a clump of firs, and, curious to know what that coppice might contain (I always have had a desire to explore the recesses of a lonely clump of trees), I turned my steps towards it, only stopping at short intervals to admire the gracefulness of the purple, blue, and yellow wild flowers with which the short, fine rabbit-grass was profusely besprent. Meanwhile the sun appeared in cloudless splendour, his powerful rays dissipating the spring-like freshness of the morning and promising a most sultry day. Yet as I drew nearer the dark fastness of the coppice I felt a chill, an actual physical sensation of cold. At the same time there arose within me a positive repugnance to draw any closer to that deep shade. This unaccountable change only made me angry with myself for being capable of feeling such a nonsensical, unexplainable hindrance to my purpose. So I took hold of it with both hands, and cast it from me, striding onward with quickened step until I really seemed to be breasting a strong tide. Panting with the intensity of my inward struggle, I reached the shadow cast by that solemn clump of pines, and saw the pale outlines of a wall in their midst. Now curiosity became paramount, and, actually shivering with cold, I pressed on until I stood in front of a fairly large house, surrounded by a flint wall on all sides, but at some yards distance from it. Through large holes in the encircling wall the wood-folk scampered or fluttered merrily but noiselessly; rabbits, hares, squirrels, and birds, and as I drew nearer there was a sudden whiff of strong animal scent, and a long red body launched itself through one of the openings, flitting past me like a flash of red-brown light. Although I had never seen an English fox before on his native heath, I recognized him from his pictures, and forgave him for startling me. Skirting the wall, I came to a huge gap with crumbling sides, where once had been a gate, I suppose. It commanded a view of the front of the house, which I now saw was a mere shell, its walls perforated in many places by the busy rabbits, which swarmed in and out like bees upon a hive. No windows remained, but the front door was fast closed and barred by a thick trunk of ivy, which had once overspread the whole building, but was now quite in keeping with it, for it was dead. The space between the wall and the house was thickly overgrown with nettles to nearly the height of a man, but there was no sign of any useful plant, and even the roof of the building, which was of red tiles and intact, had none of that kindly covering of house-leek, stone-crop, and moss, which always decks such spaces with beauty in the country. Upon a sudden impulse I turned, and behind me I saw with a shudder that only a few feet from where I stood there was a sheer descent of some thirty feet, a veritable pit some ten yards wide, but with its farther margin only a few feet high. Tall trees sprang from its bottom and sides, their roots surrounding a pool of black-looking water that seemed a receptacle for all manner of hideous mysteries. Involuntarily I shrank into myself, and looked up for a glint of blue sunlit sky, but it was like being in a vault, dark and dank and cold. Still, the idea never entered my head to get out until I had seen all that might be there to be seen, although I confess to comforting myself, as I have often done on a dull and gloomy day, with the reminder that just outside the sun was shining steadily.

Turning away from that grim-looking pit, I thrust myself through the savage nettle-bed, my hands held high so that I could guard my face with my arms, until I reached the first opening in the house wall that offered admission. With just one moment's hesitation I stepped within, and stood on the decayed floor of what had once been the best room. And then

I had need of all my disbelief in ghosts, for around me and beneath me and above were a congeries of all the queer noises one could conjure up. Soft pattering of feet, hollow murmurings as of voices, the indefinite sound of brushing past that always makes one turn sharply to see who is near. I found my mouth getting dry and my hands burning, in spite of the chill that still clung to me; but still I went on and explored every room in the eerie place, noting a colony of bats that huddled together among the bare roof-beams, prying into the numerous cavities in floors and walls made by the rabbits and the rats, but seeing nothing worthy of note until I reached a sort of cellar which looked as if it had been used as a bakehouse. Upon stepping down the decrepit ladder which led to it, I startled a great colony of rats, that fled in all directions with shrill notes of affright, hardly more scared than myself. The place was so dark that I thankfully remembered my box of wax matches, and, twisting two or three torches out of a newspaper I found in my jacket pocket, I soon had a good light.

It revealed a cavity in the floor just in front of a huge baker's oven, into the dim recesses of which I peered, finding that it extended for some distance on either side of the opening. Lighting another torch, I jumped down and found—three oblong boxes of rude construction, and across them the mouldering frame of what had once been a man. At last I had seen enough, and with something tap-tapping inside my head, I scrambled hastily out of the hole, my body shaking as if with ague, and my lungs aching for air. I looked neither to the right nor the left as I went, nor paused, regardless of the nettle grove, until I emerged upon the bright hilltop, where I flung myself down and drank in great gulps of sweet air until my tremors passed away and the tumult of my mind became appeased.

Without casting another look back at that lonely place, or attempting to speculate upon what I had seen, I departed for home, and, after a hasty breakfast, sought out a friend in the next village, Longbridge Deverill, who had already given me many pleasant hours by retailing scraps of local history reaching back for hundreds of years. I found him in his pretty garden enjoying the bright day, with a look of deep content upon his worn old face—the afterglow of a well-spent life. Staying his rising to greet me, I flung myself down on the springy turf by his side, and almost without a word of preface, gave him a hurried account of my morning's adventure. He listened in grave silence until I had finished, and then began as follows.

CHAPTER II

It is certainly a strange coincidence that you should stumble across that sombre place, because, after what you told me the other day about your family connection with this part of the country, I have no doubt whatever that the unhappy tenants of Pertwood Farm (as it is called even now) were nearly related to yourself. Their tragical story is well known to me, although its principal events happened more than sixty years ago, when I was a boy. The house had been built and enclosed, and the trees planted, by a morose old man who wished to shut himself off from the world, yet was by no means averse to a good deal of creature comfort. He lived in it for some years, attended only by one hard-featured man, who did apparently men and women's work equally well—lived there until local rumour had grown tired of inventing fables about him, and left him to the oblivion he desired. Then one day the news began to circulate that Pertwood had changed hands, that old Cusack was gone, and that a middle-aged man with a beautiful young wife had taken up his abode there, without any one in the vicinity knowing aught of the change until it had been made. Then the village tongues wagged loosely for awhile, especially when it was found that the new-comers were almost as reserved as old Cusack had been. But as time went on Mr. Delambre, whose Huguenot name stamped him as most probably a native of these parts (you have noticed how very frequent such names are hereabout), leased several good-sized fields lower down the hill towards Chicklade, and began to do a little farming. This, of course, necessitated his employing labour, and consequently, by slow degrees, scraps of personalia about him filtered through the sluggish tongues of the men who worked for him. Thus we learned that his wife (your grandmother's sister, my boy) was rarely beautiful, though pale and silent as a ghost. That her husband loved her tigerishly, could not bear that any other eyes should see her but his, and it was believed that his fierce watchful jealousy of her being even looked upon was fretting her to death. Quite a flutter of excitement pervaded the village here not long after the above details became public property, by one of the labourers from Pertwood coming galloping in on a plough-horse for old Mary Hoddinot, who had nursed at least two generations of neighbours in their earliest days. She was whisked off in the baker's cart, but the news remained behind that twin boys had arrived at Pert'ood, as it was locally called, and that Delambre was almost frantic with anxiety about his idol. The veil thus hastily lifted dropped again, and only driblets of news came at long intervals. We heard that old Mary was in permanent residence, that the boys were thriving sturdily, and that the mother was fairer than ever and certainly happier. So things jogged along for a couple of years, until an occasional word came deviously from Pertwood to the effect that the miserable Delambre was now jealous of his infant boys. Self-tortured, he was making his wife a living martyr, and such was his wild-beast temper that none dare interfere. At last the climax was put upon our scanty scraps of intelligence by the appearance in our midst of old Mary, pale, thin, and trembling. It was some time before we could gather her dread story, she was so sadly shaken; but by degrees we learned that after a day in which Delambre seemed to be perfectly devil-possessed, alternately raging at and caressing his wife, venting savage threats against the innocent babes "who were stealing all her affection away from him," he had gone down the hill to see after enfolding some sheep. He was barely out of sight before his wife, turning to old Mary, said, " Please put your arms round me, I feel *so* tired." Mary complied, drawing the fair, weary head down upon her faithful old bosom, where it remained until a chill struck through her bodice. Alarmed, she looked down and saw that her mistress was resting indeed.

Although terrified almost beyond measure, the poor old creature retained sufficient presence of mind to release herself from the dead arms, rush to the door, and scream for her employer. He was returning, when her cries hastened his steps, and, breaking into a run, he burst into the room and saw! He stood stonily for a minute, then, turning to the trembling old woman, shouted " go away." Not daring to disobey, she hurried off, and here she was. After much discussion, my father and the village doctor decided to go to Pertwood and see if anything could be done. But their errand was in vain. Delambre met them at the door, telling them that he did not need, nor would he receive, any help or sympathy. What he did require was to be left alone. And slamming the door in his visitors' faces, he disappeared. Even this grim happening died out of men's daily talk as the quiet days rolled by, and nothing more occurred to arouse interest. We heard that the boys were well, and were often seen tumbling about the grass-plot before the house door by the farm labourers. Rumour said many things concerning the widower's disposal of his dead. But no one knew anything for certain, except that her body had never been seen again by any eye outside the little family. Delambre himself seemed changed for the better, less harsh and morose, although as secretive as ever. He was apparently devoted to his two boys, who throve amazingly. As they grew up he and they were inseparable. He educated them, played with them, made their welfare his one object in life. And they returned his care with the closest affection, in fact the trio seemed never contented apart. Yet they never came near the village, nor mixed with the neighbours in any way.

In this quiet neighbourhood the years slip swiftly by as does the current past an anchored ship, and as unnoticeably. The youthful Delambres grew and waxed strong enough to render unnecessary the employment of any other labour on the farm than their own, and in consequence it was only at rare intervals that any news of them reached us in roundabout fashion through Warminster, where old Delambre was wont to go once a week on business. So closely had they held aloof from all of us that when one bitter winter night a tall swarthy young man came furiously knocking at the doctor's door, he was as completely unknown to the worthy old man as any new arrival from a foreign land. The visitor, however, lost no time in introducing himself as George Delambre, and urgently requested the doctor to accompany him at once to Pertwood on a matter of life and death. In a few minutes the pair set off through the heavy snow-drifts, and, after a struggle that tried the old doctor terribly, arrived at the house to find that the patient was mending fast.

A young woman of about eighteen, only able to mutter a few words of French, had been found huddled up under the wall of the house by George as he was returning from a visit to the sheepfold. She was fairly well dressed in foreign clothing, but at almost the last gasp from privation and cold. How she came there she never knew. The last thing that she remembered was coming to Hindon, by so many ways that her money was all spent, in order to find a relative, she having been left an orphan. Failing in her search, she had wandered out upon the downs, and the rest was a blank.

In spite of convention she remained at Pertwood, making the dull place brighter than it had ever been. But of course both brothers fell in love with the first woman they had ever really known. And she, being thus almost compelled to make her choice, with all a woman's inexplicable perversity, promised to marry dark saturnine George, although her previous behaviour towards him had been timid and shrinking, as if she feared him. To the rejected brother, fair Charles, she had always been most affectionate, so much so, indeed, that he was perfectly justified in looking upon her as his future wife, to be had for the asking. This cruel blow to his almost certain hopes completely stunned him for a time, until his brother with grave and sympathetic words essayed to comfort him. This broke the spell that had bound him, and in a perfect fury of anger he warned his brother that he looked upon him as his deadliest enemy, that the world was hardly wide enough for them both; but, for his part, he would not, if he could help it, add another tragedy to their already gloomy home, and to that end he would flee. Straightway he rushed and sought his father, and, without any warning, demanded his portion. At first the grim old man stared at him blankly, for his manner was new as his words were rough; then, rising from his chair, the old man bade him be gone—not one penny would he give him; he might go and starve for ought he cared.

"Very well," said Charles, "then I go into the village and get advice as to how I shall proceed against you for the wages I have earned since I began to work. And you'll cut a fine figure at the Warminster Court."

The threat was efficient. With a face like ashes and trembling hands the father opened his desk and gave him fifty guineas, telling him that it was half of his total savings, and with an evidently severe struggle to curb his furious temper, asked him to hurry his departure. Since he had robbed him, the sooner he was gone the better. The young man turned and went without another word.

That same night old Delambre died suddenly and alone. And Louise, instead of clinging to her promised husband, came down to the village, where the doctor gave her shelter. The unhappy George, thus cruelly deserted, neglected everything, oscillating between the village and his lonely home. The inquest showed that the old man had died of heart disease;

and George then, to every one's amazement, announced his intention of carrying out his father's oft-repeated wish, and burying him beneath the house by the side of his wife.

CHAPTER III

AND now we must needs leave Pertwood Farm and its doubly bereaved occupant for a while, in order to follow the fortunes of the self-exiled Charles. His was indeed a curious start in life. Absolutely ignorant of the world, his whole horizon at the age of twenty years bounded by that little patch of lonely Wiltshire down, and his knowledge of mankind confined to, at the most, half a dozen people. He had great native talent, which, added to an ability to keep his own counsel, was doubtless of good service to him in this breaking away into the unknown. His total stock of money amounted to less than £50, to him an enormous sum, the greater because he had never yet known the value of money. His native shrewdness, however, led him to husband it in miserly fashion, as being the one faithful friend upon which he could always rely.

And now the salt strain in his mother's blood must have asserted itself unmistakably, if mysteriously, for straight as a homing bee he made his way down to the sea, finding himself a week after his flight at Poole. I shall never forget the look upon his face as he told me how he first felt when the sea revealed itself to him. All his unsatisfied longings, all the heart-wrench of his rejected love, were forgotten in present unutterable delight. He was both hungry and weary, yet he sat contentedly down upon the verge of the cliffs and gazed upon this glorious vision until his eyes glazed with fatigue, and his body was numbed with the immovable restraint of his attitude. At last he tore himself away, and entered the town, seeking a humble lodging-place, and finding one exactly suited to his needs in a little country public-house on the outskirts of the town, kept by an apple-cheeked dame, whose son was master of a brigantine then lying in the harbour. She gave the handsome youth a motherly welcome, none the less warm because he appeared to be well able to pay his way.

Against the impregnable fortress of his reserve she failed to make any progress whatever, although in the attempt to gratify her curiosity she exerted every simple art known to her. On the other hand he learned many things, for one of her chief wiles was an open confidence in him, an unreserved pouring out to him of all she knew. He was chiefly interested in her stories of her son. Naturally she was proud of that big swarthy seaman, who, when he arrived home that evening, loomed so large in the doorway that he appeared to dwarf the whole building. As Englishmen will, the two men eyed one another suspiciously at first, until the ice having been broken by the fond mother, Charles in his turn began to pump his new acquaintance. Captain Jacks, delighted beyond measure to find a virgin mind upon which to sow his somewhat threadbare stock of yarns, was gratified beyond measure, and thenceforward until long after the usual hour for bed, the young man was simply soaking up like a sponge in the rain such a store of wonders as he had never before even dreamed of. At last the old dame, somewhat huffed by the way in which Charles had turned from her garrulity to her son's, ordered them both to bed. But Charles could not sleep. How was it possible? The quiet monotone of his life had been suddenly lifted into a veritable Wagner concert of strange harmonies, wherein joy and grief, pleasure and pain, love and hate, strove for predominance, and refused to be hushed to rest even by the needs of his healthful weariness.

Out of it all one resolve arose towering. He would, he must go to sea. That alone could be the career for him. But he would write to Louise. Knowing nothing of her flight from the old home or of his father's death, he felt that he must endeavour to assert a claim to her, more just and defensible than his brother's, even though she had rejected him. And then, soothed by his definite settlement of future action, he fell asleep, nor woke again until roused by his indignant landlady's inquiry as to whether "'ee wor gwain t' lie abed arl daay." Springing out of bed, he made his simple toilet in haste, coming down so speedily that the good old dame was quite mollified. A hasty breakfast ensued, and a hurried departure for the harbour in search of Captain Jacks' brigantine. Finding her after a short search, he was warmly welcomed by the gallant skipper, and, to his unbounded delight, succeeded in inducing that worthy man to take him as an extra hand without pay on his forthcoming voyage to Newfoundland. Then returning to his lodging, he made his small preparations, and after much anxious thought, produced the following letter, which he addressed to Louise, care of the old doctor at Longbridge.

"My Dearest Loo,

"Though you chose George instead of me I don't mean to give you up. I mean to do something big, looking forward to you for a prize. I believe you love me better than you do George in spite of what you did. You will never marry him, never. You'll marry me, because you love me, and I won't let you go. I know you'll get this letter, and send me an answer to Mrs. Jacks, Apple Row, Poole. And you'll wait for my reply, which may be late a coming, but will be sure to come.

"Yours till death,

"Charles Delambre."

A few minutes afterwards he was on his way down to the Mary Jane, Captain Jacks' brigantine. He was received with the gravity befitting a skipper on shipping a new hand, and after bestowing his few purchases in a cubby-hole in the tiny cabin, returned on deck in his shirt-sleeves, to take part in whatever work was going on, with all the ardour of a new recruit. Next morning at daylight the Mary Jane departed. Under the brilliant sky of June the dainty little vessel glided out into the Channel, bounding forward before the fresh north-easterly breeze, as if rejoicing to be at home once more, and freed from the restraint of mooring chains and the stagnant environment of a sheltered harbour.

Charles took to his new life wonderfully, feeling no qualms of sea-sickness, and throwing himself into every detail of the work with such ardour that by the time they had been out a week he was quite a useful member of the ship's company. And then there arrived that phenomenon, a June gale from the northwest. Shorn of all her white wings but one, the little brigantine lay snugly enough, fore-reaching against the mighty Atlantic rollers that hurled themselves upon her like mountain ranges endowed with swiftest motion. So she lay throughout one long day and far into the night succeeding, until just at that dread hour of midnight when watchfulness so often succumbs to weariness at sea, a huge comber came tumbling aboard as she fell off into the trough of the sea. For a while she seemed to be in doubt whether to shake herself clear of the foaming mass, and then splendidly lifting herself with her sudden burden of a deck filled with water, she resumed her gallant struggle. Just then it was discovered that her lights were gone. Before they could be replaced, out of the darkness came flying an awful shape, vast, swift, and merciless. One of the splendid Yankee fliers of those days, the Columbia, of over a thousand tons register, was speeding eastward under every stitch of sail, at a rate far surpassing that of any but the swiftest steamships. A good look out was being kept on board of her, for those vessels were noted for the excellence of their discipline and careful attention to duty. But the night was pitchy dark, the Mary Jane had no light visible, and before anything could be done her doomed crew saw the Columbia's bow towering over their vessel's waist like some unthinkable demon of destruction. Up, up, up, she soared above them, then descending, her gleaming bow shone clean through the centre of the Mary Jane's hull, tearing with it the top-hamper of masts and rigging, and rushing straight through the wreckage without a perceptible check. One wild cry of despair and all was silent. Over the side of the Columbia peered a row of white faces gazing fearfully into the gloom, but there was nothing to be seen. The sea had claimed her toll.

As usual, after such a calamity, there was a hushed performance of tasks, until suddenly one of the crew shouted, "Why, here's a stranger." And there was. Charles had clutched instinctively at one of the martingale guys as the Columbia swept over her victim, and had succeeded in climbing from thence on board out of the vortex of death in which all his late shipmates had been involved. Plied with eager questions, his simple story was soon told, and he was enrolled among the crew. The Columbia was bound to Genoa, a detail that troubled him but little; so long as he was at sea he had no desire to select his destination. But he found here a very different state of things obtaining. The crew were a hard-bitten, motley lot, prime seamen mostly, but "packet rats" to a man, wastrels without a thought in life but how soon they might get from one drinking-bout to another, and at sea only kept from mutiny, and, indeed, crime of all kinds, by the iron discipline imposed upon them by the stern-faced, sinewy Americans who formed the afterguard. There were no soft, sleepy-voiced orders given here. Every command issued by an officer came like the bellowing of an angry bull, and if the man or men addressed did not leap like cats to execute it, a blow emphasized the fierce oath that followed.

Charles now learned what work was. No languid crawling through duties with one ear ever cocked for the sound of the releasing bell, but a rabid rush at all tasks, even the simplest, as if upon its immediate performance hung issues of life or death. "Well fed, well driven, well paid," was the motto on board those ships, albeit there were not wanting scoundrelly skippers and officers, who, in ports where fresh hands were to be obtained cheaply, were not above using the men so abominably that they would desert and leave all their cruelly-earned wages behind. Strangely enough, however, Charles became a prime favourite. This son of the soil, who might have been expected to move in clod-hopper fashion, developed an amazing smartness which, allied to a keenness of appreciation quite American in its rapidity, endeared him specially to the officers. In the roaring fo'c's'le among his half-savage shipmates he commanded respect, for in some mysterious way he evolved masterly fighting qualities and dogged staying powers that gave him victory in several bloody battles. So that it came to pass, when Genoa was reached, that Charles was one day called aft and informed that, if he cared to, he might shift his quarters aft and go into training for an officer, holding a sort of brevet rank as supernumerary third mate. He accepted, and was transferred, much to the disgust of his shipmates forward, who looked upon his move aft as a sort of desertion to the enemy. But they knew Charles too well to proceed further with their enmity than cursing him among themselves, so that as much peace as usual was kept.

From this port Charles wrote lengthily to Louise at Longbridge as before, and to Poole to Mrs. Jacks, breaking her great misfortune to her, and begging her to write to him and send him at New York any letters that might have arrived for him. And then he turned contentedly to his work again, allowing it to engross every thought. He was no mere dreamer of dreams, this young man. In his mind there was a solid settled conviction that, sooner or later (and it did not greatly matter which), he would attain the object of his desires. This granitic foundation of faith in his future saved him all mental trouble, and enabled him to devote all his energies to the work in hand, to the great satisfaction of his skipper. Captain Lothrop, indeed, looked upon this young Englishman with no ordinary favour. A typical American himself, of the best school, he concealed under a languid demeanour energy as of an unloosed whirlwind. His face was long, oval, and olive-brown, with black silky beard and moustache trimmed like one of Velasquez's cavaliers, and black eyes that, usually expressionless as balls of black marble, would, upon occasion given, dart rays of terrible fire. Contrasted with this saturnine stately personage, the fair, ruddy Charles looked like some innocent schoolboy, the open, confiding air he bore being most deceptive. He picked up seamanship, too, in marvellous fashion, the sailorizing that counts, by virtue of which a seaman handles a thousand-ton ship as if she were a toy and every one of her crew but an incarnation of his will. But this very ability of his before long aroused a spirit of envy in his two brother officers that would have been paralyzing to a weaker man. Here, again, the masterly discipline of the American merchantman came to his aid, a discipline that does not know of such hideous folly as allowing jealousy between officers being paraded before the crew, so that they with native shrewdness may take advantage of the house divided against itself. When in an American ship one sees a skipper openly deriding an officer, be sure that officer's days as an officer are numbered; he is about to be reduced to the ranks. So, in spite of a growing hatred to the —— Britisher, the two senior mates allowed no sign of their feelings to be manifested before the crew. Perhaps the old man was a bit injudicious also. He would yarn with Charles by the hour about the old farm and the sober, uneventful routine of English rural life, the recital of these placid stories evidently giving him the purest pleasure by sheer contrast with his own stormy career.

In due time the stay of the Columbia at Genoa came to an end, and backward she sailed for New York. In masterly fashion she was manœuvred out through the Gut of Gibraltar, and sped with increased rapidity into the broad Atlantic. But it was now nearly winter, and soon the demon of the west wind made his power felt. The gale settled down steadily to blow for weeks apparently, and with dogged perseverance the Columbia's crew fought against it. Hail, snow, and ice scourged them, canvas became like planks, ropes as bars of iron. Around the bows arose masses of ice like a rampart, and from the break of the forecastle hung icicles which grew like mushrooms in a few hours of night. The miserable crew were worn to the bone with fatigue and cold, and had they been fed as British crews of such ships are fed they would doubtless have all died. But, in spite of their sufferings, they worked on until one night, having to make all possible sail to a " slant " of wind, they were all on deck together at eight bells—midnight. With the usual celerity practised in these ships, the snowy breadths of canvas were rising one above the other, and the Columbia was being flung forward in lively fashion over the still heavy waves, when Charles, who was standing right forward on the forecastle, shouted in a voice that could be heard distinctly above the roar of the wind and sea and the cries of the seamen, " Hard down! " Mechanically the helmsman obeyed, hardly knowing whither the summons came, and the beautiful vessel swung up into the wind, catching all her sails aback, and grinding her way past some frightful obstruction to leeward that looked as if an abyss of darkness had suddenly yawned in the middle of the sea, along the rim of which the Columbia was cringing. The tremendous voice of Captain Lothrop boomed out through the darkness, " What d'ye see,

Mister Delamber, forrard there?" "We've struck a derelict, sir," roared Charles, and his words sounded in the ears of the ship's company like the summons of doom. The ship faltered in her swing to windward, refused to obey her helm, and swung off the wind again slowly but surely, as if being dragged down into unknown depths by an invisible hand whose grip was like that of death.

CHAPTER IV

In this hour of paralyzing uncertainty Charles rose to the full height of his manhood. Passing the word for a lantern, and slinging himself in a bowline, he ventured into the blackness alongside, and presently reappeared with the cheering news that no damage was done. A few strokes of an axe and they would be set free. And arming himself with a broad axe, he again disappeared into the outer dark, this time under the watchful eye of the skipper, and presently, with a movement which was like a throb of returning life to every soul on board, the Columbia regained her freedom. Charles was hauled on board through the surf alongside like a sodden bundle of clothing, unhurt, but entirely exhausted, having made good his claim to be regarded as one of the world's silent heroes, a man who to the call of duty returns no dubious answer, but renders swift obedience.

This last adventure seemed to exhaust the Columbia's budget of ill-luck for the voyage. Although the wind was never quite fair, it allowed them to work gradually over to the westward, and with its change a little more genial weather was vouchsafed to them. They arrived in New York without further incident worthy of notice, and Charles found himself not only the guest of the skipper, but honoured by the owner, who, as an old skipper himself, was fully alive to the glowing account given him by Captain Lothrop of Charles's services to the Columbia. The other two officers left early, and Charles, now a full-blown second mate, saw his prize almost within his grasp. The more so that a letter (only one) awaited him; it was from Louise, and contained only these words—

"DEAR CHARLES,

"It is that I am yours. Whenever it shall please you to come for me, I am ready. I leave the house to the day of your parting, for your father is dead immediately, and I go not there any more. I wait for you only.

"LOUISE."

He accepted this news with perfect calmness, as of one who knew that it would come, and turned again to his work with a zest as unlike that of a love-sick youth as any one ever saw. Not a word did he say of his affairs even to his good friend the skipper, and when, their stay in New York at an end, they sailed for China, that worthy man was revolving all sorts of projects in his mind for an alliance between Charles and his wife's sister, who, during Charles' stay in New York, had manifested no small degree of interest in the stalwart, ruddy young Englishman. He, however, took no advantage of the obviously proffered opportunity, and in due course the Columbia sailed for Hong Kong, petroleum laden. Captain Lothrop carried his wife with him this voyage, and very homely indeed the ship appeared with the many trifles added to her cabin by feminine taste. A new mate and third mate were also shipped—the former a gigantic Kentuckian, with a fist like a shoulder of mutton, a voice like a wounded buffalo bull, and a heart as big and soft as ever dwelt in the breast of mortal man. Yet, strangely enough, he was a terror to the crew. Long training in the duty of running a ship "packet fashion" had made him so, made him regard the men under his charge as if they were wild beasts, who needed keeping tame by many stripes and constant, unremitting toil. The third mate was a Salem man, tall enough, but without an ounce of superfluous flesh on his gaunt frame. He seemed built of steel wire, so tireless and insensible to pain was he. With these two worthies Charles was at home at once. Good men themselves, they took to him on the spot as an Englishman of the best sort, who is always beloved by Yankees—that is, genuine Americans—and loves them in return in no half-hearted fashion.

It was well for them all that this solidarity obtained among them, for they shipped a crowd in New York of all nationalities, except Americans or English, a gang that looked as if they had stepped direct from the deck of a pirate to take service on board the Columbia. The skipper was as brave a man as ever trod a quarter-deck; but his wife was aboard, and his great love made him nervous. He suggested at once that each of his officers should never be without a loaded six-shooter in their hip-pockets by night or day, and that they should watch that crowd as the trainer watches his cage of performing tigers. Fortunately the men were all prime seamen, and full of spring, while the perfect discipline maintained on board from the outset did not permit of any loafing about, which breeds insolence as well as laziness, that root of mischief at sea. So, in spite of incessant labour and the absence of any privileges whatever, the peace was kept until the ship, after a splendid passage of one hundred days, was running up the China Sea under as much canvas as she could drag to the heavy south-west monsoon. All the watch were busy greasing down, it being Saturday, and, unlike most English ships, where, for fear of the men grumbling, this most filthy but necessary work is done by the boys or the quiet men of the crew, here everybody took a hand, and the job was done in about twenty minutes from the word "go." A huge Greek was busy at the mizzen-topmast, his grease-pot slung to his belt, when suddenly the pot parted company with him and fell, plentifully bespattering sails and rigging as it bounded and rebounded on its way down, until at last it smashed upon the cabin skylight and deposited the balance of its contents all around.

"Come down here, ye Dago beast!" bellowed the mate. Slowly, too slowly, 'Tonio obeyed. Hardly had he dropped from the rigging on to the top of the house when Mr. Shelby seized him by the throat, and, in spite of his bulk (he was almost as big as the mate himself), dragged him to the skylight, and, forcing his head down, actually rubbed his face in the foul mess. 'Tonio struggled in silence, but unavailingly, until the mate released him; then, with a spring like a lion's, he leaped at his tormentor, a long knife, never seen till then, gleaming in his left hand. Mr. Shelby met him halfway with a kick which caught his left elbow, paralyzing his arm, the knife dropping point downwards and sticking in the deck. But the fracas was the signal for a general outbreak. The helmsman sprang from the wheel, the rest of the watch slid down backstays, and came rushing aft, bent on murder, all their long pent-up hatred of authority brought to a climax by the undoubted outrage perpetrated upon one of their number. But they met with a man. His back to the mizzen-mast, Mr. Shelby whipped out his revolver, and, as coolly as if engaged in a day's partridge-shooting ashore, he fired barrel after barrel of his weapon at the rushing savages. Up came the skipper and the other two officers, not a moment too soon. A hairy Spaniard clutched at Charles as he appeared on deck, but that sturdy son of the soil grappled with his enemy so felly, that in a few heart-beats the body of the Latin went hurtling over the side. Then the fight became general. The ship, neglected, swung up into the wind and was caught aback, behaving herself in the fashion of a wounded animal, while the higher race, outnumbered by four to one, set its teeth and fought in primitive style. The groans of the wounded, the hissing oaths of the combatants, and the crack of revolver shots made up a lurid weft to the warp of sound provided by the moaning wind and murmuring sea. Then gradually those of the men who could do so crawled forrard, leaving the bright yellow of the painted deck aft all besmeared with red, and the victory was won for authority.

But a new danger threatened. Attracted, perhaps, like vultures, by the smell of blood, several evil-looking junks were closing in upon the Columbia, and but for the tremendous exertions of the officers, aided by the cook and steward and the captain's wife, who, pale but resolute, took the wheel, there is no doubt that the Columbia would have been added to the list of missing ships. That peril was averted by the ship being got before the wind again, when her speed soon told, and she hopelessly out-distanced the sneaking, clumsy junks. And before sunset a long smear of smoke astern resolved itself into one of the smart little gunboats which, under the splendid St. George's Cross, patrol those dangerous seas. In answer to signals, she came alongside the Columbia, and soon a boat's crew of lithe men-o'-war's-men were on board the American ship, making all secure for her safe passage into Hong Kong. There she arrived two days later, and got rid of her desperate crew, with the exception of two who had paid for their rash attempt the only price they had—their lives.

From Hong Kong the Columbia sailed for London, arriving there after an uneventful passage of one hundred and twenty days. Charles, turning a deaf ear to the entreaties of the captain and his fellow-officers, determined to take his discharge. A loadstone of which they knew not anything was drawing him irresistibly into the heart of Wiltshire, and, with all his earnings carefully secreted about him, he left the great city behind, and set his face steadfastly for Longbridge Deverill. There he suddenly arrived, as if he had dropped from the sky, just as the short winter's day was closing in. The few straggling villagers peered curiously at the broad, alert figure that strode along the white road with an easy grace and manly bearing quite foreign to the heavy slouch of their own men-folk. There was, too, an indefinable foreign odour about him which cut athwart even their dull perceptions and aroused all their curiosity. But none recognized him. How should they? They had hardly ever known him, except by rumour, which, during his absence of nearly two years, had died a natural death for want of something to feed upon. Straight to the old doctor's house he went as a homing pigeon would. To his confident knock there appeared at the door Louise, the light of love in her eyes, her arms outstretched in gladdest welcome. Neither showed any surprise, for both seemed to have been in some unexplainable way in communion with the other. Yet, now the first speechless greeting over, the first caresses bestowed, instead of contentment most profound came unease, an indefinite fear lest this wonderful thing that had befallen them should by the sheer perversity of fate be swept away, leaving them in the outer dark.

The quavering voice of the old doctor removed them from each other's close embrace, and shyly, yet with a proud air of ownership, Louise led the way into the cosy parlour, where the good old man sat enjoying the rest and comfort he so fully deserved. He looked up inquiringly as with dazzled eyes the big man entered the room, hesitatingly, and with a rush of strange memories flooding his brain.

"Who is it, Loo?" said the doctor. "I don't recognize the gentleman."

And, rising stiffly from his armchair, he took a step forward.

"It's Charles, doctor, Charles Delambre," faltered Louise.

"Yes, doctor; and I've come to take away your treasure. Also to thank you with my whole heart for your loving kindness in taking care of her. Without you what would she have done, me being so far away?"

Almost inarticulate with joy, the old man caught Charles's hands in both his own, and pushed him into a chair. Then sinking back into his own, he gasped breathlessly—

"Ah, my boy, my boy, how I have longed for your return! It has given me more pain than you can think—the idea that I might die and leave this poor child friendless and alone in the world. But she has had no fear. She knew you would come, and she was right. But, Charley, my boy, before we say another word—your brother. You mustn't forget him, and if, as I fear, your quarrel was fierce, you must forgive.

His sufferings have been great. Never once has his face been seen in the village since you left, and, except that we hear an occasional word of him brought by a tramp, he might be dead. Go to him, Charles, and make it up, and perhaps the good Lord will lift the cloud of misery that has so long hung heavily over your house."

Charles heard the kindly doctor's little speech in respectful silence, then, speaking for the second time since entering the house, he said—

"You are right, doctor. I will be friends with George if he'll let me. But I must first secure my wife. After all that has passed, I dare not waste an hour until we are married."

Louise sat listening with the light of perfect approval on her fine face; and the doctor also in vigorous fashion signified his entire acquiescence. The rest of that happy evening was devoted to a recital of Charles's wanderings, his escapes, and his good fortune, until, wearied out, those three happy people went to bed.

Next day Charles was busy. A special license had to be procured, and Louise must procure her simple wedding array. The facilities of to-day did not exist then, and the impatient young lover chafed considerably at the delay involved. But in due time the wedding came off, with the dear old doctor as guardian to give the bride away. The village was in a state of seething excitement; the labourers left their work, their wives left their household tasks, and all discussed with an eagerness that was amazingly different to their usual stolidity of demeanour the romantic happenings in their midst. Then, when the newly-married pair had returned to the doctor's roomy house, and the villagers had drifted reluctantly homeward again, the ripples of unwonted disturbance gradually smoothed out and subsided. Charles and his wife sat side by side in the doctor's parlour as the evening shadows fell, their benefactor's glowing face confronting them, and the knowledge that half his home was theirs removing all anxiety for the immediate future from their minds.

They sat thus, holding each other's hands in silence, until Louise, looking up in her husband's face, said, "Charles, let us go and see George. I feel I must before I sleep." And Charles answered, "Yes, dear; it was in my heart too to do so, but I'm glad you spoke first." So, gently disregarding the remonstrances of the doctor, who protested that the morrow would be a more appropriate time, they departed, warmly wrapped up against the piercing cold, and carrying a lantern. As they passed from the village on to the shoulder of the swelling down a few soft snow-flakes began to fall. . . .

All through that night the large round flakes fell heavily incessantly, until, when the pale cold dawn straggled through the leaden clouds, the whole country was deep buried in a smooth garment of spotless white. For three days the terrible, silent fall went on. The poor folk almost starved in their homes, and all traffic throughout the country was stopped. When at last communications could be opened, the old doctor, his heart aching with worry and suspense, made his way, accompanied by my father, to Pertwood Farm.

There they found only a few hastily scribbled sheets of paper on the kitchen table. They contained words to the effect that George had been startled by a long wailing cry at a late hour on the night of the first snow. He had gone to the door, and there, on the very spot where she had lain years before, was his lost love. But this time she was dead. He had buried her by the side of his parents, and hoped to join the party soon.

A little search revealed the fact that after writing those lines he had gone down into the cellar and died, for his body lay across the rude box containing the remains of Louise. But of Charles nothing was ever again seen or heard. *I* have always felt that he might have been found at the bottom of that dank tarn among the pines, into which he may have fallen on that terrible night. But I don't know, the mystery remains.

YOU SING

CHAPTER I

REGARDED collectively, the Chinese may safely be classified under the head of unpleasant races. Most people who have had personal dealings with them will doubtless admit that, while there are to be discovered among them a tiny sprinkling of really decent men and women, taken "by and large" they are, to Westerns at any rate, anathema. And yet, when due allowance is made for environment, and for hereditary peculiarities of many strange kinds—for which, of course, the individual is in no way responsible—it may not be too bold an assertion that the Chinese are a people who only need a little real leadership on Western lines to become a truly great nation. They possess all the necessary qualifications for such a splendid future and few of the drawbacks. Many virtues that are among us only inculcated by much laborious tuition are with the Chinese *sui generis*. No one will deny that they know how to die; were it possible to teach them how to live, such a revolution would be felt in the progress of the world as it has never yet witnessed. Of course, this does not touch the vast question as to whether such a resurrection of China is to be welcomed or dreaded.

But my intention in these pages is far from that of discussing the economic future of China. Such a task would be indefinitely beyond my powers, besides being utterly unnecessary and out of place here. Besides, I do not really feel sufficiently interested in the Chinese collectively. My story is about a single Chinaman who played a very important part in my own history, and who well deserved a far more powerful testimony than any I am able to bear to his virtues.

But, first, in order to launch my story properly, I must premise that in one of my vagrom voyages, while I was only a puny lad of thirteen, I was flung ashore in Liverpool, penniless, and, of course, friendless. For many days I lived—or, rather, I did not die—by picking up, bird-like, such unvalued trifles of food as chance threw in my way while I wandered about the docks; but as there were many more experienced urchins with sharper eyes than mine on the same keen quest, it may be well imagined that I did not wax overfat upon my findings. Unfortunately my seafaring instincts kept me near the docks at all times, where most of my associates were as hunger-bitten as myself; had I gone up town I should probably have fared better.

However, I had put a very keen edge indeed upon my appetite one bitter November afternoon, when, prowling along the Coburg Dock Quay, I was suddenly brought up "all standing".by a most maddening smell of soup. With dilated nostrils I drew in the fragrant breeze, and immediately located its source as the galley of a barque that lay near, loading. I must have looked hungry as I swiftly came alongside of her, for the broad-faced cook, who was standing at his galley-door swabbing his steaming face after his sultry sojourn within, presently caught sight of me and lifted a beckoning finger. I was by his side in two bounds, and before I had quite realized my good fortune I was loading up at a great rate from a comfortably-sized dish of plum soup. My benefactor said nothing as the eager spoonfuls passed, but lolled against the door placidly regarding me with much the same expression as one would a hungry dog with a just-discovered bone. When at last I was well distended, he asked me a few questions in a queer broken English that I immediately recognized as the German version. What was I? Where did I come from? Would I like to go to sea? And so on. Eagerly and hopefully I answered him, much to his amazement; for, like every other seaman I fell in with in those days, he found it hard to believe that I had already been nearly two years at sea, so small and weak did I appear. But the upshot of our interview was that he introduced me to the skipper, a burly North German, who, looking stolidly down upon me, between the regular puffs of smoke from his big pipe, said—

"Vell, poy; ju dinks ju like du komm in a Cherman scheep—hein?"

I faltered out a few words, not very coherently, I am afraid, for the prospect of getting any ship at all was just like a glimpse of heaven to me. Fortunately for my hopes, Captain Strauss was a man of action, so, cutting short my faltering reply, he resumed: "All righdt. Ve yoost loosd a leedle Engelsch boy lige ju. He pin mit me more as ein jeer, gabin-poy, und mein vife lige him fery vell. Ju do so goot as him, ju vas all righdt. Vat ju call jorselluf—hein?"

"Tom, sir," I answered promptly.

"Ya; den ve call ju Dahn. Dat oder poy ve calls Dahn, und so ju gomes all der same for him—aind it?"

That seemed to settle the matter, for he turned away abruptly and was gone. I hastened to my friend the cook, and told him what the skipper had said, with the result that in another five minutes I was busy laying the cloth for dinner in the cabin as if I had been the original Dan just come back. A pretty, fair-haired little girl of about ten years of age watched me curiously from a state-room door with the frank, straightforward curiosity of a child; and I, boy-like, was on my mettle to show her how well I could do my work. Presently she came forward and spoke to me; but her remarks being in German, I could only smile feebly and look foolish; whereupon she indignantly snapped out, "*Schaafskopf*," and ran away. She returned almost directly with her mother, a buxom, placid-looking dame of about thirty-five, who addressed me in a dignified tone. Again I was in a hole, for she spoke only German also; and if ever a poor urchin felt nonplussed, I did. This drawback made my berth an uncomfortable one at first; but, with such opportunities as I had and such a powerful inducement to spur me on, I soon picked up enough to understand what was said to me, and to make some suitable reply.

The vessel was a smart-looking, well-found barque of about six hundred tons, called the Blitzen, of Rostock, and carried a crew of fourteen all told. Each of the other thirteen was a master of mine, and seldom allowed an opportunity to slip of asserting his authority; while the skipper's wife and daughter evidently believed that I ought to be perpetually in motion. Consequently my berth was no sinecure; and, whatever my qualifications may have been, I have no doubt I earned my food and the tiny triangular lair under the companion-ladder wherein I crept—I was going to say when my work was done—but a rather better term to use would be, in the short intervals between jobs.

Now, the story of the next nine months on board the Blitzen is by no means devoid of interest; but I have an uneasy feeling that I have already tried the reader's patience enough with necessary preliminaries to the story of You Sing. After calling at several ports in South America, looking in at Algoa Bay, visiting Banjœwangie and Cheribon, we finally appeared to have settled down as a Chinese coaster, trading between all sorts of out-of-the-way ports for native consignees, and carrying a queer assortment of merchandise. Finally we found ourselves at Amoy, under charter for Ilo-Ilo with a full cargo of Chinese "notions." Owing, I suppose, to the docility of the German crew, and the high state of discipline maintained on board, we still carried the same crew that we left

England with; but I must say that, while I admired the good seamanship displayed by the skipper and his officers, I was heartily weary of my lot on board. I had never become a favourite, not even with the little girl, who seemed to take a delight in imitating her father and mother by calling me strange-sounding Teutonic names of opprobrium; and I was beaten regularly, not apparently from any innate brutality, but from sheer force of habit, as a London costermonger beats his faithful donkey. The only thing that made life at all tolerable was that I was fairly well fed and enjoyed robust health; while I never lost the hope that in some of our wanderings we should happen into an English port, where I might be able to run away. That blissful idea I kept steadily before me as a beacon-light to cheer me on. Happily, dread of losing my wages in such an event did not trouble me, because I had none to lose as far as I knew; I did not stipulate for any when I joined.

It was on a lovely night that we swung clear of Amoy harbour and, catching a light land-breeze, headed across the strait towards Formosa. Many fishing *sampans* were dotted about the sleeping sea, making little sepia-splashes on the wide white wake of the moon. Little care was taken to avoid running them down; nor did they seem to feel any great anxiety as to whether we did so or not, and as a consequence we occasionally grazed closely past one, and looked down curiously upon the passive figures sitting in their frail craft like roosting sea-birds upon a floating log. Without any actual damage to them, we gradually drew clear of their cruising-ground, and, hauling to the southward a little, stood gently onward for Cape South, the wind still very light and the weather perfect. But suddenly we ran into a strange heavy mist that obscured all the sea around us, and yet did not have that wetness that usually characterizes the clinging vapour of the sea-fog. Through this opaque veil we glided as if sailing in cloudland, a silence enwrapping us as if we had been mysteriously changed into a ghostly ship and crew. Then a quick, strong blast of wind burst out of the brume right ahead, throwing all the sails aback and driving the vessel stern foremost at a rate that seemed out of all proportion to its force.

For a few moments the watch on deck appeared to be stupid with surprise. Then the skipper, roused by the unusual motion, rushed on deck, and his deep, guttural voice broke the spell as he issued abrupt orders. All hands were soon busy getting the vessel under control, shortening sail, and trimming yards. But, to everybody's speechless amazement, it was presently found that entangled alongside lay a small junk, a craft of some twenty to thirty tons, upon whose deck no sign of life was visible. All hands crowded to the rail, staring and muttering almost incoherent comment upon this weird visitor that had so suddenly arisen, as it were, out of the void. As usual, the skipper first recovered his working wits, and ordered a couple of the men to jump on board the junk and investigate. They obeyed unquestionably, as was their wont, and presently reported that she was unmanned, but apparently full to the hatches of assorted Chinese cargo in mats and boxes. The skipper's voice took an exultant ring as he ordered the vessel to be well secured alongside, and her contents to be transferred on board of us with all possible despatch. Meanwhile the strange mist had vanished as suddenly as it had arisen, and the full bright moon shone down upon the toiling men, who with wonderful celerity were breaking out the junk's cargo and hurling it on to our decks. Such was their expedition that in half an hour our decks were almost impassable for the queer-looking boxes and bales and bundles of all shapes disgorged from the junk's hold. Then they invaded the evil-scented cabin, and ransacked its many hiding-places, finding numerous neatly-bound parcels wrapped in fine silky matting. And, last of all—they declared he must have suddenly been materialized, or words to that effect—they lighted upon a lad of probably sixteen years of age. He showed no surprise, after the fatalistic fashion of his countrymen, but stood gravely before them like some quaint Mongolian idol carved out of yellow jade, and ready for any fortune that might await him. With scant ceremony, he too was man-handled on deck, for the command was urgent to finish the work; the busy labourers followed him, and the junk was cast adrift.

Some sort of rough stowage was made of the treasure-trove thus peculiarly shipped; and, the excitement that had sustained their unusual exertions having subsided, the tired crew flung themselves down anywhere and slept—slept like dead men, all except the officer of

The toiling men were breaking out the junk's cargo.

the watch and the helmsman. They had at first little to do that might keep them from slumber, for the wind had dropped to a stark calm, which in those sheltered waters, remote from the disturbing influence of any great ocean swell, left the ship almost perfectly motionless, a huge silhouette against the glowing surface of a silver lake. But presently it dawned upon the mate who was in charge of the deck that, although the vessel had certainly not travelled more than a mile since the junk was cast adrift, that strange craft was nowhere to be seen; and, stern martinet though he was, the consciousness of something uncanny about the recent business stole through him, shrinking his skin and making his mouth dry, until for relief he sought the helmsman and entered into conversation with him on the subject. That worthy, a stolid, unemotional Dutchman named Pfeiffer, scanned the whole of the palpitating brightness around before he would assent to the mate's theory of any sudden disappearance of our late companion; but, having done so, and failed to discover the smallest speck against that dazzling surface, he, too, was fain to admit that the thing was not comforting. Right glad were those two men when the interminably long watch was over, and the sharp, business-like notes of the bell seemed to dissipate in some measure the chilling atmosphere of mystery that hemmed them in. To the second mate the retiring officer said nothing of his fears, but hastened below, hurriedly scratched a perfunctory note or two on the log-slate, and bundled, " all standing "—that is, dressed as he was—into his bunk, pulling the upper feather-bed right over his head, as if to shut out the terror that was upon him. Slowly the remainder of the night passed away; but when at last the tiny suggestion of paleness along the eastern horizon gave the first indication of the day's approach, no change, not even the slightest, had occurred to increase the mystery whose environment all felt more or less keenly. As the advancing glory of the new day displaced the deep purple of the night, the awakening crew recalled, as if it had been a lifetime ago, the strange happening of the past few hours. But it was not until the clear light was fully come that the significance of the whole affair was manifest. For there, seated upon a mat-bound case, stamped all over with red "chops," was the Chinese youth, whose existence had up till now been unnoticed from the time he was first bundled on board. Impassive as a wooden image, he looked as if the position he had held throughout the night had left him unwearied, and, to all appearance, the strange and sudden change in his environment possessed for him no significance whatever. But now, when the surly-looking mate approached him and looked him over with evident distaste, he slid off his perch, and, kneeling at the officer's feet, kissed the deck thrice in manifest token of his entire submission to whatever fate might be dealt out to him. The mate stood silently looking down upon him, as if hardly able to decide what to do with him. While this curious little episode was being enacted the skipper appeared, and, hastening to the mate's side, addressed the grovelling Celestial in what he supposed to be the only possible medium of communication—"pidgin" English, which, coupled to a German accent, was the queerest jargon conceivable.

"Vell," he said, "vot pelong ju pidgin—hay? Ju savvy vork, vun dime?"

Lifting his yellow mask of a face, but still remaining on his knees, the waif made answer—

"No shabbee. You Sing."

CHAPTER II

"You Sing" conveyed no meaning to anybody; but, after various extraordinary attempts to extend the conversation had entirely failed, it was tacitly agreed that You Sing must be his name. Whether it was or not, the taciturn pagan answered to it immediately it was uttered, or rather he came instantly to whoever mentioned it. So, seeing that it was hopeless to think of getting any information from him as to the why and wherefore of the strange circumstances under which we had found him, the skipper decided promptly to put him to work as a steward, believing that he would make a good one. To that end he was handed over to me for tuition, much to my delight, for now I felt that I should have a companion who was certainly not more than my equal, and who would not be likely to ill-treat me in any way, as most of the crew did when opportunity arose. His coming was to me a perfect godsend. He was so willing, so docile, and withal so eminently teachable, that it was a pleasure to be with him. And the incongruity of being placed under such an urchin as myself did not appear to strike him at all, for he looked upon me from the first day of our acquaintance as the one creature that stood between him and the outer dark—although it must be said that, as far as could be judged by his attitude to all with whom he came in contact, he regarded every member of the ship's company as in some sort his saviour. All could command him, and he would instantly obey; and although he understood no word of what was said to him, he watched so keenly, his desire to please was so intense, and his natural ability so great, that his efforts to do what was required of him were generally successful. Unfortunately, his willingness often got him into serious trouble, since he always obeyed the last order, not being able to discriminate between those who had the first claim upon him and those who had no right to his services whatever. But when he was beaten for neglecting tasks that he had been called away from, he never murmured or showed sign of pain or resentment; all treatment was borne with the same placid equanimity, as if he were a perfectly passionless automaton. With one exception—myself. When with me his usually expressionless eyes would shine, and his yellow face wear a peculiarly sweet smile that had quite a fascination for me. I found myself growing so much attached to him that my rage against his persecutors often drove me nearly frantic—such wrath as it had never occurred to me to feel on my own behalf.

Meanwhile the Blitzen, sorely hampered by calms

and variable winds, crept slowly and painfully towards her destination. I was so much absorbed with the education and company of You Sing that I lost all my usual interest in the progress of the vessel, and did not even wonder when we were going to reach our next port—a speculation that had hitherto always had great charms for me. But one morning before breakfast I was dreadfully affrighted to hear a fierce altercation on deck. It had always been my ill-fortune hitherto to find myself the ultimate vicarious sacrifice in all cases of trouble, and even to this day the old feeling of dread still exists—a feeling that whatever row is going on I shall presently be made to suffer for it; and the well-remembered sensation of sinking at the pit of the stomach comes back, making me for the moment quite ill. So, trembling all over, I peered out of the pantry window on to the main deck, and saw the mate confronting three men of his watch, who, with inflamed faces and fierce gestures, were evidently threatening his life. Now, there had never before been the slightest sign of insubordination on board, the discipline seeming as near perfection as possible, and therefore this sudden outbreak was most alarming. A swift step passed the pantry door, and instantly I saw the skipper rushing forward. Without a word he plunged into the midst of the angry four, and seizing the foremost seaman by the throat and waist hurled him crashing against the bulwarks. At the same moment the mate sprang at another man, as if to serve him in the same manner; but, missing his grasp, he stumbled and fell on his knees. A stifled scream burst from my dry lips as I saw the glint of steel; the seaman attacked had drawn his knife, and as the mate fell the weapon descended with fearful force between his shoulders. I heard the ugly sound right aft, and it remains with me to-day. The skipper, however, with the agility of a porpoise, instantly flung himself on the two men, and fought as if he had the sinews of ten.

Compared with the noise of the preliminary quarrel, this life-and-death struggle was silence itself; but I could hear the laboured breathings of the combatants coming in hoarse gasps, and the cracking of the joints as the writhing bodies knotted and strained. There was a scream behind me, a rustle of skirts, and out of the cabin rushed the skipper's wife, with flying hair and outstretched arms. But before she was halfway to the spot there was a swoop as of some huge bird past her, and the second mate, the youngest officer in the ship and the biggest man, alighted in the fray like a hungry tiger. I did not see the other watch of the crew arrive, but they were there, and fighting as fiercely as the rest.

Now, the first flush of fear having gone from me, I became interested—somewhat coldly critical, indeed, of the various points of the battle, finding myself, to the wonder of some other corner of my brain, siding with the officers, and hoping they would be victorious. The surprise of this backwater of thought was probably owing to the fact that all the officers had treated me with steady brutality, while the men, though not kind, seldom touched me, although that was probably only lack of opportunity. But with all my keen watching I could not yet forecast the upshot of this awful encounter. The mass of bodies seemed to me inextricably entangled, heaving and writhing like a basket of wounded eels; while all around them, frantically clutching at the labouring body of her husband, and shrieking pitifully, hovered the unhappy wife and mother.

Suddenly it dawned upon me that the little Elsie was alone, and probably frightened to death; and, though I was never a favourite with even her, it seemed good to go and comfort her if possible. So I turned away from the window, and there behind me was You Sing, calmly cleaning the knives, as unmoved by any external occurrence as a piece of machinery. As I unblocked the window he caught my eye, and the peculiarly winsome smile he always wore for me lit up his solemn face. His lips opened, and he murmured softly with an indescribable accent the only two English words I had succeeded in teaching him, "'Ullo, Tommy." I could only smile back in return as I hurried off to the skipper's state-room aft, feeling as if, with the shutting out of that savage sight, a load had been lifted off my brain. A quick revulsion of sympathy thrilled me as I found the pretty child fast asleep in placid unconsciousness of the terrible scene in progress outside. I stood for a minute looking at her with a tenderness I had never before felt towards her, all her childish dislike and funny little ways of showing it, borrowed from her parents, utterly forgotten. Then, softly closing the door, I hurried back to the pantry, finding You Sing still busily employed.

Scrambling to the window, I peered forrard again, seeing, to my horror, only a heap of bodies lying still. I stood there as if frozen, trying hard to think, endeavouring to realize the position, but unable to control my disorganized brain. How long I stood staring thus I have no idea; but I was recalled to usefulness again by You Sing's gentle touch upon my back. Turning slowly round, I faced him, while he pointed out his finished work and intimated to me in the sign language we always employed that he awaited instructions what to go on with. Impatiently I made a great effort to show him that all ordinary work was now at an end, and, pulling him to the window, pointed out the awful heap on the main hatch. He looked, and I believe understood the situation, for he turned again to me and patted my face, pointed first to me and then to himself, as if to intimate that upon us two, me as master and he as servant, the conduct of affairs now rested.

Then, taking my courage in both hands, I softly stepped out on deck and approached the scene of conflict, though trembling so violently that I could scarcely go. But when I reached the entwined heap of bodies I did not know what to do, standing helplessly staring at the grim spectacle. A faint groan startled me, and I bent down over the nearest body, which happened to be the skipper's, hearing him murmur faintly, "*Wasser, lieber Gott! Wasser.*" Hastily motioning to You Sing to fetch some water, I tried to drag the skipper into a sitting position; but it was too much for my strength. The effort, however, was apparently all that was needed to shake the last faint breath from his body, for, with wide dilated nostrils and open mouth, he gave his final gasp. Then all was still, for all were dead.

The whole waist was like the veriest shambles, and the fearful savagery of the fight was manifest in many hideous details that need not be reproduced. Suddenly a hope dawned upon me that *one* man might still be left—the helmsman; and, rushing aft, I bounded up on to the poop, only to find the wheel swinging idly to and fro: there was no one there. Then I ran forward, unheeding You Sing's dog-like wistful look after me, and ransacked the forecastle and galley; but both were deserted. We were quite alone.

This tremendous fact broke in upon me with good effect after the strain to which I had recently been subjected, for it braced me up to action. Calling upon You Sing to help me, I tackled the ghastly heap, tugging and straining at the limp bodies, and getting all gory as they were. The sweat ran down blindingly; I felt my sinews crack with my desperate exertions; but at last all the bodies were separated and laid side by side, the captain's wife last of that sad row. Not a sign of life was to be found in any one of them; and, having at last satisfied myself of this, I dropped upon the crimsoned tarpaulin exhausted, to rack my brains for some reason why this sudden tragedy should have been enacted. Gradually the conviction forced itself upon me that the whole horrible outbreak was due to some quarrel over the junk's cargo; but as that had all been overhauled and stowed away without my knowing anything of its nature, it was only a blind guess. Something, however, of tremendous importance must have occurred to make a body of men fight with such fury among themselves that not one of them remained alive.

But urgent necessity was laid upon me to be up and doing, the first duty that demanded attention being the disposal of the dead. So I called upon You Sing—who, standing near, never seemed to take his eyes off me—and the pair of us triced up one of the bulwark ports and dragged the first of the corpses up to it. Then by a sudden impulse I flung off my cap, and, kneeling down on the red deck, said the Lord's Prayer and the final Collect in the Church Service—all I could then remember; while my heathen helper stood gravely by making no sign but *looking* a very well-spring of sympathy. Strangely cheered and uplifted, I seized the poor piece of clay, and motioning my helpmate, launched it through the yawning port, listening shudderingly to the dull splash that followed. And so with the rest, until we two stood alone, panting and distressed with our heavy task. A few minutes' rest, and then, with draw-bucket and broom, we laboured to cleanse away the blood that besmeared so wide a space of the decks. At this work we toiled for a long time, and when at last we gave over, because I was tired out, we had only partially succeeded in removing the fearful evidence of that great fight. By this time I was so far myself as to feel hungry. The feeling of nausea, that had been coming and going like waves over me ever since I first left the cabin, had left me, and I ordered You Sing to get breakfast. He set about the job immediately, leaving me seated on the damp hatch wondering what would become of us. Then suddenly it occurred to me for the first time that the ship was entirely left to herself. There was a faint breeze blowing steadily, all sail being set, and the yards canted a couple of points, for what wind existed was on the quarter. I rose and went aft to the wheel, finding that she came up and fell off about three points, so that she was practically steering herself, and making a fairly average course S.S.E. This was satisfactory so far, because it relieved me of any necessity for immediate action. I knew how to steer, and, as far as my strength went, could handle sails, besides understanding fairly well how a ship was worked; for I had been over two years at sea, and always a deck-boy until this voyage, so that, unless I had been a very idiot, I must know something about sailoring.

Everything being so quiet and favourable, I remembered little Elsie, and with a sinking heart went down below to break the dreadful news to her. How it was to be done I didn't know, my stock of German being pitifully scanty, and she, poor child! not knowing one word of English. As I turned the handle of the state-room door I heard her calling, "*Mutter, wie bist du?*" and in spite of my efforts some big tears burst from my eyes. But I went in and stood by her cot, racking my brains for some way of making her understand what had happened. As soon as she saw me she began, as usual, to scold me for being there

—where, indeed, I was never allowed to enter—and ordered me with much dignity to go and call her mother.

It would be useless for me to attempt any description of the scene that followed. I could not, do what I would, make her understand what an awful change had taken place since she went to sleep. She at last made up her mind that I must be crazy, and, thoroughly frightened, sprang out of her cot, and rushed into the cabin screaming frantically for "*Mutter, Mutter! Vater, Vater!*" I followed her carefully, puzzled beyond measure to know what to do; but she fled on deck, up the ladder and on to the poop, still calling with all her voice for those who were for ever deaf to her cries.

Of course, I dared not pursue her, for fear of adding to her terror; so I waited anxiously until she had explored every vacant corner of the ship, and at last, exhausted with her efforts, she returned slowly to the cabin. Then I quietly brought her some food, and begged her to eat a little; but, as I might have expected, that was impossible. However, she was so far quieted that she plied me with questions, which I answered as well as I was able, until I succeeded in making her understand the grim truth. She burst into such a passion of weeping when she comprehended the case that at first I feared for her life; but presently I saw that this outbreak was the best thing that could have happened, for it relieved her poor little brain; and soon, utterly worn out, she went off into a heavy sleep.

Then I searched the cabin thoroughly, with the dim idea in my mind of finding some cause for the mutiny in accordance with my suspicions. Sure enough, I had been right, for in various hiding-places I came upon such treasures as I had never even dreamed of before—coined gold in boxes, in bags, in bundles: sovereigns, eagles, onzas, and napoleons; jewellery of every variety of make, glittering with precious stones of which I had never heard the name. At last I came upon a crucifix nearly two feet in length, apparently of solid gold, and encrusted with large gems, a marvel of costliness and beauty. I showed it to You Sing, who, for the first time in my acquaintance with him, showed signs of horror, and tried hard to induce me to throw the magnificent thing overboard.

CHAPTER III

THIS discovery marked a new departure in our relations towards each other. Hitherto I had looked upon You Sing as I might have done upon a big faithful dog, but never dreamed of crediting him with any intelligent initiative. His behaviour so far had certainly justified me in this opinion; but now he became completely transformed. In the most energetic pantomime, and with strangely severe struggles to enunciate a few words of my language, he endeavoured to explain to me the origin of all these treasures. I did not find it hard to understand the general drift of his attempt to enlighten me, because I had already suspected something of what I was now gathering from him. Roughly, it was to the effect that the cargo we had relieved the junk of was the accumulated hoard of a nest of pirates who had long been preying upon such seafarers as they dared attack without fear of reprisals, and who were all deliberately slain after they had been plundered and their vessels scuttled. Then the wretches had turned their bloody hands against each other, and by so doing somewhat atoned for their innumerable crimes by ridding the world of two-thirds of the gang. The survivors then loaded up all the most valuable of the stored plunder into the most seaworthy junk they possessed, and, divesting her of all suspicious appearance, sailed for some port where they intended to dispose of their loot. Again Nemesis overtook them; they had befouled the seas too long. They stealthily murdered one another as opportunity served, until there were hardly enough of them left to handle the junk. You Sing was a slave who had done their cooking, having been spared for that purpose alone out of the entire crew of a large barque they had surprised one night. Doubtless his turn to perish had nearly arrived, when, going down into their store-room under the cabin for some rice, he found himself in a sort of trap from which he was unable to escape. There he would certainly have perished of starvation, instead of sharing the unknown fate of the remnant of his tyrants, but for our intervention. And in various quaint ways he gave me to understand that he considered his life to belong to this ship and her crew, of whom the child asleep and my small self were now the sole representatives.

I could not bring myself to the point of heaving all those pretty things overboard; but seeing what a dread he had of them, I stowed them all in the late skipper's berth under his bed-place, in two large drawers, which I locked, and hung the key round my neck. Then, for the first time, I began to think about working the ship. Unfortunately, I had not the faintest idea of which was the best direction to steer in, for I did not know, within at least a thousand miles, our position. I imagined, of course, that we were somewhere south of Formosa, and between that great island and the Philippines; but that was vague in the extreme. And I was in hourly terror of being sighted by a wandering junk of whatever character, feeling certain of a barbarous death at the hands of any of You Sing's countrymen who might happen to find such a prize as the Blitzen. How I longed for the sight of a smoke-wreath festooning the horizon! That vision would have nearly sent me crazy with joy. But I suppose we were far out of the track of steamers, for we saw no sign of one.

Aided most manfully and sensibly by You Sing, I clewed up the royals and topgallant sails with a view of making the vessel easier to handle, and with a great deal of labour managed to haul up the courses (mainsail and foresail) as well, taking the gear to the capstan where it was too heavy for our united efforts, until those great squares of canvas hung snug as they could be without being actually furled. Then, after long cogitation, I decided to make for the coast of China, which I knew must be west of us, and trust to a merciful God to bring us in sight of either some civilized port or ship before any of those calm, merciless pagans came across us. Now we each took a regular trick at the wheel (You Sing learned to do so in less than half an hour); and little Elsie, all her high spirits gone, and docile as You Sing himself, even took a spell at steering when we would let her. Heaven alone knows what our track would have looked like on the chart, but it's my belief that we *were* getting to the westward at the rate of about twenty miles a day for the best part of a week (I lost all count of time); and, though it seems hard to believe, I was actually beginning to feel quite important as the commander of a big vessel on the high seas. We fed well and we slept well—at least Elsie and I did; as for You Sing, I don't know whether he ever slept at all. He did all the cooking, kept everything clean and tidy, and was ever ready when called upon. Besides all this, he had won his way into the affections of Elsie; and I almost felt a pang of jealousy when I heard her clear laugh at some of the quaint antics he cut in order to amuse her. Had it not been for the one haunting dread of being overhauled by a junk, I believe we should have been quite happy; for the terror of the past tragedy had faded from our minds, and the sea was kind and gentle, the soft breeze blew sweetly, though it varied a great deal, making our task of trimming the yards in order to keep the vessel somewhere near her course—due west—an uncommonly heavy one.

You Sing

Then it fell a flat calm. Now, I had, even at that early age, all a sailor's horror of a calm, and this one troubled me more than any I had yet experienced. The silence was almost unbearable. I could not rest day or night—it lasted three days—for more than an hour or so at a time; and when I fell asleep from sheer weariness, I always woke with my heart thumping furiously and in an icy sweat of fear. The inaction got upon my nerves, so that I began to hear strange noises, and to imagine that the dead crew were among us, grieving because we were yet alive, and scheming to secure our company. This state of mind grew upon me to such an extent that at last I dared not leave You Sing, clinging to him as the one hope I had of ever again seeing the land of the living. He—grave, careful, and kind as ever—accepted this entire change in our relative positions with the same serene behaviour as before; and in my worst mental trouble I had only to look into his eyes to be completely comforted. Elsie, strange to say, seemed quite happy. She was carelessly kind to me; but she loved our Chinese friend. A word or two from him, in an unintelligible jargon, would set her dancing with delight, and it was only during his unavoidable absence from her for a short time that she ever seemed to feel the misery of our position.

On the tenth evening (I think) of our loneliness, and the third of the calm, I was lolling against the useless wheel watching, with eyes that observed naught, the fantastic efforts of You Sing to amuse Elsie, when an appalling feeling of dread suddenly came over me. It was as if I was going to be violently sea-sick, and affected my limbs to such an extent that I slid down from the wheel to the deck. This disabling sensation was happily only momentary in its effect, so that I was able to rise to my feet again almost immediately, though trembling violently. Whatever mysterious cause had thus affected me I could not tell, and it was evidently peculiar to myself, for my two shipmates were still merry at their play. But I was desperately uneasy, fearing that I was going to be very ill. I left the deck, and descended into the cabin, seeing, to my astonishment, several rats prowling uneasily about. They took scarcely any notice of me, and I was too upset to obey the momentary impulse to chase them. I sank down on a settee and tried to collect myself, but I was too uneasy to sit still, and soon wandered out on the main-deck again.

Aimlessly I slouched forrard and climbed up on the forecastle head. As soon as I reached it, on looking ahead, I saw a sight that thickened my blood. Right before the vessel rose a dense mass of inky cloud, extending over an arc of the horizon of about one-sixth of its circumference. It was dome-shaped, and upon its apex rested the descending sun, his glowing disc changed into a dull bronze-green ball that shed no light around. It looked as if the glorious orb was sick unto death. As I watched with growing anxiety, the painfully changed luminary sank slowly into that black mountain of gloom and disappeared. But above it the clear sky reflected its ghastliness, not by reason of its rays ascending, for it appeared to have none, but as if some unknown light from the bowels of the earth had broken through the sea, and was thus disfiguring the beautiful face of the heavens.

Tearing myself away from the disabling fascination of the sight, I returned to the poop, noticing with much satisfaction that my trembling had almost ceased. I found You Sing and Elsie sitting on a hen-coop, watching with solemn faces the rising gloom ahead in perfect silence, all their pleasant play at an end. Meeting You Sing's eye, I read therein a reflection of my own concern, and in an instant we understood each other. Doubtless, it being his native country, he understood the ominous signs far better than I, although even the child could see and feel that something terrible was impending; and as I went up to her to coax her below he murmured in my ear two words of pure Chinese, which, because they have passed into the English language, I understood at once: "*Ty foong!*" They rang through my brain like a sentence of death; but I actually felt some relief at knowing the worst. For if we were about to encounter a typhoon in our utter helplessness either to prepare for it by furling sail, or to handle the vessel in any way, what hope could there be of our survival? But there *is* a certain satisfaction in knowing that, whatever happens, it is no fault of yours; that you can do nothing of any service, but just endure and hope. And that was exactly our position.

We got Elsie down below without alarming her, laid in a stock of fresh water in the cabin, and barricaded the doors opening on to the main-deck. Then we got some old sails up from the locker and covered the cabin skylight, lashing it down as securely as we knew how. The cabin being as secure as we could make it, we braced the yards sharp up on the starboard tack (although I don't know why I chose that side, I'm sure), for I had a dim idea that we should stand a better chance so than with the yards square as they were, since I knew very well that in heavy gales of wind a vessel ought to be hove to, and that that was always effected by bracing the yards forrard. Then I let go the topsail-sheets and lowered the upper topsails down on the cap. We also hauled all the jibs and staysails down, making them as snug as we could. Last of all, I put the helm hard down, and lashed it there. My hope was that in the first burst of the tempest the big sails that were loose would blow away, and that the vessel would then heave herself to naturally, although I knew well enough that if caught by the lee she would probably capsize or drive under stern foremost.

While we had been thus busy the rising pall of clouds had imperceptibly grown until exactly half of the concave above was perfectly black—black as the adit of a coal-mine. The other half astern was of an ugly green tint, as unlike the deep violet of the night sky in those latitudes as could well be imagined. Its chief peculiarity, though, was its light. That segment of the sky was full of glare, diffused light that was even reflected on to the vessel, and yet could not be traced to any definite source. The contrast between this uncanny radiance and the crêpe-like darkness of the other half of the sky was tremendous, and of itself enough to inspire fear in the breast of any creature living.

Presently, as we watched in strained silence, came the beginning of what we were to know; a twining golden webwork of electric fires all over the swart roof of cloud, or whatever that gloom was built of, and in a hot puff of wind the destroying genie of the tropics uplifted the opening strains of his song. All cries of uttermost woe were blended in it as it faintly fell upon our ears, indistinctly, as if echoed and re-echoed from immeasurable distances, but growing louder and wilder with every burning breath. Then, in one furious blast, accompanied by a cracking blaze of lightning, the typhoon burst upon us. It was just sufficiently on the starboard bow to avoid catching us aback, and the vessel paid off, heeling over to its force until her lee rail was awash, and the gleaming foam toppled inboard in a smother of pale light. Lower and lower the sky descended, until it seemed as if we might have reached upward and touched it; and, unable to bear the sight any longer, I fled below, followed by You Sing, and securely fastened the scuttle behind us.

Elsie was asleep when I peeped into her room, for which I felt profoundly thankful; since how could we have comforted her? I sat down by You Sing's side and looked up wonderingly into his impassive face which, as usual, was lighted by a tender smile as he met my troubled gaze. He took hold of my hand and patted it, murmuring his shibboleth, " 'Ullo, Tommy;" and, in spite of my terrors, I smiled. Outside, the uproar was beyond description; but except that we lay over at a most dangerous angle we were fairly steady. The force of the wind did not permit the sea to rise, and so between sleeping and waking that awful night passed.

CHAPTER IV

Having no means of knowing the time—for the clock had never been wound, owing to my not being able to find the key—I cannot tell when the change came; but I think it must have been about eight next morning. The vessel suddenly righted, and then began to tumble about in so outrageous a fashion that I thought she must go all to pieces. Elsie awoke screaming with fright; and with all You Sing's cat-like capacity for holding on, it was some minutes before he could get to her to comfort her. He had not left my side more than ten minutes, when, with a tremendous lurch, the vessel was hurled over to starboard, and I knew that my greatest fear was realized—she had been caught aback! Over, over she went, until it was almost possible to stand upright upon the lee bulk-heads of the cabin. In sea-phrase, she was on her beam-ends.

I now gave all up for lost, and waited, hardly breathing, for the crash of the end. The water on deck burst in through every crevice, and rose upon the lee-side until I was obliged to climb up to the fast-clamped settees to windward to avoid being drowned. The uproar on deck was louder than ever, and I fancied that I could hear every now and then through the tumult the rending and crashing of spars, and feel the shattering blow of their great masses against the hull alongside. But still the vessel appeared staunch, although every inch of her framework visible in the cabin was all awork.

After what seemed like a whole day, but could only have been two or three hours, she began to right herself, and the din outside grew less deafening. Rapidly the howl of the wind moderated, although the vessel still tossed and tumbled about in frantic fashion, until my anxiety to see daylight again got the better of my fears, and I painfully made my way up the companion, opened it, and stepped on to the poop. The sight I beheld took away my breath. The Blitzen was a complete wreck. Not a stick was standing except the three jagged stumps of the lower masts; the bulwarks were stripped from her sides for their entire length, the house on deck had clean disappeared, and everything that could be torn from its fastenings about the decks had gone also. It was a clean sweep. A cold shiver went through me, such as one might feel upon awakening to find his house roofless and all his household goods exposed to the glare of day. But the sky was clear, the sea was going down, and we were still afloat. A great wave of thankfulness came over me, suddenly checked by the paralyzing thought that perhaps we had sprung a leak. I stood still for a moment while this latest fear soaked in; then, bracing myself up to learn the worst, I hurried forrard to try and find the rod to sound the well. But it had gone, among the rest of the carpenter's gear, with the deck-house, and I was obliged to give up the idea. Returning aft, I uncovered the cabin skylight and went below, finding You Sing busy preparing some food. Then I suddenly remembered that I was ravenously hungry, and we all three sat down and ate our fill cheerfully and gladly. But while we were swallowing the last morsels of our meal, You Sing gravely lifted his hand and sat listening intently. There was a strange sound on deck, and it made me almost helpless with fear; for it sounded like the singing chatter of Chinese. We sat for a few moments as if suddenly frozen, listening with every faculty, and hardly breathing. Then, ghost-like, You Sing rose, and, taking the two of us by the arms, gently persuaded us into one of the state-rooms at hand, and signed to us to keep close while he went to investigate. Noiselessly he glided away from us and was gone, leaving us a prey to the most harrowing sensations in the belief that all our cruel forebodings were about to be proved true. For some time not a sound could be heard in our hiding-place except the soothing creak of the timbers or the wash of the caressing waves outside the hull. Yet I remember curiously how even in that agony of suspense I noticed that the motion of the ship was changed. She no longer seemed to swing buoyantly from wave to wave, but solemnly, stolidly, she rolled, as if the sea had taken possession of her, and bereft her of her own grace of mastery.

A confused thudding sound reached us from above, as if caused by the pattering of bare feet on deck;

but there were no voices, nor, indeed, any other noises to give us a clue as to what was going on. Very soon even that slight sound ceased, and we were left again to the dumbness of our surroundings. The child went to sleep; and I, after perhaps half an hour of strained listening, felt that I could bear this condition of things no longer, for it had seemed like a whole day to my excited imaginings. So, as silently as had You Sing long ago, I stole from the little state-room and across the saloon. With all my terrors weighing me down, I crawled, worm-like, up the companion-ladder, and wriggled on to the deck on all-fours. The sea, and the sky, and the barren deck all lay in perfect silence, which pressed upon me like one of those nightmares in which you feel that unless you can scream you must die. After two or three attempts, I moistened my parched mouth and called, "You Sing!" There was no voice of any one that answered. But that I think the limit of my capacity for being terrified had been reached some time before, I believe this irresponsiveness, with its accompanying sensation of being utterly alone, would have made me an idiot. As it was, I only felt numbed and tired. Slowly I stood up upon my feet, and went forrard to the break of the poop, learning at once the reason of You Sing's silence; for by the side of the after-hatch lay three Chinese, naked and dead, bearing on their bodies the grim evidences of the method of their ending. Close to the cabin door, as if he had dragged himself away from his late antagonists in the vain hope of reaching his friends again, lay You Sing. As I looked down upon him he moved slightly. In a moment, forgetting everything else, I was by his side, and lifted his head upon my knee. He opened his glazing eyes and looked up into my face with his old sweet smile, now with something of highest satisfaction in it. His dry lips opened, and he murmured, "'Ullo, Tommy; all litee." Then the intelligence faded out of his eyes, and he left me.

It must have been hours afterwards when I again realized my surroundings. Elsie was sitting by the piece of yellow clay that had been You Sing, perfectly still, but with an occasional tearing sob. She must have been crying for a long time. Gradually the whole of the past came back to me, and I saw how our dead friend had indeed paid in full what he considered to be his debt to us; although how that mild and gentle creature, in whom I never saw even so much as a shade of vexation, much less anger, could have risen to such a height of fighting valour as to slay three men in our defence was utterly beyond my powers of comprehension. For, without attempting any eloquence of panegyric, that was precisely what he had done, and with his opponent's own weapons, too. To say that I had not really felt lonely and helpless until now only faintly conveys the appalling sense of loss that had come upon me. As for the poor child, she crouched by the side of the corpse, scarcely more alive than it was, manifesting no fear or repugnance at the presence of death; indeed, she appeared unable to realize the great fact in its full terror.

How long we both sat in this dazed condition it is impossible to say with any definiteness. No doubt it was for several hours, for we both seemed only partially alive; and, for my part, the only impression left was that all besides ourselves were dead. That feeling carried with it a dim anticipation that we too might expect to find our turn to depart confronting us at any moment; but in this thought there was no fear, rather relief.

How often, I wonder, has it been noted that in times of deep mental distress, when the mind appears to have had a mortal blow, and all those higher faculties which are our peculiar possession are so numbed that they give no definite assistance to the organism, the animal needs of the body have instinctively asserted themselves, and thus saved the entire man or woman from madness or death? It must surely be one of the commonest of experiences, although seldom formulated in so many words. At any rate, this was now the case with me. Gradually the fact that I was parched with thirst became the one conscious thing; and, without thinking about it, without any definite idea even, I found myself on my feet, swaying and staggering as I crossed the bare deck to where the scuttle-butt used to be lashed. Finding it gone, I stood helplessly staring at the ends of the lashings that had secured it, with a dull, stupid anger of disappointment. *Then* I began to think; I had to, for my need was imperative. I remembered that You Sing had brought into the cabin before the typhoon a store of water sufficient for days. This mental effort was bracing, doing much to restore me again to some show of usefulness. I soon found the water, and hurried on deck once more, for the cabin was no place to stay in now. It was tenanted by shapes of dread, full of inaudible signs of woe; and right glad was I to regain the side of the little girl for living companionship. I offered her some water. She looked at it dully, as if unable to attach any idea to it; and it was only by repeatedly rousing her that I managed to awaken any reason in her injured mind at all. In the absence of any such compulsion, I think she would have just sat still and ceased to live, painlessly and unconsciously.

Now that the needs of another were laid upon me, I began to move about a little more briskly, and to notice our condition with returning interest. For some time the strange steadiness of the ship had puzzled me without arousing any definite inquiry in my mind as to the cause of it. But in crossing the deck to re-enter the cabin the true significance of that want of motion suddenly burst upon me, for I saw the calm face of the water only a few inches from the deck-line. The Blitzen was sinking. During the typhoon she must have received tremendous injuries from the wreckage of her top-hamper, that, floating alongside, entangled in the web of its rigging, was as dangerous as so many rocks would have been. There was urgent need now for thought and action also, for there was nothing of any kind on deck floatable. Boats, spars, hen-coops, all had gone. A thousand futile thoughts chased one another through my throbbing brain, but they ran in circles that led nowhere. There seemed to be no possible means of escape. Yet somehow I was not hopeless. I felt a curious reliance upon the fact that we two small people had come through so much unhurt in any way, and this baseless unreasoning faith in our good (?) fortune forbade me to despair. So that I cannot say I felt greatly surprised when I presently saw on the starboard side forrard a small *sampan* floating placidly, its grass painter made fast to the fore-chains. There was no mystery about its appearance. It had brought those awful visitors whose defeat caused You Sing his life, and was probably the only surviving relic of some junk that had foundered in the storm. The sight of it did me a world of good. Rushing to Elsie, I pointed out the fact of our immediate danger, and of the hope left us, and after some little difficulty succeeded in getting her into the *sampan*. The Blitzen was now so low in the water that my remaining time was countable by seconds. I flew into the cabin, snatched up a few biscuits and the large can of water that stood in the bathroom, and rushed for the boat. As I scrambled into her with my burden I noticed shudderingly that the ship was beginning to move, but with such a motion! It was like the death-throe of a man—a physical fact with which of late I had been well acquainted. Every plank of her groaned as if in agony; she gave a quivering sideway stagger. My fingers trembled so that I could hardly cast adrift the painter, which I was compelled to do, having no knife. I got the clumsy hitches adrift at last, and with one of the rough oars gave our frail craft a vigorous shove off, Elsie staring all the while at the huge hull with dilating eyes and drawn white face. Presently the Blitzen seemed to stumble;

a wave upreared itself out of the smooth brightness of the placid sea and embraced her bows, drawing them gently down. So gently, like a tired woman sinking to rest, did the Blitzen leave the light, and only a few foam-flecked whorls and spirals on the surface marked for a minute or two the spot where she had been.

Happily for us who were left, our troubles were nearly at an end. One calm night of restless dozing under the warm sky, trying not to think of what a tiny bubble we made on the wide sea, we passed not uncomfortably. Just before dawn I felt rather than heard a throbbing, its regular pulsations beating steadily as if inside my head. But they had not lasted one minute before I knew them for the propeller-beat of a steamer, and strained my eyes around through the departing darkness for a sight of her. Straight for us she came, the watchful officer on the bridge having seen us more than a mile off. In the most matter-of-fact way we were taken on board, and Elsie was soon mothered by the skipper's wife, while I was being made much of by the men. And that was all. Of all that mass of treasure that had caused the sacrifice of so many lives not one atom remained where it could ever again raise the demon of murder in human breasts. And although I could not realize all this, I really did not feel sorry that I had not succeeded in saving the slightest portion of it, my thankfulness at being spared alive being so great.

There were no passengers on board to make a fuss, so none was made. Three days afterwards we were at Hong Kong, and Elsie was handed over to the German

Consul, who gravely took down my story, but I could see did not believe half of it. I bade good-bye to Elsie, having elected to remain by the steamer, where I was being well treated, and in due time reached England again, a step nearer to becoming a full-fledged seaman.

THE DEBT OF THE WHALE

Elisha Cushing, skipper of the Beluga, South Seaman, of Martha's Vineyard, was a hard-bitten Yankee of the toughest of that tough race. Even in the sternest of mankind there is usually to be found some soft spot, some deeply-hidden well of feeling that at the touch of the right hand will bubble up in a kindly stream, even though it be hermetically sealed to all the world beside. But those who knew Captain Cushing best were wont to say that he must have been cradled on an iceberg, spent his childhood in a whaler's fo'c's'le, hardened himself by the constant contemplation and practice of cruelty, until, having arrived at the supreme position of master of his own ship, he was less of a man than a pitiless automaton who regarded neither God nor devil, and only looked upon other men as an engineer might upon the cogs of a machine. Few, indeed, are the men who, throughout a voyage lasting from three to four years, shut up within the narrow bounds of a small ship, could entirely do without human companionship, could abstain from some friendly intercourse, however infrequent, with those around them. Yet Captain Cushing was even such a man. No one knew how he passed his abundant leisure. He was never seen reading, he did not smoke, no intoxicating drink was ever allowed on board his ship; in fact at all times, except when whale-fishing was being carried on, he was to all appearance a body without a mind, a figure of a man who moved and ate and slept mechanically, yet whom to offend was to court nothing less than torture. Those unspeculating eyes missed nothing; not a member of the crew but felt that in some not-to-be-explained fashion all his doings, almost his very thoughts, were known to the grim commander, and hard, indeed, was the lot of any unfortunate who in any way came athwart the stern code of rules that appeared to govern Captain Cushing's command. Nevertheless he had one virtue—he did not interfere. So long as the business of the ship went on as goes a good clock, there was peace. The discipline was perfect; it reduced the human items that composed the Beluga's crew to something very nearly resembling a piece of carefully constructed mechanism, for Captain Cushing's genius lay that way. Out of the many crews that he had commanded during his thirty years' exercise of absolute power he was wont to winnow officers that were a reflex of his own mind, and it mattered not how raw were the recruits bundled on board his ship at the last moment before leaving home, the Cushing system speedily reduced them to a condition of absolute mindlessness as far as any wish of their own was concerned. They became simply parts of the engine whereby Captain Cushing's huge store of dollars was augmented.

It was an article of religion among the afterguard of the Beluga, handed on to each new-comer by some unspoken code of communication, that the "old man's" being and doing might never be discussed. The subject was "tabu," not to be approached upon any pretext, although nothing could be more certain than that it lay uppermost in every officer's mind. Among the crew, in that stifling den forrard where thirty men of almost as many differing nationalities lived and sometimes died, the mystery of the grim skipper's ways, coupled with queer yarns about his antecedents, was occasionally commented upon with bated breath in strange mixtures of language. But somehow it always happened that, closely following upon any conversation of the kind, the injudicious talkers ran butt up against serious trouble. No charges were made, no definite punishments were awarded; but loss of rest, dangerous and unnecessary tasks, kickings and stripes exhibited casually, were their portion for a season. These things had the effect of exciting an almost superstitious reverence for the captain's powers of knowing what was going on, coupled with a profound distrust of each other among the foremast hands, that made for their subjection perhaps more potently than even the physical embarrassments which formed so liberal a part of their daily lot. And yet, such is the perversity of human nature, whenever the Beluga gammed another whaler, and the wretched crowd got a chance to talk to strangers, they actually indulged in tall talk, "gas" about their skipper's smartness as a whaleman, his ability as a seaman, and, strangest of all, his eminence as a hard citizen who would "jes' soon killer man's look at 'im." Every fresh device of his for screwing extra work out of his galley-slaves, every mean and low-down trick played upon them for the lessening of their scanty food or robbing them of their hard-earned lay, only seemed to increase their admiration for him, as if his diabolical personality had actually inverted all their ideas of right and wrong.

The man himself, the centre of this little cosmos of whose dreary round pleasure formed not the minutest part, was apparently about 55 years of age. He had been tall, above the average, but a persistent stoop had modified that particular considerably. The great peculiarity about his appearance was his head, which was shaped much like a fir-cone. From the apex of it fell a few straggling wisps of hay-coloured hair that did not look as if they belonged there, but had been blown against the scalp and stuck there accidentally. Wide, outstanding ears, pointed at the top like a bat's, eyes that were just straight slits across the parchment face, from between whose bare edges two inscrutable pupils of different but unnameable colours looked out, a straight, perfectly shaped nose, so finely finished that it looked artificial, and another straight lipless slit for a mouth completes his facial portrait. His arms were abnormally long, and his legs short, while his gait, from long walking upon greasy decks, was a bear-like shuffle. It was whispered in the fo'c's'le that his strength was gigantic, and there was a tradition extant of his having wrung a recalcitrant harpooner's neck with his bare hands as one would a fowl's; but none of his present crew had seen him exert himself at all.

What impressed them most, however, was his voice. Ordinarily he spoke in almost a faint whisper, such as a dying man might be supposed to utter, but it must have been very distinct in articulation, as he was never known to speak twice. Yet, if at any time it became necessary for him to hail a boat or a passing ship, that strange opening in his head would unclose, and forth from it would issue a strident sound that carried farther than the bellow of any angry bull.

His "luck" was proverbial. None of his officers ever knew, any more than did the meanest member of the ship's company, whither he was bound, nor in what unfrequented areas of ocean he sought the valuable creatures from which he was amassing so much wealth. Of course, they knew, as all sailors do from close observation of courses made, land seen, weather, etc., within a few hundred miles or so, but their knowledge was never ample enough to have enabled them afterwards to take another ship along the same tracks that the Beluga had found so richly frequented by payable whales. But Elisha Cushing added to his so-called luck almost superhuman energy. If he did not spare his unhappy slaves, he was no more merciful to himself. Never a boat was lowered after whales, no matter what the weather or how few the prey, but he was foremost; as if he loved (if it be admissible to mention love in connection with this emotionless man) the chase for its own sake, or, knowing that he carried a charmed life, dared to take risks that no ordinary man would do except under compulsion. There was one marked feature of his whaling, however, that was noticed by all his crew, if, owing to the difficulties hinted at before, it was seldom discussed. Whenever the boats approached either a single whale or a whale school, Captain Cushing would surely be seen standing high on the two quarter-cleats in the stern-sheets of his boat, searching with sparkling, almost glaring eyes among them for *something*. It was believed that the boats never " went on a whale " until the skipper had first passed them (the whales) all in review, and fully satisfied himself that the object of his search, whatever it might be, was not there. His scrutiny over, the game commenced, and surely never, since the bold Biscayan fishermen first attacked the questing rorquals that visited their shores, with bone and flint pointed lances, was there ever seen such whale-hunting as that carried on by Elisha Cushing. Without changing colour, or raising his voice above its usual low murmur, he would haul his boat up alongside of the mountainous mammal, order her to be held there, and then, disregarding the writhings and wallowing of the great creature, he would calmly feel for the ribs or the shoulder-blades with the lance point. And having found an interspace, the long arms would straighten out, and four feet of the lance would glide like a slender bright snake into the mighty vitals, only to be withdrawn on the instant and plunged home again and again and again, each thrust taking a new turn within, and causing the black, hot blood to burst from the wound as from the nozzle of a fire-hose. Or, quietly seated on the gunwale, he would select his spot, and probe with the lance as a surgeon might seek for a bullet in the body of an insensible patient. Should the boat swerve away from the whale ever so slightly until he gave the signal, he would look round, and on the instant five men, albeit in the very shadow of death, would feel a creeping at the pit of their stomachs, and a frantic desire to avert his anger; for he had been known to reach across the boat and snatch a man from his thwart with one hand, flinging him, a limp, ragged bundle, far out of the boat, and not caring where. The only signs that he ever showed of anything unusual being toward, was a faint blue patch that appeared in the middle of his otherwise yellow cheek, and a reddish glint in his eyes. In spite of his peculiarities, his men were proud to be members of his boat's crew, for his skill was of so high an order that his apparent recklessness never got him a boat stove or lost him a man; while his officers, though the pick and flower of whalemen, had their usual share of casualties.

About two years of the cruise had gone by, and the Beluga's hold was already more than two-thirds full of oil, in spite of the fact that several shipments home had been made during the voyage. After a season on the Vasquez ground in the South Pacific, where she had averaged two whales a week, she was now steering an easterly course with a little south in it—not cruising, but making a passage apparently for the "off-shore grounds," on the coast of Chili. One morning at daybreak the cry of "sail-ho" from the crow's-nest reached Captain Cushing in his cabin, and before the officer on deck had time to answer, his deep breathed tones were heard welling up from below in reply, " Where away." The stranger was a whaling barque also, lying hove-to right ahead, as if expecting and waiting for the Beluga. When the two vessels were within three miles of each other, Captain Cushing ordered his boat away, and with an order to the mate to " keep her jes 's she is," he departed. No sooner had his crew put him alongside than he climbed on board, and, contrary to the usual practice, ordered them away from the stranger, telling them to lie on their oars at a little distance until he should call them. The skipper of the stranger (still an unknown ship to the Beluga's crew, as she had no name visible) met Captain Cushing at the gangway, presenting as complete a contrast to that inscrutable man as could well be imagined. A dumpy, apple-faced little fellow, with a lurking smile in every dimple, and a mat of bright red curls covering his round head. Snatching the languidly offered paw of his visitor, he burst forth, " Wall, ef this ent grate! I be tarnally ding-busted ef I wa'nt a talkin' 'bout ye las' night, talkin' t' meself that is," he hastily interjected, upon seeing the look that Cushing turned upon him. " But kem along daown b'low n'hev—wall I wonder wut y' *will* hev. Don' seem sif y' ever hev anythin'. Nev' mine, less git b'low anyhaow." And together they descended.

For a long time the little man did all the talking —after the manner of a trusted manager of a thriving business making his report to his principal. He told of whales caught, of boats stove, of gear carried away —quite the usual routine—while Cushing listened with his impenetrable mask, through which it was impossible to see whether he was interested or not. It was like talking to a graven image. But still, as the tale went on, and it appeared that the little talker had been fairly successful, there was a slight relaxing of the rigid pose, which to the eye of the initiate spelt satisfaction. For all unknown to any one except the ruddy skipper talking to him, Cushing was really the owner of this unnamed ship—a vessel that he had stolen from an anchorage in the Pelew Islands, while all her crew were ashore on a furious debauch which had lasted for several weeks, and had ever since been running her in this mysterious fashion by the aid of the one man in the wide world in whom he could be said to repose any confidence. That story is, however, too long to be told here.

The recital was apparently finished, when suddenly, as if he had just remembered an important part of his report, the narrator resumed, his jolly red face assuming an air of gravity that was strangely out of harmony with it. "An' cap'," said he, "I'd eenamost fergot—I met up with the spotted whale of the Bonins las' cruise. I——"

But there was a sudden change, an unearthly brightening into copper colour of Cushing's face, as he sprang to his feet, and, with his long fingers working convulsively, gurgled out, "'R ye sure? Don't ye mislead me, Silas, 'r ye'd be better dead every time. Naow yew jest gi' me th' hull hang o' this thing 'fore y' say 'nother word 'bout anythin'!"

There was no mask of indifference now. The man

was transformed into a living embodiment of eager desire, and bold indeed would any have been that would have dared to thwart him. No such idea was in his hearer's thoughts, at any rate, for no sooner had he done speaking than Silas leaned forward and said—

"Yes, cap', I *am* sure, not thet it's hardly wuth while sayin' so, fur yew couldn't imagine me bein' mistook over a critter like thet. 'Twas this way. Ev' since *thet* affair I've scurcely ever fergot yew're orders—t' look eout fer Spotty an' let ye' know fust chance whar he uz usin' roun', but at this perticler lowerin' we jest had all eour soup ladled eout fer us an' no mistake. Ther'd ben a matter o' a dozen ships ov us in compny, 'n I wuz bizzy figgerin' haow t' git rid'r some ov 'em befo' we struck whale. I noo they wuz abaout; the air wuz jest thick up with whale smell, 'n every one ov my boys wuz all alive. Wall, we hove to thet night 's ushal till midnight, 'n then I sez t' myself, sez I, ef I don't up-stick 'n run south I'm a horse. Fur, ye see, 'twuz born in 'pon me thet whales wuz comin' up from the line away, 'n a big school too. I doan' know why, ov course not, but thar twuz—y' know how 'tis yerself.

"Sure 'nough by dayspring they wa'nt a ship in sight of us, but at seven bells we raised whale, 'n b' gosh I reckon they was mos' a thousan' of 'em spread all out to looard of us more like a school o' porps than hunderd bar'l whales—which they wuz every last one ov 'em, cep them thet wuz bigger. They wa'nt much wind, 'n we lowered five boats 'n put f'r them whales all we knew. Tell y' wut, cap', I've seen some tall spoutin', but that mornin's work jest laid raight over all I ever heer tell ov, much less see. We all got fas' on the jump, 'n then we cut loose agen. Reason why, we couldn't move fur 'em. They jest crowded in on us, quite quiet; they wa'nt a bit er fight in one ov 'em, and we handled the lances on the nearest. That patch o' sea wuz jest a saladero now I'm tellin' ye. We never chipped a splinter ner used ten fathom o' tow line, 'n be *my* recknin we killed twenty whales. Gradjully the crowd drawed off, leavin' us with all that plunder lyin' roun' loose, an I wuz beginnin' t' wish I hadn't run so fur away from the fleet. Fur I knew we couldn' handle sech a haul's thet—more'n haef ov em 'd be rotten 'fore we c'd cut in ef we'd worked f'r a week on eend 'thout a minnit's rest.

"While we wuz jest drawin' breth like after th' war, and the shipkeepers 'uz a workin' her daown t' us, my harponeer sings out 'sif he'd a ben snake bit, 'Blow-w-s 'n breaches! Ee'r sh' white waterrs. Madre di Gloria, Capena, lookee what come.' 'N thar shore nuff he uz comin'; Spotty fur true. I know, cap. I never see him afore. All I knoo 'bout him uz wut ye told me, an' I doan mine ownin' up naow at I thought y' mout ha ben a bit loony on thet subjec, but I tek it all back, 'n 'umbly axes yer pardin.

"Yaas, sir, he come; like all hell let loose. He jes flung himself along the top er th' sea like a dolphin, 'n I reckin we all felt kiender par'litic. Soon's I got me breath I sings out t' cut adrif', fur we'd all got towlines fast to flukes ready to pass abroad, and handle bomb-guns quick. Then when he come within range t' let him have 'em full butt 'n put f'r th' ship. Don't say I felt very brash 'baout it, but twuz the best I c'd think ov. He kem, oh yes, sir, he kem, 'n the sight of his charge brung a verse of th' Bible (haint looked inside one f'r twenty years) into my mind. Goes suthin like this 'The mountings skipped like rams, th' little hills like young sheep.' We done all we knoo, we twisted and tarned an' pulled an' starned; but you know, cap, better'n any of us, thet the boat never was built thet c'd git out of th' way ov a spalmacitty whale when he'd made up his mine fur mischief. 'N we wa'nt no excepshin. We weakened at las', 'n took th' water, whar we knoo he wouldn't tech us, 'n b' gosh he didn' leave a plank o' one o' them thar boats whole. I doan know why he didn' foller it up or go fur th' ship. Ef he hed thar'd a ben an eend of the story, sure. But no, he just disappeared quiet 's death, 'n we all gut picked up in time. Yes, 'n we managed to rig up our spare boat 'n git five of them whales cut in too, though I'm free t' confess the last of 'em wuz middlin' gamey by th' time they got t' th' try pots. The rest jest floated erroun 'n stunk up th' North Persific Ocean till twuz like a graveyard struck be 'n erthquake. But we got six hunderd barl out of th' catch, anyway."

While the recital was proceeding, Cushing's face was a study. He listened without moving a muscle, but rage, hope, and joy chased one another over that usually expressionless mask like waves raised by sudden squalls over the calm surface of a sheltered lake. And when it was over he rose wearily, saying—

"All right, Jacob; when ye're through put fur the

old rondyvoos an' discharge. I'll be long 'bout March an' range fur next cruise. So long. I'm off t' th' Bonins full pelt."

"But, Cap'n Cushing, is ut worth huntin' up that gauldern spotty beast 'n gettin' 'tarnally smashed up fur an' idee? Why caint y' leave 'im alone? Sure's deeth he'll do ye a hurt. Take a fool's advice, cap'n, 'n let him die ov ole age or accident."

"Jacob, my man, y' fergit yerself. When I want yew're advice, I'll seek it. Till then don't ye offer it. Tain't t' my likin', fur I'm accustomed to take no man as my counsellor. So long once more, 'n don't fergit y'r orders."

In two strides he reached the top of the companion-ladder, and with that wide-breathed cry of his that we knew so well had summoned his boat. She sprang to the nameless barque's side like a living thing, Captain Cushing stepped into her, and the queer gam was over. Back alongside he came, standing erect as a monolith in the stern-sheets, and, hardly allowing time for the boat to be hooked on, issued rapid orders for all sail to be made; the helm was put hard up, and away we went N.W. No one ventured an opinion upon this sudden change, but every one looked volumes of inquiry. And no one dared even hint to his fellow the wonder, the painful curiosity, he felt as, day after day, before a strong south-east trade, the Beluga did her steady seven knots an hour, nor stayed for anything. Again and again the cry of "blow" came ringing down from the crows'-nests, and as often as it was heard the old man mounted aloft with his glasses, and stayed until he had apparently satisfied himself of something. But never a halt did we make. No, and as if the very whales themselves knew of our pre-occupation, a school actually rose near and accompanied us for a whole watch, gambolling along massively within gun-shot on either side. They might as well have been a thousand miles away for all the notice the old man took of them. He just leaned upon the weather-rail, gazing with expressionless face at the unchanging ring of the horizon—a fathomless enigma to all of us. The proximity of those whales, however, troubled the officers more than anything else had done, and it took all their inbred terror of the old man to keep them from breaking into open mutiny. Even among us, who had little interest in the voyage from a monetary point of view, and to whom the capture of whales only meant a furious outburst of the hardest work, the feeling of indignation at the loss of so grand an opportunity was exceedingly hard to bear.

Onward we sped until we got among the islands, but no slackening of haste, except when the wind lulled, was indulged in. By day or by night we threaded those mazy archipelagoes as if the whole intricate navigation was as familiar to the skipper as the rooms of his cabin. Such ship-handling surely never was seen. Perched upon the fore-yard, the only light visible being the blazing foam spreading widely out on either bow and ahead where the staunch old ship plunged through those phosphorescent waters, the glowing patches cropping up hither and thither all around as the indolent Pacific swell broke irritably over some up-cropping coral patch, and the steely sparkles of the stars in the blue-black sky above, Captain Cushing conned the ship as easily and confidently as a pilot entering New York harbour on midsummer day, his quiet voice sounding down from where he crouched invisible as if we were being celestially directed. There was no feeling of apprehension among us, for our confidence in his genius was perfect, making us sure that whatever of skill in navigation was required he surely possessed it.

Nevertheless, the mystery of our haste across the whole vast breadth of the Pacific fretted every man, even the dullest. It was outside all our previous experience. Perhaps the only thing that made it bearable was the knowledge that not one of the officers was any better informed than we were. Foremast hands are always jealous of the information obtainable in the cuddy, and even though it may not be of the slightest use to them, any scrap they may obtain gives to the lucky eavesdropper a sort of brevet-rank for the time being. Here, however, all that was to be known as to our movements, the reason for them, and the ultimate object of our long passage, with its unprecedented haste, was locked up in one man's mind, and that man a graven image for secretiveness.

Such was the expeditiousness of our passage that seven weeks after gamming the nameless whaler on the " off-shore " ground, we sighted one of the Volcano group of islands which lie near the Bonins in the great eddy of the Kuro Siwo or Japanese current, and form one of the landmarks of what was once the busiest sperm whaling-ground on the globe. The shape of the island, more like the comb of a cock than anything else, was familiar to many of us, and gave us for the first time for months a clear idea of our position. So we were on the Japan ground. It was a relief to know that much, certainly; but why—why had we, contrary to all whaling precedent, made a passage of several thousand miles in such haste? No answer. But having arrived, our usual whaling tactics were immediately resumed. With a difference. Instead of being kept hard at work during all the hours of daylight scrubbing, polishing, cleaning, until the old oil-barrel of a ship was as spick and span as a man-o'-war, the word was passed that the watch on deck were to keep a look-out for whale—every man of them except him at the wheel. And the watchers in the crows'-nest were provided each with a pair of binoculars—a thing unheard of before. So the ship became a veritable argus. It is safe to say that nothing, not even a frond of seaweed, or a wandering sea-bird, ever passed within range of sight without being seen and noted. After a few days of this most keen outlook came another surprise in the shape of a speech from the old man.

Calling all hands aft, he faced us for a minute in silence, while every heart beat a trifle quicker as if we were on the threshold of a mystery deeper than any that had yet worried us. He spoke quietly, dispassionately, yet with that blue patch in the middle of each yellow cheek that was to us the symbol of his most intense excitement. "I've kem up hyar aefter *one* whale, 'n ef I git him th' v'yge is over. He's big, bigger'n enny man here's ever seen, I guess, an' he's spotted with white on brown like a pieball horse. Yew kaint mistake him. I'll give five hundred dollars t' th' man that raises him first, 'n I'll divide five thousand among ye 'cordin t' grade ef I kill him. An' when we've cut him in we'll up-stick f'r Noo Bedford. Naow, ef this is enny indoocement t' ye, keep y'r eyes skinned by day and night. Moreover, I warn ye thet this ship doan't see civilization agen• until I git wut I'm after, 'r I go under. Thet'll do, all haends."

In any other ship this harangue would have been succeeded by a buzz of chat as soon as the fellows got forward, but here not a word was spoken. Thenceforward, though it was evident that not a thought could be spared, not a look wasted from scanning the wide circle of blue around, by night and by day the watch never slackened, and men would hardly sleep for eagerness to be the first to claim the prize. Yet, as so often happens, it fell to one who had the least opportunity of obtaining it, the mulatto steward whose duties kept him below most of the time. About ten days after the skipper's offer the steward crept on deck one evening about eight bells, his long day's work just over, and slouching forward into the waist leaned over the side and began to fill his pipe. It was a heavenly evening, hardly a breath of air breaking the sleekiness of the sea-surface, the slightest perceptible swell giving us a gentle undulatory motion, and overhead the full moon hung in the cloudless dome like an immense globe glowing with electric light. The steward had finished filling his pipe, and was just feeling for a match when he stopped suddenly and said to his nearest neighbour, " Oliver, what in thunder's thet right in the moon-glade?" The whisper ran round the ship as if on a telephone, and in less than a minute all the night-glasses were on the spot. The skipper's voice broke the silence—hardly broke it—so quiet yet audible was it. " 'Way boats. Th' first man thet makes a noise, I'll cripple him f'r life. Stoord, g'lang b'low 'n git y'r money; ye'll find it on my bunk-shelf."

Like a crew of ghosts, we sped to our stations, hanging over side and booming the boats off as they were lowered with the utmost caution lest there should be a rattle of a patent block or a splash as they took the water. In five minutes we were all away, five boats, the skipper leading and every man, except the officers steering, wielding an Indian paddle as if his life depended upon utter silence. As we sat facing forrard every eye was strained for a glimpse of the enemy, but at that low level and in the peculiar glare of a moonlit tropical night we could see nothing. Moreover, we were paddling along the glittering path cast upon the sea by the moon, and a few minutes' steady gaze upon that stretch of molten silver made the eyes burn and throb, so that it was an intense relief to close them for a while. At every dip of the paddles there was an additional flash in the water, behind each boat and far beneath myriads of dancing gleams disported themselves, while in ever-accumulating numbers wide bands of pale fire radiating from opaque bodies keeping company with us told us of the shark hosts mustering for the fight wherein they, at any rate, were likely to fall heirs to goodly spoil.

Without a pause for rest, and in the same utter stillness, we toiled on for at least two hours. It was back-breaking work, and but for the splendid training we were in we could not possibly have held out. Then suddenly from ahead came a yell of wild laughter, the most blood-chilling sound surely ever heard. Immediately following it we saw a veritable hill of light upraise itself out of the sea ahead, and realized that at last our quarry was brought to bay. "In paddles, out oars!" yelled the officers, and as we obeyed we were aware that a terrific commotion was in progress ahead. The greenish-glaring spray ascended in long jets, and the dull boom of mighty blows reverberated over the hitherto quiet sea. Pulling till our sinews cracked, we reached the storm-centre, and, by what seemed a miracle, actually succeeded in getting fast to the whale—every boat did that, although it seemed to many of us a suicidal policy under the circumstances. Shouts and curses resounded until a voice was heard that enforced silence, the far-reaching tones of Captain Cushing, who was nearest to the foe, but for all his ability was unable to do more once he had got fast. For now the whale had settled down into a steady straightforward rush at the rate of about fourteen knots an hour, the five boats sweeping along in his wake like meteors glancing across the deep darkness of the night. The whale could not be seen. Only at long intervals did he slant upwards and, with a roar like the lifting of an overloaded safety-valve, disappear again.

So on we went through the warm quiet night without the slightest sign of slackening until the gladsome light of dawn quickened on the sea-rim, and showed us that we were alone—there was no sign of the ship. A gaunt and haggard crew we looked, anxiety scoring deep furrows in our wan faces. And as the sun sprang into the sky we suddenly came to a dead stop. The strain on the line compelled us to pay out, and thus we hovered in a circle, bows awash, and awaited the pleasure of our foe. There was a sudden upspringing of all boats, a hasty manœuvring to clear one another as far as might be, and, before any of us could have imagined it possible, high into our midst leaped the spotted whale, his awful jaws agape, and his whole body writhing in its evolution. Straight for the skipper's boat he came, taking it diagonally, and, with a crash that set all our teeth on edge, she disappeared. A mist arose before our sight, the spray of the conflict filling the air, but, fired beyond fear by the wholesale tragedy we believed had taken place, we bent to our oars till they cracked, thirsting for that monster's blood. As we came bounding to the spot he disappeared, and, to our unspeakable amazement (though we had no time to show it) all the destroyed boat's crew reappeared. But if Captain Cushing had looked dangerous before, his appearance now was that of a demoniac. His cap was gone, so that the yellow dome of his head loomed strangely in the early morning light, his clothing hung from him in ribbons, and his right arm dangled as if only held by a few sinews. He had come right out of the whale's jaws. All the others were scathless.

To all offers of help he turned a savage scowl, and seizing a bomb-gun in his uninjured hand he jammed himself in the boat's bows, his voice, unaltered save for being a little higher in pitch, being heard and obeyed among the other boats on the instant. The whale returned. At the captain's orders all cut their lines, and the real fight began. Truly Captain Cushing was fit to be a leader of men, for his eyes missed nothing. At his orders all four boats advanced, retreated, backed, circled, stopped dead. He seemed able to penetrate the misleading medium of the water, where a whale at twenty fathoms' depth looks like a salmon, and whatever move the monster made, his counter-move baffled the savage intent. Yet all the time we were strictly on the defensive. Our long night's tow, want of food and drink, and since daylight the tremendous strain upon our nerves, was surely telling against us, and our adversary was apparently tireless. Not only so, but his ingenuity never flagged. Ruse after ruse was tried by him, but no two were alike. And without a doubt our hopes of coming alive out of this battle were growing fainter and fainter every moment.

Things were in this gloomy stage when, with a most appalling roar, the whale suddenly broke water on his back, and launched himself at the captain's boat. The wide sea boiled like a pot as he came, but, to our horror, the boat lay still, as if anchored to the spot. The crash came, and amidst its uproar we heard the sharp report of a gun. Like a great whirlpool the waters foamed and rose, nothing being distinguishable in the midst of the vortex until it gradually subsided, and we saw the fragments of the boat idly tossing upon the crimson foam. Hastening to the rescue, we found six men still alive, but all sadly hurt. The seventh was gone. At last Captain Cushing had paid in full the debt that had been owing. We were now completely overborne with fatigue as well as overloaded with helpless men—utterly unfit to compete any further with so fearful a foe. While we lay thus helplessly awaiting what all felt must be the end, the whale again broke water about twenty yards away. Up, up, up into the air he rose, effortless, majestically; and as he soared aloft every heart stood still to see the body of our late commander hanging limply at the angle of that yawning mouth. The yellow visage was towards us, the same savage grin frozen upon it, but the will against which everything had shivered was now but the will of the drift-weed round about; that clammy piece of clay was tenantless.

Down came the gigantic form, tearing up the sea into foam and disappeared from our sight, to be seen no more. Long and wearily we waited, hungry and thirsty, and some in agony from their injuries, until twenty-four hours later the Beluga found us, and all were safely taken on board. Strangely transformed the old ship appeared. At first we went about as we had been wont, not daring to exchange thoughts with one another. But gradually the blessed truth soaked in. We were freed from a tyranny more dire than any of us had realized—a tyranny over mind as well as body. Officers and men rejoiced together, for all had suffered. And it was at once decided to return home in leisurely fashion, calling at well-known ports on the way, and endeavouring to make up by a little joy of life for past miseries.

What the true inwardness of Captain Cushing's desire of revenge on the spotted whale was we never rightly knew, but many rumours were current among ships that we gammed that he had, with his own hand many years before, killed the whale of a small pod, or company of whales, of which the spotted whale was the leader, and that they had met on several occasions afterwards, their meeting always being attended by some grave disaster to Cushing's ship and crew. This had wrought upon his mind until it had become a mania, and he was willing to risk all for the chance of slaying his redoubtable foe. But we had no doubt that the whale was merely the instrument chosen by Providence for meting out to him a death he richly deserved for his many crimes.

THE SKIPPER'S WIFE

Stories of the Sea have in my humble opinion been quite unfairly dealt with by the majority of their narrators. Told for the benefit of non-seafaring folk by writers, who, however great their literary gifts, have had merely a nodding acquaintance with the everyday doings on board ship, they generally lack proportion, and fail to convey to shore folk an intimate sense of the sea-atmosphere. Especially has this been so with books for young people, as was no doubt to be expected. So much has this been the case that sailors generally despise sea-stories, finding them utterly unlike anything they have ever experienced themselves. Of late years there have been some notable exceptions among sea story writers, most of them happily still living and doing splendid service. One cunning hand is still, that of James Runciman, whose yarns are salt as the ocean, and have most truly held the mirror up to Nature in a manner unexcelled by any other marine writer living or dead. Freedom from exaggeration, clarity of expression, and sympathetic insight into sea-life were his main features, and no one hated more than he the utterly impossible beings and doings common to the bulk of sea-fiction.

Whether it be from lack of imaginative power or

an unfertile inventiveness I cannot say, but it has always appeared to me as if one need never travel outside the actual facts of his experience, however humdrum it may appear to the casual observer, to find matters sufficiently interesting to hold any intelligent reader enthralled, always providing that matter be well presented. And in that belief I venture to tell a plain tale here, into which no fiction enters except proper names.

Drifting about the world, as the great fucus wanders from shore to shore, having once been dislodged from its parent rock, I one day found myself ashore at Quilimane, desperately anxious to get a berth in any capacity on board ship for the sole purpose of getting away. My prospects were not very rosy, for the only vessels in the hateful place were two or three crazy country craft with Arab crews, that looked exceedingly like slavers to me. At last, to my intense relief, a smart looking barquentine entered the port and anchored. I was, as usual, lounging about the beach (it seemed the healthiest place I could find) and my longing eyes followed every move of the crew as they busied themselves in getting the boat out. When the captain stepped ashore I was waiting to meet him, and the first words he heard were—

"*Do* you want a hand, cap'n?"

Taking keen stock of me, he said, "What sort of a berth do you want?"

"Well, sir," I replied, "I've got a second-mate's ticket, but I'll go as boy for the chance of getting away from here, if necessary."

" I want a cook-and-steward," he murmured dubiously, " and as I've got my wife aboard the cooking's rather important."

" I'm your man, sir," I cried, " if I can't cook you can dump me overboard. I never shipped as cook yet, but I've had to teach a good few cooks how to boil salt water without burning it."

He smiled pleasantly at this, and said, " I must say I like your looks and—well there, jump into the boat. I'll be back directly."

Sure enough, in a couple of hours I was busy in her cosy galley, while the chaps were rattling the windlass round with a will, anxious enough to get clear of that sweltering coast. From the first my relations with all hands were of the pleasantest kind. They had suffered many things at the hands of several so-called cooks during the eighteen months they had been away from home, each dirty destroyer of provisions being worse than his predecessor. But especially were my efforts appreciated in the cabin. The skipper had with him his wife and two little girls, aged four and five respectively, who made that little corner of the ship seem to a homeless, friendless wanderer like myself a small heaven. Mrs. Brunton was a sweet-faced grey-eyed woman of about thirty, with a quiet tenderness of manner and speech that made a peaceful atmosphere about her like that of a summer Sunday evening in some tiny English village. Her husband was a grand specimen of a British seaman, stalwart and fair-haired, with a great sweeping beard and bright blue eyes that always had a lurking smile in their depths. The pair appeared to have but one mind. Their chief joy seemed to be in the silent watching of their children's gambols, as, like two young lambs, they galloped round the decks or wriggled about the cramped fittings of the small saloon. The charm of that happy home-circle was over all hands. You might say that the ship worked herself, there was so little sign of the usual machinery of sea-life.

So the days slipped away as we crept down towards the Cape, bound round to Barbadoes, of all places in the world. Then in the ordinary course of events the weather got gradually worse, until one night it culminated in a following gale of hurricane fierceness, thundering down out of an ebony sky that almost rested on the mastheads. By-and-by the swart dungeon about us became shot with glowing filaments that quivered on the sight like pain-racked nerves, and the bass of the storm fell two octaves. Sail had been reduced to the fore lower topsail and the fore-topmast staysail, which had the sheet hauled flat aft in case of her broaching-to. Even under those tiny rags she flew before the hungering blast like a hare when the hounds are only her own length behind. The black masses of water gradually rose higher alongside as they bellowed past until their terrible heads peered inboard as if seeking the weakest spot. They began to break over all, easily at first, but presently with a sickening crash that made itself felt in one's very bowels. At last two menacing giants rose at once on either side, curving their huge heads until they overhung the waist. Thus, for an appreciable fraction of time, they stood, then fell

Gently she covered their ruddy faces.

—on the main-hatch. It cracked—sagged downward —and every man on deck knew that the foot-thick greenheart fore-and-after was broken, and that another sea like that would sink us like a saucer. Hitherto the skipper had been standing near the cuddy scuttle, in which his wife crouched, her eyes dim with watching her husband. Now he stooped and whispered three words in her ear. With one more glance up into his face she crept down into their berth, and over to where the two little ones were sleeping soundly. Gently, but with an untrembling hand, she covered their ruddy faces with a folded mosquito net and turned out the light. Then she swiftly returned to her self-chosen post in the scuttle, just reaching up a hand to touch her husband's arm, and let him know that she was near. The quiver that responded was answer enough. He was looking astern, and all his soul was in his eyes. For there was a streak of kindly light, a line of hope on the murky heaven. It broadened to a rift, the blue shone through, and stooping he lifted his wife's head above the hatch, turning her face so that she too might see and rejoice. She lifted her face, with streaming eyes, to his for a kiss, then fled below, turned up the light again, and uncovered the children's faces. Five minutes later she heard his step coming down, and devoured him with her eyes as he walked to the barometer, peered into it and muttered "thank God."

A fortnight later I was prowling up and down the cabin outside their closed state-room door, my fingers twitching with nervousness, and a lump continually rising in my throat that threatened to choke me; for within that tiny space, the captain, all unaided except by his great love and quiet common sense, was elbowing a grim shadow that seemed to envy him his treasure. Now and then a faint moan curdled round my heart, making it ache as if with cold. Beyond that there was no sign from within, and the suspense fretted me till I felt like a bundle of bare nerves. Overhead I could hear the barefooted step of the mate, as he wandered with uncertain gait about the lee side of the poop under the full glow of the passionless moon. At last, when I felt as worn as if I had been swimming for hours, there came a thin, gurgling little wail—a new voice that sent a thrill through the curves of my brain with a sharp pang. And then I felt the hot tears running down my face—why, I did not know. A minute later the door swung open, and the skipper said, in a thick, strange tone, "It's all right, Peter; I've a son. And she's grand, my boy, she's grand." I mumbled out something; I meant well, I'm sure, but no one could have understood me. He knew, and shook hands with me heartily. And presently I was nursing the bonny mite as if I had never done aught else—me that never had held a baby before. It was good, too; it lay in my arms on a pillow, and looked up at me with bright, unwinking eyes.

Then came three weeks of unalloyed delight. Overhead the skies were serene—that deep, fathomless blue, that belongs of right to the wide, shoreless seas of the tropics, where the constant winds blow unfalteringly to a mellow harmony of love. On board, every thought was drawn magnet-wise to the tiny babe who had come among us like a messenger from another sphere, and the glances cast at the tender mother as she sat under the little awning, like a queen, holding her court, were almost reverential. Never a man of us will forget that peaceful time. Few words were spoken, but none of them were angry, for every one felt an influence at work on him that, while it almost bewildered him, made him feel gentle and kind. But into the midst of this peaceful time came that envious shadow again. How it happened no man could tell; what malign seed had suddenly germinated, after so long lying dormant, was past all speculation of ours. The skipper himself fell sick. For a few days he fought man-fashion against a strange lassitude that sapped all his great strength and overcame even his bright cheery temper until he became fretful as a sickly babe. At last there came a day when he could not rise from his cot. With a beseeching look in his eyes he lay, his fine voice sunk to a whisper and his sunny smile gone. His wife hovered about him continually, unsparing of herself, and almost forgetting the first claim of the babe. The children, with the happy thoughtlessness of their age, could not be kept quiet, so, for the most part, they played forward with the crew, where they were as happy as the day was long. Every man did his best to entertain them; and when sailors make pets of children, those children are favoured by fortune. Meanwhile, in the cabin, we fought inch by inch with death for our friend. But our hands were tied by ignorance, for the rough directions of the book in the medicine chest gave us no help in dealing with this strange disease. Gradually the fine frame of the skipper dwindled and shrank, larger and more wistful grew his eyes, but after the first appalling discovery of his weakness he never uttered a complaining word. He lay motionless, unnoticing, except that into the deep wells of his eyes there came an expression of great content and peace whenever his wife bent over him. She scarcely ever spoke, for he had apparently lost all power of comprehension as well as speech, except that which entered his mind by sight. Thus he sank, as lulls the sea-breeze on a tropical shore when twilight comes. And one morning at four, as I lay coiled in a fantastic heap upon one of the settees near his door, sleeping lightly as a watch-dog, a long, low moan tugged at my heart-strings, and I sat up shivering like one in an ague-fit, although we were on the Line. Swiftly I stepped into his room, where I saw his wife with one arm across his breast and her face beside his on the pillow. She had fainted, and so was mercifully spared for a little while the agony of that parting—for he was dead.

Up till that time every device that seamanship could suggest had been put into practice to hurry the ship on, so that she was a perfect pyramid of canvas rigged wherever it would catch a wasting air. But all was of little use, for the wind had fallen lighter and lighter each day until, at the time of the skipper's passing, it was a stark calm. Then, as if some invisible restraint had been suddenly removed, up sprang the wind, strong and steady, necessitating the instant removal of all those fragile adjuncts to her speed that had been rigged everywhere possible aloft. So that no one had at first any leisure to brood over our great loss but myself, and I could only watch with almost breathless anxiety for the return of that sorely-tried, heroic woman to a life from which her chief joy had been taken away. She remained so long in that death-like trance that again and again I was compelled to reassure myself, by touching her arms and face, that she was still alive, and yet I dreaded her re-awakening. At last, with a long-drawn sigh, she lifted her head, looked steadfastly for a while at the calm face of her dead husband, then stooped and kissed him once. Then she turned to me as I stood at the door, with the silent tears streaming down my face, and said, in a perfectly steady voice (I can hear it now), "Are my children well?" "Yes, ma'am," I answered, "they are all asleep." "Thank you," she murmured; "I will go and lie down with them a little while. I feel so tired. No" (seeing I was about to offer), "I want nothing just now but rest." So she turned into their little cabin and shut the door. I went on deck and waited until the mate (now skipper) was free, and then told him how she was. He immediately made preparations for the burial, for we were still a week's sail from port. In an hour all was ready, and silently we awaited the re-appearance of the chief mourner. She came out at breakfast-time, looking like a woman of marble. Quietly thanking the new skipper for what he had done, she resumed her motherly duties, saying no word and showing no sign of the ordeal she was enduring.

All through the last solemn scene, except for a convulsive shudder as the sullen plunge alongside closed the service, she preserved the same tearless calm, and afterwards, while she remained on board—which was only until we arrived at Barbadoes—she preserved the same automaton-like demeanour. The mail steamer arrived the day after we anchored, and we took her on board for the passage to England; her bitter tragedy moving most of the passengers to tears as the history of it spread like wildfire among them. And as the Medway steamed out of the harbour, we all stood on the poop of our own vessel, with bared heads, in respectful farewell to, and deepest sympathy for, our late captain's wife.

A SCIENTIFIC CRUISE

FIVE and twenty minutes, I believe, was the extreme limit of time it took me to discover that my new ship was likely to provide me some of the queerest experiences I had yet met with in all my fishing. But after a month's weary munching the bread of the outward-bounder, and in Calcutta too, I was so hungry for a berth that I would have shipped as mess-room steward in a Geordie weekly boat, and undertaken to live on the yield of the dog-basket from the engineers' table, if nothing better had offered. So when Romin Dass, a sircar that I was very chummy with, hailed me one morning at the corner of the Radha Bazaar, with a quotation from Shakespeare to point his information that he had heard of a second-mate's berth for me on board the Ranee, a fine iron ship moored off Prinseps Ghât, I was so glad that I promised him the first five dibs I could lay hands on. Trembling with eagerness, I hurried down to the ghât and wheedled a dinghy-wallah into putting me on board. The mate, a weary looking man, about my own age, met me at the foot of the gangway ladder with that suspicious air common to all mates of ships abroad, especially when they see an eager looking stranger with a nautical appearance come aboard uninvited. In a diffident uncertain way, born of a futile attempt, to conceal my anxiety and look dignified, I inquired for Captain Leverrier.

"He isn't aboard," snarled the mate, "an' not likely to be to-night. What might your business be?"

"Well, you see—the fact is—I thought—that is," I blundered, getting red in the face as I saw a sarcastic grin curdling the mate's face. "I—I thought you wanted a second mate, an' I——"

"Oh, why the devil didn't you say so, 'thout gay-huppin' about it like that. I begun ter think you was some beach-comber tryin' on a new bluff. Come an' have a drink."

Greatly relieved I followed him into the saloon, which was almost as gorgeous as a yacht's, carpets, and mirrors, and velvet settees, piano and silver-plated metal work till you couldn't rest. A gliding Hindoo came salaaming along with a bottle and glasses and some ice in a bowl at a word from the mate, and solemnly, as if pouring a libation, we partook of refreshment. Then, offering me a Trichie, the mate began to cross-examine me. But by this time I had got back my self-possession, and I soon satisfied him that I shouldn't make half a bad shipmate. I happened to have sailed with an old skipper of his, I knew two or three fellows that he did, or at least I thought I knew them, and before half an hour had passed we were on quite confidential terms. No, not quite; for two or three times I noticed that he checked himself, just when he was on the point of telling me something, although he let drop a few hints that were totally unintelligible to me. At last he said—

"You might as well stay to supper an' keep me company, unless you've got to get back anywhere."

"Anywhere's just the right word, Mr. Martin," I broke in; "anywhere but ashore again in this God-forsaken place. If you'd been ashore here for six weeks, looking for a pierhead jump as I have, you'd think it was heaven to get aboard a ship again. It'd be a mighty important engagement that 'ud take you up town again."

"All right, my boy. Hullo, what do you want?" to the suppliant steward, who stood in a devotional attitude awaiting permission to speak.

"Dinghy-wallah, sab, waitin' for speaky gentyman, sab."

I went cold all over. That infernal coolie was after me for his fare, and I hadn't a pice. I'd forgotten all about him. I did the only thing possible, owned up to the mate that I had a southerly wind in my pockets, and he came to the rescue at once, paying the dinghy-wallah a quarter of what he asked (two rupees), and starting him off. Then we sat down to a sumptuous supper, such as I had not tasted for many months, for I came out before the mast, and the grub in the Sailors Home (where I had been staying) was pretty bad. Over the pleasant meal Mr. Martin thawed out completely, and at last, in a burst of confidence, he said—

"Our ole man's scientific, Mr. Roper."

As he looked at me like a man who has just divulged some tremendous secret, I was more than a little puzzled what to say in reply, so I looked deeply interested, and murmured, " Indeed."

" Indeed, yes," growled the mate; " but I'll bet you a month's wages you won't say ' indeed ' like that when we've ben to sea a few days. I'll tell you what it is, I've been with some rum pups of skippers in my time, but this one scoops the pot. He's a good enough sailor man, too. But as fer his condemn science—well, he thinks he's the whole Royle Serciety an' Trinity House biled down into one, an' I'm damfee knows enough to come in when it rains. He's just worryin me bald-headed, that's what he is. Why, if it wasn't fer the good hash and bein' able to do pretty much as I mind to with the ship, I'd a ben a jibbin mainyac 'fore now, I'm dead shore o' that. Looky here," and he sprang up and flung a state-room door wide open, " djever see anythin' like that outen a mewseeum? "

I stared in utter amazement at a most extraordinary collection of queer looking instruments, models, retorts, crucibles, and specimen glasses, turning round after completing my scrutiny, and gazing into the mate's face without speaking.

He was peering at me curiously, and presently said, interrogatively, " Well? "

Seeing that I was expected to make some sort of a reply, I said, with a cheerful air—

" 'Looks as if the skipper was no end of a scientific pot, I must confess; but, after all, Mr. Martin, it's a harmless fad enough, isn't it? "

" Harmless! Well, of all the—— Good heavens,

man, you hain't the least idea—but, there, what's the use er talkin'. Better letcher wait 'n see fer yerself. Come on up onter the poop 'n git a whiff er fresh Calcutta mixtcher, dreadful refreshin', ain't it?"

A long confab succeeded to the accompaniment of many cigars and sundry pegs, but not another word about the skipper and his hobbies did the mate let slip. No; we discussed, as housewives are said to do when they meet, the shortcomings of those over whom we were put in authority, compared notes as to the merits and demerits of skippers we had served under, and generally sampled the gamut of seafaring causeries, until, with my head buzzing like a mosquito in a bottle, I gave the mate good-night, and retired to my bunk in an enviable state of satisfaction at my good fortune. Next morning I was up at coffee-time, and while sitting on the after-hatch coamings enjoying the enlivening drink and chatting with the mate, a most unearthly howl fairly made my whiskers bristle. I looked at Mr. Martin, whose face wore a sarcastic grin, but never a word spake he. Another nerve-tearing yell resounded, starting me to my feet, while I exclaimed—

"Whatever is it, Mr. Martin? I've never heard such a devilish noise in my life."

"Oh, it's only some o' the ole man's harmless fads he's a exercisin'. You'll git used ter them chunes presently."

He *was* going to say something else, but just then the steward emerged from the saloon—that is to say, he shot out as if he had been fired from a balista.

When I saw him a few minutes before he was a suave olive-complexioned Hindoo, cat-like in his neatness, and snowy in his muslin rig. Now he was a ghastly apparition, with streaming scalp-lock and glaring eye-balls, his face a cabbage-water green, and his lank body as bare as a newly-scalded pig. Apparently incapable of flight, he crouched where he fell, salaaming with trembling hands, and chattering almost monkey-like. While the mate and I stood silently regarding him, and indignation at the poor wretch's plight was rapidly ousting my alarm at the manner of his appearance, a mild and benevolent looking man of middle-age dressed in pyjamas appeared at the saloon door.

"Good morning, Mr. Martin," said the skipper, for it was himself, "did you see where that heathen landed?"

"Oh yes, sir," drawled the mate, "'eer 'e is, what's left ov 'im."

"Ah," replied the skipper, with a placid smile, "he's a bit startled I see. He trod on the plate of my new battery, and got a slight shock, I think. But where's his close?"

"The Lord only knows," piously ejaculated the mate. "Looks ter me 'sif he'd ben shot clean out ov 'em, puggree an' all."

By this time the luckless steward, finding, I suppose, that he had not reached Jehannum yet, began to pull himself together, and, doubtless ashamed of his being all face in the presence of the all-powerful sahibs, writhed his way worm-like towards the other door of the saloon, and disappeared within, the skipper regarding him meanwhile with gentle interest as if he were a crawling babe. Then turning his attention to me, the old man courteously inquired my business, and finding that I suited him, engaged me there and then as second mate.

During the short stay we made in port after my joining, nothing further occurred to change the opinion I had already formed that I was in a very comfortable ship. The fellows forward seemed fairly well contented and willing. The food both fore and aft was wonderfully good, and so was the cooking, for a marvel. But that was because we had a Madrassee cook who had served an arduous apprenticeship in P. and O. boats, from which excellent service he had been driven by some amiable inability to comprehend the laws of meum and tuum. Here there was no chance for him to steal, and every inducement for him to earn a good name by pleasing his many masters. The result was singularly happy for all of us. The foremast hands were fairly divided into Britons and Scandinavians, all good seamen and quiet, well-behaved men. One thing, however, was noticeable, they all seemed nervously anxious to avoid the after part of the ship as much as possible. All seamen before the mast have an inbred sense of reverence for the quarter-deck, walking delicately thereon, and studiously keeping to the lee-side, unless compelled by duty to go to windward. But in the Ranee, whenever a man came aft for any purpose whatever, his movements were much like those of a man visiting a menagerie for the first time alone, and morbidly suspicious that some of the cage doors were unfastened. This behaviour was highly amusing to me, for I had never seen anything like it before, and I couldn't help wondering how the helmsman would hang out a trick at the wheel when we got to sea.

All preparations complete, we unmoored, and in tow of the Court Hey proceeded majestically down the Hooghly, waking all the echoes and scaring the numberless pigeons of the King of Oude's palace with the exultant strains of "Sally Brown." One of those majestic creatures, the Calcutta pilots, paced the poop in awful state, alone, the skipper being nowhere visible. Presently, my lord the pilot, feeling slightly fatigued, I suppose, threw himself into the old man's favourite chair, an elaborately cushioned affair of peculiar shape and almost as long as a sofa. No sooner had he done so than, with a most amazing movement, the whole fabric changed its shape, and became one of the most bewildering entanglements conceivable, gripping the astounded pilot in so many places at once that he was in imminent danger of being throttled. I rushed to his assistance, and exerted all my strength to set him free, but my energetic efforts only seemed to hamper him more, and fearing lest I should break him all to pieces, I rushed below for the skipper. That gentleman was busy in his laboratory, making carburetted hydrogen, I should judge, from the "feel of the smell," as the Scotch say, but in answer to my agitated call he emerged, serene and bland, to inquire my business. Faith, I could hardly tell him, what with the reek, my haste, and the anxiety I felt. Somehow I managed to convey to him that the pilot was being done to death in his chair, and as I did so I noticed (or thought I did) a momentary gleam of satisfaction in his starboard eye. But he mounted the companion, and gliding to the spot where the unhappy man, voiceless and black in the face, was struggling, he stooped, touched a spring, and that infernal chair fell out flat like a board. I stooped to assist the victim, but, unluckily for me, he sprang to his feet at the same moment, and his head catching me under the chin, I had urgent business of my own to attend to for some little time. When I got quite well again, I heard conversation. In fact I might almost say the coolies in the jungle heard it. The pilot was expressing his opinion upon his recent experience, and from his manner I concluded that he was annoyed. When at last he had finished, and the lingering echoes had died away, the old man, looking as happy as a lamb, offered to show him the beauty and ingenuity of the mechanism. But the pilot merely suggested that the only sight that could interest him just then would be the old man dangling by the neck at the cro'jack yard-arm, with that something (I didn't quite catch the adjective) chair jammed on to his legs. And then the unreasonable man walked forward, leaving the skipper looking after him with a puzzled, yearning expression upon his pleasant face. Perhaps it is hardly necessary to say that thenceforward relations between the pilot and the captain were somewhat strained. At any rate, the former potentate refused to come below, taking his meals on deck with an air as of a man whose life was at the mercy of irresponsible beings, and when at last we hauled up at the mouth of the river for the pilot brig to send a boat for our pilot, he left the ship looking supremely relieved. To the skipper's outstretched hand he was blind, and to that gentleman's kindly good-bye he said naught but "thank God, I'm safe out of your ship." Away he went, never once looking back to where we were busily setting sail for the long homeward passage.

For some days everything went on greased wheels. Except for an air of mystery that overhung the ship, and which puzzled me not a little, she was the most comfortable craft I ever sailed in. The skipper scarcely ever appeared, although sundry strange noises and unpleasant odours proceeding from his laboratory were evidence all-sufficient that he was on the alert. I was somewhat aggrieved though by the mate's sardonic grin every time he relieved me, and made the usual remark, "still alive, eh?" Still, as each quiet day succeeded a quieter night my wonderment became dulled, and I thought that either the mate was mistaken or that he had been trying to fool me.

One evening, however, when we were drawing near the line, I came on deck at four bells to find the mate's watch busy rigging up a sort of theatre aft. An awning had been stretched over the front of the poop, weather cloths were hung along each side, and seats arranged. As soon as I appeared, looking round me in astonishment, the mate approached me and said, "th' entertainment's goin' ter begin." Before I had time to question him as to his meaning, the old man emerged from the cabin loaded with sundry strange-looking machines, and followed by the steward bearing more. For a few minutes he was mighty busy placing his menagerie in order, and then he turned to me and said briskly, " Now, Mr. Roper, I'm all ready, go forrard and invite the hands aft to the lecture." " Aye, aye, sir," I answered mechanically, and departed. I found all hands outside the forecastle, evidently waiting for the summons, but looking as unlike men expecting a treat as one could possibly picture. But they all shambled aft in silence, and took their seats with eyes fixed upon the strange-looking assemblage of machinery in the centre.

It was a lovely evening, the sails just drawing to a steady air, while the sea was so smooth that the vessel was almost as motionless as if in dock. As it was my watch on deck, I mounted the poop, glanced at the standard compass, cast my eye aloft to see that all was as it should be, and then turned my gaze with intense interest upon the scene below. And what a scene it was to be sure. All hands were glaring upon the high priest of the mysteries as if mesmerised, every expression gone from their faces but that of painful anxiety to know what was going to happen. The skipper was as busy as two people about his wheels and things, and the unhappy steward like an image of fear obeyed mechanically the various commands of his dread master. At last a whirring sound was heard like the humming of some huge imprisoned bee, and to this accompaniment the skipper took up his parable and proceeded to talk. I frankly confess that I know no more what he said than I should have done had he been speaking in Sanskrit, and I am perfectly sure that none of his audience were in any better case. Indeed, from what I could see of their faces, I believe every other sense was merged in the full expectation of an explosion, and they couldn't have taken their strained eyes off the buzzing gadget in their midst for any consideration whatever. Suddenly a dark shadow glided across the patch of deck behind the skipper, which I recognized as a monkey belonging to one of the crew. It reached the machine, and then—— What really happened nobody is ever likely to know, for in a moment there was a shriek, a perfect shower of blue sparks and a writhing, kicking, biting heap of skipper, monkey, and steward. Some of the fellows, acting upon impulse, forgot their fears and rushed to the rescue, but only succeeded in adding to the infernal riot, as they too became involved in the mysterious calamity. Others, wiser in their generation, fled forward to the fo'c'sle, from whence they gradually crept aft again near enough to watch in safety the devil's dance that was going on. I looked on in a sort of coma of all the faculties, until the mate touched me on the shoulder, and said in a sepulchral voice—

"Now, Mr. Roper, djever strike anythin' o' this kind before. *Ain't* it scientific? Ain't he a holy terror at science? What I'd like ter know is, where do I come on in this Gypshun Hall business? Damfime goin' ter be blame well paralyzed, or whatever it is, for all the skippers erflote, n' yet—n' yet; I *don't* like ter see sech ungodly carryins on aboard of any ship I'm mate of."

I hadn't time to answer him—besides I couldn't, I was all shook up like; but while I was trying to get my thinking-gear in order, there was a bang, all the sufferers yelled at once, and then all was quiet. Both the mate and myself sprang into the arena, fully expecting to find all the actors dead, but, bless you, they were all laying round looking as if they'd been having no end of a spree. All except the monkey, that is. He was a very unhandsome little corpse, and I picked him up by the tail to throw him overboard, getting a shock through my right arm that took all the use out of it for quite a while. Presently the fellows began to get up one by one and slink away forrard, still with that half-drunk smile on their heads, but when we came to the skipper, although he wore a wide smile too, he hadn't any get up about him. Not he. He lay there as comfy as you please, taking no notice of anything we said, or any heed of the deliberate way in which the mate was pushing the remains of his machinery out through the gaping port with a broom. We couldn't move him. He was just charged jam full of electricity, and one of the men who *did* touch him let a yell out of him fit to call D. Jones, Esq., up from below, but it didn't change the skipper's happy look one fragment. Well, he laid there all night alongside of the steward, and in the morning he gets up just before wash-deck time, and, says he, " Mr. Roper, I shan't give any more scientific exhibitions this trip; I think they're immoral." With that he hobbled into his cabin, and we saw no more of him for a week. When we did, you couldn't have got a grain of science out of him with a small-tooth comb, and the mate looked as glad as if he'd been appointed Lord High Admiral. And from thenceforward she was, as I had at first imagined she would be, the most comfortable vessel I ever sailed in.

A GENIAL SKIPPER

CAPTAIN SCOTT was as commonplace a little man as ever commanded an old wooden tub of a barque lumbering her way forlornly from port to port seeking freight as a beggar seeks pence. His command, the Sarah Jane, belonged to a decayed firm of shipowners that, like many other old-fashioned tradesmen, had not kept pace with the times, and were now reduced to the possession of this ancient pauper and a still older brig, all the rest of their once stately fleet having been sold or lost or seized to satisfy mortgages. Yet they still retained a keen sense of respectability, and when Captain Scott applied for the command of the Sarah Jane they were exceedingly careful to ascertain that he was strictly sober and trustworthy. He not only succeeded in satisfying them on these points, but in some mysterious manner persuaded them also that he was exceedingly pious, and would certainly hold service on board every Sunday, weather permitting. That settled his appointment, for the senior member of the firm was a good, honest Dissenter, who, if a trifle narrow and bigoted in his religious views, was sincerely anxious to live up to the light he had. Beyond all question the Sarah Jane was the best-found vessel of her class in the food line that we chaps forrard had ever sailed in. It would have been hard to find a more agreeably surprised little crowd than we were when the first meal appeared in the fo'c'sle, for our preliminary view of the ship certainly gave us the idea that we were in for "plenty pump and velly flat belly," as a quaint little Italian A. B. said while we were selecting bunks.

But no, she was a comfortable ship. There was certainly "plenty pump," but the grub was so good that there was never a growl heard among us, and a pleasanter passage out to Algoa Bay than we enjoyed could hardly be imagined. The Sunday services were held, too—that is to say, twice; after that they were quietly dropped without any reason assigned. No one felt sorry, for there was an air of unreality and constraint about the whole thing that was puzzling and unsatisfactory; and on several occasions there was wafted across the poop, as the skipper emerged from the companion, a tantalizing odour which none of us could mistake—the rich bouquet of old Jamaica rum. This gave rise to many discussions in the fo'c'sle. The port watch took sides against the starboard, insisting that the old man had fallen from grace, if, which was problematical, he had ever possessed any of that mysterious quality. We of the starboard, or skipper's watch, as in duty bound, stood up for him, accounting for the thirst-provoking smell that came wafting upwards from the cabin periodically by the theory of the Sarah Jane having been an old sugar drogher for many years, until her timbers were saturated with the flavour of rum, and, according as the wind tended to diffuse it, we were favoured with it on deck.

Never was a skipper watched more closely by his crew than Captain Scott was by us, for the steward and the officers were unapproachable upon the subject, and it was only by catching him really drunk that our continual dispute could be settled. After we had crossed the Line, and were getting rapidly to the suth'ard, I began to lose faith, for, although I could not determine whether the skipper's peculiar gait was or was not the regular nautical roll accentuated by some physical peculiarity, there was no mistaking the ever-deepening hue of his face. When we left home it was fresh-coloured, but as the weeks went by it took on the glow of burnished copper—especially after dinner—and sometimes his nose looked warm enough to light one's pipe at it. However, we reached Algoa Bay without settling our argument—openly, that is. In truth, we of the starboard watch were looking eagerly for some way of retreat from what we all felt was getting to be an untenable position. Still, no agreement was arrived at until we had been at anchor off Port Elizabeth for a week, during which time we had never seen our respected skipper once.

Then there arrived alongside, on a Saturday afternoon, after we had washed decks and were dabbing out our own few bits of duds for Sunday, a surf-boat, in the stern of which sat precariously a very drunken man. He was truculently drunk, and the big cigar, which was stuck in one angle of his protruding lips, pointed upwards like an old collier's jibboom. Both his hands were thrust deep into his pockets, and his top-hat was jammed hard down on the back of his head. As the boat bumped alongside, his insecure seat failed him, and he lurched massively forward upon the crown of his hat, which caved in after its brim had passed his ears, adding to the picturesqueness of his outfit. The boatmen seized and reinstated him upon a thwart, receiving for their pains an address that reeked of the pit. For variety of profanity we all admitted it to be far beyond anything of the kind that we had ever heard, and one of our number suggested that he had been founding a new church during his absence, his outbreak of peculiar language being part of the liturgy thereof. We only had an ordinary side ladder of the usual type carried in those ships—two ropes with wooden rungs seized between them—which was suspended perpendicularly from the rail. This kind of approach is not easy of negotiation by anybody but a sober sailor; it was impossible now to Captain Scott. He gazed upwards fiercely at the anxious face of the mate, and, with many flowers of speech, insisted that a whip should be rigged on the mainyard for him—blasphemously sharp, too, or he would, yes, he would, when he *did* get aboard.

So we rigged a single whip at the mate's order, not without many audible comments upon this new development and recriminations between the members of the two disputing watches. With many a bump, as the vessel rolled to the incoming swell, we hoisted our commander on board, letting him come down on deck with a jolt that must have well-nigh started all his teeth. Released from his bonds, he rose swaying to his feet, and, glaring round upon the assembled crew, roared thickly, "All han's short'n sail!" There was a shout of laughter at this maniacal command, which infuriated him so much that he seemed transformed into a veritable demon. His face went purple, he ground his teeth like a fighting boar, and would no doubt have had some sort of fit but for a diversion made by the boatmen who had brought him off. One of them approached him, saying abruptly but quite civilly—

"If you don't want us any more, sir, we sh'd like our fare, so's we can get ashore again."

Peculiarly, this interruption changed his mood into the coldly sarcastic. With an air of exquisite politeness he turned to the boatman, and, with a bear-like bow, said—

"Ho, indeed; Hi 'ave much pleasure in 'earin' ov it. An' may we take th' hopportunity hof harskin' oo th' 'ells a-preventin' hof yer frum goin' t' the devil hif ye likes." (Be it noted that when sober he spoke fairly correct English.) "Has ter a-wantin' hof ye hany more, Hi wouldn't 'ave a barge-load hof yer fur a gift; Hi wouldn't carry yer fur ballast, there! Might come in 'andy for dunnagin' carsks—but there, I don' know. Anyway, get t' 'ell houter this."

Of course, it could hardly be expected that such sturdy independent souls as Algoa Bay boatmen would be likely to take contumely of this sort meekly in exchange for their hard labours. At any rate, if such a thing had ever been expected, the expectation was doomed to instant disappointment. Turning to the rail, the boatman who had spoken to the skipper gave a shout which brought the six of his mates on deck. Just a word or two of explanation, and they advanced threateningly towards their debtor. We stood in passive enjoyment of what we felt was soon to be a due meting out of reward to a man who deserved such recompense richly. The two mates made a feeble attempt to interfere, but were roughly thrust aside, while the enraged boatmen seized the burly form of our skipper, and were about to manhandle him over the side when he roared for mercy, saying that he would pay all their demand. He did so, and they departed, not without a full and complete exposition of what they considered to be all his characteristics, mental and physical. They had hardly left the side when the skipper ordered the windlass to be manned, and, in spite of his drunken condition, no long time elapsed before we were under way and standing rapidly out to sea.

But that night a black south-easter sprang up, to which we set all the sail we could stagger under for our northward passage to Pondicherry, but towards morning the wind backed to the northward, and blew so hard as to necessitate the sudden taking in of all the sail we had set except a tiny storm-staysail. But, while we were, all hands of us, in the throes of our conflict with the slatting topsails, a curious thing happened. Sharp snapping noises were heard, and flashes of light totally unlike lightning were seen on deck. Cries were heard, too, that were disconcerting, for it seemed as if a row was going on for which we could imagine no cause. Suddenly the little Italian, who was manfully struggling by my side to get the topsail furled, yelled at the pitch of his voice something in his own language, at the same time disappearing to a dangling position on the foot-rope. This was strange, but almost immediately after something with a sharp "ping" struck the yard by my side, and the horrible truth flashed into my mind that somebody on deck was shooting at us poor wretches struggling aloft. It is difficult, indeed, to express what the conditions of our minds were upon making this discovery. The handling of sails by a weak crew in a gale of wind at night is no child's play at any time, but when to that great fight is added the peculiar complication of a drunken madman amusing himself by taking pot-shots at the men aloft, the condition of things is, to say the least, disconcerting. The sails were let go. Incontinently we slid down on deck, taking refuge behind whatsoever shelter we could find. Happily, Natalie, the poor little Italian, managed to get down too, having, as we presently discovered, a bullet through the fleshy part of his arm. The sails blew to pieces, the ship tumbled about helplessly, the helmsman having run from his post, and it appeared as if a terrible calamity was about to overtake us, but presently the two mates came forrard, saying, "It's all right, men. We've knocked him down, and, although we couldn't find his revolver, we have locked him up in his cabin. For God's sake, turn to and get the ship in hand."

With many muttered curses and desires of taking the skipper's life we resumed our duties, and soon had got the rags of sail still left on the yards snugly secured. Then the watch entitled to go below retired. Natalie had his wound dressed, and peace reigned for a time. In the morning the skipper, being sober, begged piteously to be released. All of us protested strongly against any such piece of folly being perpetrated. However, after he had been confined a week our hearts relented towards him, and, upon his making a solemn assurance that he had no more ammunition or grog, which latter disturbing element the mates assured us they had searched for and were unable to find, it was agreed that he should resume command.

During the rest of our passage to Pondicherry there was certainly nothing to complain of. More, she was as comfortable a ship as one could wish to be on board of. Evidently, with a view to mollifying our feelings towards him, Captain Scott allowed us to fare as well as he and his officers did, so that by the time we anchored in Pondicherry we had, with the short memory for previous sufferings peculiarly characteristic of sailors, apparently entirely forgotten his amiable little outbreak. Nor during her stay at Pondicherry did we have anything to complain of. Then came the welcome news that we were homeward bound. On a glorious morning, just at daybreak, the order was given to man the windlass, and, with the singing that old-time shanty of "Hurrah, my boys, we're homeward bound," we were all lustily engaged in tearing out the big mud-hook, when suddenly, to our unspeakable horror, Captain Scott emerged from the cabin, his outstretched hands each grasping a huge navy revolver, and almost immediately after bullets were flying like hail. Like frightened rabbits, we bolted for even the most impracticable holes and corners—anywhere, indeed, out of that withering fire. The situation was desperate, but, happily for us, a British gunboat was lying near. The officer in charge of her deck, hearing the fusillade, with naval promptitude sent a boat's crew on board to inquire into the cause of this strange occurrence.

It so happened that the inquirers arrived just as Captain Scott was recharging his revolver, and they lost no time in taking him prisoner. We, the luckless crew, emerging from our various hiding-places, laid the matter before them with much wealth of detail, and the result that we presently had the satisfaction of seeing our vivacious commander, bound hand and foot, being lowered into the boat for conveyance on board the man-o'-war. Her commander held an inquiry immediately into Captain Scott's conduct, examining us closely as to the reasons for this outbreak, if we could give any. Strange to say, our recollection of his good treatment outweighed our immediate resentment against him, and we agreed that if only he could be rendered incapable of either getting drunk or shooting, we should be glad to finish the voyage with him. So, after a thorough search for fire-arms and rum, resulting in the discovery of no less than four more revolvers, quite a large box of ammunition, and an extraordinarily large quantity of the potent liquor, all of which was duly confiscated by the naval authorities, we returned to our duties, got under way, and sailed for home.

The Sarah Jane was a most fortunate ship, as far as weather was concerned, at any rate. Catching the first breath of the north-eastern monsoon immediately outside the harbour, under all canvas we bowled briskly down to the line, crossed it with a steady, if light breeze from the northward, and, without experiencing any calm worth mentioning, presently found ourselves in the tender embrace of the south-east trade-winds, and being wafted steadily at the rate of about five knots an hour across the vast placid bosom of the Indian Ocean.

Life at sea under such conditions is very pleasant. For the vicissitudes of a sailor's life only become hard to bear when weather is bad, food scanty, and officers brutal. When the opposites of these three conditions obtain, the sailor can gladly put up with many evil qualities in the ship itself. The leakiness of our old vessel troubled us not at all as long as the pleasant conditions of which I have spoken continued. Even when we reached the stormy latitudes adjacent to the Cape of Good Hope we were favoured by fair winds until we arrived off Simons Bay, when the wind fell away, and a perfect calm ensued with lowering, ugly-looking weather. But our good fortune still remained. The great sweep of the Agulhas current carried us round the Cape of Storms homeward without any wind worth taking notice of coming upon us out of the leaden-looking sky, and so we rounded the Cape, and with a fine southerly breeze pointed the Sarah Jane jibboom homeward.

The usual routine work of cleaning ship was indulged in. Nothing worthy of notice occurred until losing the trades. In about 7° N. lat. a calm of a week's duration ensued. Here we fell in with several other ships, and our captain, apparently with a view of getting a little amusement, had a boat out, and went ship-visiting. This suited us admirably. Sailors always enjoy it, perhaps because they get so little of it on board merchant ships. The first two ships we visited were evidently strongly teetotal, for we noticed that while our captain returned on board perfectly sober, he always looked exceedingly glum and disappointed. But at last we spoke a vessel whose captain was in dire want of a little fresh water. We had plenty to spare, and in no long time had filled a couple of puncheons, lowered them over the side into the water, and towed them to the other ship. Her captain's gratitude was great; in fact, he seemed hardly able to reward us sufficiently. Among other gifts we received a huge hog, two cases of preserved beef, a barrel of cabin biscuits, and two large cases of what appeared to us to be lime-juice. We returned on board, and hoisted in our spoils.

That night a breeze sprang up, and the little company of vessels that had clustered together in the vortex made by the "trades" separated, and pursued their various ways. Next morning we were alone, our ship was by herself on the face of the deep. The steward went to call the captain as usual, but could get no response. Alarmed, he came and reported the matter to the mate, whose watch on deck it was at the time. The mate went down, and, after repeated knockings at the captain's door which failed to obtain any response, took violent measures, and burst the door open.

The captain was not there. A search was immediately made without result, but presently, to the horror of every one on board, the steward, a rather feeble-minded mulatto, rushed on deck shouting "Fire!" It need not be said how terrible this cry at sea always is, but it is never more so than when on board a badly-found wooden ship. However, all hands rushed aft at the call of the mate, and prepared to do everything that was possible for the subdual of the fire when it should be located. The smoke appeared to be rising from the lazarette, a store-room in the after part of the ship beneath the cabin. The mate and a couple of men tore off the hatch, and, half choked with the smoke that burst up in a great volume, made their way below, only to scramble out again in double quick time and fall fainting on the deck.

Meanwhile everybody was wondering what had become of the captain, until suddenly an awful-looking figure was seen emerging from a ventilator on deck at the fore part of the cabin. It was the captain, who announced his presence with a series of horrible yells. His clothes were in ribands, his face was black, his eyeballs glared. Several of us made a rush at him, conceiving him to have suddenly gone mad, but he eluded our grasp, and, nimble as a monkey, rushed up aloft, and sat mowing on the mainyard. A couple of us started after him, but were recalled by the second mate, who said—

"Let the old —— alone. We have got something else to do if we want to save our lives."

And indeed we had. The feeble pump in the bows of the ship, which we used for washing decks, was not of the slightest service as a fire-engine, and drawing water overside by buckets is a tedious process. We could hear the roaring of the flames underneath our feet, we could feel the decks getting hot, and as it appeared that our labour was utterly in vain, and that if we wished to save our lives we must waste no time in getting the boats provisioned and lowered, we turned all our energies in that direction. By the most tremendous exertions we succeeded in getting a fairly satisfactory amount of food and water into the two boats, along with some clothing, a compass, and a sextant. Hardly had we done so before a sudden outburst of flame from the cabin of furious violence warned us that it was time to be gone.

Meanwhile the skipper had been raging, a howling madman, on the mainyard. What was to be done about him? Truth compels me to state that the majority of us were for leaving him to his fate, realizing that to him we owed all our misfortunes. But still, *that* we could hardly bring ourselves to do when the time came. The ship herself solved the question for us. She seemed to suddenly burst into flame fore and aft, the inflammable cargo, most of which was of cotton and various grasses, burning almost like turpentine. Indeed, some of us were compelled to spring into the sea and clamber on board the boats as best we could. Having done so, it became necessary to put a goodly distance between us and the ship with little delay, for the heat was terrible. And there sat the skipper on the mainyard, while the long tongues of flame went writhing up the well-tarred rigging. Suddenly we saw him spring to his feet, balancing himself for a moment on the yard, and then, with a most graceful curve, he sprang into the sea. He reappeared, swimming strongly, and the mate's boat picked him up. And here occurred the strangest part of the whole matter, for no sooner was he in the boat than all the previous occurrences seemed to be wiped clean out of his mind, and he was as sane as any man among us. We stared at him in amazement, but he took no notice, saying a word or two on the handling of the boat or the direction in which she was to be steered, but making no comment upon the sudden catastrophe that had overtaken us.

Fortunately for us all, the weather remained perfectly fine, and as we knew we were directly in the track of ships, we were under no apprehensions as to our safety, but we certainly looked upon the skipper as, to say the least of it, uncanny. We watched him closely by day and by night, lest in some new maniacal outbreak he should endanger the lives of us all once more, and this time without hope of recovery. But he remained perfectly quiet and sensible, nor did he betray by any sign whatever any knowledge of what had happened. On the third day we sighted a barque right astern. She came up grandly, and very soon we were all safely on board of the same vessel from which we had received the provisions. Then we found that the two cases we had supposed to contain lime-juice had really been full of lime-juice bottles of rum—which explained matters somewhat.

And now another astonishing thing happened. Captain Scott suddenly conceived the notion that the Jocunda was his own ship, nor could any arguments convince him that he was wrong. The captain humoured him for a while, but at last his mania reached such a height that it became necessary to confine him in irons, and thus he was kept under restraint until our arrival in Plymouth, where no time was lost in placing him in a lunatic asylum.

What became of him I do not know, but at the Board of Trade inquiry all hands had the greatest difficulty in persuading the officials that we were not joined in a conspiracy of lying, and I for one felt that we could hardly blame them.

MAC'S EXPERIMENT

"MAHN, A'am nae carin' a snap wut ye think aboot ma. A'am a Scoetchman, ye ken, fra Fogieloan; an' them 'at disna laik ma th' wye Ah aam, c'n juist dicht ther nebs an' ma bachle-vamps. Tha rampin', roarin' lion uv Auld Scoetland aye gaed his ain wye, an' A'am thinkin' 'at maist o' his weans 'll dae the same thing. An' if tha canna dae't yin day, they'll dae't the neist, an' muckle Auld Hornie himsel' winna stap them a'thegither."

It was a long speech for Jock MacTavish, our taciturn shipmate aboard the Yankee whaling-barque Ursus. Like several other luckless deep-water sailors, he had been "shanghaied" in San Francisco, awaking from the combined effects of a drug that would have killed anybody but a sailor, and sundry ugly blows on the head, to find himself booked for a cruise in a "spouter" for an indefinite length of time, and at a remuneration that none of us were ever able to understand. This was bad enough, in all conscience, but it might easily have been much worse, for the Ursus was a really good ship, as whalers go.

At the time when this yarn begins, we had been employing a slackness in the fishing by having a thorough clean up. It was very nearly time, for she was beginning to stink so badly that every morsel of food we ate seemed saturated with rancid whale-oil. So we worked, if possible, harder than usual, with sand and ley, to remove the clotted fat from decks, bulwarks, and boats, until on Christmas Eve she was almost her old clean self again. There remained only the tryworks, but they were certainly in a vile condition of black grease.

At knock-off time (all hands had been working all day) we began discussing our chances of having a merry Christmas on the morrow, and, with the usual argumentativeness of sailors, had got a dozen different theories started. But running through them all there seemed to be a fixed idea that no notice whatever would be taken of a day that we all regarded as the one festival of the year which could, by no possible means, be allowed to pass unhonoured.

No, not all, for when the discussion was at its height, Conkey, a lithe Londoner, whose epithet of Cockney had somehow taken this form, suddenly looked straight to where Mac was sitting stolidly munching a gigantic fragment of prime East India mess beef (it hadn't been round Cape Horn more than four times), and said, "Wot d'yer sye, Mac? Ain't 'erd from yer. 'Ow d'yer feel abart workin' a Crissmuss dye?"

There was an instant silence, while every one fastened his eyes on Mac and awaited his answer. Slowly, as if the words were being squeezed out of him, he replied, "It disna matter a snuff tae me what wye 'tis. Ah belong tae the Free Kirk o' Scoetland, an' she disna gie ony suppoert tae siccan heathen practusses as th' obsairvin' o' days, an' months, an' yeers."

Conkey sprang to his feet full of fury, and, in choicest Mile End, informed Mac that, " hif 'e thawt 'e wuz blanky well goin' ter call 'im a bloomin' 'eathen an' not goin' ter git bashed over it, 'e wuz a bigger blank fool then 'e'd ever seen a-smokin' tea-leaves ter sive terbacker." To this outburst Mac only said what begins this yarn, and, in so saying, brought all hands down on him at once. Conkey was restrained from his meditated attack while one after another tried to argue the point with Mac, and to convince him that no man who neglected to keep Christmas Day as a feast of jollity and respite from all work, except under the direst pressure of necessity, could possibly be a Christian.

The contract we had on hand, though, was much too large for us. Metaphorically speaking, Mac wiped the fo'c'sle deck with each of us in succession. His arguments, in the first place, were far too deep for our capacity, had they been intelligible; but couched in the richest Aberdeenshire dialect, and bristling with theological terminology utterly foreign to us, we stood no chance. One by one we were reduced to silence. It was broken by Conkey, who said finally, " Hi don't know wot 'e bloomin' well sez, but Hi c'n punch 'is hugly carrotty mug for 'im, an' 'ere goes."

Again we restrained our shipmate's primitive instincts, while Mac slowly rose from his donkey, wiped his sheath-knife deliberately on his pants, put it away, and then, quietly as if it had just occurred to him, turned to the raging Conkey, saying, " See heer, ma laddie, A'al mak' y' an oafer. A'al fecht ye. If ye gie ma a lickin' A'al hae naethin' mair tae dae wi' the business; bud if Ah lick you, A'al dae aal Ah can tae get, no juist the day aff, but a guid blow-out o' vittles in the bairgin, altho' Ah misdoot ma muckle ther's naethin' aft that ye cud mak' a decent meal o'. Hoo diz that shoot ye?"

For all answer Conkey, breaking away from those who had held him, sprang at Mac, dealing, as he came, two blows, right and left, like flashes. Mac did not attempt to parry them, but seemed to stoop quietly; and suddenly Conkey's heels banged against the beam overhead. Immediately afterwards there came the dull thump of his head upon the floor. Mac just disengaged himself, and stood waiting till his opponent should feel able or willing to resume.

Truly the latter's head must have been as thick as his courage was high, for, before any of us had begun to offer assistance, he had struggled to his feet, looking a bit dazed, it is true, but evidently as full of fight as ever. He had learned a lesson, however—that caution in dealing with his sturdy adversary was necessary, and that he must accommodate his undoubted boxing powers to new conditions.

In a crouching attitude, and with two arms held bow-wise in front, he moved nearer the rugged, square-set figure of the Scotchman, who, as before, stood strictly on the defensive. There was a feint by Conkey—we saw Mac's head go down again—but then came a sharp thud and a swinging, sidelong blow from

Conkey, and Mac seemed to crumble into a heap, for, as he stooped to repeat his former successful grip, Conkey had shot upward his right knee with such force that Mac's nose was a red ruin, and the blow on the ear from Conkey's left could have done Mac very little good. So far, the advantage undoubtedly lay with the Londoner, but, after a brief spell, Mac pulled himself together, and the two clinched again. Locked together like a pair of cats, except that they neither bit, scratched, nor made a sound, they writhed all over the fo'c'sle unable to strike, but so equally matched that neither could loose himself. Had they been alone, I believe only death would have parted them; but at last, in sheer admiration for the doggedness of their pluck, we laid hold on them and tore them apart, declaring that two such champions ought to be firm friends. As soon as they got their breath, Conkey held out his hand, saying, "Scotty, me cock, ye're as good a man as me, but Hi'm —— hif ye're a better. If yer think y'are, wy, we'll just ply the bloomin' 'and art, but if ye're satisfied, Hi am." Taking the proffered hand, Scotty replied, "Mahn, A'am no thet peticklar. Ah haena a pickle o' ambeeshun tae be thocht a better mahn than ma neebours, neither am Ah a godless fule that henkers aefther fechtin' for fechtin's sake; but as ye say, we're baith 's guid 's yin anither, an' there's ma han' upo' th' maetter. Ah dinna see 'at we're ony forrader wi' oor bairgin tho'."

Then a regular clamour of voices arose, all saying the same thing, viz. that the heroes should "pull sticks"—that is, one should hold two splinters of wood concealed in his hand with the ends just protruding for the other to choose from, and whichever got the shortest piece should be the loser. It is a time-honoured fo'c'sle way of settling disputes or arranging watches.

They drew, and Scotty won. All faces fell at this, for if we were going to make a bold bid for our Christmas privileges we needed unity, and especially we wanted such a tough nut as Jock MacTavish actively enlisted on our side. The winner lifted our gloom by saying quietly, "Sae A'm with ye, aefther aal, ut seems." Then, noting the surprise on our faces, he went on, "What's the differ, think ye, whether Ah win at fechtin' or drawin'. Ah said Ah'd be with ye if Ah won, sae that's a' richt." And, easy in our minds, we separated, the watch below to their bunks, and the rest to their stations.

* * * * * * * *

Morning broke in glory, such a day as we see, perhaps, two of during a year in our hard, grey climate at home. After wetting down the decks as usual, the mate gave the order to turn-to at cleaning the try-works—a step which brought us all up "with a round turn," as we say. Closing together we faced the amazed officer, and Mac, stepping a little in advance, said, "Div ye no ken, Maister Winsloe, 'at this is the day o' days tae all true Chreestyin' men. Suner than Ah'd dae ae han's turrn on Chrissmus Da,—except, af coorse, in the wye o' neceesary seamen's duties, sic as a trick at the wheel, furrlin' sail, or the like—Ah'd gae ashore this meenut!"

The skipper produced from his hip-pocket a revolver.

At this we couldn't help chuckling, for the nearest land was about three miles beneath our keel, vertically, and at least a thousand horizontally. But the mate was like Lot's wife after she looked back. The thing was outside his mental dimension altogether. As the real significance of it filtered through, his eyes gleamed, and, with a yell like a Pawnee, he leaped for Scotty—and missed him; for Scotty was a born dodger, and had an eye like a gull's. The officer's spring carried him right into our midst, however; and, with a perfect hurricane of bad words, he struck out right and left as if we were the usual mixed gang of Dagoes, Dutchmen, and Kanakas he had been used to. Pluck he certainly did not lack, but his judgment had turned sour.

In a minute he was flat on deck on his face, with Conkey sitting on his head, and the rest of us were marching aft to make an end of the matter with the old man. He reached the deck from below just as we arrived; and, although the most unusual sight might well have given him pause, he showed no sign of surprise.

Advancing to meet us, he said quietly, "Well?" Again Mac was to the fore, and, facing the stately, impassive figure of the skipper, he said, "We've juist daundert aeft, sir, tae wuss ye a Murry Chrismuss, an' tae thenk ye in advance-like for the bit extry vittles, an' maybe a drap o' somethin' cheerin' tae drink ye're health in an sic an ahspeeshus occashin."

For an answer the skipper produced from his hip-pocket a revolver, which he pointed straight at Scotty's head, while with the other hand he made a comprehensive gesture, which we obeyed by falling back from that dangerous vicinity. As we did so, there was a rioting behind us, and into our midst burst the mate and Conkey, fiercely struggling.

In a moment there was as pretty a rough-and-tumble among us as any fighting-man would wish to see, for the harpooners and the other three mates had sprung in from somewhere, and were making up for lost time with vigour.

Apart from the struggling crowd the skipper stood fingering his shooting-iron, apparently irresolute—indeed, it was hard to decide for a moment what to do. Bloodshed was evidently most distasteful to him, yet there could be no doubt that he would not shrink from it if necessary. But the whole affair was so grotesque, so causeless, that he was undecided how to deal with it, the more especially as his officers were every one mixed inextricably with the crew in a writhing mass.

The problem was solved for him and for us in a most unexpected way. In the midst of the riot there was a tremendous shock, as if the Ursus had suddenly struck a rock while going at full speed; but, as she had barely been going through the water at the rate of two knots an hour, that was an impossible explanation. The concussion, whatever it was, flung every man to the deck, and in one moment all thoughts were switched off the conflict with one another and on to this mysterious danger. All hands rushed to the side and looked overboard, to see the blue of the sea streaked with bands of blood, while not twenty feet away, on the starboard beam, a huge sperm whale lay feebly exhaling breath that showed redly against the blue of the water. Like a trumpet-blast the old man's voice rang out, " Lower 'way boats! " and with catlike celerity every man flew to his station, the falls rattled, and with an almost simultaneous splash three boats took the water.

" Hold on, starboard bow boat! " roared the old man again, seeing that there was no need of it, and taking that advantage of keeping it in its place given him by the third mate being a few seconds slower than the others in getting away.

Before we had time to realize what a change had come over us all, we were furiously assaulting the monster, but he was in no condition to retaliate. Had we left him alone, he must have died in a few minutes, for protruding from the side of his massive head was a jagged piece of timber, showing white and splintered where it had been freshly broken away.

We had little time to speculate upon the strangeness of the occurrence, for suddenly we were aware that urgent signals were being made from the ship; and, leaving one boat to pass the fluke-line ready for hauling our prize alongside, the other two sped back to the ship. Arriving alongside, we clambered swiftly on board, to hear the skipper's deep voice calling, " Leave the boats and man the pumps! " A cold shudder ran through us at the words, for in a moment all knew that our ship had received a deadly blow from the wounded whale, and that it was a portion of her that we had seen protruding from his head. And we remembered the awful loneliness of that part of the Pacific, far away from the track of all ships except an occasional whaler, so occasional that our chances of falling in with one was infinitesimal.

The wind fell to a dead calm. There was not a cloud in the heavens, and the sea in our immediate vicinity was not only smooth, but silky, from the slight oiliness we exuded, so that looking down into it was almost like looking up at the sky. After the first alarm had subsided it was evident that we could have several relays at the pumps, their structure not admitting of more than eight men working conveniently at one time. The skipper stood by with the sounding-rod, waiting, in grim silence, to see whether we or the leak were gaining, when Mac, sidling up to him, made some remark that we could not hear. The skipper turned to him and nodded; and immediately we saw our pawky shipmate shedding his two garments. Next thing we knew he was climbing over the side, and those of us who were resting mounted the rail and watched him. I have seen Kanakas diving for pearl-shell, and Malays diving for pearls, but never an olive-skinned amphibian of them all could have held a candle to Jock MacTavish. He swam about under the ship's bottom, examining her just as coolly as if in Lambeth Baths, his wide, open eyes glaring upward through the water with a most uncanny look in them—like the eyes of a man long dead. Suddenly he popped up alongside, not at all distressed, and, wringing the water from his nose, mounted the side and approached the skipper.

With one accord the clang of the pumps ceased to hear his words, for we felt that they were a verdict of life or death for all of us. "She'll be a' recht, sir," said he. "Ther's a muckle hole in th' garburd straake, an' aboot twenty fit o' the fause keel awa'; bit a poke fu' o' shakins 'll bung it up brawly wi' a len'th o' chain roond her tae keep it in's plaace." The pumping was resumed with all the energy of hope renewed, while busy hands made ready a bagful of soft rope-yarns and got up a spare fluke-chain. The bag was made fast in the bight of a rope, which, weighted with a lump of sandstone attached by a slipping lashing of spunyarn, was passed under her bottom. Again Mac went overboard and guided the plug into its place.

Then the chain was passed round her, and placed over the plug by Scotty. On deck we hove it taut, and in four hours we had sucked her out.

Then the skipper called all hands aft, and said, "Boys, ye're the whitest crowd I've ever struck. The best dinner I k'n scare up 's waitin' for ye, 'n I've raided the medsun chest for the only drop of licker thar is aboard. I don't tech fire-water meself, but I'll wish ye a Merry Christmas with all me heart. Ther's only one thing I'd like t' know; an' that is, haow a Scotchman comes to risk his life for a Christmas dinner?" "We'el, cap'n," drawled Mac, "'twus juist a wee bit seekoeloegical expeerimunt."

Time's up; but I must add that we humoured the old barky back to 'Frisco—and we didn't lose that whale either.

ON THE VERTEX

NOT the least curious to the uninitiated of the ways by which shipmasters navigate their vessels over the trackless wastes of ocean is that known to the navigator by the name of Great Circle Sailing. Lest the timid reader take alarm at the introduction of so high-sounding a technical term, let me hasten to assure him or her that I have no deep-laid designs upon innocent happiness by imposing a trigonometrical treatise upon them in the guise of an amusing or interesting story. To such baseness I cannot stoop, for one very good reason at any rate, because I have such a plentiful lack of trigonometry myself. Nevertheless, I do think that much more interest might be taken in the ways of our ships and their crews by the people of this essentially maritime nation than is at present the case if, in the course of sea-story telling, the narrators were not averse to giving a few accurate details as to the why and how of nautical proceedings.

Having, I trust, allayed all tremors by these preliminary remarks, let me go on to say that while all sane civilized persons believe this earth of ours to be more or less globular in shape, it probably occurs to but few that the shortest distance from point to point on a globe is along a curve. But in order to get any substantial gain out of this knowledge in the direction of shortening a ship's passage, it is necessary first of all to have a considerable stretch of sea whereon to draw your curve, which is after all a straight line, since it is the shortest distance between two points. Even the fine open ocean between England and America is hardly sufficient to induce navigators to make use of Great Circle Sailing on outward or homeward passages, the gain being so small. When, however, the captain of an outward bound ship has wriggled through the baffling belt of hesitating winds that have hindered his progress southward from the equator to Cape, and begins to look for the coming of the brave westerly gales that shall send him flying before them to Australia or New Zealand, an opportunity occurs as in no other part of the world for putting the pretty Great Circle theory into practice.

It may be necessary to remind the reader that Great Circles are those which divide a globe into two equal parts, such as the equator and the meridians. If, then, the navigator at Cape in South America draws a thread tightly on a terrestrial globe between that point and, say, the south-east cape of Tasmania, the line it describes will be the arc of a Great Circle, and consequently the shortest distance between the two places. But when he comes to lay down the track which that thread has described upon his Mercator chart he finds that, instead of steering almost a straight course between the two places, he must describe a huge curve, with its vertex or highest southerly point well within the Antarctic circle. Now, no sane seaman would dream of seeking such a latitude upon any voyage but one of exploration, since it is well known what kind of weather awaits the unfortunate mariner there. But, without saying that Captain Jellico was a lunatic, it is necessary to remark that he was no ordinary shipmaster, and those who knew him best often prophesied that one day his persistent pursuit of hobbies and fads would involve him and all his unfortunate crew in some extraordinary disaster.

On the present voyage he commanded an ancient teak built barque that had long ago seen her best days, and was, besides, so slow that any of the ordinary methods of economizing time were a ridiculous waste of energy when applied to her. Of course, she carried stunsails, those infernal auxiliaries that are or were responsible for more sin on board ship than any other invention of man. She was bound to Auckland, and by the time she had waddled as far south as Cape had already consumed as many days as a smart clipper ship would have needed to do the whole passage. Yet Captain Jellico was so proud of the ugly old tub (bathing machine, the men called her), principally because he was half-owner of her, that he was perfectly blind to her slothful and unhandy qualities. Day by day he held forth to his disgusted mate upon the beauty of the Great Circle problem, and the desirability of putting it into practice, announcing his firm intention of carrying it out in its entirety this trip. He wasn't going to piffle with any "composite" Great Circle track, not he. Half-hearted seamen might choose to follow the great curve down as far as 50° S.

or so, and then shirk the whole business by steering due east for a couple of thousand miles, but he would do the trick properly, and touch the vertex, unless, indeed, it happened to be on the mainland of Antarctica. After an hour or two of this sort of talk the mate would go on deck feeling mighty sick, and muttering fervent prayers that his commander would meet with some entirely disabling accident soon, one that would effectually hinder him from carrying out his oft-reiterated intention. But no such answer was afforded to Mr. Marline's impious aspirations. The steadfast westerly wind began as usual, and the clumsy old Chanticleer, under every rag of canvas, stunsails and all, began to plunder along that hateful curve, steering about south-east by south. Gradually the wind strengthened, until, much to the delight of the scanty crew, the fluttering rags that hung precariously at the yard-arms were taken in and stowed snugly away, the booms and irons were sent down from aloft, and lashed along the scuppers with the spare spars and stunsail carrying, for that passage, at any rate, became only a wretched memory. Sterner and stronger blew the wind as day succeeded day and higher latitudes were successively reached, until, although it was the Antarctic summer, all hands were wearing nearly every garment they possessed in the vain endeavour to keep a little warmth in their thin blood.

One topic now overlaid every other in the endless causeries that were held in the gloomy den where the sailors lived. It was the course steered. The position of the ship is always more or less a matter of conjecture to the men forward, except when some well-known island or headland is sighted, but all sailors are able to judge fairly well from the courses steered what track is being made, and the present persistence in a southerly direction was disquieting in the extreme to them all. The weather worsened every day, and occasional icebergs showed their awful slopes through the surrounding greyness, making every man strain his eyes when on the look-out or at the wheel in painful anxiety lest the ship should suddenly come full tilt upon one of them. A deep discontent was heavy upon the heart of every member of the crew, with the sole exception of the skipper. Snugly wrapped in a huge fur-lined jacket, and with an eared sealskin cap drawn down over his ears, he paced the poop jauntily, as merry as Father Christmas, and utterly oblivious of everything and everybody but the grand way in which he was following up his Great Circle. At last, when a dull settled misery seemed to have loaded all hands so that they appeared to have lost the heart even to growl, a dense mist settled fatefully down upon the ship, a white pall that was not dispelled again by the strong, bitter wind. The skipper hardly ever left the deck, but his almost sleepless vigilance had no effect upon his high spirits. Suddenly at mid-day, when by dead reckoning he was within a day's sail of the vertex, the sea, which had been running in mountainous masses for weeks past, occasionally breaking over all and seething about the sodden decks, became strangely smooth and quiet, although the wind still howled behind them. Such a change sent a thrill of terrible dread through every heart. Even the skipper, with all his stubborn fortitude, looked troubled, and faltered in his unresting tramp fore and aft the poop. Then gradually the wind failed until it was almost calm, and the enshrouding mist closed down upon the ship so densely that it was hardly possible to see a fathom's length away. The silence became oppressive, all the more so because underlying it there was the merest suggestion of a sound that always has a fateful significance for the mariner, the hoarse, unsatisfied murmur of the sea sullenly beating against an immovable barrier. And thus they waited and endured all the agony and suspense born of ignorance of the dangers that they knew must surround them, and utter incapability to do anything whatever. Full thirty-six hours crept leaden-footed away before there came any lightening of their darkness. Then gradually the rolling wreaths of mist melted away and revealed to them their position. At first they could hardly credit the evidence of their senses, believing that what they saw hemming them in on every side was but the reluctant fog taking on fantastic shapes of mountain, valley, and plateau. But when at last the wintry sun gleamed palely, and they could discern the little surf glittering against the bases of the ice-cliffs, all elusive hopes fled, and they became fully aware of their horrible position. The vessel lay motionless in a blue lake bounded on every side by white walls of ice, the snowy glare of their cliffs contrasting curiously with the deep blue of the sea. Some of the peaks soared to a height of over one thousand feet, others again rose sheer from the water for several hundreds of feet, and then terminated in flat table-like summits of vast area. But all were alike in their grim lifelessness. They looked as if they had thus existed for ages; it was impossible to imagine any change in their terrible solidity.

After the first shock of the discovery had passed, the relief that always comes from knowing the worst came to them, and they began to speculate upon the manner in which they could have entered this apparently ice-locked lake. Presently the skipper, in a strangely altered voice, ordered the long boat to be got out, a task of great difficulty, since, as in most vessels of the Chanticleer's class, the long boat was, besides being hampered up by a miscellaneous collection of all the rubbish in the ship, secured as if she was never intended to be used under any circumstances. But the tough job gave the hands something to take their minds off their unhappy position, while the exertion kept off the icy chill of their surroundings. When at last the boat was in the water, although she was so leaky that one man was kept constantly baling, the skipper entered her, and, with four oarsmen, started to explore their prison. With the utmost caution, they surveyed every fathom of the sea line, no detail of the ice-barrier escaping their anguished scrutiny; but when at last, after six hours' absence, they returned on board, they had been unable to discover the slightest vestige of a passage, no, not so much as would admit their boat. The only conclusion that could be arrived at was that they had passed in through the opening of a horseshoe-shaped berg of enormous area, and that another smaller berg had drifted in after them and turned over in the channel, effectually closing it against their return. Slowly and sadly they had returned to the ship, the skipper looking heart-broken at this tragic termination to his enthusiastic scheme of navigation. After ascertaining his position by means of an artificial horizon, he called all hands aft, and thus addressed them, " Men, we'm all fellow-sufferers now, I reckon, and the only thing to do 'es to wait God's good time for lettin' us get out. I find we'm in 61° S., 50° E., and I reckon our only hope lies in the fact that this can't be no shore ice; it must be a floatin' berg, ef 'tes a most amazin' big un. Consequently it must be a driftin' to the norrard a little; they all do, and sooner or later the sun 'll melt us out. One good job, we got 'nough pervisions in the cargo ter las' us six years, an' as for water, well, I reckon there's more fresh water froze around us than all the ships in the world 'ud ever want. So we'll just take care of ourselves, try an' keep alive, 'n look after the old barky, for we shall certinly sail away in her yet." His speech was received in silence, but all hands looked brighter and happier than they had done for a long time. They towed the vessel into a sort of cove, and moored her firmly with kedges and hawsers to the ice, then turned their attention to the invention of all sorts of expedients for preventing the time hanging too heavily. Better feeding became the order of the day, for the old man at once drew upon the cargo, which included an immense assortment of preserved food of the best brands, as well as many luxuries. And every day there was a slight change in the position, showing that, as the skipper had said, the whole body of ice was drifting north as well as east. So uneventfully and tediously two months passed away, leaving everything pretty much the same, except that the skipper seemed to have aged ten years.

Then one afternoon, when the enwrapped mist was so thick that even the deck beneath their feet was scarcely visible, there came a tremendous crash that made the old vessel quiver from keel to truck. It was followed by loud splashes as of falling blocks of ice, and strange sounds that resembled human voices. Presently the fog lifted, and revealed a great gap in the ice-wall just ahead of the vessel, and on one side of its cliffs the wreck of a splendid ship, whose crew were huddled upon the precipitous crags of the berg. The sight sent all hands into frantic activity on the instant. Toiling like giants, they rescued all the nearly frozen men, who were in such evil case that they could hardly ask whence their rescuers had come, and then, as if incapable of fatigue, they strained every ounce of strength they possessed to warp their long-imprisoned ship out of that terrible dock. Once escaped, it is hardly necessary to say that Captain Jellico lost no time in getting north and running his easting down upon a parallel of 42° S. Great Circle Sailing had lost all its charms for him. And in due time the Chanticleer arrived at Auckland, two hundred and forty-six days out from home, with all her passengers and crew in the best of health and mutually pleased with each other.

A MONARCH'S FALL

GLORIOUS in all his splendid majesty, the great sun issued forth of his chamber, and all the wide sea basked in his beams with a million million smiles. Save the sea and the sun and the sky, there was nought apparently existing—it might well have been the birthday of Light. Also the one prevailing characteristic of the scene to a human eye, had one been there to see, was peace—perfect stainless peace. But we are, by the very fact of our organization, true impressionists, and only by a severe course of training, voluntary or otherwise, do we realize aught but the present fact, the past is all forgotten, the future all unknown. So it was here, beneath that sea of smiling placid beauty a war of unending ferocity was being waged, truceless, merciless; for unto the victors belong the spoils, and without them they must perish—there was none other food to be gotten.

But besides all this ruthless warfare carried on inevitably because without it all must die of hunger, there were other causes of conflict, matters of high policy and more intricate motive than just the blind all-compelling pressure of hunger. The glowing surface of that morning sea was suddenly disturbed simultaneously at many points, and like ascending incense the bushy breathings of some scores of whales became visible. Perfectly at their ease since their instincts assured them that from this silent sea their only enemy was absent, they lay in unstudied grace about the sparkling waters, the cows and youngsters gambolling happily together in perfect freedom from care. Hither they had come from one of their richest feeding-grounds, where all had laid in a stock of energy sufficient to carry them half round the globe without weariness. So they were fat with a great richness, strong with incalculable strength, and because of these things they were now about to settle a most momentous question. Apart from the main gathering of females and calves by the space of about a mile lay five individuals, who, from their enormous superiority in size, no less than the staid gravity of their demeanour, were evidently the adult males of the school. They lay almost motionless in the figure of a baseless triangle whereof the apex was a magnificent bull over seventy feet in length, with a back like some keelless ship bottom up, and a head huge and square as a railway car. He it was who first broke the stillness that reigned. Slowly raising his awful front with its down-hanging, twenty-foot lower jaw exposing two gleaming rows of curved teeth, he said, "Children, ye have chosen the time and the place for your impeachment of my overlordship, and I am ready. Well, I wot that ye do but as our changeless laws decree, that the choice of your actions rests not with yourselves, that although ye feel lords of yourselves and desirous of ruling all your fellows, it is but under the compelling pressure of our hereditary instincts. Yet remember, I pray you, before ye combine to drive me from among ye, for how many generations I have led the school, how wisely I have chosen our paths, so that we are still an unbroken family as we have been for more than a hundred seasons. And if ye must bring your powers to test now, remember, too, that I am no weakling, no dotard weary of rule, but mightiest among all our people, conqueror in more than a thousand battles, wise with the accumulated knowledge of a hundred generations of monarchy. Certainly the day of my displacement must come; who should know that better than I? but methinks it has not yet dawned, and I would not have ye lightly pit your immature strength against mine, courting inevitable destruction. Ponder well my words, for I have spoken."

A solemn hush ensued, just emphasized by the slumbrous sound of the sparkling wavelets lapping those mighty forms as they lay all motionless and apparently inert. Yet it had been easy to see how along each bastion like flank the rolling tendons, each one a cable in itself, were tense and ready for instantaneous action, how the great muscle mounds were hardened around the gigantic masses of bone, and the flukes, each some hundred feet in area, did not yield to the heaving bosom of the swell, but showed an almost imperceptible vibration as of a fucus frond in a tide rip. After a perfect silence of some fifteen minutes an answer came—from the youngest of the group, who lay remote from the chief. "We have heard, O king, the words of wisdom, and our hearts rejoice. Truly we have been of the fortunate in this goodly realm, and ingrates indeed should we be had our training under so terrible a champion been wasted upon us. But therefore it is that we would forestall the shame that should overtake us did we wait until thy forces had waned and that all-conquering might had dwindled into dotage ere we essayed to put thy teaching into practice. Since thy deposition from this proud place must be, to whose forces could'st thou more honourably yield than to ours, the young warriors who have learned of thee all we know, and who will carry on the magnificent traditions thou hast handed down to us in a manner worthy of our splendid sire! And if we be slain, as well may be, remembering with whom we do battle, the greater our glory, the greater thine also."

A deep murmur like the bursting of a tidal wave against the sea-worn lava rocks of Ascension marked the satisfaction of the group at this exposition of their views, and as if actuated by one set of nerves the colossal four swung round shoulder to shoulder, and faced the ocean monarch. Moving not by a barnacle's breadth, he answered, "It is well spoken, oh my children, ye are wiser than I. And be the issue what it will, all shall know that the royal race still holds. As in the days when our fathers met and slew the slimy dragons of the pit, and, unscared by fathom-long claws or ten-ply coats of mail, dashed them in pieces and chased them from the blue deep they befouled, so to-day when the world has grown old, and our ancient heritage has sorely shrunken, our warfare shall still be the mightiest among created things."

A Monarch's Fall

Hardly had the leviathan uttered the last word when, with a roar like Niagara bursting its bonds in spring, he hurled his vast bulk headlong upon the close gathered band of his huge offspring. His body was like a bent bow, and its recoil tore the amazed sea into deep whirls and eddies as if an island had foundered. Full upon the foremost one he fell, and deep answered unto deep with the impact. That awful blow dashed its recipient far into the soundless depths while the champion sped swiftly forward on his course, unable to turn until his impetus was somewhat spent. Before he could again face his foes, the three were upon him, smiting with Titanic fluke strokes, circling beneath him with intent to catch the down-hanging shaft of his lower jaw, rising swiftly end on beneath the broad spread of his belly, leaping high into the bright air and falling flatlings upon his wide back. The tormented sea foamed and hissed in angry protest, screaming sea-birds circled low around the conflict, ravening sharks gathered from unknown distances, scenting blood, and all the countless tribes of ocean waited aghast. But after the first red fury had passed came the wariness, came the fruitage of all those years of training, all the accumulated instincts of ages to supplement blind brutal force with deep laid schemes of attack and defence. As yet the three survivors were but slightly injured, for they had so divided their attack even in that first great onset, that the old warrior could not safely single out one for destruction. Now the youngest, the spokesman, glided to the front of his brethren, and faced his waiting sire—

"What! so soon weary. Thou art older than we thought. Truly this battle hath been delayed too long. We looked for a fight that should be remembered for many generations, and behold——" Out of the corner of his eye he saw the foam circles rise as the vast tail of the chief curved inward for the spring, and he, the scorner, launched himself backwards a hundred fathoms at a bound. After him, leaping like any salmon in a spate, came the terrible old warrior, the smitten waves boiling around him as he dashed them aside in his tremendous pursuit. But herein the pursued had the advantage, for it is a peculiarity of the sperm whale that while he cannot see before him, his best arc of vision is right astern. So that the pursuer must needs be guided by sound and the feel of the water, and the very vigour of his chase was telling far more upon his vast bulk than upon the lither form of his flying enemy. In this matter the monarch's wisdom was of no avail, for experience could not tell him how advancing age handicaps the strongest, and he wondered to find a numbness creeping along his spine—to feel that he was growing weary. And suddenly, with an eel-like movement the pursued one described a circle beneath the water, rising swift as a dolphin springs towards his pursuer, and dashing at the dangling, gleaming jaw. These two great balks of jaw met in clashing contact, breaking off a dozen or so of the huge teeth, and ripping eight or ten feet of the gristly muscle from the throat of the aggressor. But hardly had they swung clear of each other than the other two were fresh upon the scene, and while the youngest one rested, they effectually combined to prevent their fast-weakening foe from rising to breathe. No need now for them to do more, for the late enormous expenditure of force had so drained his vast body of its prime necessity that the issue of the fight was but a question of minutes. Yet still he fought gallantly, though with lungs utterly empty—all the rushing torrent of his blood growing fetid for lack of vitalising air. At last, with a roar as of a cyclone through his head, he turned on his side and yielded to his triumphant conquerors, who drew off and allowed him to rise limply to the now quiet sea-surface. For more than an hour he lay there prone, enduring all the agony of his overthrow, and seeing far before him the long, lonely vista of his solitary wanderings, a lone whale driven from his own, and nevermore to rule again.

Meanwhile the three had departed in search of their brother, smitten so felly early in the fight that he had not since joined them. When they found that which had been him it was the centre of an innumerable host of hungry things that fled to air or sea-depths at their approach. A glance revealed the manner of his end—a broken back, while already, such had been the energy of the smaller sea people, the great framework of his ribs was partly laid bare. They made no regrets, for the doing of useless things finds no place in their scheme of things. Then the younger said—

"So the question of overlordship lies between us three, and I am unwilling that it should await settlement. *I* claim the leadership, and am prepared here and now to maintain my right."

This bold assertion had its effect upon the two hearers, who, after a long pause, replied—

"We accept, O king, fully and freely, until the next battle-day arrives, when the succession must be maintained by thee in ancient form."

So the matter was settled, and proudly the young monarch set off to rejoin the waiting school. Into their midst he glided with an air of conscious majesty, pausing in the centre to receive the homage and affectionate caresses of the harem. No questions were asked as to the whereabouts of the deposed sovereign, nor as to what had become of the missing member of the brotherhood. These are things that do not disturb the whale-people, who in truth have a sufficiency of other matters to occupy their thoughts besides those inevitable changes that belong to the settled order of things. The recognition complete, the new leader glided out from the midst of his people, and pointing his massive front to the westward moved off at a stately pace, on a straight course for the coast of Japan.

Long, long lay the defeated one, motionless and alone. His exertions had been so tremendous that every vast muscle band seemed strained beyond recovery, while the torrent of his blood, befouled by his long enforced stay beneath the sea, did not readily regain its normally healthful flow. But on the second day he roused himself, and raising his mighty head swept the unbroken circle of the horizon to satisfy himself that he was indeed at last a lone whale. Ending his earnest scrutiny he milled round to the southward and with set purpose and steady fluke-beat started for the Aucklands. On his journey he passed many a school or smaller "pod" of his kind, but in some mysterious manner the seal of his loneliness was set upon him, so that he was shunned by all. In ten days he reached his objective, ten days of fasting, and impelled by fierce hunger ventured in closely to the cliffs, where great shoals of fish, many seals, with an occasional porpoise, came gaily careering down the wide-gaping white tunnel of his throat into the inner darkness of dissolution. It was good to be here, pleasant to feel once more that unquestioned superiority over all things, and swiftly the remembrance of his fall faded from the monster's mind. By day he wandered lazily, enjoying the constant easy procession of living food down his ever-open gullet; by night he wallowed sleepily in the surf-torn margin of those jagged reefs. And thus he came to enjoy the new phase of existence, until one day he rose slowly from a favourite reef-patch to feel a sharp pang shoot through his wide flank. Startled into sudden, violent activity, he plunged madly around in the confined area of the cove wherein he lay in the vain endeavour to rid himself of the smart. But he had been taken at a disadvantage, for in such shallow waters there was no room to manœuvre his vast bulk, and his wary assailants felt that in spite of his undoubted vigour and ferocity he would be an easy prey. But suddenly he headed instinctively for the open sea at such tremendous speed that the two boats attached to him were but as chips behind him. He reached the harbour's mouth, and bending, swiftly sought the depths. Unfortunately for him a huge pinnacle of rock rose sheer from the sea bed some hundred fathoms below, and upon this he hurled himself headlong with such fearful force that his massive neck was broken. And next day a weary company of men were toiling painfully to strip from his body its great accumulation of valuable oil, and his long career was ended.

THE CHUMS

WHAT a depth of mystery is concealed in the phenomena of likes and dislikes! Why, at first sight, we are attracted by one person and repelled by another, independently, to all outward seeming, of personal appearance or habits of observation. This is, of course, a common experience of most people, but one of the strangest instances I have ever known was in my own affection for Jack Stadey and all that grew out of it.

Stadey was a Russian Finn, one of a race that on board ship has always had the reputation of being a bit wizard-like, credited with the possession of dread powers, such as the ability to raise or still a storm, become invisible, and so on. The bare truth about the seafaring Finns, however, is that they make probably the finest all-round mariners in the world. No other sea-folk combine so completely all the qualities that go to make up the perfect seaman. Many of them may be met with who can build a vessel, make her spars, her sails, and her rigging, do the blacksmith work and all the manifold varieties of odd workmanship that go to complete a ship's equipment, take her to sea, and navigate her on soundest mathematical principles, and do all these strange acts and deeds with the poorest, most primitive tools, and under the most miserable, poverty-stricken conditions. But, as a rule, they are not smart; they must be allowed to do their work in their own way, at their own pace, and with no close scrutiny into anything except results. Now, Jack Stadey was a typical Finn, as far as his slow ungainly movements went, but none of that ability and adaptiveness which is characteristic of his countrymen was manifest in him. To the ordinary observer he was just a heavy, awkward " Dutchman," who couldn't jump to save his life, and who would necessarily be put upon all the heaviest, dirtiest jobs, while the sailorizing was being done by smarter men. With a long, square head, faded blue eyes, and straggling flaxen moustache, round shoulders, and dangling, crooked arms, he seemed born to be the butt of his more favoured shipmates. Yet when I first became acquainted with him in the fo'c'sle of the old Dartmouth, outward bound to Hong Kong, something about him appealed to me, and we became chums. The rest of the crew, with one notable exception, were not bad fellows, and Jack shuffled along serenely through the voyage, quite undisturbed by the fact that no work of any seamanlike nature ever came to his share. I came in for a good deal of not ill-natured chaff from the rest for my close intimacy with him, but it only had the effect of knitting us closer together, for there is just that strain of obstinacy about me that opposition only stiffens. And as I studied that simple, childlike man, I found that he had a heart of gold, a nature that had no taint of selfishness, and was sublimely unconscious of its own worth.

We made the round voyage together, and on our return to London I persuaded him to quit the gloomy environment of sailor-town to come and take lodgings with me in a turning out of Oxford Street, whence we could sally forth and find ourselves at once in the midst of clean, interesting life, free from the filthy importunities of the denizens of Shadwell that prey upon the sailor. My experiences of London life were turned to good account in those pleasant days, all too short. Together we did all the sights, and it would be hard to say which of us enjoyed ourselves most. At last, our funds having dwindled to the last five pounds, we must needs go and look for a ship. I had "passed" for second mate, but did not try very hard to get the berth that my certificate entitled me to take, and finally we both succeeded in getting berths before the mast in a barque called the Magellan, bound for New Zealand. To crown the common-sense programme we had been following out, we did a thing I have never seen deep-water sailors do before or since—we took a goodly supply of such delicacies on board with us as would, had we husbanded them, have kept us from hunger until we crossed the line. But sailor Jack, with all his faults, is not mean, and so all hands shared in the good things until they were gone, which was in about three days. To our great disgust, Jack and I were picked for separate watches, so that our chats were limited to the second dog-watch, that pleasant time between six and eight p.m. when both watches can fraternize at their ease, and discuss all the queer questions that appeal to the sailor mind.

Jack never complained, it wasn't his habit, but, unknown to me, he was having a pretty bad time of it in the starboard watch. Of course, the vessel was short-handed—four hands in a watch to handle an over-sparred brute of nearly a thousand tons—and as a consequence Jack's ungainly want of smartness was trying to his over-worked watchmates, who were, besides, unable to understand his inability or unwillingness to growl at the hardness of the common lot. The chief man in that watch was a huge Shetlandman, Sandy Rorison, who, broadly speaking, was everything that Jack was not. Six feet two in his stocking vamps, upright as a lower mast, and agile as a leading seaman on board a man-o'-war, there was small wonder that Sandy was sorely irritated by the wooden movements of my deliberate chum. But one day, when, relieved from the wheel, I came into the forecastle for a "verse o' the pipe," I found Sandy bullying him in a piratical manner. All prudential considerations were forgotten, and I interfered, although it was like coming between a lion and his kill. Black with fury, Sandy turned upon me, tearing off his jumper the while, and in choking monosyllables invited me to come outside and die. I refused, giving as my reason that I did not feel tired of life, and admitting that I was fully aware of his ability to make cracker-hash of me. But while he stood gasping, I put it to him whether, if he had a chum, any consideration for his own safety would stop him from risking it in the endeavour to save that chum from such a dog's life as he was now leading Jack Stadey. Well, the struggle between rage and righteousness in that big rough man was painful to see. It lasted for nearly five minutes, while I stood calmly puffing at my pipe with a numb sense of "what must be will be" about me. Then suddenly the big fellow went and sat down, buried his face in his hands, and was silent. I went about my work unmolested, but for nearly a week there was an air of expectation about the whole of us—a sense that an explosion might occur at any moment. Then the tension relaxed, and I saw with quiet delight that Rorison had entirely abandoned his hazing of Jack.

After a most miserable passage of a hundred and ten days we arrived at our port, and almost immediately after came an opening for me to join a fine ship as second mate. It could not be disregarded, although I had to forfeit to the knavish skipper the whole of my outward passage earnings for the privilege of being discharged. So Jack and I parted, making no sign, as is the custom of men, of the rending pain of our separation. When next I saw Jack, several years after, I had left the sea, but on a periodical visit to the docks —a habit I was long curing myself of—I met him, looking for a ship. How triumphantly I bore him westward to my little home I need not say, but when in the course of conversation I found that he and Rorison had been chums ever since I left the Magellan, I was dumbfounded. The more because, in spite of the change in Rorison after my risky interference on that memorable afternoon, I had passed many unhappy hours, thinking, in my conceit and ignorance of the nobleness of which the majority of human kind are capable, given the proper opportunity for showing it, that Jack would have but a sorry time of it after *I* had left him. Malvolio thought nobly of the soul, and I have had reason, God knows, to think nobly of my fellow-men, even of those who upon a casual acquaintance seemed only capable of exciting disgust. I believe that few indeed are the men and women who have not within them the germ of as heroic deeds as ever thrilled the hearts and moistened the eyes of mankind, although, alas! myriads live and die wanting the occasion that could fructify the germ. Made in His own image, although sorely battered out of the Divine likeness, the Father does delight in showing how, in spite of the distance men generally have placed between themselves and Him, the type still persists, and self-sacrifice, soaring above the devilish cynicism that affects to know no God but self-interest, blazes forth to show to all who will but open their eyes that "God's in His Heaven, all's right with the world."

Two more strangely assorted chums surely seldom foregathered than Sandy and Jack. I remember none in real life, though the big trooper George Rouncewell and Phil have been immortalized by Dickens in "Bleak House," and the probability is that such a friendship had been known to that marvellous man. How the bond between the Shetlandman and the Finn gradually grew and toughened I had no means of knowing, for Jack was a man of so few words, that even my eager questioning never succeeded in drawing from him the information that I thirsted for. However, to resume my story, the pair succeeded in obtaining berths in the same ship again, a big iron clipper, the Theodosia, bound to Melbourne. I did not succeed in meeting Sandy before they sailed, though I tried hard in my scanty leisure to do so. But I determined that when they returned I would have them both home to my little place, and devote some of my holidays to entertaining them. I watched carefully the columns of the Shipping Gazette for news of the ship, and succeeded in tracing her home to Falmouth for orders from Port Pirie. Thence in due time she departed, to my great disappointment, for Sunderland. And the rest of the story must be told as I learned it long afterwards.

It was in the late autumn that they sailed from Falmouth, leaving port on a glorious afternoon with that peerless weather known to west-country fishermen as a "fine southerly." Up the sparkling Channel they sped with every stitch of canvas set, and a great contentment reigning on board at the prospect of the approaching completion of the voyage under such favourable conditions. Being foul, the Theodosia made slow progress, but so steady was the favouring wind that in two days she picked up her Channel pilot off Dungeness. He was hardly on board before a change came. One of those sudden gales came howling down the stern North Sea, and gradually the labouring ship was stripped of her wings, until in a perfect whirl of freezing spindrift she was groping through the gloom across the Thames estuary. But no uneasiness was felt, because the pilot was on board, and the confidence felt in the well-known skill and seamanship of those splendid mariners makes even the most timid of deep-water sailors feel secure under their charge. No man is infallible, however, and just before midnight a shock, which threw all hands, then standing by to wear ship, off their feet, brought the huge vessel up all standing. Not many minutes were needed to show every man on board that she was doomed. Lying as she was on the weather edge of the Galloper Sand (though her position was unknown even to the pilot), she was exposed to the full fury of the gale, and the blue lights and rockets made but the faintest impression upon the appalling blackness. All hands worked with feverish energy to free the long-disused boats from their gripes, although they were often hurled headlong from this task by the crushing impact of those inky masses of water that rose in terrible might all around. And as the boats were cleared, so they were destroyed until but one remained seaworthy and afloat upon the lee-side, fast by the end of the forebrace. One by one the beaten, bruised, and almost despairing men succeeded in boarding that tiny ark of refuge as it strained and plunged like a terrified creature striving to escape from the proximity of the perishing leviathan. When it appeared that all hands were crowded into the overburdened boat, the watchful skipper mounted the lee rail, and, waiting his opportunity, leapt for his life.

"Cast off, cast off," shouted a dozen voices as the captain struggled aft to the place of command, but one cry overtopped them all, the frenzied question of

Rorison, "Where's Jack Stadey?" A babel of replies arose, but out of that tumult one fact emerged, he was not among them. The next moment, as a mountainous swell lifted the boat high above the ship's rail, Rorison had leapt to his feet, and, catching hold of the drooping mainbrace above his head, was hauling himself back on board again. And the boat had gone. Doubtless in the confusion, some man had succeeded in casting the end of the rope adrift that held her, not knowing what had happened, so that the next vast roller swept her away on its crest a hundred fathoms in an instant. The wide mouth of the dark engulfed her. All unheeding the disappearance of the boat, Rorison fought his way about the submerged and roaring decks, peering with a seaman's bat-like power of vision through the dark for any sign of his chum. Buffeted by the scourging seas, conscious that he was fast losing what little strength remained to him, he yet persisted in his search until, with a cry of joy, he found poor Stadey jammed between the fife-rail and the pumps, just alive, but with a broken leg and arm. Not a word passed between them, but with a sudden accession of vigour, Sandy managed to drag his chum aft and lash his limp body to one of the poop hencoops. He then cast another coop adrift, and secured it to the side of the first. Having done this, he lashed himself by Stadey's side, and with one hand feeling the languid pulsation of his chum's heart, awaited the next comber that should sweep their frail raft away into the hissing sea.

Next morning, under a sky of heavenly glory, two

Harwich fishermen found the tiny raft, still supporting the empty husks of those two faithful souls, undivided even unto the end of their hard life, and together entered into rest.

With these two exceptions all hands were saved.

ALPHONSO M'GINTY

Who is there among British seafarers that does not know the "chain-locker"—that den just opposite the Mint like an exaggerated bear-pit? The homeward-bounder, his heart light as thistle-down with the first taste of liberty after his voyage's long imprisonment, takes no heed of its squalor; no, not even in the drear December slushiness, following upon a Shadwell snowstorm. If he does glance around shudderingly at the haggard faces of the unshipped for a moment, the feel of the beloved half-sheet of blue foolscap ostentatiously displayed in his club-fingered right hand brings the departing look of satisfaction back swiftly enough. It is his "account of wages," his passport within the swing doors of the office, which he will presently exchange for the few pieces of gold for which he has given such a precious slice of his life.

But the outward-bounder, his hands thrust deep into empty pockets, the bitter taste of begrudged bread parching his mouth, and the scowling face of his boarding master refusing to pass from his mind's eye; he it is who feels the utter desolation of the crowded "chain-locker" corrode his very soul. After a long day's tramp around the docks, sneaking on board vessels like a thief, and asking the mate for a "chance" with bated breath, as if begging for pence, unsuccessful and weary, he returns to this walled-in pit of gloom, and jealously eyes the company of miserables like himself, as if in each one he saw a potential snatcher of his last hope of a berth.

Outward-bounders have little to say to each other in the "chain-locker." They wait, not like honest labourers seeking legitimate employment, but like half-tried prisoners awaiting sentence. This characteristic is so universal that, although we who bided the coming of the Gareth's skipper had all got our discharges in, and so felt reasonably sure of her, we had not exchanged half a dozen words among the fourteen of us.

But there suddenly appeared in our midst a square-built, rugged-faced man of middle height, whose grey eyes twinkled across his ruined nose, and whose mouth had that droll droop of the lower lip that shows a readiness, not only to laugh in and out of season, but almost pathetically invites the beholder to laugh too. He it was who broke the stony silence by saying in the richest brogue, "Is it all av us bhoys that does be goin' in the wan ship, I wondher?" Even the most morose among us felt an inclination to smile, we hardly knew why, but just then the swing door of the engaging office burst open, and a hoarse voice shouted, "Crew o' the Gareth here."

The words, like some irresistible centripetal force, sucked in from the remotest corner of the large area every man, and in a moment all of us, who had, as we thought, secured our chances by lodging our discharges beforehand, were seized with something of a panic lest we should lose the ship after all. Heavens! how we thrust and tore our way into the office, past the burly policeman who held every one of us at the pinch of the door until he was satisfied of our right to enter. Once within, we felt safe, and stood nervously fingering our caps while the clerk gabbled over the usual formula, to which none of us gave the slightest heed. "Signing on" began and proceeded apace, to the accompaniment of a running fire of questions as to age, nationality, last ship, etc., to which answers, if not promptly forthcoming, were, I am afraid, supplied by the questioner. There was a subdued chuckle, and the man who had spoken outside stood at the counter.

"What name?" snapped the clerk.

"Alphonso M'Ginty, yer anner," was the answer. No exquisite witticism ever raised a more wholesome burst of laughter. It positively brightened that dull hole like a ray of sea-sunshine.

"How old?" said the clerk, in a voice still tremulous.

"God befrind me, I forgot! Say tirty-five, sor."

"Your discharge says twenty-five?" returned the clerk.

"Ah yes, yer anner, but it's said that for the last tirty years!"

"Isn't it time it was altered then?" retorted the clerk, magisterial again, as he entered fifty-five on the articles. The old fellow's quaint speech, added to an indefinable aureole of good humour about him, had completely changed the sullen aspect of our crowd, so that for the moment we quite forget that but fourteen of us were engaged to take the 4000-ton ship Gareth to New Zealand first, and then to any other part of the world, voyage not to exceed three years.

So, with even the Dutchmen laughing and chuckling in sympathy with the fun they felt, but didn't understand, we all dispersed with our advance notes to get such discount as fate and the sharks would allow. In good time we were all aboard, for ships were scarce, and all of us anxious to get away. But when we saw the vast, gaunt hull well down to Plimsoll's Mark, and the four towering steel giants of masts with their immense spreading branches, and thought of the handful we were to manage them, we felt a colder chill than even the biting edge of the bitter east wind had given us.

We mustered in the dark, iron barn of the fo'c'sle, and began selecting bunks temporarily, until we were picked for watches, when our attention was arrested by the voice of M'Ginty, saying—

"Bhoys!"

All turned towards him where he stood, with a bottle of rum and a tea-cup, and no one needed a second call. When the bottle was empty, and our hearts had gone out to the donor, he said, clearing his throat once or twice—

"Bhoys, fergive me, I'm a —— imposhtor. I broke me right knee-cap an' five ribs comin' home from 'Frisco in the Lamech—fell from the fore-t'gal-ant yard—an' I bin three months in Poplar Hospital. I can't go aloft, but I didn't think what a crime it wuz goin' to be agin ye all until I see this awful over-sparred brute here. Don't be harrd on me, bhoys; ye wouldn't have me starrve ashore, wud yez now, or fret me poor owld hearrt out in the wurrkhouse afther forty-five year on the open sea?"

He stopped and looked around distressfully, and in that moment all our hearts warmed to him. We were a mixed crowd, of course, but nearly half of us were British, and there would have been a stormy scene if any of the aliens had ventured to raise a protest against M'Ginty's incapacity. We didn't express our sympathy, but we felt it, and he with native quickness knew that we did. And never from that day forward did the brave old chap hear a word of complaint from any of us about having to do his work.

Just then the voice of the bos'un sounded outside, "Turn to!" and as we departed to commence work, although not a word was said, there was a fierce determination among us to protect M'Ginty against any harshness from the officers on account of his disablement. There was too much of a bustle getting out of dock for any notice to be taken of his stiff leg, which he had so cleverly concealed while shipping, but the mate happening to call him up on to the forecastle head for something, his lameness was glaringly apparent at once to the bos'un, who stood behind him. For just a minute it looked like trouble as the bos'un began to bluster about his being a —— cripple, but we all gathered round, and the matter was effectually settled at once.

We never regretted our consideration. For, while

it was true that he couldn't get aloft, and those mighty sails would have been a handful for double our number in a breeze of wind, there never was a more willing, tireless worker on deck, and below he was a perfect godsend. His sunny temper, bubbling fun, and inexhaustible stock of yarns, made our grey lives happier than they had ever been at sea before. If we would have allowed it, he would have been a slave to all of us, for we carried no boys, and all the odd domestic jobs of the fo'c'sle had to be done by ourselves. As it was, he was always doing something for somebody, and as he was a thorough sailor in his general handiness and ability, his services were highly appreciated. He made the Gareth a comfortable ship, in spite of her manifold drawbacks.

In due time we reached the "roaring forties" and began to run the easting down. The long, tempestuous stretch of the Southern Ocean lay before us, and the prospect was by no means cheering. The Gareth, in spite of her huge bulk, had given us a taste of her quality when running before a heavy breeze of wind shortly after getting clear of the Channel, and we knew that she was one of the wettest of her class, a vessel that welcomed every howling sea as an old friend, and freely invited it to range the whole expanse of her decks from poop to forecastle. And, in accordance with precedent, we knew that she would be driven to the last extremity of canvas endurance, not only in the hope of making a quick passage, but because shortening sail after really hard running was such an awful strain upon the handful of men composing the crew. So that when once the light sails were secure, an attempt would always be made to " hang on " to the still enormous spread of sail remaining, until the gale blew itself out, or we had run out of its vast area. But for some days the brave west wind lingered in its lair, and we slowly crept to the s'uthard and east'ard with trumpery little spurts of northerly and nor'-westerly breeze. We had reached 47° S. and about 10° E. when, one afternoon, it fell calm.

One of the most magnificent sunsets imaginable spread its glories over the western sky. Great splashes of gorgeous colouring stained the pale blue of the heavens, and illuminated the fantastic crags and ranges of cloud that lay motionless around the horizon, like fragments of a disintegrated world. A long, listless swell came solemnly from the west at regular intervals, giving the waiting ship a stately rhythmical motion in the glassy waters, and making the immense squares of canvas that hung straight as boards from the yards slam against the steel masts with a sullen boom. Except for that occasionally recurring sound, a solemn stillness reigned supreme, while the wide mirror of the ocean reflected faithfully all the flaming tints of the sky. Quietly all of us gathered on the fo'c'sle head for the second dog-watch smoke, but for some time all seemed strangely disinclined for the desultory chat that usually takes place at that pleasant hour. Pipes were puffed in silence for half an hour, until suddenly M'Ginty broke the spell (his voice sounding strangely clear and vibrant, by saying—

" I had a quare dhrame lasht night."

No one stirred or spoke, and after a few meditative pulls at his pipe, he went on—

"I dhreamt that I was a tiny gorsoon again, at home in owld Baltimore. I'd been wandherin' and sthrayin', God alone knows where, fur a dhreadful long while, it seemed, until at lasht, whin I wuz ready t' die from sheer weariness an' fright, I hearrd me dear mother's sweet voice cryin', 'Where's Fonnie avic iver got to this long while?' Oh! 'twas as if an angel from hiven shpoke to me, an' I cried wid all me hearrt an' me tongue, 'Here, mother, here I am!' An' she gathered me up in her arrums that wuz so soft an' cosy, till I felt as if I was a little tired chick neshtlin' into its mother's feathers in the snuggest of nests. I didn't go to sleep, I just let meself sink down, down into rest, happy as any saint in glory. An' thin I woke up wid a big, tearin' ache all over me poor owld broken-up body. But bad as that wuz, 'twuz just nothin' at all to the gnawin' ache at me hearrt."

Silence wrapped us round again, for who among us could find any words to apply to such a story as that? And it affected us all the more because of its complete contrast to M'Ginty's usual bright, cheery, and uncomplaining humour. Not another word was spoken by any one until the sharp strokes on the little bell aft cleft the still air, and, in immediate response, one rose and smote the big bell hanging at the break of the forecastle four double blows, ushering in the first watch of the night. The watch on deck relieved wheel and look-out, and we who were fortunate enough to have the "eight hours in," lost no time in seeking our respective bunks, since in those stern latitudes we might expect a sudden call at any moment. We had hardly been asleep five minutes, it seemed, when a hoarse cry came pealing in through the fo'c'sle door of "All hands on deck! Shorten sail!" And as we all started wide awake, we heard the furious voice of the southern tempest tearing up the face of the deep, and felt the massive fabric beneath our feet leaping and straining under the tremendous strain of her great breadths of canvas, that we had left hanging so idly at eight bells.

Out into the black night we hurried, meeting the waiting mate at the foremast, and answering his first order of "man the fore tops'ls downhaul" with the usual repetition of his words. Weird cries arose as we hauled with all our strength on the downhauls and spilling lines, while overhead we could hear, even above the roar of the stôrm, the deep boom of the topsails fiercely fighting against the restraining gear. Then, with a hissing, spiteful snarl, came snow and sleet, lashing us like shotted whips, and making the darkness more profound because of the impossibility of opening the eyes against the stinging fragments of ice. But, after much stumbling and struggling, we got the four huge tops'ls down, and, without waiting for the order, started aloft to furl, the pitiful incapacity of our numbers most glaringly apparent. The pressure of the wind was so great that it was no easy matter to get aloft, but clinging like cats, we presently found ourselves (six of the port watch) on the fore topsailyard.

The first thing evident was that the great sail was very slightly subdued by the gear; it hovered above the yard like a white balloon, making it both difficult and dangerous to get out along the spar. The storm scourged us pitilessly, the great round of the sail resisted all our attempts to " fist " it, and we seemed as helpless as children. Some bold spirits clutched the lifts, and, swinging above the sail, tried to stamp a hollow into it with their feet; but against the increasing fury of the tempest we seemed to be utterly impotent. We were so widely separated, too, that each man appeared to be essaying a giant's task single-handed, and that horrible sense of fast-oozing strength was paralyzing us. Feeling left our hands; we smote them savagely against that unbending sail without sensation, and still we seemed no nearer the conclusion of our task. But suddenly the ship gave a great lurch to windward, and just for one moment the hitherto unyielding curve of the sail quivered. In that instant every fist had clutched a fold, and with a flash of energy we strained every sinew to conquer our enemy.

* * * * * * * *

Tugging like a madman to get the sail spilled, I glanced sideways, and saw to my horror, by a jagged flash of lightning, the rugged face of M'Ginty.

I had hardly recognized him when, with a roar like the combined voices of a troop of lions, the sail tore itself away from us, and with bleeding hands I clutched at the foot-rope stirrup as I fell back. But at the same moment M'Ginty's arms flew up. He caught at the empty gloom above him, gasping, " *In manus tuas, Domine*——" and fell. Far beneath us the hungry

He gasped "In manus tuas, Domine," and fell.

sea seethed and whirled, its white glare showing ghastly against the thick darkness above. For two or three seconds I hung as if irresolute whether to follow my poor old shipmate or not; then the heavy flapping of the sail aroused me, and springing up again, I renewed my efforts. The ship had evidently got a "wipe up" into the wind, for the sail was now powerless against us, and in less than five minutes it was fast, and we were descending with all speed to renew our desperate fight with the mizen and jigger topsails. The decks were like the sea overside, for wave after wave toppled inboard, and it was at the most imminent risk to life and limb that we scrambled aft, quite a sense of relief coming as we swung out of that turbulent flood into the rigging again.

But I was almost past feeling now. A dull aching sense of loss clung around my heart, and the patient, kindly face of my shipmate seemed branded upon my eyes, as he had lifted it to the stormy skies in his last supplicatory moan. I went about my work doggedly, mechanically; indifferent to cold, fatigue, or pain, until, when at last she was snugged down, and, under the fore lower topsails and reefed foresail, was flying through the darkness like some hunted thing, I staggered wearily into the cheerless fo'c'sle, dropped upon a chest, and stared moodily at vacancy.

Somebody said, "Where's M'Ginty?" That roused me. It seemed to put new life and hope into me, for I replied quite brightly, "He's gone to the rest he was talking about in the dog-watch. He'll never eat workhouse bread, thank God!"

Eager questioning followed, mingled with utter amazement at his getting aloft at all. But when all had said their say one feeling had been plainly manifested—a feeling of deep thankfulness that such a grand old sailor as our shipmate M'Ginty was where he fain would be, taking his long and well-earned rest.

THE LAST STAND OF THE DECAPODS

PROBABLY few of the thinking inhabitants of dry land, with all their craving for tales of the marvellous, the gloomy, and the gigantic, have in these later centuries of the world's history given much thought to the conditions of constant warfare existing beneath the surface of the ocean. As readers of ancient classics well know, the fathers of literature gave much attention to the vast, awe-inspiring inhabitants of the sea, investing and embellishing the few fragments of fact concerning them which were available with a thousand fantastic inventions of their own naïve imaginations, until there emerged, chief and ruler of them all, the Kraken, Leviathan, or whatever other local name was considered to best convey in one word their accumulated ideas of terror. In lesser degree, but still worthy compeers of the fire-breathing dragon and sky-darkening "Rukh" of earth and sky, a worthy host of attendant sea-monsters were conjured up, until, apart from the terror of loneliness, of irresistible fury and instability that the sea presented to primitive peoples, the awful nature of its supposed inhabitants made the contemplation of an ocean journey sufficient to appal the stoutest heart. A better understanding of this aspect of the sea to early voyagers may be obtained from some of the artistic efforts of those days than anything else. There you shall see gigantic creatures with human faces, teeth like foot-long wedges, armour-plated bodies, and massive feet fitted with claws like scythe-blades, calmly issuing from the waves to prey upon the dwellers on the margin, or devouring with much apparent enjoyment ships with their crews, as a child crunches a stick of barley-sugar. Even such innocent-looking animals as the seals were distorted and decorated until the contemplation of their counterfeit presentment is sufficient to give a healthy man the nightmare, while such monsters as really were so terrible of aspect that they could hardly be "improved" upon were increased in size until they resembled islands whereon whole tribes might live. To these chimæras were credited all natural phenomena such as waterspouts, whirlpools, and the upheaval of submarine volcanoes. Some imaginative people went even farther than that by attributing the support of the whole earth to a vast sea-monster; while others, like the ancient Jews, fondly pictured Leviathan awaiting in the solitude and gloom of ocean's depths the glad day of Israel's reunion, when the mountain ranges of his flesh would be ready to furnish forth the family feast for all the myriads of Abraham's children.

Surely we may pause awhile to contemplate the overmastering courage of the earliest seafarers, who, in spite of all these terrors, unappalled by the comparison between their tiny shallops and the mighty waves that towered above them, set boldly out from shore into the unknown, obeying that deeply rooted instinct of migration which has peopled every habitable part of the earth's surface. Those who remember their childhood's dread of the dark, with its possible population of bogeys, who have ever been lost in early youth in some lonely place, can have some dim conception, though only a dim one, after all, of the inward battle these ancients fought and won, until it became possible for the epigram to be written in utmost truth—

"The seas but join the nations they divide."

But, after all, we are not now concerned with the warlike doings of men. It is with the actualities of submarine struggle we wish to deal—those wars without an armistice, where to be defeated is to be devoured, and from the sea-shouldering whale down to the smallest sea-insect every living thing is carnivorous, dependent directly upon the flesh of its neighbours for its own life, and incapable of altruism in any form whatever, except among certain of the mammalia and the sharks. In dealing with the more heroic phases of this unending warfare, then, it must be said, once for all, that the ancient writers had a great deal of reason on their side. They distorted and exaggerated, of course, as all children do, but they did not disbelieve. But moderns, rushing to the opposite extreme, have neglected the marvels of the sea by the simple process of disbelieving in them, except in the case of the sea-serpent, that myth which seems bound to persist for ever and ever. Only of late years have the savants of the world allowed themselves to be convinced of the existence of a far more wondrous monster than the sea-serpent (if that " loathly worm " were a reality), the original Kraken of old-world legends. Hugest of all the mollusca, whose prevailing characteristics are ugliness, ferocity, and unappeasable hunger, he has lately asserted himself so firmly that current imaginative literature bristles with allusions to him, albeit oftentimes in situations where he could by no possibility be found. No matter, he has supplied a long-felt want; but the curious fact remains that he is not a discovery, but a re-appearance. The gigantic cuttle-fish of actual, indisputable fact is, in all respects except size, the Kraken; and any faithful representation of him will justify the assertion that no imagination could add anything to the terror-breeding potentialities of his aspect. That is so, even when he is viewed by the light of day in the helplessness of death or disabling sickness, or in the invincible grip of his only conqueror. In his proper realm, crouching far below the surface of the sea in some coral cave or labyrinth of rocks, he must present a sight so awful that the imagination recoils before it. For consider him but a little. He possesses a cylindrical body reaching in the largest specimens yet recorded as having been seen, a length of between sixty and seventy feet, with an average girth of half that amount. That is to say, considerably larger than a Pullman railway-car. Now, this immense mass is of boneless gelatinous matter capable of much greater distension than a snake; so that in the improbable event of his obtaining an extra-abundant supply of food, it is competent to swell to the occasion and still give the flood of digestive juices that it secretes full opportunity to dispose of the burden with almost incredible rapidity. Now, the apex of this mighty cylinder—I had almost said "tail," but remembered that it would give a wrong impression, since it is the part of the monster that always comes first when he is moving from place to place, is conical, that is to say, it tapers off to a blunt point something like a whitehead torpedo. Near this apex there is a broad fin-like arrangement looking much like the body of a skate without its tail, which, however, is used strictly for steering purposes only. So far there is nothing particularly striking about the appearance of this mighty cylinder except in colour. This characteristic varies in different individuals, but is always reminiscent of the hues of a very light-coloured leopard; that is to say, the ground is of a livid greenish white, while the detail is in splashes and spots of lurid red and yellow, with an occasional nimbus of pale blue around these deeper markings. But it is the head of the monster that appals. Nature would seem in the construction of this greatest of all molluscs to have combined every weapon of offence possessed by the rest of the animal kingdom in one amazing arsenal, disposing them in such a manner that not only are they capable of terrific destruction, but their appearance defies adequate description.

The trunk at the head end is sheath-like, its terminating edges forming a sort of collar around the vast cable of muscles without a fragment of bone which connects it with the head. Through a large opening within this collar is pumped a jet of water, the pressure of which upon the surrounding sea is sufficiently great to drive the whole bulk of the creature, weighing perhaps sixty or seventy tons, *backwards* through the water, at the rate of sixteen to twenty miles per hour, not in steady progression, of course, but by successive leaps. At will, this propelling jet is deeply stained with sepia, a dark-brown inky fluid, which, mingling with the encompassing sea, fills all the neighbourhood of the monster with a gloom so deep that nothing, save one of its own species, can see either to fight or whither to fly. The head itself is of proportionate size. It is rounded underneath, and of much lighter hue than the trunk. On either side of it is set an eye, of such dimensions that the mere statement of them sounds like the efforts of one of those grand old mediæval romancers, whose sole object was to make their reader's flesh creep. It is perfectly safe to say that even in proportion to size, no other known creature has such organs of vision as the cuttle-fish, for the pupils of such an one as I am now describing are fully two feet in diameter. They are perfectly black, with a dead white rim, and cannot be closed. No doubt their enormous size is for the purpose of enabling their possessor to discern what is going on amidst the thick darkness that he himself has raised, so that while all other organisms are groping blindly in the gloom, he may work his will among them. Then come the weapons which give the cuttle-fish its power of destruction, the arms or tentacles. These are not eight in number, as in the octopus, an ugly beast enough and spiteful withal, but a babe of innocence compared with our present subject. Every schoolboy should know that *octopus* signifies an eight-armed or eight-footed creature, and yet in nine cases out of ten where writers of fiction and would-be teachers of fact are describing the deadly doings of the gigantic cuttle-fish they call *him* an octopus; whereas he is nothing of the kind, for, in addition to the eight arms which the octopus possesses, the cuttle-fish flaunts two, each of which is double the length of the eight, making him a *decapod*. This confusion is the more unpardonable, because even the most ancient of scribes always spoke of this mollusc as the " ten-armed one," while a reference to any standard work on Natural History will show even the humbler cuttle-fish with their full complement of arms—that is, ten. But this is digression.

Our friend has, then, ten arms springing from the crown of his head, of which eight are forty feet in length, and two are seventy to eighty. The eight each taper outward from the head, from the thickness of a stout man's body at the base to the slenderness of a whip-lash at the end. On their inner sides they are studded with saucer-like hollows, each of which has a fringe of curving claws set just within its rim. So that in addition to their power of holding on to anything they touch by a suction so severe that it would strip flesh from bone, these cruel claws, large as those of a full-grown tiger's, get to work upon the subject being held, lacerating and tearing until the quivering body yields up its innermost secrets. Each of these destroying, serpent-like arms is also gifted with an almost independent power of volition. Whatever it touches it holds with an unreleasable grip, but with wonderful celerity it brings its prey inwards to where, in the centre of all those infernal purveyors lies a black chasm, whose edges are shaped like the upper and lower mandibles of a parrot, and these complete the work so well begun. The outliers, those two far-reaching tentacles, unlike the busy eight, are comparatively slender from their bases to near (within two feet or so of) their ends. There they expand into broad paddle-like masses, thickly studded with *acetabulæ*, those holding sucking-discs that garnish the inner arms for their entire length. So, thus armed, this nightmare monstrosity crouches in the darkling depths of ocean, like some unimaginable web, whereof every line is alive to hold and tear. Its digestion is like a furnace of dissolution, needing a continual inflow of flesh, and nothing living that inhabits the sea comes amiss to its never-satisfied cravings. It is very near the apex of the pyramid of interdependence into which sea-life is built, but not quite. For at the summit is the sperm whale, the monarch of all seas, whom man alone is capable of meeting in fair fight and overcoming.

The head of the sperm whale is of heroic size, being in bulk quite one-third of the entire body, but in addition to its size it has characteristics that fit it peculiarly to compete with such a dangerous monster as the gigantic decapod. Imagine a solid block of crude indiarubber, between twenty and thirty feet in length, and eight feet through, in shape not at all unlike a railway-carriage, but perfectly smooth in surface. Fit this mass beneath with a movable shaft of solid bone, twenty feet in length, studded with teeth, each protruding nine inches, and resembling the points of an elephant's tusks. You will then have a fairly complete notion of the equipment with which the ocean monarch goes into battle against the Kraken. And behind it lies the warm blood of the mammal, the massive framework of bone belonging to the highly developed vertebrate animal, governed by a brain impelled by irresistible instinct to seek its sustenance where alone it can be found in sufficiently satisfying bulk. And there for you are the outlines of the highest form of animal warfare existing within our ken, a conflict of Titans, to which a combat between elephants and rhinoceri in the jungle is but as the play of schoolboys compared with the gladiatorial combats of Ancient Rome.

This somewhat lengthy preamble is necessary in order to clear the way for an account of the proceedings leading up to the final subjugation of the huge molluscs of the elder slime to the needs of the great vertebrates like the whales, who were gradually emerging into a higher development, and, finding new wants oppressing them, had to obey the universal law, and fight for the satisfaction of their urgent needs. Fortunately, the period with which we have to deal was before chronology, so that we are not hampered by dates; and, as the disposition of sea and land, except in its main features, was altogether different to what we have long been accustomed to regard as the always-existing geographical order of things, we need not be greatly troubled by place considerations either. What must be considered as the first beginning of the long struggle occurred when some predecessors of the present sperm whales, wandering through the vast morasses and among the sombre forests of that earlier world, were compelled to recognize that the conditions of shore life were rapidly becoming too onerous for them. Their immensely weighty bodies, lumbering slowly as a seal over the rugged land surface, handicapped them more and more in the universal business of life, the procuring of food. Not only so, but as by reason of their slowness they were confined for hunting-grounds to a very limited area, the slower organism upon which their vast appetites were fed grew scarcer and scarcer, in spite of the fecundity of that prolific time. And in proportion as they found it more and more difficult to get a living, so did their enemies grow more numerous and bolder. Vast dragon-like shapes, clad in complete armour that clanged as the wide-spreading bat-wings bore them swiftly through the air, descended upon the sluggish whales, and with horrid rending by awful shear-shaped jaws, plentifully furnished with foot-long teeth, speedily stripped from their gigantic bodies the masses of succulent flesh. Other enemies, weird of shape and swift of motion although confined to the earth, fastened also upon the easily attainable prey that provided flesh in such bountiful abundance, and was unable to fight or flee.

Well was it, then, for the whales that, living always near the sea, they had formed aquatic habits, finding in the limpid element a medium wherein their huge bulk was rather a help than a hindrance to them. Gradually they grew to use the land less and less as they became more and more accustomed to the food provided in plenty by the inexhaustible ocean. Continual practice enabled them to husband the supplies of air which they took in on the surface for use beneath the waves; and, better still, they found that whereas they had been victims to many a monster on land whose proportions and potentialities seemed far inferior to their own, here in their new element they were supreme, nothing living but fled from before them. But presently a strange thing befell them. As they grew less and less inclined to use the dry land, they found that their powers of locomotion thereon gradually became less and less also, until at last their hind legs dwindled away and disappeared. Their vast and far-reaching tails lost their length, and their bones spread out laterally into flexible fans of toughest gristle, with which they could propel themselves through the waves at speeds to which their swiftest progress upon land had been but a snail's crawl. Also their fore legs grew shorter and wider, and the separation of the toes disappeared, until all that was left of these once ponderous supports were elegant fan-like flippers of gristle, of not the slightest use for propulsion, but merely acting as steadying-vanes to keep the whole great structure in its proper position according to the will of the owner. All these radical physical changes, however, had not affected the real classification of the whales. They were still mammals, still retained in the element which was now entirely their habitat the high organization belonging to the great carnivora of the land. Therefore it took them no long period of time to realize that in the ocean they would be paramount, that with the tremendous facilities for rapid movement afforded them by their new habitat they were able to maintain that supremacy against all comers, unless their formidable armed jaws should also become modified by degeneration into some such harmless cavities for absorbing food as are possessed by their distant relatives, the mysticetæ, or toothless whales.

With a view to avoiding any such disaster, they made good use of their jaws, having been taught by experience that the simple but effectual penalty for the neglect of any function, whether physical or mental, was the disappearance of the organs where such functions had been performed. But their energetic use of teeth and jaws had a result entirely unforeseen by them. Gradually the prey they sought, the larger fish and smaller sea-mammals, disappeared from the shallow seas adjacent to the land, from whence the whales had been driven; and in order to satisfy the demands of their huge stomachs, they were fain to follow their prey into deeper and deeper waters, meeting as they went with other and stranger denizens of those mysterious depths, until at last the sperm whale met the Kraken. There in his native gloom, vast, formless, and insatiable, brooded the awful Thing. Spread like a living net whereof every mesh was armed, sensitive and lethal, this fantastic complication of horrors took toll of all the sea-folk, needing not to pursue its prey, needing only to lie still, devour, and grow. Sometimes, moved by mysterious impulses, one of these chimæras would rise to the sea-surface and bask in the beams of the offended sun, poisoning the surrounding air with its charnel-house odours, and occasionally finding within the never-resting nervous clutching of its tentacles some specimens of the highest, latest product of creation, man himself. Ages of such experiences as these had left the Kraken defenceless as to his body. The absence of any necessity for exertion had arrested the development of a backbone; the inability of any of the sea-people to retaliate upon their sateless foe had made him neglect any of those precautions that weaker organisms had provided themselves with, and even the cloud of sepia with which all the race were provided, and which often assisted the innocent and weaker members of the same great family to escape, was only used by these masters of the sea to hide their monstrous lures from their prey.

Thus on a momentous day a ravenous sperm whale, hunting eagerly for wherewithal to satisfy his craving, suddenly found himself encircled by many long, cable-like arms. They clung, they tore, they sucked. But whenever a stray end of them flung itself across the bristling parapet of the whale's lower jaw it was promptly bitten off, and a portion having found its way down into the craving stomach of the big mammal, it was welcomed as good beyond all other food yet encountered. Once this had been realized, what had originally been an accidental entrapping changed itself into a vigorous onslaught and banquet. True, the darkness fought for the mollusc, but that advantage was small compared with the feeling of incompetence, of inability to make any impression upon this mighty impervious mass that was moving as freely amid the clinging embarrassments of those hitherto invincible arms as if they were only fronds of sea-weed. And then the foul mass of the Kraken found itself, contrary to all previous experience, rising involuntarily, being compelled to leave its infernal shades, and, without any previous preparation for such a change of pressure, to visit the upper air. The fact was that the whale, finding its stock of air exhausted, had put forth a supreme effort to rise, and found that, although unable to free himself from those enormous cables, he was actually competent to raise the whole mass. What an upheaval! Even the birds that, allured by the strong carrion scent, were assembling in their thousands, fled away from that appalling vision, their wild screams of affright filling the air with lamentation. The tormented sea foamed and boiled in wide-spreading whirls, its deep sweet blue changed into an unhealthy nondescript tint of muddy yellow as the wide expanse of the Kraken's body yielded up its corrupt fluids, and the healthful breeze did its best to disperse the bad smells that rose from the ugly mass. Then the whale, having renewed his store of air, settled down seriously to the demolition of his prize. Length after length of tentacle was torn away from the central crown and swallowed, gliding down the abysmal throat of the gratified mammal in snaky convolutions until even that great store-room would contain no more. The vanquished Kraken lay helplessly rolling upon the wave while its conqueror in satisfied ease lolled near, watching with good-humoured complacency the puny assault made upon that island of gelatinous flesh by the multitude of smaller hungry things. The birds returned, reassured, and added by their clamour to the strangeness of the scene, where the tribes of air and sea, self-bidden to the enormous banquet, were making full use of their exceptional privilege. So the great feast continued while the red sun went down and the white moon rose in placid beauty. Yet for all the combined assaults of those hungry multitudes the tenacious life of that largest of living things lay so deeply seated that when the rested whale resumed his attentions he found the body of his late antagonist still quivering under the attack of his tremendous jaws. But its proportions were so immense that his utmost efforts left store sufficient for at least a dozen of his companions, had they been there, to have satisfied their hunger upon. And, satisfied at last, he turned away, allowing the smaller fry, who had waited his pleasure most respectfully, to close in again and finish the work he had so well begun.

Now, this was a momentous discovery indeed, for the sperm whales had experienced, even when fish and seals were plentiful, great difficulty in procuring sufficient food at one time for a full meal, and the problem of how to provide for themselves as they grew and multiplied had become increasingly hard to solve. Therefore this discovery filled the fortunate pioneer with triumph, for his high instincts told him that he had struck a new source of supply that promised to be inexhaustible. So, in the manner common to his people, he wasted no time in convening a gathering of them as large as could be collected. Far over the placid surface of that quiet sea lay gently rocking a multitude of vast black bodies, all expectant, all awaiting the momentous declaration presently to be made. The epoch-making news circulated among them in perfect silence, for to them has from the earliest times been known the secret that is only just beginning to glimmer upon the verge of human intelligence, the ability to communicate with one another without the aid of speech, sight, or touch—a kind of thought transference, if such an idea as animal thought may be held allowable. And having thus learned of the treasures held in trust for them by the deep waters, they separated and went, some alone and some in compact parties of a dozen or so, upon their rejoicing way.

But among the slimy hosts of the gigantic Mollusca there was raging a sensation unknown before—a feeling of terror, of insecurity born of the knowledge that at last there had appeared among them a being proof against the utmost pressure of their awful arms, who was too great to be devoured, who, on the other hand, had evinced a greedy partiality for devouring them. How this information became common property among them it is impossible to say, since they dwelt alone, each in his own particular lair, rigidly respected by one another, because any intrusion upon another's domains was invariably followed by the absorption of either the intruder or the intruded upon by the stronger of the two. This, although not intended by them, had the effect of vastly heightening the fear with which they were regarded by the smaller sea-folk, for they took to a restless prowling along the sea-bed, enwreathing themselves about the mighty bases of the islands, and invading cool coral caverns where their baleful presence had been till then unknown. Never before had there been such a panic among the multitudinous sea-populations. What could this new portent signify? Were the foundations of the great deep again about to be broken up, and the sea-bed heaved upward to replace the tops of the towering mountains on dry land? There was no reply, for there were none that could answer questions like these.

Still the fear-smitten decapods wandered, seeking seclusion from the coming enemy, and finding none to their mind. Still the crowds of their victims rushed blindly from shoal to shoal, plunging into depths unfitted for them, or rising into shallows where their natural food was not. And the whole sea was troubled, until at last there appeared, grim and vast, the advance-guard of the sperm whales, and hurled itself with joyful anticipation upon the shrinking convolutions of those hideous monsters that had so long dominated the dark places of the sea. For the whales it was a time of feasting hitherto without parallel. Without any fear, uncaring to take even the most elementary precautions against a defeat which they felt to be an impossible contingency, they sought out and devoured one after another of these vast uglinesses, already looked upon by them as their natural provision, their store of food accumulated of purpose against their coming. Occasionally, it is true, some rash youngster, full of pride, and rejoicing in his preeminence over all life in the depths, would hurl himself into a smoky network of far-spreading tentacles which would wrap him round so completely that his jaws were fast bound together, his flukes would vainly essay to propel him any whither, and he would presently perish miserably, his cable-like sinews falling slackly and his lungs suffused with crimson brine. Even then, the advantage gained by the triumphant Kraken was a barren one, for in every case the bulk of the victim was too great, his body too firm in its build, for the victor, despite his utmost efforts, to succeed in devouring his prize. So that the disappointed Kraken had perforce to witness the gradual disappearance of his lawful prize beneath the united efforts of myriads of tiny sea-scavengers, secure in their insignificance against any attack from him, and await with tremor extending to the remotest extremity of every tentacle, the retribution that he felt sure would speedily follow.

This desultory warfare was waged for long, until, driven by despair to a community of interest unknown before, the Krakens gradually sought one another out with but a single idea—that of combining against the new enemy; for, knowing to what an immense size their kind could attain in the remoter fastnesses of ocean, they could not yet bring themselves to believe that they were to become the helpless prey of these new-comers, visitors of yesterday, coming from the cramped acreage of the land into the limitless fields of ocean, and invading the immemorial freeholds of its hitherto unassailable sovereigns. From the remotest recesses of the ocean they came, that grisly gathering —came in ever-increasing hosts, their silent progress spreading unprecedented dismay among the fairer inhabitants of the sea. Figure to yourselves, if you can, the advance of this terrible host. But the effort is vain. Not even Martin, that frenzied delineator of the frightful halls of hell, the scenes of the Apocalypse, and the agonies of the Deluge, could have done justice to the terrors of such a scene. Only dimly can we imagine what must have been the appearance of those vast masses of writhing flesh, as through the palely gleaming phosphorescence of the depths they sped backwards in leaps of a hundred fathoms each, their terrible arms, close-clustered together, streaming behind like Medusa's hair magnified ten thousand times in size, and with each snaky tress bearing a thousand mouths instead of one.

So they converged upon the place of meeting, an area of the sea-bed nowhere more than 500 fathoms in depth, from whose rugged floor rose irregularly stupendous columnar masses of lava hurled upwards by the cosmic forces below in a state of incandescence and solidified as they rose, assuming many fantastic shapes, and affording perfect harbourage to such dire scourges of the sea as were now making the place their rendezvous. For, strangely enough, this marvellous portion of the submarine world was more densely peopled with an infinite variety of sea-folk than any other; its tepid waters seemed to bring forth abundantly of all kinds of fish, crustacea, and creeping things. Sharks in all their fearsome varieties prowled greasily about, scenting for dead things whereon to gorge, shell-fish from the infinitesimal globigerina up to the gigantic clam whose shells were a yard each in diameter; crabs, lobsters, and other freakish varieties of crustacea of a size and ugliness unknown to day lurked in every crevice, while about and among all these scavengers flitted the happy, lovely fish in myriads of glorious hues matching the tender shades of the coral groves that sprang from the summits of those sombre lava columns beneath. Hitherto this happy hunting-ground had not been invaded by the sea-mammals. None of the air-breathing inhabitants of the ocean had ventured into its gloomy depths, or sought their prey among the blazing shallows of the surface-reefs, although no more favourable place for their exertions could possibly have been selected over all the wide sea. It had long been a favourite haunt of the Kraken, for whom it was, as aforesaid, an ideal spot, but now it was to witness a sight unparalleled in ocean history. Heralded by an amazing series of under-waves, the gathering of monsters drew near. They numbered many thousands, and no one in all their hosts was of lesser magnitude than sixty feet long by thirty in girth of body alone. From that size they increased until some—the acknowledged leaders

—discovered themselves like islands, their cylindrical carcases huge as that of an ocean liner, and their tentacles capable of overspreading an entire village.

In concentric rings they assembled, all heads pointing outward, the mightiest within, and four clear avenues through the circles left for coming and going. Contrary to custom, but by mutual consent, all the tentacles lay closely arranged in parallel lines, not outspread to every quarter of the compass, and all a-work. They looked, indeed, in their inertia and silence, like nothing so much as an incalculable number of dead squid of enormous size neatly laid out at the whim of some giant's fancy. Yet communication between them was active; a subtle interchange of experiences and plans went briskly on through the medium of the mobile element around them. The elder and mightier were full of disdain at the reports they were furnished with, utterly incredulous as to the ability of any created thing to injure them, and, as the time wore on, an occasional tremor was distinctly noticeable through the whole length of their tentacles, which boded no good to their smaller brethren. Doubtless but little longer was needed for the development of a great absorption of the weaker by the stronger, only that, darting into their midst like a lightning streak, came a messenger squid, bearing the news that a school of sperm whales, numbering at least ten thousand, were coming at top-speed direct for their place of meeting. Instantly to the farthest confines of that mighty gathering the message radiated, and as if by one movement there uprose from the sea-bed so dense a cloud of sepia that for many miles around the clear blue of the ocean became turbid, stagnant, and foul. Even the birds that hovered over those dark-brown waves took fright at this terrible phenomenon, to them utterly incomprehensible, and with discordant shrieks they fled in search of sweeter air and cleaner sea. But below the surface under cover of this thickest darkness there was the silence of death.

Twenty miles away, under the bright sunshine, an advance-guard of about a hundred sperm whales came rushing on. Line abreast, their bushy breath rising like the regular steam-jets from a row of engines, they dashed aside the welcoming wavelets, every sense alert, and full of eagerness for the consummation of their desires. Such had been their despatch that throughout the long journey of 500 leagues they had not once stayed for food, so that they were ravenous with hunger as well as full of fight. They passed, and before the foaming of their swift passage had ceased, the main body, spread over a space of thirty miles, came following on, the roar of their multitudinous march sounding like the voice of many waters. Suddenly the advance-guard, with stately elevation of the broad fans of their flukes, disappeared, and by one impulse the main body followed them. Down into the depths they bore, noting with dignified wonder the absence of all the usual inhabitants of the deep, until, with a thrill of joyful anticipation which set all their masses of muscle a-quiver, they recognized the scent of the prey. No thought of organized resistance presented itself; without a halt, or even the faintest slackening of their great rush, they plunged forward into the abysmal gloom; down, down withal into that wilderness of waiting devils. And so, in darkness and silence like that of the beginning of things, this great battle was joined. Whale after whale succumbed, anchored to the bottom by such bewildering entanglements, such enlacement of tentacles, that their vast strength was helpless to free them; their jaws were bound hard together, and even the wide sweep of their flukes gat no hold upon the slimy water. But the Decapods were in evil case. Assailed from above while their groping arms writhed about below, they found themselves more often locked in unreleasable hold of their fellows than they did of their enemies. And the quick-shearing jaws of those enemies shredded them into fragments, made nought of their bulk, revelled and frolicked among them, slaying, devouring, exulting. Again and again the triumphant mammals drew off for air and from satiety, went and lolled upon the sleek oily surface, in water now so thick that the fiercest hurricane that ever blew would have failed to raise a wave thereon.

So through a day and a night the slaying ceased not, except for these brief interludes, until those of the Decapods left alive had disentangled themselves from the débris of their late associates and returned with what speed they might to depths and crannies, where they fondly hoped their ravenous enemies could never come. They bore with them the certain knowledge that from henceforth they were no longer lords of the sea, that instead of being, as hitherto, devourers of all things living that crossed the radius of their outspread toils, they were now and for all time to be the prey of a nobler race of creatures, a higher order of being, and that at last they had taken their rightful position as creatures of usefulness in the vast economy of Creation.

THE SIAMESE LOCK

EVEN in these prosaic days of palatial passenger steamers, running upon lines from port to port almost as definite as railway metals, and keeping time with far more regularity than some railway trains that it would be easy to name, there are many eddies and backwaters of commerce still remaining where the romance of sea-traffic retains all the old pre-eminence, and events occur daily that are stranger than any fiction.

Notably is this the case on the Chinese coast, in whose innumerable creeks and bays there is a never-ceasing ebb and flow of queer craft, manned by a still queerer assortment of Eastern seafarers. And if it were not for that strange Lingua Franca of the Far East, to which our marvellous language lends itself with that ready adaptability which makes it one of the most widely-spoken in the world, the difficulties awaiting the white man who is called upon to rule over one of those motley crews would be well-nigh insuperable. As it is, men of our race who spend any length of time "knocking about" in Eastern seas always acquire an amazing *mélange* of tongues, which they themselves are totally unable to assign to their several sources of origin, even if they ever were to seriously undertake such a task. Needless, perhaps, to say that they have always something more important on hand than that. At least I had when, after a much longer spell ashore in Bangkok than I cared for, I one day prevailed upon a sturdy German skipper to ship me as mate of the little barque he commanded. She flew the Siamese flag, and belonged, as far as I was ever able to ascertain, to a Chinese firm in the humid Siamese capital, a sedate, taciturn trio of Celestials, who found it well worth their while to have Europeans in charge of her, even though they had to pay a long price for their services. My predecessor had been a "towny" of the skipper's, a Norddeutscher from Rostock, who, with the second mate, a huge Dane, had been with the skipper in the same vessel for over two years. On the last voyage, however, during his watch on deck, while off the Paracels, he had silently disappeared, nor was the faintest inkling of his fate obtainable. When the skipper told me this in guttural German-English, I fancied he looked as if his air of indifference was slightly overdone, but the fancy did not linger—I was too busy surmising by what one of the many possible avenues that hapless mate had strolled out of existence. I was glad, if the suggestion of gladness over such a grim business be admissible, to have even this scanty information, since any temptation to taking my position at all carelessly was thereby effectually removed. Before coming on board I invested a large portion of my advance in two beautiful six-shooters and a good supply of ammunition, asking no questions of the joss-like Chinaman I bought them from as to how he became possessed of two U. S. Navy weapons and cartridges to match. I had, besides, a frightfully dangerous looking little kris, only about nine inches long altogether, but inlaid with gold, and tempered so that it would almost stab into iron. I picked it up on the beach at Hai-phong six months before, but had only thought of it as a handsome curio until now.

Thus armed, but with all my weapons well out of sight, I got aboard, determined to take no more chances than I could help, and to grow eyes in the back of my head if possible. The old man received me as cordially as he was able—which isn't saying very much—introduced me to Mr. Boyesen, the second mate, and proposed a glass of schnapps and a cheroot while we talked over business. I was by no means averse to this, for I wanted to be on good terms with my skipper, and I also had a strong desire upon me to know more about the kind of trade we were likely to be engaged in, for I didn't even know what the cargo was, or what port she was bound to—the only information the skipper gave me when I shipped being that she was going "up the coast," and this state of complete ignorance was not at all comfortable. I hate mystery, especially aboard ship—it takes away my appetite; and when a sailor's off his feed he isn't much good at his work. But my expectations were cruelly dashed, for, instead of becoming confidential, Captain Klenck gave me very clearly to understand that no one on board the Phrabayat—"der Frau" *he* called her—but himself ever knew what was the nature of the trade she was engaged in or what port she was bound to. More than that, he told me very plainly that he alone kept the reckoning; the second mate and myself had only to carry out his instructions as to courses, etc., and that so long as we kept her going through our respective watches as he desired, he was prepared to take all the risk. And all the time he was unloading this stupefying intelligence upon me, he kept his beady eyes on mine as if he would read through my skull the nature of my thoughts. Had he been able so to do, they would have afforded him little satisfaction, for they were in such a ferment that I "wanted out," as the Scotch say, to cool down a bit. I wanted badly to get away from Bangkok, but I would have given all I had to be ashore there again and well clear of the berth I had thought myself so lucky to get a day or two ago. But that was out of the question. The old man helped himself to another bosun's nip of square-face, and, rising as he shipped it, said—

"Ve ked her onder vay mit vonce, Meesder Fawn, und mindt ju keeb dose verdammt schwein coin shtrong. Dey vants so mooch boot as dey can get, der schelm."

Glad of any chance of action to divert my mind, I answered cheerily, "Ay, ay, sir!" and, striding out of the cabin, I shouted, "Man the windlass!" forgetting for the moment that I was not on board one of my own country's ships, free from mysteries of any kind. My mistake was soon rectified, and for the next hour or so I kept as busy as I knew how, getting the anchor and making sail. The black, olive, and yellow sailors worked splendidly, being bossed by a " serang " or " bosun " of herculean build and undiscoverable nationality. I think he must have been a Dyak. Now, it has always been my practice in dealing with natives of any tropical country to treat them as men, and not, as too many Europeans do to their loss, behave towards them as if they were unreasoning animals. I have always found a cheery word and a smile go a long way, especially with negroes, wherever they hail from —and, goodness knows, unless you are liverish, it is just as easy to look pleasant as glum. At any rate, whether that was the cause or not, the work went on greased wheels that forenoon, and I felt that if they were all the colours the human race can show, I couldn't wish for a smarter or more willing crowd. When she was fairly under way and slipping down to the bar at a good rate, I went aft for instructions, finding the old man looking but sourly as he conned her down stream. Before I had time to say anything he opened up with—

" Bei Gott, Meesder Fawn, ju haf to do diffrunt mit dese crout ef ju vaunts to keep my schip coin. I tondt vant ter begin ter find fault, but I ain't coin to haf no nicker-cottlin abordt de Frau. Ju dake id from me."

This riled me badly, for I knew no men could have worked smarter or more willingly than ours had, so I replied quietly, " Every man knows his work and does it, Cap'n Klenck. I know mine, and I'll do it, but I must do it my own way, or not at all. If you've got any fault to find, find it, but don't expect me to spoil a decent crew and chance getting a kris between my brisket bones in the bargain."

He gave me one look, and his eyes were like those of a dead fish. Then he walked away, leaving me standing simmering with rage. But no more was said, and at dinner he seemed as if he had forgotten the circumstance. And I, like a fool, thought he had, for the wish was ever father to the thought with me, especially in a case of this kind, where what little comfort I hoped to enjoy was entirely dependent upon the skipper. He, astuteness itself, gave no sign of his feelings towards me, being as civil as he was able in all our business relations; but beyond those he erected a barrier between us, all the more impassable because indefinite. Thrown thus upon my own resources, I tried to cultivate an acquaintance with Mr. Boyesen; but here again I was baffled, for he was the greatest enigma of all. I never knew a man possessing the power of speech who was able to get along with less use of that essentially human faculty. He was more like a machine than a man, seeming to be incapable of exhibiting any of the passions or affections of humanity. I have seen him grasp a Siamese sailor by the belt and hurl him along the deck as if he were a mere bundle of rags; but for any expression of anger in his pale blue eyes or flush upon his broad face, he might as well have been a figure-head. So that after a brief struggle with his immobility I gave up the attempt to make a companion of him, coming to the conclusion that he was in some way mentally deficient.

The Siamese Lock

Thus I was perforce driven to study my crew more than I perhaps should have done, particularly the neat-handed, velvet-footed Chinese steward, Ah Toy, who, although at ordinary times quite as expressionless as the majority of his countrymen, generally developed a quaint contortion of his yellow visage for me, which, if not a smile, was undoubtedly meant for one. We were the best of friends; so great, indeed, that whenever I heard the old man beating him—that is, about once a day—I felt the greatest difficulty in restraining myself from interference. I was comforted, however, by noticing that Ah Toy seemed to heed these whackings no more than as if he had been made of rubber; he never uttered a cry or did anything but go on with his work as if nothing had happened. I had eight men in my watch: two Chinese, four Siamese, one Tagal, and a Malay; a queer medley enough, but all very willing and apparently contented. For some little time I was hard put to it to gain their confidence, their attitude being that of men prepared to meet with ill-treatment and to take the earliest opportunity of resenting it (although they accepted hearty blows from the Serang's colt with the greatest good nature). But gradually this sullen, watchful demeanour wore off, and they became as cheerful a lot of fellows as I could wish, ready to anticipate my wishes if they could, and as anxious to understand me as I certainly was them. This state of things was so far satisfactory that the time, which had at first hung very heavily, now began to pass pleasantly and quickly, although I slept, as the saying is, with one eye open, for fear of some development of hostility on the skipper's part. Because, in spite of my belief that he meant me no ill, having, indeed, no reason to do so as far as I knew, I could not rid myself of an uneasy feeling in my mind that all was not as it should be with him.

We had wonderfully fine weather, it being the N.E. monsoon, but made very slow progress, the vessel being not only a dull sailer at the best of times, but much hindered by the head wind. This tried my patience on account of my anxiety to get some inkling of our position, which the old man kept as profound a secret as if millions depended upon no one knowing it but himself. And although we sighted land occasionally, I was not sufficiently well up in China coast navigation to do more than guess at the position of the ship. At last, when we had been a fortnight out, I was awakened suddenly in my watch below one night by the sound of strange voices alongside. I sprang out of my bunk in the dark, striking my head against the door, which I always left open, but which was now closed and locked. I felt as I should imagine a rat feels in a trap. But the first thrill of fear soon gave place to indignation at my treatment, and, after striking a light, I set my back against the door and strove with all my might to burst it open. Failing in the attempt, I remembered my little bag of tools, and in a few seconds had a screw-driver at work, which not only released me, but spoiled the lock for any future use. Of course, my revolvers were about me; I always carried *them*. Still hot with anger, I marched on deck to find the ship hove-to, a couple of junks alongside, the hatches off, and a rapid exchange of cargo going on. Silence and haste were evidently the *mots d'ordre*, but, besides, the workers were the smartest I had ever seen; they handled the stuff, cases, bags, and bales of all sorts and sizes, with a celerity that was almost magical. I stood looking on like a fool for quite two or three minutes, in which every detail of the strange scene became indelibly stamped upon my brain. The brilliant flood of moonlight paling all the adjacent stars, the wide silvern path of the moon on the dark water broken by a glistening sand-bank over which the sullen swell broke with an occasional hollow moan, every item in the arrangement of the sails, and the gliding figures on deck; all helped to make a marvellous picture. The brief spell was broken by a hand upon my shoulder that made me leap three feet forward. It was the skipper, and in that moment I felt how helpless I was if this man desired to do me hurt. We stood facing each other silently for a breath or two, when he said quietly—

"Meesder Fawn, I tondt vant my offcers to keeb only dere own vatch. I nefer make dem vork oferdime. Ven ids your vatch an deg yu vill be gall as ushal. Goot nacht," and he stood aside to let me pass.

"But, Captain Klenck," I blurted out, "why did you lock me in my berth?"

"Ey good man, du bist nod vell, or ellas you bin hafin a—vat you call im—night-pig, ain'd it?" Then, suddenly changing his tone, he made a step towards me, and said, "Go below mid vonce, er I'm tamt ef ju see daylight any more dis foyge!"

To tell the truth, I didn't quite see my way to defying him. I felt like a beastly cur, and I knew there was some devilish business going on, but the whole thing had come on me so suddenly that I was undecided how to act, and indecision in such a predicament spells defeat. So I just inclined my head and sauntered off to my cabin in a pretty fine state of mind. Needless to say, I got no more sleep. A thousand theories ran riot in my brain as to the nature of the business we were doing, and I worried myself almost into a fever wondering whether Boyesen was in it. By the time eight bells (four a.m.) was struck I was almost crazy, a vile taste in my mouth, and my head throbbing like a piston. The quiet appearance of Ah Toy at my door murmuring "eight bell" gave me relief, for I took it as a sign that I might reappear, and I wasted no time getting on deck. I found the watch trimming the yards under the skipper's direction, but no sign of the second mate. All trace of the junks had vanished. I went for'ard to trim the yards on the fore by way of slipping into my groove, and being in that curious mental state when in the presence of overwhelmingly serious problems the most trivial details demand attention, some small object that I kicked away in the darkness insisted upon being found before I did anything else. It only lay a yard or two in front of me, a key of barbarous make with intricate wards on either side. Mechanically I picked it up and dropped it in my pocket, imagining for the moment that it must belong to one of the seamen, who each had some sort of a box which they kept carefully locked. Then I went on with my work, getting everything ship-shape and returning to the poop. The skipper greeted me as if nothing had happened, giving me a N.N.E. course if she would lay it, and, bidding me call him at once in the event of any change taking place, went below.

Left alone upon the small poop with the vessel calmly gliding through the placid sea, and the steadfast stars eyeing me solemnly, I felt soothed and uplifted. I reviewed the situation from every possible point of view I could take of it, until, sick and weary of the vain occupation, I unslung a bucket and went to the lee-side with the intention of drawing some water to cool my aching head. As I leaned over the side I saw a sampan hanging alongside, and a figure just in the act of coming aboard. By this time I was almost proof against surprises of any kind, so I quietly waited until the visitor stepped over the rail, and saluted me as if boarding a vessel in the dark while she was working her way up the China Sea was the most ordinary occurrence in the world. He was a gigantic Chinaman, standing, I should think, fully 6ft. 6in. or 6ft. 7in., and built in proportion. In excellent English he informed me that he had business with Captain Klenck, who was expecting him, and without further preliminary walked aft and disappeared down the cabin-companion quietly as if he had been an apparition. In fact, some such idea flitted across my mind, and I stepped back to the rail and peered down into the darkness alongside to see if the sampan was a reality. It was no longer there. Like one in a dream

I walked aft to where one of the Siamese stood at the wheel, and after a casual glance into the compass, from sheer force of habit, I asked the man if he had seen the visitor. He answered, "Yes," in a tone of surprise, as if wondering at the question. Satisfied that at least I was not the victim of some disorder of the brain, I went for'ard again, noting with a sense of utmost relief the paling of the eastern horizon foretelling the coming of the day.

No one realizes more than a sailor what a blessing daylight is. In a gale of wind the rising sun seems to lighten anxiety, and the prayer of Ajax trembles more frequently upon the lips of seafarers than any other. I watched the miracle of dawn with fervent thanksgiving, feeling that the hateful web of mystery that was hourly increasing in complexity around me would be less stifling with the sun upon it. And in the homely duties of washing decks, "sweating-up," etc., I almost forgot that I was not in an orderly, commonplace English ship, engaged in honest traffic. The time passed swiftly until eight bells, when a double portion of horror came upon me at the sight of Captain Klenck coming on deck to relieve me. Before I knew what I was saying I had blurted out, "Where's Mr. Boyesen?" The cold, expressionless eyes of the skipper rested full upon me as he replied slowly—

"Ju tondt seem to learn mooch, Meesder Fawn. I dells ju one dime more, undt only one dime, dat ju nodings to do mit der peezness auf dis scheep. Verdammt Englescher schweinhund, de nexd dime ju inderferes mit mein affaires will pe der lasd dime ju efer do anythings in dees vorl'. Co pelow!"

Again I had to own myself beaten, and the thought was just maddening. To be trampled on like a coolie, abused like a dog. Great heavens! how low had I fallen. I never seemed to be ready or able to keep end up when that man chose to put forth his will against mine. But, unknown even to myself, I was being educated up to the work that was before me, and the training was just what was necessary for me. I ate my breakfast alone, Ah Toy waiting on me with almost affectionate care. Several times I caught his eye, and fancied that there was a new light therein. Once I opened my mouth to speak to him, but his finger flew to his lips, and his look turned swiftly towards the skipper's berth, that closely-shut room of which I had never seen the inside. As soon as my meal was over I retreated to my cabin, closed the door, and busied myself devising some means of fastening it on the inside. For now I felt sure that for some reason or other Boyesen had been made away with, and in all probability my turn was fast approaching. Is it necessary to say that I felt no want of sleep? Perhaps not; at any rate, I spent the greater part of my watch below in such preparations as I could make for self-defence. My two revolvers now seemed precious beyond all computation as I carefully examined them in every detail, and made sure they were ready for immediate use.

While thus employed a sudden appalling uproar on deck sent my blood surging back to my heart, and, after about a second's doubt, I flung wide the door and rushed on deck, flinging off Ah Toy, who caught at me as I passed his pantry door. Springing out of the cabin, I saw the colossal Chinaman who had boarded us on the previous night standing calmly looking on, while the crew fought among themselves with a savagery awful to witness. I did not see the skipper at first, but, glancing down, I caught sight of his face distorted beyond recognition by the foot of the huge Celestial, which was planted on his throat. In that moment all my detestation of him vanished. He was a white man at the mercy of Mongols, and drawing my revolvers, I sprang towards his foe. Click went the trigger, but there was no flash or report. Both were alike useless, and my brain working quietly enough now, I realized that the man I would have saved had rendered my weapons useless while I slept, to his own bitter cost. Flinging them from me, I snatched at a hand-spike that lay at my feet; but before I could grasp it the combatants divided, half a dozen of my watch flung themselves upon me, and in a minute I was overpowered. Of course I was somewhat roughly handled, but there was no anger against me in the faces of my assailants. As for the giant, he might as well have been carved in stone for all the notice he appeared to take of what was going on.

Two Siamese carefully lashed me so that I could not move, then carried me, not at all roughly, aft to the cabin door, and sat me on the grating, where they left me and returned to the fight, which seemed to be a life and death struggle between two parties into which the crew were divided. I have no taste for horrors, and do not propose serving up a dish of them here, although the temptation to describe the wild beast fury of those yellow and black men is very great. But it must suffice to say that those who were apparently friendly to me were the victors, and having disposed of the dead by summarily flinging them overboard, they busied themselves of their own accord in trimming sail so as to run the vessel in towards the coast.

Meanwhile, the gigantic Chinaman, whose advent had so strangely disturbed the business of our skipper, quietly lifted that unhappy German as if he had been a child, and carried him into the cabin. Ah Toy, doubtless ordered by some one in authority, came and set me free, his face fairly beaming upon me as he told me that it was entirely owing to my humane treatment of the fellows that my life had been spared. To my eager questionings as to what was going to be done with the skipper and the ship, he returned me but the Shibboleth of the East, "No shabee him; no b'long my pidgin."

I went on with the work of the ship as usual, finding the survivors quite as amenable to my orders as they had ever been, and contenting myself with keeping her on the course she was then making until some way of taking the initiative should present itself. I had given up studying the various problems that had so recently made me feel as if I had gone suddenly mad, and went about in a dull, animalized state, too bewildered to think, and prepared for any further freak of Fate. While thus moodily slouching about, Ah

Toy came on deck and informed me that the huge Chinaman was anxious to see me in the cabin. Instinctively I felt that whatever, whoever he was, I could not afford to offend him, so I went on the instant, finding him sitting in the main cabin contemplating the lifeless body of Captain Klenck, which lay on the deck by his side. Although prepared for anything, as I thought, I could not repress a shudder of horror at this spectacle, which did not pass unnoticed by the giant. Turning a grave look upon me, he said, in easy, polished diction—

"This piece of carrion at my feet had been my paid servant for the last two years. He was necessary to me, but not indispensable, and he fell into the fatal error of supposing that not only could I not do without him, but that, in spite of the enormous salary I paid him, he could rob me with impunity. I am the senior partner in the Bangkok firm owning this vessel, and also a fleet of piratical junks that range these seas from Singapore to Hong Kong, and prey upon other junks mostly, although wherever it is possible they have no scruples in attacking European vessels. It is a lucrative business, but a good deal of business acumen is needed in order to dispose of the plunder realized. In this the late Captain Klenck was a very useful man, and, knowing this, we paid him so well that he might very soon have realized a fortune from his salary alone. Now my men, who, as you have seen, without any assistance from me, have easily disposed of the gang Klenck had engaged to further his ends, tell me that they are very fond of you. They say that you have treated them like men, of your own free will, and I am prepared to offer you the command of the Phrabayat at the same salary as Klenck enjoyed. What do you say?"

For a moment I was stunned at the story told me, and, besides, very much annoyed because I hadn't seen it all before. It looked so simple now. But one thing dominated all the rest—who or what was this suave, English educated Celestial, who trafficked in piracy and yet spoke as if imbued with all the culture of the West? He actually seemed as if he read my thoughts, for with something approaching a smile he said—

"I see you are wondering at my English. I am a graduate of Cambridge University, and was at one time rather lionized in certain fashionable circles in London. But circumstances made it necessary for me to go into this business, which pleases me very well. You have not yet answered my question, though."

"I am aware that I run considerable risk at present by so doing," I replied; "but, in spite of that, I must give you an unqualified refusal. I am rather surprised at your offer!"

A look of genuine astonishment came over his face as he said, "Why? Surely you are not so well off that you can afford to play fast and loose with such a prospect as I hold out to you?"

Then, as if it had suddenly dawned upon him, he shrugged his shoulders and murmured, "I suppose you have some more scruples. Well, I do not understand them, but for the sake of my foolish men I suppose I must respect them. There is one other point, however, upon which I think you can enlighten me or help me. This carrion here," and he kicked contemptuously at the skipper's dead body, "has secreted quite a treasure in pearls and gold, and I cannot now compel him to tell me where. Did you enjoy his confidence at all?"

I hastened to assure my questioner that nothing could well be farther from the late skipper's thoughts than to place any confidence in me; but, as I was speaking, I suddenly remembered the odd-looking key I had picked up, and diving into my pocket I produced it, saying, "This may open some secret locker of his. I found it on deck last night, just after the transhipment of cargo in the middle watch."

His eyes gave one flash of recognition, and he said quietly, "I know that key. Come, let us see what we can find by its aid."

Then, for the first time, I saw the inside of the skipper's state-room. No wonder he kept it fast closed. It was honeycombed with lockers of every shape and size; but, strangest of all, there were three rings in the deck as if to lift up level-fitting hatches. These took my eye at once, and, upon my pointing them out, the Chinaman stooped and essayed to lift one. He had hardly taken hold of the ring, though, when he saw a keyhole at one edge, and muttering, "I didn't know of this, though," he tried my key in it. It fitted, unlocking the hatch at once. But neither he nor I was prepared for what we found. There, in a space not more than four feet square and five feet deep, was a white man, a stranger to me. The giant at my side reached down and lifted the prisoner out of his hole as if he had been a child, and, placing him gently on a settee, regarded him with incurious eyes. He was just alive, and moaning softly. I called Ah Toy, who evinced no surprise at seeing the stranger; but, after he had brought some water at my order, and given the sufferer some drink, he told me that this was the missing mate. Ah Toy assisted me to get the unfortunate man into my berth, where I left him to the ministrations of the steward, while I hurried back to the skipper's state-room. When I reached it the calm searcher had laid bare almost all its secrets.

Boyesen, the second mate, was there, looking like a man just awaking from a furious debauch, and blinking at the light like a bat. And around him on the deck were heaped treasures beyond all my powers of assessment. But their glitter had no effect upon me; I suppose I must have been saturated with surprises, so that my clogged brain would absorb no more. I turned to Boyesen and offered him my hand, which he took, and, by assistance, crawled out of that infernal den, leaving the Chinaman to sort out his wealth.

I tried hard to get some explanation of the second mate's strange disappearance from him, but, in addition to his habitual taciturnity, he was in no condition to talk; so, after a few minutes' ineffectual effort, I left him and returned on deck. Ah, how delightful was the pure air. I drew in great draughts of it, as if to dispel the foulness of that place below; I looked up at the bright sky and down at the glittering sea, over which the Phrabayat was bounding at the rate of six or seven knots an hour, and blessed God that I was still alive, and for the moment forgot how great was the danger still remaining.

Far ahead I could see the loom of the China coast. By my reckoning she would be in touch with the land before nightfall if the present fresh breeze held—and what then? A sudden resolve came upon me to ask the evident master of my destinies; for, although I felt quite sure that any compunction for whatever sufferings we white men might endure would be impossible to him, there would be a certain amount of satisfaction in knowing his intentions. I turned to go and seek him, but he was standing by my side. Without waiting for me to speak to him, he said gravely—

"In a few hours I hope to reach the creek where my agents are waiting to tranship the cargo. What then will happen depends largely upon yourself. Should you persist in refusing to take command of this vessel it may be the easiest plan to cut your throat, as you would be greatly in the way. Of course, your two companions would be disposed of in the same manner. But for the present, if you will have the goodness to call the hands aft, there are some precautions to be taken with reference to the valuables you have seen, which represent the loot that Captain Klenck anticipated making off with presently. That reminds me——" And, disappearing from my side, he slid rather than walked below. I called the hands aft, walking to the break of the poop as I did so. As I stood looking down on to the main deck, my late companion appeared with the skipper's body in his arms, which he cast over the lee-rail as if it had been a bundle of rags.

Then, turning to the waiting crew, he gave a few quiet orders, and at once they began preparing the two boats for lowering. Some of them dived below and brought up armfuls of small boxes, bags, and mats, within which coarse coverings I knew were concealed that mass of wealth lately exposed upon the deck of the state-room below.

Quite at a loss what to do, I stood listlessly watching the busy scene, until I suddenly remembered the two white men below, who had been so strangely rescued from an awful death. And as I was clearly not wanted on deck I went into the cabin, finding, with the first thrall of satisfaction I had felt for a long time, that they were both rapidly mending. It is hardly necessary to say that I soon found the stranger to be my predecessor, whose mysterious disappearance had worried me not a little. Neither he nor Boyesen were able to talk much, had they been willing; but I learned that they had both incurred the wrath of the skipper from having obtained too much knowledge of his proceedings, that they had both been drugged (at least, only in that way could they account for his being able to deal with them as he had done), and they had suffered all the torments of the lost until the yellow giant had let in the blessed daylight upon them again. But neither they nor I could understand why the skipper had not killed them offhand. That was a puzzle never likely to be unravelled now.

Neither of them appeared to take a great deal of interest in the present state of affairs, certainly not enough to assist me in concerting my plans for our safety. I was quite satisfied that we were in no immediate danger, so that I was content, having established a bond of good-fellowship between us, to wait until they were more fit for active service.

We sat quietly smoking and dropping an occasional word, when a sudden hurried pattering of bare feet overhead startled me. I rushed on deck, roused at last into something like vigorous interest, to find that all hands were quitting the ship. We were now some twenty miles (by my estimate) from the land, and what this sudden manœuvre could mean was beyond me until, looking astern, I saw a long smoke-wreath lying like a soft pencil smudge along a low mass of cumulous cloud. Not one of the departing heathen took the slightest notice of me as they shoved off, so I darted out, snatched up the glasses, and focused them on the approaching steamer. I could not make her out, but I felt sure it was her advent that had rid us of our parti-coloured masters. Down I went and told the invalids what had happened, begging them, if they could, to come on deck and lend a hand to get her hove-to, so that the steamer might the more rapidly overhaul us. Boyesen managed to make a start, but the late mate was too feeble. And Ah Toy, to my surprise, also showed up. I had no time to ask him why he had not gone with the rest, but together we hurried on deck, finding that a thick column of smoke was rising from the main hatch—those animals had set her on fire! There were, of course, no boats, and unless that vessel astern got in some pretty good speed we stood no bad chance of being roasted alive. However, we rigged up an impromptu raft, after letting go all the halyards so that her way might be deadened —we knew better than to waste time trying to put out such a fire as was raging below.

Why enlarge upon the alternations of hope and fear until the Ly-ee-moon, Chinese gunboat, overhauled us? She did do so, but not until we were cowering on the taffrail watching the hungry flames licking up the mizen-rigging. And when rescued I would not have given a dozen "cash" for our lives, but that the gunboat had an Englishman in command, to whom I was able to tell my story. He put the coping-stone upon my experiences when he told me that he had been watching for the Phrabayat for the past six months, having received much information as to her doings. And he used language that made the air smell brimstone when he realized that, after all, his prize had escaped him. I told him all I could—it was not much—of the disappearance of the crew, but he was indifferent. He "didn't expect to clap eyes on 'em any more," he said. Nor did he. Where they landed, or whether they sank, no one but themselves knew. And we three unfortunate wretches were landed in Hong Kong three weeks afterwards almost as bare of belongings as when we began the world. Ah Toy fell on his feet, for he shipped in the gunboat as the commander's servant upon my recommendation.

I had all the experience of the China coast I wanted, and shipped before the mast in a "blue-funnelled" boat for home two days after, glad to get away on any terms. The two Danes went their way, and I saw them no more.

THE COOK OF THE CORNUCOPIA

A SQUARE-SET little Norwegian with a large head, puffy face, faded blue eyes, and a beard that, commencing just below them, flowed in wavy masses nearly to his waist; the "Doctor" had already achieved a reputation among us for taciturnity and gruffness quite out of keeping with his appearance.

As a cook he was no better or worse than the average, except in one particular, his cleanliness; and as the majority of sailors in British ships do not expect such a miracle as would be necessary in order to change the bad, scanty provisions supplied into tasty food by cooking, a clean cook is pretty certain of becoming a prime favourite for'ard.

But Olaf Olsen courted no man's company or favour. To all such sociable advances as were made him by various members of the crew he returned the barest answer possible, letting it plainly be seen that he considered his own society amply sufficient for all his desires. One of the most difficult positions to maintain, however, on board ship is that of a misanthrope. Sooner or later the need of human fellowship always asserts itself, and the most sullen or reserved of men let fall their self-contained garment. Olsen was no exception to this rule.

Before we had been a month at sea, I was sitting on the spare spars opposite the galley door silently smoking during the last half-hour of the second dog-watch, in full enjoyment of the delicious evening freshness, when the cook suddenly leaned out over the half-door of his den and said—

" You looks fery quiet dis efening, ain't id ? "

I was so taken aback by his offering any remark that I let my pipe fall out of my mouth, but stooping to pick it up gave me time to collect myself and reply in a cheery word or two, feeling curiously anxious to draw him out. One word brought on another, as the common phrase has it, and five minutes after his first remark he was sitting by my side yarning away as if trying to make up for lost time. I let him talk, only just dropping a word or two at intervals so as to keep him going by showing him that I was paying attention. Presently he broke off some rambling remarks by saying abruptly—

" You efer bin t' Callyo ? "

" No, but I've heard a lot about it," I replied. " Pretty hard citizens around there, ain't they ? "

" Id's de las' place Gott Allamitey efer made, my boy, an' de deffel's ben a dumpin' all de leff-overs in de vorl' down dere efer since," grunted he. " I vas dere las' voy'ge. You know a ship call de Panama—big wooden ship 'bout fourteen hundred ton ? Vell, I vas cook apoard her, ben out in her over two yere ven ve come ofer frum Melbun in ballas'. Ve schip a pooty hard crout in de Colonies, leas, dey fancy demsellufs a tough lot, but mie Gott ! dey tidn' know

Capn Tunn. No, dey tidn', ner yet de tree mates, 'n' leas' of all dey tidn' know *me*. I like de afterguard fus'-class, me an' dem allvus ked along bully, an' ve vas all lef' of de fus' crew ship' in London.

"De Bosun, Chips, an' Sails wa'nt any count; square-heads all tree ov' em. P'raps you'se tinkin' I'm a square-head, too? Yus, but I'm f'm Hammerfes', an' dey don' breed no better men in de vorl, dan dere. Vell, I see how tings vas coin' t'be, 'fore ve ked out of Bass's Straits, 'n I dells you, my poy, dere vas dimes pooty soon. De ole man vas a Kokney, but he looks so much like me as if he been my dvin broder. He speak fery low an' soft—de mate alvus done de hollerin'; but de fus' time one of de fellers gif him some slack, he pick him from de veel like he bin a crab, unt schling him forrut along de poop so he fall ofer de break onto de main-deck vere de mate vus standin' ready ter kig him fur fallin'. De noise bring de vatch below out, an' dey all rush af', fur a plug mush. I come too, but I sail in an he'p de ole man, un' I dell you id vas a crate fight, dere vas blut unt hair flyin'.

"In den minnits ve hat it all ofer, de olt man vas de boss, unt eferybody know it. All de fellers get forrut like sheeps, un' ven de ole man sing out, 'Grog oh!' presently, dey come aft so goot as a Suntay-school. Ve haf no more trouble mit dem, but ven ve ket ter Callyo de ole man say, 'Py Gott! I ain't coin ter keep dis crout loafin' rount here fur two tree mont' vile ve vaitin' fur our turn at de Chinchees. Run 'em out, Misder Short; ve ket plenty men here ven ve vant 'em quite so goot as dese, un some blut money too!' So de mate, he vork 'em up, make 'em rouse de cable all ofer de ballas', schling 'em alof', tarrin' un schrapin' an' slushin' all day long frum coffee-time till eight bells at night, unt I feet 'em yoost de same as at sea.

"In tree day efery galoot ov 'em vas gone, unt den ve haf goot times, I dell you, de Bosun unt Chips unt Sails vashin' decks unt keepin' tings shipshape. Ve lay dere tree mont', an' den de olt man ket his per-mit fur de islan's. He vent to Bucko Yoe, de Amerigan boarding-master dat kill so many men—you hear of him before, ain't it?—unt he say, 'Yoe, I vant fifteen men to-morrow. I ton'd care a tam who dey vas s'long's dey's life sailormen, put py Gott, ef you schanghai me enny 'longshoremen, alla det men, I fills you so full of holes dat you mage a No. 1 flour tretger. Dat's all I'm coin t' say t' you.' Bucko Yoe he larf, but he know de olt man pefore, unt he pring us fifteen vite men, all blind, paralytic tronk, but anybody see dey vas sailormen mit von eye."

Just at this juncture, Sandy McFee, my especial chum, came strolling out of the fo'c'sle, his freshly-loaded pipe glowing and casting a grateful odour upon the quiet evening air. He was, like the cook, a square-set, chunky man, but he was also, in addition, one of the smartest men I ever knew. He brought up all standing at the unusual sight of the Doctor and myself enjoying a friendly cuffer, so surprised that he allowed his pipe to go out. The cook froze up promptly, and stared at the intruder stonily. It was an uncomfortable silence that ensued, broken at last by the rasping

He clutched his insulter by the beard and belt.

voice of the Aberdonian, saying, "Man Tammas, hoo d'ye manach t' open th' lips o' yon Dutch immuj? Ah'd a noshin' ut he couldna speyk ony ceevil language. Ye micht tell ma hoo ye manached it."

A certain quivering about the cook's broad shoulders was the only visible sign that he had heard and understood the mocking little speech made by Scotty, but the latter had hardly finished when the Doctor rose to his feet, remarking with a yawn, as of a man who took no interest in the subject—

"I allvus t'ought Scossmen vas dam' pigs, und now I knows it. But I nefer hear von crunt before. Vy tondt you co unt scradge yorselluf? You findt un olt proom forrut."

Down went Sandy's pipe, an articulate growl burst from his chest, and, with a spring like a grasshopper, he had clutched his insulter by the beard and belt. There was a confused whirl of legs and arms, a panting snarl deep down in the men's throats, and suddenly, to my horror, I saw the cook go flying over the rail into space, striking the sea almost immediately afterwards with a tremendous splash. It was all so sudden that for the instant I was helpless. But the splash alongside started me into life, and, grabbing the coil of the fore-sheet behind me, I hurled it overside without looking. At the same moment Sandy, horror-struck at his mad action, sprang on to the pin-rail and dived after his victim.

The ship was just forging ahead through an oily smoothness of sea to a faint upper current of air, so that there was no great danger except from a prowling shark, but the short twilight was fading fast. As if intuitively, all hands had rushed on deck and aft to the quarter, while the helmsman jammed the wheel hard down. The vessel turned slowly to meet the wind, while we watched the man who had just hurled a fellow-creature to what might easily be his death, fighting like a lion to rescue him. The cook could not swim, that was evident, but it was still more evident that he had no thought of his own danger if only he might take his enemy along with him to death. He had, however, to deal with one who was equally at home in the water as on deck, and it was wonderful to see how warily, yet with what determination the little Scotchman manœuvred until he had the furious Norwegian firmly pinned by the arms at his back, and how coolly he dipped him again and again beneath the surface, until he had reduced him to quiescence.

Getting the boat out is usually in those ships a formidable task, and it was nearly half an hour before we had the two men safely on board again. The skipper was a quiet, amiable man, and this strange outbreak puzzled him greatly. Sandy, however, expressed his contrition, and promised to avoid the Doctor and his bitter tongue in future. So with that the skipper had to be content, especially as the cook recovered so rapidly from his ducking that we heard him in another half-hour's time grinding coffee for the morning as if nothing had happened. But the strangest part of the affair to me was its outcome. Next morning, in our watch below, the Doctor came into the fo'c'sle, and, walking up to Sandy, put out his hand, saying—

"Santy, you vas a coot man, pedder as me, unt I tond vant any more row longer you. I ben coot man, too, bud I ain't any longer, only I forkedd it somedimes. I cot my soup unter vay for dinner, unt if you likes I finish dot yarn I vas tellin' Tom here lasd night."

Now Sandy was all over man, and jumping up from his chest he gripped the Doctor's paw, saying—

"Weel, Doctor, A'am as sorry as a maan can be 'at I lost ma temper wi' ye. W'en Ah see ye i' th' watter Ah feelt like a cooard, and Ah'd a loupit owerboord afther ye, even ef Ah couldna ha soomt a stroak. Ah wisht we'd a bottle o' fhuskey t' drink t' yin anither in; but never mind, we'll hae two holl evenin's thegither in Melburrun when we got thonder. But you an' me's chums fra this oot."

This happy conclusion pleased us all, and, in order to profit by this loosening of the Doctor's tongue, I said, passing over my plug of tobacco—

"Now then, Doctor, we're all anxious to hear the rest of that cuffer you was tellin' me last night. I've told the chaps all you told me, and they are just hungry for the rest, so fill up and go ahead."

"Vell, poys, you nefer see a hantier crout dan dat lot Amerigan Yoe cot schanghaied abord of us in Callyo. How he ked 'em all so qviet I ton't know. But dey vas all ofer blut, unt dere close vas tore to shakin's, so I kess dey vas some pooty hart fightin' pefore he put 'em to sleep so he could pring dem alonkside. De olt man unt his bucko crout of off'cers ton't let 'em haf time to ked spry pefore dey pegin roustin' 'em erroun'—dey know de ropes too vell fer dot. So as soon as de boardin' marsder vas gone, oudt dey comes, unt aldough it vas keddin' tark, I be tamt ef dey vasn't sdarted holystonin' de deck fore 'n aft. Dey vas haluf tedt mit knoggin' about, dey hadn't been fed, unt dey vas more as haluf poison mit bad yin, unt den to vork 'em oop like dat, I dells you vat, poys, id vas tough.

"Dey let oop on 'em 'bout twelluf o'clock unt told 'em to co below, but de poor dyfuls yoost ked into de fo'c'sle unt fall down—anyveres—unt dere dey schleep till coffee-dime. Perhaps you ton'd pelief me, but I dells you de trut, dem fellers come out ven de mate sinks oudt, 'Turn-to' like anoder crout altogeder. Efen de mate look mit all his eyes cos he don't aspect to see 'em like dat. Dey ton't do mooch till prekfuss-dime, unt den dey keds a coot feet; mags dem quite sassy.

"Unt so off ve goes to de Chinchees, unt from dat day out ve nefer done fightin'. You talk apout Yankee blood-poats unt plue-nose hell-afloats, dey wan't in it 'longside de Panama. Dem fellers vas all kinds; but dey vas all on de fight, unt, if de could only haf hang togedder, dey'd haf murder de whole lot of us aft. But dey couldn't; leas', dey didn't until long after ve lef de island, an slidin' up troo de soud-east trades tords de line. Den one afternoon I ketch one of 'em diggin' a lot er slush * outer one er my full casks. 'Course I vas mat, unt I dells him to get t' hell out er dat, unt leave my slush alone. He don't say nuthin', but he schlings de pot at me. Den it vas me un him for it, un ve fight like two rhinosros.

"Ve fight so hardt ve don't know dat all hants haf choin in, efen de man run from de veel un chip in. I bin dat mat 'bout my slush I fight like six men, unt ven de fight vas ofer I fall down on teck right vere I am, unt go to sleep. Ven I vake up aken de olt man haf got de hole crout in ierns. He say he be tam ef he coin't t' haf any mo' fightin' dis voy'ge; liddle's all fery vell, but 'nough's a plenty. So ve vork de ship home oursellufs—qvite 'nough t' do, I tell you, t' keep her coin 'n look after dat crout so vell.

"De olt man dell me he bin fery font of me, 'n he coin' t' gif me dupple pay; but ven ve ket to Grafesent 'n sent all de crout ashore in ierns, I vant t' sell my slush to a poatman—I haf fifteen parrels—unt de poatman offer me £25 for it. But de olt man he say he want haluf—haluf *my* slush vat I ben safin fery near tree years! I say to him, 'Look here, Cap'n Tunn, I luf you petter as minesellluf; but pefore I led you take away haluf my slush, I coin to see vich is de pest man, you alla me.' He don't say no more, but he valk up

* "Slush" in the merchant service is the name given to the coarse dripping, lumps of waste fat, etc., which the ship's cook has over after preparing the men's food. He is entitled to this as his perquisite, and is naturally careful to cask it down during the voyage for sale ashore, after the voyage, to wholesale chandlers and soap-boilers, or their middlemen.

to me unt make a crab at my peard, unt den it vas us two for it. But he vasn't a man, he vas ten deffels stuff into von liddle man's body. I tondt know how long ve fight, I tondt know how ve fight; but ven I vake oop I ain't any fightin' man no more. My het is crack unt haluf my teet gone, unt I haf some arms unt legs break pesides. But he gomes to see me in de 'ospital, unt he ses, 'Olsen, my poy, you bin a tam goot man, 'n I haf sell your slush for tirty poun' unt pring you de money. You haf £120 to take, unt ven you come out, tondt you go to sea no more; you puy a cook-shop in de Highvay; you make your fortune.' Den he go avay, unt I never see him any more.

"Ven I come out I traw my 150 soffrins unt puy a pelt to carry dem rount me. Unt I pig up mit a nice liddle gal from de country, unt ve haf a yolly time. Ve make it oop to ked marrit379 righd off, unt dake dat cook-shop so soon as I haf yoost a liddle run rount. Den I sdart on de spree unt I keep it oop for tree veeks, until I ked bad in my het, allvus dirsty unt nefer can't get any trinks dat seems vet. Afterwards I co vat you call oudt—off my het, unt I tond't know vedder I isn't back in de Panama agen, fightin', fightin' all day unt all night. Ven I ked vell agen, I got nuthin', no money, no close, no vife. So I tink I petter go unt look for a ship, unt ven I ked dis von I ain't eat anyting for tree days."

Then, as abruptly as he had opened the conversation, he closed it by getting up and leaving us, having, I supposed, obeyed the uncontrollable impulse to tell his story that comes now and then upon every man.

A LESSON IN CHRISTMAS-KEEPING

MORNING broke bleakly forbidding on the iron-bound coast of Kerguelen Island. Over the fantastic peaks, flung broadcast as if from the primeval cauldron of the world, hung a grim pall of low, grey-black cloud, so low, indeed, that the sea-birds drifting disconsolately to and fro between barren shore and gale-tossed sea were often hidden from view as if behind a fog-bank, and only their melancholy screams denoted their presence, until they glinted into sight again like huge snow-flakes hesitating to fall. Yet it was the Antarctic mid-summer, it was the breaking of Christmas Day.

As the pale dawn grew less weak, it revealed a tiny encampment, just a few odds and ends of drifting wreckage piled forlornly together, and yielding a dubious shelter to a huddled-up group of fourteen men, sleeping in spite of their surroundings. Presently, there were exposed, perched upon the snarling teeth of an outlying rock-cluster, the " ribs and trucks " of a small wooden ship, a barque-rigged craft of about four hundred tons. Her rigging hung in slovenly festoons from the drunkenly standing masts, the yards made more angles with their unstable supports than are known to Euclid, while through many a jagged gap in her topsides the mad sea rushed wantonly, as if elated with its opportunities of marring the handiwork of the daring sea-masters.

The outlook was certainly sufficiently discomforting; yet, as one by one the sleepers awakened, and with many a grunt and shiver crept forth from their lair, it would have been difficult to judge from the expressions upon their weather-beaten countenances how hopeless was the situation that they were in.

For they came of a breed that is strong to endure hardness, that takes its much bitter with little sweet as a matter of course, and, by dint of steady refusal to be dismayed at Fate's fiercest frowns, has built up for itself a most gallantly earned reputation for pluck, endurance, and success throughout the civilized world. They were Scotch to a man, rugged and stern as the granite of their native Aberdeenshire.

They were the crew of the barque Jeanie Deans, of Peterhead, which, while outward bound from Aberdeen to Otago, New Zealand, had, after long striving against weather extraordinarily severe for the time of year, been hurled against that terrific coast during the previous afternoon. Their escape shoreward had been as miraculous as fifty per cent. of such escapes are, and, beyond their lives, they had saved nothing. So the prospect was unpromising. Nothing could be expected from the break-up of the ship. She was loaded with ironwork of various sorts, and her stores were not in any water-tight cases which might bring them ashore in an eatable condition. But the large-limbed, red-bearded skipper, after a keen look round, said—

"Ou, ay, ther isna ower muckle tae back an' fill on, but A'am thenkin' we'll juist hae to bestir wersells an' see if we canna get some breakfas'. Has ony ane got ony matches?"

It presently appeared that of these simple yet invaluable little adjuncts to civilization there was not one among the crowd. But even this grim discovery appeared to make no great impression, and presently the mate, a tall man from Auchtermuchty, with an expressionless face and a voice like "a coo's," as he was wont to say, remarked casually—

"If ye'll scatther aboot an' see fat ye can fine tae cuik, I'se warrant ye Aa'll get ye some fire tae cuik it wi'."

No one spoke another word, but silently they separated for their quest, leaving Mr. Lowrie, with his blank face, methodically rummaging among the *débris*. Presently he sat down quietly with a piece of flat board before him about two feet long by six inches wide. In his hand he held a piece of broomstick, which in some mysterious way had got included in the flotsam. This he whittled at one end into a blunt point, carefully saving the cuttings in his trousers pocket. Then with a steady movement of his stick he commenced to chafe a groove lengthways in the board, adding occasionally a pinch of grit from the ground to assist friction.

By-and-by there was quite a little heap of brown wood-dust collected at one end of the groove. Then getting on his knees and grasping his broom-stick-piece energetically in both hands, he pushed it to and fro in the groove with all his force and speed, until suddenly he flung away the stick, and stooping over the little pile of dust, he covered it tenderly with both hands hollowed, and bending his head over it breathed upon it most gently. And by imperceptible degrees there arose from it a slender spiral of smoke.

His right hand stole to his pocket, and fetched therefrom a few slivers of wood, which he coyly introduced under the shelter of his other hand, until suddenly the Red Flower blossomed—there was fire. Now it only needed feeding to rise gloriously into that gloomy air. To this end Mr. Lowrie worked like a Chinaman, until within an hour he had a pile of burning driftwood, four feet high and fully six feet round, sending up ruddy tongues of flame and a column of smoke like a palm tree.

One by one the adventurers returned with dour faces, empty-handed save for a sea-bird's egg or two, a few fronds of seaweed which the bearers insisted was "dulse" (the edible fucus), and a brace of birds that looked scarcely enough to furnish an appetizer for one. But just as a stray sunbeam darted down upon the little gathering, while they huddled round the grateful warmth, there was a hoarse shout. All started, for it was the skipper's voice roaring—

"C'way here an' lend a han', ye louns. Fat'r ye aal shtannin there toasting yer taes fur like a pickle o' weans juist waitin' on yer mithers tae cry on ye tae come ben fur yer breakfas'?"

The men at once obeyed the familiar command, finding the skipper and the cook wrestling with a huge case, that was so stoutly built that not a plank of it had come adrift. When they had man-handled it over the rugged ground to within reach of the warmth the skipper said—

" Ah divna ken fats intilt, bit Ah min fine that Mester Broon, fan he shipped it, said it wis somethin' Ah wis tae tak unco care o'. And so 'twis lasht under th' s'loon table. C'wa, le's open't; please God ther may be somethin' useful inside o't."

Willing hands, regardless of the loss of skin from knuckles and arms, wrought at the task; but so stoutly did the case resist their efforts that it was long before they had stripped off the stout planking and revealed an air-tight lining of thick tin. This was attacked with sheath-knives, and, after much hacking and breaking of cutlery, yielded and exposed a number of queer-looking parcels most carefully packed. On the top was a letter. It ran as follows:—

" DEAR JACK,

" In full recollection of your curious Scottish prejudice against any celebration of Christmas, and also of that awful time when you and I were stranded on the Campbells, and compelled to suck raw sea-birds' eggs for our Christmas fare, I have sent you the materials for a good old-fashioned Christmas dinner, as I understand it, being a Cockney of the Cockniest. I also send you Dickens's ' Christmas Carol ' to read after dinner, and if you don't do justice to my loving Christmas Box, I solemnly swear that I will never regard you as a chum again. Here's wishing you a Merry Christmas, and as jolly a Hogmanay as ever you can get after.

"Most affectionately yours,

"JOHN BROWN."

"Em, ehmm" (no written words can adequately represent the peculiar Scottish exclamation that stands for anything you like, being strictly non-committal), "that reads no sae bad. We'll juist investigate. Fat hae we here? Et's a duff, mahn, ou ay, bit et's a boeny wan."

And as he spoke he pulled out of its nest a gorgeous Christmas pudding weighing some twenty-five pounds. Next came an enormous oblong tin case, labelled, "Fortnum and Mason. Special Christmas turkey, stuffed with capon, tongue, and forcemeat," upon reading which the skipper murmured again, "Ou ay, that's no sae dusty, ye ken." Next came a layer of bottles of green peas, alternated with bottles labelled "Turtle soup." Other queer tin cases followed, bearing inscriptions such as "Special mince-pies," "Scotch shortbread," "American biscuits"—like foam-flakes—"Dessert fruits," "York ham, best quality, ready cooked," and "Boar's head." Finally, on the ground floor, as it were, was displayed a compact array of bottles, of which six were labelled, "Extra special Scotch whisky," six "Special port, bin 50," two corpulent ones bore the signature "D.O.M.," and twelve had big-headed corks with gold foil adorning them.

Followed at last two boxes of fat-looking cigars, and the book.

That grim assembly looked down upon this tempting array with their hard features perceptibly softening, while the skipper said—

" Weel a'weel. A'am no' an advocate for specializin' Chrismuss masel, altho' Ah laik fine tae keep up Hogmanay. But A'am no a bigot, ye ken, an' A'am thenkin' that unner th' circumstances 'twad juist be flytin' Proeveedence no tae accept in a speerut o' moderashun sichn a Chrismuss Boex as thon. Bit I'll not coairce ony man. Them 'at disna approve o' keepin' Chrismuss ava can juist daunder awa'. 'S far as A'am consairned "—here he deftly knocked the top off one of the special Scotch bottles, and, looking round benignantly, said—" Here's tae wersels, boys, a blessin' on the giver o' th' feast, an' a Merry Chrismuss tae us a'."

Why particularize the proceedings that ensued? Should it not be sufficient to say that no conscientious scruples were entertained by any of those hard-grained men at this almost compulsory wrecking of their principles? Scarcely; yet passing notice may be given to the difficulties attendant upon drinking champagne out of bottle-necks, of eating concentrated turtle-soup warmed in the bottle like Pommard, of the total want of order and routine evidenced in dealing with the assorted provisions so providentially to hand—and mouth. Especially was this the case with the rotund bottles of Benedictine. One and all agreed that while the contents were " gey an' oily-like," they were " vara seductiv'," and had the effect of making the partakers thereof curiously unreserved and open to conviction as to the general satisfactoriness of things in general.

When at last, with long-drawn sighs, the unwonted Christmas-keepers sank down upon their stony seats and lit up their aromatic smokes with brands passed from hand to hand, it evidently needed no keen judge of human nature to prophesy that a unanimous vote would be given if asked for as to the desirability of keeping up Christmas English fashion.

When all had quietly settled down to the soothing influence of nicotine in its best form, the skipper lifted up his voice and said—

"Weel, ma lads, A'am thenkin' that we k'n dae nae less than gae through the haill reetual. This buik, 'A Christmas Carol,' is eevidently pairt o' th' programme, an' as A'am nae that ongratefu' I'll juist read it, fativer it coasts ma."

So he opened the volume, and read while the hard lines of the faces softened under the magic of the Master's words, and in spite of the well-worn masks of indifference an occasional dewdrop of sympathy glittered like a diamond in the furrow of a bronzed visage.

* * * * * * * *

"Ah wudna wuss tae interrup ye, sir," suddenly interjected an ordinary seaman, "bit Ah thocht ye micht laik tae ken that thers a vessel juist lookin' roun' the point."

"Man, ye're richt, there is that. Weel, A'am neerly throu', an' as thon auld deevil Scrooge has been conveencit o' th' errour of's ways (as we have), A'am of opingon we ma tak' th' lave o' th' storey as read. But 'twas a gey guid yarn, was't no?"

By this time the ship of deliverance, having hove to, was getting a boat out. That laborious business over, the boat came at fair speed towards the only practicable landing-place, until the commiserating face of the officer in charge took on an expression of bewilderment as he noted the smug complacency on the countenances of the castaways.

It did not diminish when the skipper, gravely welcoming him with one hand, held out invitingly a decapitated bottle of extra special Scotch with the other, saying, with lingering sweetness in his voice—

"Mahn dear, here's wussin' ye a Merry Chrismuss."

THE TERROR OF DARKNESS

"SOUTH 70° E., sir, weather's a bit sulky and inclined to dirt before daylight, I should think. Lot of ships about. Bishop bore N. 20° W. fifteen miles off at eight bells (4 a.m.). Good morning." And as he uttered the last words the second officer of the Kafirstan, 10,000-ton cargo steamer, London to Boston, U.S., swung his burly form down the lee-bridge ladder, and the darkness swallowed him up. The chief, who had just relieved him, mumbled out "G'mornin'" in the midst of a cavernous yawn, not because he was churlish or out of humour, but for the reason that be a man never so seasoned, the sudden transition from the cosy recesses of a warm bunk and sweet sleep to a narrow platform some forty feet above the sea, fully exposed to the wrathful edge of a winter gale at four o'clock in the morning, does not predispose him to cheerful conversation, or indeed any other of the amenities of life, until the wonderful adaptability of the human body has had time to adjust itself to the altered conditions.

No; John Furness, chief mate, was anything but a sulky man. Buffeted by the storms of Fate from his earliest youth in far fiercer fashion than ever the gales of winter had smitten him, he was now by way of esteeming himself one of the most fortunate of mankind, for, after serving as second mate for several years with a chief and master's ticket, and never getting a better berth than some thousand-ton tramp could afford him, he had suddenly taken unto himself a wife —a dear girl, as poor and as friendless as himself— with the quaint remark that the best thing to do with two lonely people was to make 'em one, on the principle that like cures like. And with his marriage his luck seemed to have turned. On the second day of his honeymoon he was taking his young wife round the docks, and pointing out to her the various ships— like introducing her to old acquaintances—when suddenly, with a bound, he left her side and disappeared over the edge of a jetty. He had caught sight of an old gentleman who had tripped his foot in a coil of rope and tumbled over it and the edge of the pier at the same time. John's promptitude cost him a wetting, but got him his present berth, the best he had ever held in his life, and his heart beat high with hope that at last he was on the high road to fortune.

Still, all these pleasant recollections didn't prevent him feeling sleepy and chilly upon relieving his shipmate. Vigorously he called up his resources of energy, peering through the thick gloom ahead at the twinkling gleams showing here and there, betokening the presence of other ships. Far beneath him the untiring engines, with their Titanic thrust and recover, kept his lofty station a-quiver as they drove the huge mass of the Kafirstan steadily onward against the fierce and increasing storm. Again and again he answered cheerily to the look-out man's taps on the bells announcing lights "All right," and as often by a word to the helmsman behind him, altered his great vessel's course a little to port or starboard in order to avoid collision with the passing ships. All this in the usual course of routine—it is what hundreds of men like him are doing this morning, thinking no more of the magnitude of the forces they control than a cabman who navigates the crowded London streets dwells upon what would happen if he should spill his fare under a passing waggon. It is, above all things, necessary at sea to refrain from dwelling upon what *may* happen. The one thing needful is to be equal to each duty as it arises. And John Furness was undoubtedly that. But suddenly an awful crash flung him backwards; his head struck against a stanchion of the bridge, a myriad lights gleamed before his glazing eyes, and he knew no more—knew nothing, that is, of the short, stern agony through which his shipmates passed as the huge fabric beneath them admitted the supremacy of the ever-watchful sea. She had met—her mass of 10,000 tons or so being hurled along at the rate of twelve miles an hour—with the Terror of the Darkness, a derelict just awash, one of those ancient Norwegian timber-scows, the refuse of the sea, that crawl to and fro across the Atlantic on sufferance, until there comes a day when the half-frozen crew are swept from the top of the slippery deck-load, the sea pours in through a hundred openings, and she becomes one of the most awful dangers known to mariners—a waterlogged derelict. Floating just awash at the will of ocean currents, she cannot be located with any degree of certainty, but solid almost as a rock she drifts silently across the great ocean highway invisible, unheard, a lier-in-wait for the lives of men.

When John Furness returned to consciousness again, he became aware of acute pains all over his body. Also that he was not drowning, although at intervals waves washed over him. Gradually he realized that he was clinging desperately, mechanically, but with such force that he could hardly unbend the grip of his hands, to a slimy rope. But where? As his mind cleared, and the certainty of the awful tragedy that had just passed over him and left him still alive became borne in upon him, he felt his heart swell. He thought of the handful of brave men, of whom he had already got to know every one, suddenly hurled into oblivion with all the hopes and love of which each was the centre. And a few heavy drops rolled out from his brine-encrusted eyes. Then he thought of Mary—his Mary—and at the same moment realized his duty: to strive after life for her sake. The impulse was needed, because that lethargy that means a loss of the desire to live was fast stealing over him. With a great effort that sent racking pains through his stiffened body he turned his face upwards, passed one hand across his face, and saw where he was. Lying upon the slope of a bank thickly overgrown with dank green weed like fine hair, and with a strong fishy smell. With awakening interest he peered at the rope he held—it, too, was thickly draped with the same growth, but in addition, beneath the weed, it was encrusted with jagged little shells. More than this he could hardly discern for the present, because it was still dark; but as his senses resumed their normal keenness of apprehension, he knew that he was afloat, and guessed the truth—that by some mysterious means he had been preserved from drowning by laying hold of the same cause that had sent all his late shipmates to their sudden end. A low, sullen murmur smote upon his ears, for the wind had gone down, and the resentful sea still rolled its broken surface violently in the direction in which it had been so fiercely driven, making John's holding-on place roll and heave in a heavy, lifeless manner. The grey, cheerless dawn struggled through the thick pall of clouds still draping the sky, and by the cold light the shivering man saw the full horror of his surroundings. He was clinging to the last rag of running-gear trailing from the short stump of the mainmast of a large ship—a ship that must, at least, have been of seventeen or eighteen hundred tons burden. She lay with one side of the deck well below the water, and the other some ten feet above it. Not a vestige of bulwarks, cabin, or fo'c'sle appeared on deck, all was flush as if mowed off by some gigantic scythe. Only a little forrard of where John lay was a gash cut into her side at right angles, revealing within sodden masses of timber also crushed and broken by the terrible impact of that blow. And as he looked at the wedge-shaped wound there came back to him, as if in a dream of some former life, the shock, the few seconds' realization of that fatal blow dealt herself by the Kafirstan, before he had lost consciousness to resume it here. And knowing the build of the steamer as he did, he had not the faintest hope of her having survived for even an hour. His chief longing was that sufficient time had been allowed his shipmates to get into the boats and pull away from the frightful vortex of the sinking Kafirstan.

The light having become sufficiently strong for him to see thoroughly well, he made another heroic effort, and commenced to explore his prison. And as soon as he did so, he realized how long this dangerous obstruction had been drifting about the ocean. For she was literally undistinguishable, except to a seaman's eye, from a worn and sea-beaten rock. Through the crevices in her deck and the gap made by the Kafirstan, he could see hosts of fish, legions of crabs of various kinds, and nowhere, except at the point where she had been run into, was there a square inch that was not thickly hidden by the sea-growth of weed and shells. He dragged himself up to the stump of the mainmast, and, bracing himself erect against it, looked long and earnestly around the lowering horizon; but he was quite alone. Not a gleam of sail or a wreath of smoke was to be seen. But he was a man who, while never very sanguine about his "luck," had a wonderful fund of hope, and in spite of the dismal outlook, he felt no despair. Nevertheless, that he might not brood, he determined to be busy, and dragging himself aft with the utmost caution that he might not slide off that slimy slope into the cold sea to leeward, he reached the yawning cavity, where once the companion or entrance to the lower cabin had been.

Peering down, the sight was not encouraging, although the dark water did not here come so close up to the deck as forward. But he was bound to explore, even if he had to swim, if only for the sake of employment; so crawling over the edge, he dropped below into water up to his waist, and immediately struggled to windward, where to his content he found he could move about above water. He entered what he took to be the skipper's cabin, noticing with a queer feeling of sympathy the few remnants of clothing hanging from hooks like silent witnesses of the tragedy of long ago. To his surprise, he found that everything was left as if in the midst of ordinary life; the owner had been carried off without a moment in which to return for anything he might value. Even the bedclothes, dank and sodden, lay as they had been jumped out of, well tucked in at the foot of the bunk by a careful steward. With a sense of sacrilege that he found it hard to shake off, John tried the drawers, and the woodwork fell away at his touch. Clothes, papers, photographs within lay in pulpy masses where the invading sea had so long drained through on to them. But the searcher turned all over, listlessly, mechanically, until the hot blood suddenly surged to his head as he heard a musical jingle. With feverish haste he pulled out the lumps of dank stuff until at the bottom of the drawer he found a heap of gold coins which he had evidently disturbed by twitching at the rotted bag which had contained them. Gathering them all together without counting, he shovelled them into the two inner pockets of his pea-coat, afterwards tearing open the lining and securing the necks of the pockets by a piece of roping twine, of which he was never without a small ball.

Then with almost frantic haste he scrambled on deck, feeling as if by being down there another minute he might be risking his chance of rescue. But when he again reached the mainmast and looked around only the same blank circle greeted him. And his mind, until then fairly calm, fiercely rebelled at the idea of being lost now, when the weight burdening him told him that should he reach home again, he would be able to secure a position for himself as captain of a ship by the hitherto impossible means of buying an interest in her. Had he waited to analyze his feelings, he would no doubt have wondered why the possession of a little gold should have the power to change his usually calm and philosophic behaviour into the fretful eager frame in which he now found himself; but at the time all his hopes, all his energies, were concentrated upon the one idea, how to save, not merely his life, but his newly gotten gold for the enjoyment of that dear one bravely waiting at home.

The long bitter day passed without other sign of life around, than the occasional deep breathing of a whale close at hand, or the frolicsome splash of a passing porpoise. His vitality, great though it was, began to fail under the combined influences of cold and hunger and thirst. So that he passed uneasily to and fro between sleeping and waking, only dimly conscious all the time of decreasing ability to resist the combined influences of these foes to life. Day faded into night, and still the wind did not rise, although the sky continually threatened, being so lowering that the night shade was almost opaque. As he lay semi-conscious some mysterious premonition smote him to his very vitals, and raised him erect with such nervous energy that he felt transformed. There, almost upon him, glared the two red and green eyes of a great ship, while, high above, the far-reaching electric beams from her fore masthead made a wide white track through the darkness. He shouted with, as it seemed to him, ten voices, "Ship ahoy." And back like an echo came the reply, "Hullo." The alarm was taken, and close aboard of the derelict the huge mail steamer came to a standstill, saved from destruction. In ten minutes John Furness was in safety, and three days after he landed in London, bringing the first news of the loss of the Kafirstan. And in three days more his treasure trove had secured for him the position he had so long fruitlessly striven to obtain by merit and hard work.

THE WATCHMEN OF THE WORLD

There is surely high inspiration in the thought that of all the mighty civilizations that have emerged in these latter days, there is none that dare claim the comprehensive title given to this paper without fear of contradiction, save ourselves. For the function of the Watchman is to keep the peace, to restrain lawlessness, to bring evil-doers to justice, and to hold himself unspotted from even the tiniest speck of injustice. At least these should be his functions, and if they seem to be counsels of perfection, the aiming thereat with persistent courage is continually bringing them nearer a perfect realization. And if this be so with individual watchmen, it is infinitely more so with those typical Watchers of the Empire, of whom I would now speak, the splendid, ubiquitous, and ever-ready British Navy. It would be an uplifting exercise for some of us, widening our outlook upon life, and enlightening us as to the majestic part our country has been called upon to play at this wonderful period of the world's history, if we were to get a terrestrial globe, a number of tiny white flags, and a list of positions of all our men-o'-war. Then by sticking in a flag for every ship wherever she was stationed, or on passage at the time, we should have a bird's-eye view as it were of the "beats" which our Empire Watchmen patrol unceasingly.

From end to end of the great Middle Sea wherein we hold but those dots upon the map, Gibraltar and Malta and Cyprus, whose shores bristle with hostile populations, our stately squadrons parade, not on sufferance, but as a right, none daring to say them nay. Their business is peaceful, although they have enormous force ready to use if need be, the duty of keeping Britain's trade routes clear, that the shuttles weaving the vast web of world-wide trade that we have built up may glide to and fro in security even though envious nations gnash upon us with their teeth, and vainly endeavour by every species of chicane and underhand meanness to rob us of the fruits of centuries of industry. In two Mediterranean countries alone are our ships of war heartily welcome. Italy and Greece remember gratefully our constant friendship. Italians of all classes are acquainted with the practical goodwill of Great Britain, and so man-o'-war Jack is sure of warm reception throughout that lovely country. Not that the manner of his reception troubles the worthy tar at all. Oh no. The keynote of the chorus that is perpetually being chanted in the British Navy is *duty*. The word is seldom mentioned, but better than that, it is lived. It enables the sailor to spend unmurmuringly long periods of absolute torture under the blazing furnace of the Persian Gulf, an oven that while it burns does not dry; where the soaking dews of the night lie thickly upon the decks throughout the scorching day, and are not dispersed because the molten air is overloaded with moisture, and life is lived in a vapour-bath. Here you will find the young men of gentle birth who govern in our fighting ships, forgetting their own physical miseries, in the brave effort to make the severe conditions more tolerable to the crews they command. Do their dimmed eyes often in the steaming night turn wistfully westward to the cool green English country-side, where the old home lies embowered amid the ancestral oaks? Why, certainly, but that does not make the young officer's zeal any weaker, does not damp his ardour to sustain the great traditions which are the pride and glory of the service to which it is his greatest delight to belong.

Or creep down the coast of East Africa, throbbing, palpitating under that fervent heat glare, and see the St. George's Cross proudly waving over the sterns of the gun-boats set by Britain to quell the bloodthirsty Arab's lust for slavery. Here is manifest such devotion to an ideal, albeit that ideal is never formulated in so many words, as should stir the most prosaic, matter-of-fact minds among us. I well remember—could I ever forget?—a visit I once paid to H.M.S. London, sometime depôt ship at Zanzibar. It was a privilege that I valued highly, not knowing then that with a high courtesy our country's men-o'-war are always accessible at reasonable times to any citizen who would see with his own eyes how his home is defended and by whom. I was then mate of a trading vessel that had brought supplies from home for the use of the East Indian fleet, and consequently my business took me on board the depôt ship often. First of all I was shown the hospital, a long airy apartment on the upper deck, kept as cool as science could devise in that burning climate, and fitted with all the alleviations for sickness that wise skill and forethought could compass. Here they lay, the heroes of the long, long fight, the never-ending battle of freedom against slavery, the men who had left their pleasant land for service under the flag of England against a foreign foe; yes, and far more than that. For we know that they who fight in the deadliest combat with lethal weapons are upheld and swept onward by the fierce joy of strife; so that death when it comes is no terror, and fear vanishes under the pressure of primitive instincts. But here there is no glitter, no glamour of battle. Forgotten by the world, unknown to the immense majority of their countrymen, these Britons suffer and die that the fair fame of their country may live. There, in that miniature hospital, on board H.M.S. London, I saw rows of pale, patient figures, their faces drawn and parchment-like with fever, the deadly malaria of that poisonous coast, while amongst them passed silently doctors and sick-bay attendants, each doing his part in the universal warfare. Passing thence on to the main deck, I came across a bronzed, busy group hoisting up a steam pinnace that had just returned from a cruise among the slimy creeks and backwaters of the mainland and adjacent islands, busily seeking for hunters of human flesh. A dozen men formed her crew, men who had once been white Anglo-Saxons, but were now, after a week's cruise under such conditions as that, so disguised by ingrained dirt, so scorched and dried by exposure to that terrible sun, that they were indistinguishable save by their clothing from the Arabs they had been set to watch. They were not happy, because having chased a dhow, which they were sure was packed with slaves, throughout a day and a night, they had been baffled upon coming up with her, by her hoisting the tricolour of France, the Flag of Liberty, Equality and Fraternity, sold for a few paltry dollars, to cover a traffic which the French nation had covenanted to assist in putting down. More than that, a deep gloom pervaded the whole ship on account of their recent loss; a loss which to them seemed irreparable. Their captain, idolized by them all, had been killed while engaged in an act of gallantry, typical of the service. He had gone off like any sub-lieutenant with all his honours to win, in a chase after a dhow, with only a weak boat's crew. The villainous Arabs in the dhow, seeing their advantage, turned and fought desperately. Outnumbered by five to one, and being moreover the attacking party, the Britons were beaten off, while a shot from one of the antiquated guns carried by an Arab slaver slew Captain Brownlow on the spot. And all his men mourned him most deeply and sincerely.

But cross over the Indian Ocean, and thread the tortuous ways of the East Indian Archipelago, and you shall find the beautiful white flag with its red cross flying in the most out-of-the-way nooks among that tremendous maze. Here with never-ceasing labours the highly trained officers of our navy work with loving care to make perfect our geographical knowledge of those intricate current-scoured channels. By reason of this long-drawn-out toil our merchant ships are enabled to pursue their peaceful way with perfectly trustworthy charts to guide them. Not only so, but, owing to the dauntless courage, energy, and perseverance of these nameless seafarers, those tortuous waters have been cleansed of the human tigers that had for so long infested them, swooping down upon hapless merchantmen of all nations, pitiless and insatiable as death itself. Within the lifetime of men of middle age those seas were like a hornet's nest. In every creek, estuary, and channel lurked Portuguese, Malay, and Chinese pirates, the terror of the Eastern seas. Now, solely through the exertions of our countrymen, or by their good example putting heart into the Chinese sailors, those waters are as safe as the English Channel. So, too, have the coasts of China itself been purged of pirates, although there, since every Chinese, of whatever grade, is a potential pirate or brigand given the opportunity, immunity from piratical raids is only purchased at the price of incessant vigilance. In the far Eastern seas, however, our stalwart fighting sailors are more than mere keepers of the peace of Britain, they stand between the crumbling Celestial Empire and the greed of the world.* Ever ready in diplomacy as in war, and with a force always sufficient to command respect as well as breed envy, they make the might of our island nation felt in all the affairs of the Far East.

Cross the Pacific, and on the western sea-board of

* This sentence was written before the recent outbreak of hostilities in China.

our vast American possessions find a naval station fully equipped for the maintenance of a fleet so far from home. From thence the peace-keepers sally forth all over the length and breadth of Northern Oceania and all down the western littoral of the great American continent, a mobile body of peace-keepers, whose business it is to keep widely opened eyes upon all the doings of other people, no matter how great or how small they may be. Hailed with delight by dusky populations, who hate impartially the Germans and the French, and look upon the war-canoes of the great white Queen of Belitani as the adjusters of disputes and the even-handed dispensers of justice between them, dreaded by the rascaldom of the Pacific; the robbers of men's bodies as well as the robbers of their produce, truly the lads under the White Ensign have a wide field in the "peaceful" ocean for their beneficent labours. Guarding that Greater England in the Southern seas, where men of every nation under heaven find the same security, the same opportunities to grow rich that men of our own race enjoy, clustering closely around that storm-centre (in a double sense), the Cape Colony, patrolling Western Africa, as well as Eastern, and ready at a word to send off a compact little army into the interior, mobile and manageable as no shore troops can ever be; among West Indian islands, as warm and fruitful as the most northerly American station is cold and arid, the great patrol goes on.

One does not need to be a rabid Imperialist or a raving Jingo to feel in every fibre of his frame the debt that we Britons owe to our navy. These brave, stalwart men, the very pick and flower of the British race, stand continually on sentry on all the shores of all the world—stand to guard our freedom, and, so far as one nation may do, strive to secure freedom for all other peoples. We see but little of them, for their parades are not held amid shouting crowds, but on the lonely waters, under an Admiral's eye, keen to discover defects where all seems to an untrained observer perfection of power and movement; their greatest deeds, done by steady presentation of an unmistakable object-lesson to our enemies—that is to say, to a full half of the world, bursting with envy at our comfort and prosperity—are hidden from most of us.

In God's name, then, let us see that we do not forget, amid the security and plenty that we enjoy, the labours of those who are watching, far out of our sight, to see that these blessings are not filched from us. Let the officers and men of the Royal Navy see that they are ever in our thoughts, that out of sight out of mind is not true in their case, but that stay-at-home Britons are fully conscious that the outposts of our Empire, the piquets of our power, are in very truth to be found on board the ships of the Royal Navy, the Watchmen of the World.

THE COOK OF THE WANDERER

ONE of the oldest, truest, and most often quoted of all sea-sayings is that "God sends meat, but the devil sends cooks." The first part of this saw is really a concession on the sailor's part, for few of them truly believe that the Deity has much to do with the strange stuff usually served out as meat on board ship. The latter half of the proverb is taken for granted, and while admitting to the full the thanklessness of the task of endeavouring to dish up tasteful meals with such unpromising materials as are usually given to sea-cooks to work upon, it certainly does seem truer than the majority of such sayings are apt to be.

But in justice even to sea-cooks let it be said that they have but a hard life of it. Cooking is a hobby of my own, and I feel a positive delight in the preparation of an appetizing dinner, which culminates when those for whom it is dressed partake of it with manifest enjoyment. Between the calm, unhindered task of shore-cooking and the series of hair-breadth escapes from scalding, burning, or spoiling one's produce that characterizes sea-cooking there is, however, a great gulf fixed, and with a full consciousness of the unromantic character of his trials, I must confess a deep sympathy with the sea-cook in his painful profession.

Even in the well-ordered kitchens of a great liner, where every modern appliance known to the art is at hand, and where the chief cook is a highly paid professional, each recurring meal brings with it much anxiety, and, when the weather is bad, much painful work also. There is no allowance made. Whatever happens, passengers and crew must be fed, although the roasting joints may be playing "soccer" in the ovens, the stew-pans tobogganing over the stove-tops, and the huge coppers leaping out of their glowing sockets. Let all who have ever gone down to the sea as passengers remember how faithfully the cooks have justified the confidence reposed in them, and how punctually the varied courses have appeared on the fiddle-hampered tables without even a hint as to the series of miracles that have produced them. Still, in large passenger steamers there is a fairly large staff of cooks, unto each of whom is given his allotted task, so that the labour, though severe, is not so complicated as it must necessarily be in vessels where one unfortunate man must needs be a host in himself. In sailing-ships on long voyages the cook's berth is perhaps the worst on board, for he has to hear the continual growling of the men at the brutal monotony of the food (which he cannot help), and he must, if he would not be badgered to death, perform the difficult task of keeping on good terms with both ends and the middle of the ship. Under the blistering sun of the tropics, or amid the fearful buffeting of the Southern seas, he must perform his duties within a space about six feet square, of which his red-hot stove occupies nearly half. And, as a pleasant change, he is liable to have the weather door of his galley burst in by a tremendous sea, and himself in a devil's dance of seething pots, and all the impedimenta of his business hurled out to leeward.

Necessarily such a service does not appeal strongly to many, and often in English vessels of small size prowling about the world begging for freight, some very queer fellows are met with filling the unenviable post of cook. In the course of a good many years of sea-service I have met with several cooks, each of whom deserves a whole chapter to deal comprehensively with his peculiarities, but chief among them all must be placed the exceedingly funny fellow designated at the beginning of this sketch. The Wanderer was a pretty brigantine of about 200 tons register, built and owned in Nova Scotia, and at the time of my joining her as an A.B. was lying in the Millwall Docks outward bound to Sydney, Cape Breton, in ballast. She had quite a happy family of a crew, while the skipper was as jolly a Canadian as it was ever my good fortune to meet with. We left the docks in tow of one of the little "jackal" tugs that scoot up and down the Thames like terriers after rats, but, owing to the vessel's small size and wonderful handiness, we dispensed with our auxiliary just below Gravesend, and worked down the river with our own sails. As soon as the watches were set all hands went to supper, or tea, as it would be called ashore, and going to the snug little galley with my hook-pot for my modicum of hot tea, I made the acquaintance of the cook. He was a young fellow of about two and twenty, able-looking enough, but now evidently ill at ease. And when, with trembling hand, he baled my tea out of a grimy saucepan with another saucepan lid, I regarded him with some curiosity, fancying that he had the air of a man to whom his surroundings were the most unfamiliar possible. Supper consisted of some cold fresh meat and " hard tack," so that any deficiency in the cookery was not manifest beyond a decidedly foreign flavour in the tea, making it unlike any beverage ever sampled by any of us before. But we were a good-natured crowd, willing to make every allowance for a first performance, and aware that the " Doctor," as the cook is always called at sea, had only joined on the previous day. Nevertheless, we discussed him in some detail, arriving at the conclusion that by all appearances he would be found unable to boil salt water without burning it, which, according to the sea phrase, marks the nadir of culinary incompetence.

Next morning it was my " gravy-eye " wheel, the " trick " that is, from four to six a.m. The cook is always called at four a.m. in order to prepare some hot coffee by two bells, five a.m., and, as may be expected, the comforting, awakening drink is eagerly looked forward to, although it usually bears but a faint resemblance to the fragrant infusion known by the same name ashore. Two bells struck, and presently, to my astonishment, sounds of woe arose forward, mingled with many angry words. I listened eagerly for some explanation of this sudden breach of the peace, but could catch no connected sentence.

Presently one of my watchmates came aft to relieve me, as the custom is, to get my coffee, and I eagerly questioned him as to the nature of the disturbance. With a sphinx-like air he took the spokes and muttered, "You'll soon see." I hastened forward, got my pannikin, and going to the galley held it out for my coffee. The cook had no light, but he silently poured me out my portion, and wondering at his strange air I returned to the fo'c'sle. I sugared my coffee, and put it to my lips, but with a feeling of nausea spat out the mouthful I had taken, saying, "What in thunder is this awful stuff?" Then the other fellows laughed mirthlessly and loud, saying, "You'd best go'n see ef you kin fine out. Be dam' 'fenny ov us can tell." I hastened back to the galley and said coaxingly, "Doctor, you ain't tryin' to poison me, are ye?" He looked at me appealingly, and I saw traces of recent tear-tracks adown his smoke-stained cheeks. "Mahn," he said, "Ah've niver dune ony cookin' afore, an' ah must hev made some awfu' mistake, but ah'll sweer ony oo-ath ah dinna ken wut's wrang wi' the coaphy." And he wept anew. "For Heaven's sake, don't cry, man," I put in hastily; "you'll make me sea-sick if you do. Let me have a look at it." I stepped into his den, and striking a match explored the pot with a ladle. And I found that he had been stewing green unroasted coffee beans. The colour was brought somewhat near that of the usual product by reason of the remains of some burnt porridge at the bottom of the saucepan, but the taste was beyond description evil.

This was but a sorry beginning to our voyage, since so much of our comfort depended upon the cooking of our victuals, and it was well for the unfortunate cook that all hands, with the sole exception of the mate, were of that easy-going temper that submits to any discomfort rather than ill-use a fellow-creature. For Jemmie (the quondam cook) was not only ignorant of the most elementary acquaintance with cookery—he was also unclean and unhandy to the uttermost imaginable possibility of those bad qualities. Yet he did not suffer any grievous bodily harm until an excess of new-found zeal brought him one day into contact with the mate. As the only way in which we could hope to get anything beyond hard tack to eat, we had all taken turns to cook our own meals. Even the skipper, with many uncouth, unmeant threats, used to visit the galley and try his hand, while the trembling Jemmie stood behind him watching with eager eyes the mysterious operations going on. One morning the skipper fancied some flap-jacks, a sort of primitive pancake of plain flour and water fried in grease, and eaten with molasses. He had hardly finished a platter full and borne it aft, when Jemmie seized the bowl, and mixing some more flour, proceeded to try his hand. He managed after several failures to turn out half a dozen quite creditable-looking patches of fried batter, and intoxicated with his success rushed aft with them to where the mate and his watch were busy scrubbing the poop. Timidly approaching the energetic officer, Jemmy said, " Wou'd ye like a flap-jack, sir? they're nice an' hot."

For one fearful moment the mate glared at the offender, then as the full area of the enormity enveloped him he uttered a hyena-like howl and fell upon him. Snatching the flap-jacks from his nerveless grasp, the mate overthrew him, and frantically burnished his face with the smoking dough, holding him down on the deck by his hair the while. Then when the last fragments had been duly spread over Jemmie's shining visage, the mate dragged him to the break of the poop, and with many kicks hurled him forward to make more flap-jacks should he feel moved so to do.

So his education proceeded, until one day he felt competent to essay the making of some soup for us forward. By the time his preparations were complete he was a gruesome object, and withal so weary that he sat down on the coal-locker and went fast asleep. He awoke just before the time the soup was due to be eaten to find it as he left it, the fire having gone out. In a terrible fright he rushed aft and smuggled a tin of preserved meat forward—a high crime and misdemeanour—since that was only kept in case of bad weather rendering cooking impossible. However, he succeeded in stealing it, but when he had got it he was little better off. For he didn't know how to shell it, as it were, how to get the meat out of the tin. I happened to be passing by the galley-door at the time, and saw him with the tin lying on its side before him, while he was insanely chopping at it with a broad axe, all unheeding the spray of fat and gravy which flew around at each swashing blow. I gave him such assistance as I could, and took the opportunity thus afforded of asking him however he came to offer himself as a ship's cook. I learned then that his previous sea experience had been limited to one trip to Iceland as a bedroom steward on board a passenger steamer from Leith—that having come to London to seek his fortune, he had foregathered with an old friend of his father's, who had obtained for him this berth, and who, in answer to his timid demur as to his being able to do what should be required of him, stormed at him so vigorously for what he called his " dam' cowardice " that he took the berth, and resigned himself to his fate, and ours. His fates were kind to him in that he fell among easy-going fellows, for I shudder to think what would have befallen him in the average " Bluenose " or Yankee. A description of it would certainly have been unprintable.

Yet, like so many other people ashore and afloat, he was ungrateful for the many ways in which we, the sailors, helped and shielded him, and one day when I found him laboriously drawing water from our only wooden tank by the quarter pint for the purpose of *washing* potatoes, in answer to my remonstrance he was exceeding jocose and saucy, even going so far as to suggest that while my advice was doubtless well meant, it irked him to hear, and I had better attend to my own business. Now, to use fresh water where salt water will serve the same purpose is at sea the unpardonable sin; and where (as in our case) a few days' difference in the length of the passage might see us all gasping for a drink, it merits a severe punishment. So I was indignant, but swallowed my resentment as I saw the mate coming down from aloft with his eyes fixed upon the criminal.

I must draw a veil over what followed, only adding that by the time the cook had recovered from his injuries we were in port, and, with the luck of the incompetent, no sooner had he been bundled ashore than he obtained a good berth in an hotel at about treble the salary he would ever earn. But we held a praise-meeting over our happy release.

THE GREAT CHRISTMAS OF GOZO

On the eve of the nativity of our Blessed Lord A.D. 1551 there was profound peace in Gozo.

The assaults of the infidel had for so long a time been intermitted, that the simple hardy islanders had almost come to believe that they would always be left in peace to cultivate their tiny fields, to worship God after their own sweet manner, and to rest quietly in their little square stone dwellings, secure from the attacks of the swarthy, merciless monsters that, not content with the possession of their own sunny lands, had so often swarmed across the bright blue stretches of sea separating the Maltese Islands from Africa.

Over the main thoroughfare of Rabato, the principal town of the tiny island that hung like a jewel in the ear of Malta the Beautiful, the great square citadel of the knights kept grim watch and ward. It rose sheer from the street for one hundred feet of height, a mass of quarried stone cemented into a solidity scarcely less than that of the original rock from whence its ashlar had been hewn with such heavy toil, a mountainous fortress, to all outward seeming impregnable. Upon its highest plateau towered the mighty cathedral, fair to view without in its stately apparel of pure white stone, and all glorious within by reason of the numberless gifts showered upon it by the loving hands of those who desired thus to show their gratitude to God.

In truth it was a goodly fane. Not merely because of the blazing enrichments of gold and silver and precious stones with which it glowed and sparkled, but because of the many signs of loyalty and truth evidenced in the sculptured tombs of the illustrious dead. The knights who kept vigilant watch around its sacred walls and came daily to worship within its cool aisles were never left without a solemn witness to the fealty of those who had gone before them. The most careless among them could not help being impressed by the fact that here in the midst of the Great Sea had been planted an outpost of Christendom of which they were the custodians—a fortress of the utmost value for the keeping back of the Paynim hordes who bade fair to overwhelm all Christian countries, and bring them under the abhorrent rule of Mahomed the Accursed One.

In this there is no exaggeration. If there be one fact more clearly established than any other, amid the welter of misleading rubbish that floods the world to-day, it is this, that the fearless self-sacrifice of the knights of Malta, buttressed by the devotion of those over whom they held no gentle sway, saved Europe from being overrun by the pitiless Mussulman, saved Europe from being to-day a depraved, debased, and miserable land, wherein all the horrors of Eastern Africa would have their full and awful outcome.

Raimondo de Homedes, only son of the Grand

She was to him brightest and best of all damsels.

Master of that name, Juan de Homedes, was on this most momentous Christmas Eve in command of the Gozo garrison. The general feeling was one of security. The last attack of the infidel in 1546 had been repulsed with such terrible loss to the invader that the high-spirited garrison could not help coming to the conclusion that it would be at least a generation before any such attempt would again be made.

Raimondo de Homedes, then, went the rounds of his great command in the citadel of Gozo with a carefree heart. His thoughts were mainly occupied with the question of how soon he should be free to meet his lady-love, the stately daughter of Alfonso de Azzopardi, chief of all the notables in Gozo. She was, to him at least, brightest, best of all the damosels whose charms fired the palpitating hearts of those warriors of the Cross who were holding these islands for the commonweal of Christian Europe.

While he thus meditated, receiving the replies to his perfunctory challenges of the sentries on guard with an ear that hardly conveyed to his brain the meaning of the words, there came running to him a page, a lad of parts who was an especial favourite. Breathless, panting with excitement, the child (he was scarcely more) gasped out, "Messer Raimondo, the sentinel on the eastern tower says that since you passed his guard-house he has been mightily exercised by the appearance of some black masses on the sea. He knows not what they can be, but he fears they are galleys and that they can be coming for no good purpose. He prays you to return and look for yourself, in case there should be any mischief intended of which we have had no warning by our spies."

Raimondo listened, with a concentration of all his mental faculties, but as he did so he could not help a contemptuous smile crinkling his features. "Just another bad dream of old Gianelli's. But never mind; I will go and set his troubled soul at rest."

It wanted but two hours of midnight. The moon was full and almost in the meridian, pouring down through the cloudless serene a flood of light like molten silver. So dazzling was the radiance that when the commandant and his companion stepped forth upon the highest plateau of all into its full glare, their shadows glided by their sides as if carved in solid ebony, and every object around them was as clearly visible as if it had been noonday. With a quick springing step, Raimondo mounted the half-dozen steps of stone leading into the eastern tower, meeting Gianelli's challenge with the countersign of the night, "Mary." Then Raimondo burst impetuously into speech, saying—

"What ails thee, Gianelli? Surely dreams trouble thee; and in thy nervous anxiety to be counted most faithful of all our faithful guards, thou hast conjured up a band of spectres to torment thyself withal. What hast thou seen and where?"

For all answer Gianelli bowed low, and, straightening himself immediately, stretched out his long left arm towards the west in the direction of Tunis. And there, in that blazing tract of silvern light shed upon the darkling sea by the moon, was distinctly to be seen a row of objects that could be nothing else but galleys, although it was evident that they were of the smallest size.

An instantaneous change took place in the attitude of the young commandant. "By the Holy Sepulchre," he muttered, "thou art right, Gianelli, and I did thee grievous wrong to ridicule thy well-known fidelity and watchfulness."

"Say no more about it, my lord; I love thee far too well to be over-pained by what I know is but the natural free speech of a high-spirited youth. But what thinkest thou, my lord? Is it possible that some of our own galleys may be returning from a secret raid upon the infidel strongholds?"

"No, Gianelli, it is not; for my latest information, coming yesterday morning, was to the effect that all the smaller galleys had been recalled, and were safely housed in the Grand Harbour. Their crews have been given leave for the great festival, only the slaves remaining by them under guard. No; this must be a matter of far more serious import. Sound the summons to arms and light the beacon while I haste to the Council Chamber. Luigi, my lad, run thou to the church and pass the word for all my officers to leave their vigil around the altars at once."

Thus saying, Raimondo hastened away, noting as he did so, with grim satisfaction, the leaping flames from the summit of the tower being answered by twinkling points of light all over the black masses of rock that lay to the eastward, showing that already the alarm had been sounded in every fortress from Rabato to St. Elmo.

Within the great church were gathered most of the garrison not on guard. All the gorgeous details with which the church loves to welcome in the Day of days had been lovingly attended to. There was the stable, the manger, the waiting cattle, the worshipping Eastern kings. Mary, in her mighty meekness, cradled her Divine infant upon her virgin bosom; Joseph, careworn and travel-stained, looked upon her with a solemn wonder in his honest eyes; while around and above jewels and gold and silver flashed in all their splendour by the light of a thousand tall candles. A thin blue haze of incense gave all things an air of mystery, and the perfume laid upon the senses a strange exaltation.

Suddenly there was a hush, a bated breathing by all, as the archbishop, in his marvellous vesture, arose from his knees and spoke.

" My brethren, from the preparation for the advent of the day whereon we celebrate the human birth of our Divine Redeemer, ye are called to do battle with His most terrible foes. My lord the Commandant of Gozo informs me that the galleys of the infidel are approaching us, in the hope, he supposes, of finding us all so enwrapped in our devotions that he will have of us an easy prey. My children, let him learn that we watch as well as pray. Show him once again that we count it our most precious privilege to pour out our blood in defence of our most Holy Faith, that we look upon our dying in this high endeavour to protect Christendom from the infidel as the most glorious fate that could befall us. Receive at my hands the blessing of the Most High. Go forth, each of you, fully equipped, not merely with material armour, but with the knowledge that upon you rests the special benevolence of God the Son, under whose banner you fight."

All heads bowed for an instant as the solemn benediction was spoken, then with a clanging of armour and a clashing of swords the great assembly sprang to their feet and departed each to his post of honour and utmost danger.

It was high time. Already those snaky galleys laden with men of the most bloodthirsty type, fired with fanaticism and lured by the promises of an endless paradise of sensual delight, had crept into the many little sheltered bays of the island, and were vomiting forth their terrible crews.

Already a quick ear might catch the varied cries in strange tongues floating upward through the silken smoothness of the night air, predominant over them all the oft-reiterated shout of "Allah!" Already the keen-sighted watchers could discern dark-moving masses of men, from the midst of which came an occasional silvery gleam as the molten flood of moonlight touched a spear-tip or sword-blade.

Onward they came, marvelling doubtless at the ease with which they had been permitted thus to assemble upon the enemy's territory, and for the most part utterly unconscious of the reception that awaited them at the goal of their hot desire. Suddenly there arose from the town beneath the citadel walls a long-drawn cry of anguish. The careless ones who had not fled for shelter to the common refuge had been found by the invader, and were being ruthlessly slaughtered. Their cries made bearded lips tighten, nervous hands grasp more firmly their weapons, and all hearts above to beat higher and more resolute to repay these murderers in full tale when the opportunity so to do should arrive.

Out from the highest belfry of the cathedral pealed the twelve strokes of the midnight hour, and before their sound had died away there uprose from the citadel a mighty chorus of welcome to Christmas Day—Gloria in excelsis Deo.

Before it had ended the first of the invaders had reached the walls, and, mad with fanatic fury and lust of blood, were swarming like ants up its steep sides, clinging with desperate tenacity to every plant and projection that afforded the slightest foot or hand hold. Regardless of the avalanche of stones hurtling down upon them, unheeding the dreadful rain of boiling lead and scalding water, they came indomitably on. Their numbers seemed incalculable, their courage, buttressed by unreasoning faith, invincible. But they were met at every point by men whose hearts were as well fortified as their own, and who possessed, besides the inestimable advantage of discipline and long training in warlike matters, the invaluable position of being defenders.

Downwards by hundreds the invaders were hurled, their spurting blood staining the pure whiteness of the walls with long black-red smears, which the shuddering moonlight revealed in all their ghastliness. Already the reinforcements were compelled to mount upon mounds of dead to get their first hold; the street of the little town, but lately so peaceful, was defiled by heaps upon heaps of frightfully mangled corpses, representatives of all the savage tribes of Northern Africa. "For Mary and her Son"—the war-cry of the night—rang out clearly and defiantly, soaring high above the shrill yells of the savages and the monotonous howl of "Allahhu!"

So far all seemed to have gone well, until suddenly a shudder ran through the whole garrison as the news spread that by the treachery of a vile renegade the secret subterranean passage into the citadel from a point near the shore had been laid open, and that already a torrent of the infidels were pouring through it.

The commandant, who had approved himself on this occasion a man of the very highest ability and courage, no sooner heard this awful news than, summoning around him his most trusted knights, he placed himself at their head and hurried to the spot. And the first sight that met his eyes was the beautiful form of her he loved borne high upon the shoulders of a gigantic heathen in black armour who, apparently feeling her weight not at all, was brandishing a huge scimitar in his right hand, and yelling words of encouragement in some guttural Eastern tongue to his followers.

Forgetful of all else, his brain on fire at the sight, Raimondo sprang ahead of his men, his keen blade whirling round his head. By the sheer fury of his onslaught he burst through the grim ranks of the heathen, and smiting with all his vigour at the head of the captor of his beloved one, slew, not his foe, alas! but her for whom he would gladly have given his life. The terrible blow cleft her fair body almost in twain, as the heathen giant held her before himself shieldwise to meet it. The distracted commandant's first impulse was to fling himself upon that beloved corpse and accompany her spirit to heaven, but that thought was conquered by the knowledge of his high responsibilities. And with a shout of "Mary" he recovered his blade, sprang at the foul Paynim's throat, and cleft him in sunder through gorget and vant brace.

All the followers of the young knight were fired in like manner, and like avenging angels before whom no mere flesh and blood could possibly stand for a moment, they hewed their gory way through the masses of the heathen, halting not until the last of their foes had gasped out into the darkness of eternal night his guilty soul.

And as it was in the heart of the citadel, so it had been on the battlements, not one heathen had survived his footing upon those sacred walls. And as it appeared that the whole force had devoted themselves to death in default of victory there was not one left alive.

So that the great fight ceased with the death of the last invader, and the blessed sun rose upon a scene of carnage such as even these blood-stained islands had never before witnessed. But in the hour of victory there arose a great cry. Raimondo the gallant commandant was missing. His devoted friends rushed hither and thither in the pearly light of the new day, seeking him where the heaps of dead lay thickest, but for a long time their search was in vain. At last he was found before the manger in the church, lying with face hidden on the bosom of his beloved, whose cold mangled body was clutched in an unreleasable embrace. He was to all human sight unwounded, but even the most ignorant and callous of his command knew that he had died of a broken heart.

Yet it must be believed that he went gladly to join his beloved one, knowing full well that as a gallant soldier of the Cross he had nobly sustained his high part, and only when his duty was done had he permitted himself to sink into eternal rest in the arms of her whom he had so fondly loved.

DEEP-SEA FISH

AMONG shore-dwellers generally there obtains an idea that the ocean, except in the immediate vicinity of land, is an awful solitude, its vast emptiness closely akin to the spaces above. But while admitting fully that there is little room for wonder at such a speculative opinion, it must be said that nothing could well be farther from the truth. Indeed, we may even go beyond that statement, and declare that the fruitful earth, with its unimaginable variety and innumerable hosts of living things, is, when compared to the densely populated world of waters, but a sparsely peopled desert. A little knowledge of the conditions existing at great depths, may well make us doubt whether any forms of life exist able to endure the incalculable pressure of the superincumbent sea; but leaving all the tremendous area of the ocean bed below 200 fathoms out of the question, there still remains ample room and verge enough for the justification of the statement just made.

Nothing has ever excited the wonder and admiration of naturalists more than this prodigious population of the sea—these unthinkable myriads of hungry things which are shut up to the necessity of preying upon each other since other forms of food do not exist.

The mind recoils dismayed from a contemplation of their countlessness, as it does from the thought of timelessness or the extent of the stellar spaces, shrinkingly admitting its limitations and seeking relief in some subject that is within its grasp. But without touching upon the lower forms of life peopling the sea, and so escaping the burden of thought which the slightest consideration of their myriads entail, it is possible to note, without weariness, how, all over the waste spaces of a remote and unhearing ocean, fish of noble proportions and varying degrees of edibility disport themselves, breeding none know where, and revealing their beauties to the passing seafarer as they gather companionably around his solitary keel. Excluding all the varied species of mammals that form such an immense portion of the sea-folk, it may roughly be said that the majority of deep-sea fish belong to the mackerel family, or *Scombridæ*. They possess, in an exaggerated form, all the characteristics of that well-known edible fish that occasionally gluts our markets and gladdens the hearts of our fishermen.

One of the least numerous, but from his size and prowess probably the monarch of all sea *fish*, is the sword-fish, *Xiphias*. This elegant fish attains an enormous size, specimens having been caught weighing over a quarter of a ton; but owing to the incomparable grace of its form, its speed and agility are beyond belief. It is often—in fact, generally—confounded with the "saw-fish," a species of shark; the principal reason of this confusion being the great number of "saws" or beaks of the latter, which are to be found in homes about the country. Yet between the sword of the Xiphias and the "saw" of the *Pristiophoridæ* there is about as much similarity as there is between the assegai of a Zulu and the waddy of a black-fellow. The one weapon is a slender, finely pointed shaft of the hardest bone, an extended process of the skull, about two feet long in a large specimen. Impelled by the astounding vigour of the lithe monster behind it, this tremendous weapon has been proved capable of penetrating the massive oaken timbers of a ship, and a specimen may be seen in the Museum of Natural History at South Kensington, at this present time, transfixing a section of ship's timber several inches in thickness. The "saw," on the other hand, is, like all the rest of a shark's skeleton, composed of cartilage, besides being terminated at the tip by a broad, almost snout-like end. Unlike the round lance of the sword-fish, the "saw" has a flat blade set on both sides with sharp teeth with considerable gaps between them. As its name and shape would imply, it is used saw-wise, principally for disembowelling fish, for upon such soft food the saw-fish is compelled to feed owing to the shape of his mouth and the insignificance of his teeth. Thus it will be seen that apart from the radical differences between the two creatures, nothing being really in common between them, except that they are both fish, there is really no comparison possible between "saw" and "sword." Fortunately for the less warlike inhabitants of the deep sea, sword-fish are not numerous, there are none to cope with them or keep their numbers down if they were prolific. Sometimes—strange companionship—they join forces with the killer whale and the thresher shark in an attack upon one of the larger whales, only avoiding instinctively that monarch of the boundless main, the cachalot.

Next in size and importance among deep-sea fish, excluding sharks, about which I have said so much elsewhere that I do not propose dealing with them here, is the albacore, tunny or tuña, all of which are sub-varieties of, or local names for the same huge mackerel. They abound in every tropical sea, and are also found in certain favourable waters, such as the Mediterranean and Pacific coast of America. Like the sword-fish their habits of breeding are unknown, since they have their home in the solitudes of the ocean. But they are one of the fish most frequently met with by seafarers, as, like several others of the same great family, they are fond of following a ship. A sailing ship that is, for the throb of the propeller, apart from the speed of the vessel, is effectual in preventing their attendance upon steamers, so that passengers by steamships have few opportunities of observing them. But in sailing vessels, gliding placidly along under the easy pressure of gentle breezes, or lying quietly waiting for the friendly wind, ample scope is given for study of their every-day life. Very occasionally too, some seaman, more skilful or enterprising than his fellows, will succeed in catching one by trolling a piece of white rag or a polished spoon with a powerful hook attached. Yet such is the vigour and so great is the size of these huge mackerel, some attaining a length of six feet and a weight of five hundred pounds, that their capture from a ship is infrequent.

In size, beauty, and importance, the "dolphin" easily claims the next place to the albacore. But an unaccountable confusion has gathered around this splendid fish on account of his popular name. The dolphin of mythological sculpture bears no resemblance either to the popularly named dolphin of the seaman and the poets, or the scientifically named dolphin of the natural histories, which is a mammal, and identical with the porpoise. One thing is certain, that no sailor will ever speak of the porpoise as a dolphin, or call *Coryphena hippuris* anything else. Of this lovely denizen of the deep sea, it is difficult to speak soberly. Even the dullest of men wax enthusiastic over its glories, feeling sure that none of all beautiful created things can approach it for splendour of array. I have often tried to distinguish its different hues, watching it long and earnestly as it basked alongside in the limpid blue environment of its home. But my efforts have always been in vain, since every turn of its elegant form revealed some new combination of dazzling tints blending and brightening in such radiant loveliness that any classification of their shades was impossible. Then a swift wave of the wide forked tail-fin would send the lithe body all a-quiver in a new direction, where, catching a stray sunbeam it would blaze like burnished silver reflecting the golden gleam, and the overtaxed eye must needs turn away for relief. Then suddenly the marvellous creature would spring into activity, launching itself in long vibrant leaps through the air after its prey, a fleeting school of flying fish, that with all their winged speed could not escape the lethal jaws of their splendid pursuer. Having read of the wondrously changing colours of a dying dolphin I watched with great eagerness the first one that ever I saw caught. Great was my disappointment and resentment against those who had perpetrated and perpetuated such a fable. Compared with the glory of the living creature, the fading hues of its vesture when dying were as lead is to gold. Only by most careful watching was it possible to distinguish the changing colour schemes, faint and dim, as if with departing vitality they too were compelled to fade and die away into darkness. On the utilitarian side too the dolphin is beloved by the sailor, for its flesh is whiter and more sapid than that of any other deep-sea fish except the flying fish, which are too small and too infrequently got hold of on board ship to be taken much account of for food. Yet, in spite of its wondrous speed, the dolphin, when congregated in considerable numbers, often falls a prey to the giant albacore, which hurls itself into their midst, clashing its great jaws and destroying many more than it devours.

Commonest of all deep-water fish, but only found in the warm waters of the tropical seas or fairly close to their northern or southern limits is the bonito, another member of the mackerel family, but much inferior in size to the albacore. "Bonito" is a Spanish diminutive equivalent to beautiful, and beautiful the bonito certainly is, although compared with the dazzling glory of the dolphin it looks quite homely. It is a most sociable fish, keeping company with a slow-moving sailing ship for days together, and quite easily caught with a hook to which a morsel of white rag is fastened to simulate a flying fish. For its size —the largest I have ever seen being less than thirty pounds weight—its strength is incredible, as is also the quantity of warm blood it contains. On account of these two characteristics, it is usual when fishing for bonito off the end of the jibboom to take out a sack and secure it to the jib-guys with its mouth gaping wide so that the newly caught fish may be promptly dropped therein to kick and bleed in safety and cleanliness. My first bonito entailed upon me considerable discomfort. I was a lad of fourteen, and had stolen out unobserved to fish with the mate's line, which he had left coiled on the boom. I hooked a large fish which, after a struggle, I succeeded in hauling up until I embraced him tightly with both arms. His vibrations actually shook the ship, and they continued until my whole body was quite benumbed, and I could not feel that a large patch of skin was chafed off my breast where I hugged my prize to me. And not only was I literally drenched with the fish's blood, but the flying jib, which happened to be furled on the boom, was in a truly shocking condition likewise. Nevertheless I rejoice to think that I held on to my fish and successfully bore him inboard to the cook, although I shook so with excitement and fatigue that I could scarcely keep my feet. Nor was my triumph much discounted by the complete rope's-ending I got the same evening, when upon hoisting the jib, its filthy condition was made manifest, and at once rightly attributed to me. The flesh of the bonito is coarse and dark, tough, and with little flavour. But still it comes as a welcome change to the worse than pauper dietary served out to crews of sailing ships generally, while the ease with which the fish may be caught, and the frequency of its companionship make it one of the most appreciated by seamen of all the denizens of the deep sea. One other virtue it possesses which makes it even more of a favourite than the dolphin, in spite of all the latter's superior palatability—it is never poisonous, unless after exposure to the rays of the moon. Dolphin have often been known to inflict severe suffering upon those eating their flesh, and no one who has ever experienced the enormously swollen head and agonizing pain consequent upon a meal off a poisonous dolphin is ever likely to think even of such a meal again without a shudder.

Another exceedingly pretty fish found in all deep tropical waters is the skip-jack. Smaller than the average bonito, yet in the details of its form closely resembling the great albacore, this elegant fish is less sociable than any of those mentioned in the preceding lines. Therefore, it is seldom caught, although in calm weather in the doldrums thousands may often be seen making the short vertical leaps into the air from which peculiar evolution they derive their trivial name. Both the bonito and the skip-jack are subject to being devoured by the albacore, whose voracity, swiftness, and size make him the terror of all his smaller congeners.

Occasionally after a few days' calm some delicate little fish, also belonging to the mackerel tribe—a species of caranx—will be seen huddling timorously around the rudder of a ship, as if in momentary dread of being devoured, a dread which is exceedingly well founded. The wonder is how any of them escape the ravenous jaws of the larger fish since they must find it well-nigh impossible to get away from such pursuers. They may be easily caught by a fine line and hook, and are very dainty eating. So, too, with the lovely little caranx familiar to all readers as the pilot fish. What peculiar instinct impels this beautiful tiny wanderer to attach himself to a shark is one of the mysteries of natural history, and the subject of much ignorant incredulity on the part of those who are often found ready to believe some of the most absurd travellers' yarns. But the pilot fish and its habits deserves a whole paper to itself—it is far too interesting a subject to be dealt with in the brief space now remaining. This, too, must be said of the flying-fish, one of the most wonderful of all the inhabitants of the deep seas, yet not so important to the seaman from a utilitarian point of view, since the occasional stragglers that do fly on board ship in their blind haste to escape from their countless foes beneath, usually fall to the lot of the ship's cat. Pussy is swift to learn that the sharp " smack " against the bulwarks at night, followed by a rapid rattling flutter means a most delicious meal for her, and smart indeed must be the sailor who finds the hapless fish before pussy has commenced her banquet.

One more important member of the true ocean fish must be mentioned, although it also frequents many shores, and is regularly caught for market on widely separated coasts. It is the barracouta or sea-pike, a large fish of delicious flavour, much resembling the hake of our own southern coasts. As I have caught this voracious fish all over the Indian Ocean, I have no hesitation at including it among deep-sea fish, although perhaps many well-informed seafarers would disagree with me. But if any seaman, still pursuing his vocation, doubts my statement, let him on his next East Indian voyage keep a line towing astern with a shred of crimson bunting hiding a stout hook at its end, as soon as the ship hauls to the nor'ard after rounding the Cape. And I can assure him that he will have several tasty messes of fish before she crosses the Line.

A MEDITERRANEAN MORNING

FROM my lofty roof-top here, in the highest part of Valetta, it is possible to take in at one sweeping glance a panorama that can hardly be surpassed for beauty and interest.

Intensely blue, the placid sea curdles around the rock bases of this wonderful little island as if it loved them. There are no rude breakers, no thundering, earth-shaking on-rushings of snowy-crested waves, leaping at the point of impact into filmy columns of spray.

Overhead the violet, star-sprinkled splendours of the night are just beginning to throb with returning light. One cannot say that the beams are definite, rather it is a palpitating glow that is just commencing to permeate the whole solemnity of the dome above, as does the first impulse of returning joy relax the lines of a saddened face. Far to the north may be seen a tiny cluster of fleecy cloudlets nestling together as if timid and lonely in that vast expanse of clear sky. But as the coming day touches them they put on garments of glory and beauty. Infinite gradations of colour, all tender, melt into one another upon their billowy surfaces until they spread and brighten, investing all their quadrant of the heavens with the likeness of the Gardens of Paradise.

At my feet lie the mighty edifices of stone that have, by the patient unending labour of this busy people, grown up through past ages, until now the mind reels in the attempt to sum up the account of that labour. A sea of white roofs, punctuated here and there with the dome and twin steeples of a church, the only breaks in the universal fashion of roof architecture. Away beneath, the white, clean streets—so strangely silent that the far-off tinkle of a goat-bell on the neck of some incoming band of milk-bearers strikes sharply athwart the pellucid atmosphere, like the fall of a piece of broken glass on to the pavement below. A few dim figures, recumbent upon the wide piazza of the Opera House, stir uneasily as the new light reaches them, and gape, and stretch, and fumble for cigarettes. A hurried, furtive-looking labourer glides past, his bare feet arousing no echo, but making him pass like a ghost. And then, from the direction of the Auberge de Castile, comes a solemn sound of music.

Its first faint strains rise upon the sweet morning calm like some lovely suggestion of prayer, but they are accompanied by an indefinite pulsation as of a beating at the walls of one's heart. More and more distinct the strains arise until recognizable as Chopin's " Marche Funèbre," and suddenly in the distance may be discerned, turning into the Strada Mezzodi, row after row of khaki-clad figures moving, oh, so slowly. Deadened and dull the drum-beats fall, more and more insistent wails that heart-rending music, and close in its rear appears the only spot of colour in the sad ranks, the brilliant folds of the Union Jack, hiding that small oblong coffer which holds all that was mortal of Private No. ——. Perhaps in life he was rather an insignificant unit of his regiment, at times a troublesome one, familiar with "pack-drill," "C.B.," and "clink," but now he has been brevetted, for a fleeting hour his fast-decaying remains are greeted with almost Royal honours.

Nearer and nearer creeps the solemn and stately procession, so slowly that the strain becomes intolerable. How do his comrades bear it? We who knew him not at all find ourselves choking, gasping in sympathy. While that silent escort is filing past we have traced his history, as it might be, his babyhood in some fair British village far away, his schooldays, his pranks, his mother's pride. Then his aspirations, what he would do when he was a man. Or perhaps he came from the slums of a great town, where, neglected, unwanted, he wallowed in the gutters, living like the sparrows, but less easily, and only surviving the rough treatment by dint of a harder grip of life than so many of his fellows. He knew no love, was coarse of speech, given to much drink and little repentance. But who thinks of that now? He is our dear brother departed, and his comrades follow him home, for the time at least solemnized at the presence among them of that awful power before whom all heads must bow.

Now, the so lately slumbering street has filled. Swarthy Maltese, Sicilians, Indians, men of all occupations, and of none, stand with bared heads and downcast faces as the King goes by. Oh that they would hasten on! But no. As if the procession would never end, it files through the Porta Reale, and at last is lost to view, although for long afterwards those muffled drums still beat upon the heart.

As if rejoicing at the passing of death, the street suddenly awakens. A very hubbub of conversation arises. Incoming crowds of workmen, striding along with that peculiarly easy gait common to the barefooted, jostle each other, and fling jest and repartee in guttural Maltese. Country vehicles, laden with all manner of queer produce, their bitless stallions swaying tinkling bells, encumber the way. Presently all make clear the crown of the road for the passage of a company of mounted infantry, which, in the almost blatant pride of fitness and workmanlike appearance, sallies forth into the country for exercise beyond the walls. But hark! martial strains are heard, a joyous blare of brass, a gleeful clatter of cymbal and drum. Hearts beat quicker, the foot taps, involuntarily acknowledging the power of music to elevate or depress the mind. Swinging into view strides a jaunty company, with heads erect and splendid swagger, and in their midst the plain imitation gun-carriage, which so short a time ago was burdened with the flag-enwrapped dead, is gaily trundled along. The moments of mourning are ended. We have hidden our dead out of our sight, and, with a spring of relief, are back again with the duties and pleasures of the living.

The great sun is soaring high, and already his beams are heating the stones so that we can hardly bear to touch them. The sea is rejoicing, for with the sun a little breeze has risen and covered that gorgeous expanse of sapphire with an infinity of wavelets, each crested with a spray of diamonds. A few barbaric-looking feluccas, their great pointed sails gleaming like snow against the blue sea, are creeping in from Gozo or Sicily, laden with fruit and fish for hungry Valetta. Far out, a long black stain against the clear sky betokens the presence of a huge steamship, homeward bound from the East, and avoiding these bright shores carefully because of stringent quarantine regulations. The very mention of the dread word "plague" is enough to cause a panic here, and if the most rigorous exclusion, at whatever cost, of vessels from infected ports, will keep us free, we will see to it that such exclusion is practised.

But what is this long, phantom-like vessel, her colour so blending with the blue of the sea, that she is difficult to distinguish? Occasionally from one of her three irregularly placed funnels there is a burst of black smoke, but otherwise she is as nearly invisible as careful painting can make her. Up there at the lofty look-out station the signalmen are discussing her with many epithets of dislike. They know her well, and all her kindred; know well, too, with what jealous, longing eyes those on board peer at the prosperous island, and with what accents of hatred they speak of the insolent, perfidious Briton, who dare to thus maintain a station of such strength, a naval base of such inestimable value, in the midst of what should be a Latin-governed sea.

But the treasure so coveted is not only guarded by all the deadly devices known to modern warfare, it is made doubly secure in that these swarthy speakers of a strange tongue know and love their rulers too well to exchange them, save at the cost of almost utter annihilation, for masters whom they equally well know and hate.

The morning freshness has gone. Valetta, never quite asleep at any time, only drowsing occasionally, is wide awake now. The bright waters of the harbour are alive with "disós," gondola-like boats, and small steamers. The hurrying thousands have swarmed into their appointed places in the dockyard, the never-finished stone-hewing is going briskly forward, the market is a howling vortex of clamour and heat and excitement; and in its niche of living rock the tabernacle of him who yesterday was Private ——, of her Majesty's army, lies quietly oblivious of it all.

ABNER'S TRAGEDY

OUR quaint little Guamese was vociferously cheered at the close of his yarn, although in some parts it had been most difficult to follow, from the bewildering compound of dialects it was delivered in. Usually that does not trouble whalers' crews, much accustomed as they are to the very strangest distortions of the adaptable English language. "The next gentleman to oblige" was, to my utter amazement, Abner Cushing, the child of calamity from Vermont, who had been hung up by the thumbs and flogged on the outward passage. Up till then we had all looked upon him as being at least "half a shingle short," not to say downright loony, but that impression now received a severe shock. In a cultivated diction, totally unlike the half-intelligible drawl hitherto affected by him, he related the following story.

"Well, boys, I dare say you have often wondered what could have brought me here. Perhaps (which, come to think of it, is more likely) you haven't troubled your heads about me at all, although even the meanest of us like to think that we fill some corner in our fellow's mind. But if you have wondered, it could not be considered surprising. For I'm a landsman if ever there was one, a farmer, who, after even such a drilling as I've gone through this voyage, still feels, and doubtless looks, as awkward on board as any cow. My story is not a very long one, perhaps hardly worth the telling to anybody but myself, but it will be a change from whaling 'shop' anyhow, so here goes.

"My father owned a big farm in the old Green Mountain state, on which I grew up, an only son, but never unduly pampered or spoiled by the good old man. No; both he and mother, though fond of me as it was possible to be, strove to do me justice by training me up and not allowing me to sprout anyhow like a jimpson weed to do as I darn pleased with myself when and how I liked. They were careful to keep me out of temptation too, as far as they were able, which wasn't so difficult, seeing our nearest neighbour was five miles away, and never a drop of liquor stronger than cider ever came within a day's journey of home. So I suppose I passed as a pretty good boy; at least there were no complaints.

"One day, when I was about fifteen years old, father drove into the village some ten miles off on business, and when he came back he had a little golden-haired girl with him about twelve years old. A pale, old-fashioned little slip she was, as staid as a grandmother, and dressed in deep black. When I opened the gate for the waggon, father said, 'This is your cousin Cicely, Abner, she's an orphan, an' I cal'late to raise her.' That was all our introduction, and I, like the unlicked cub I must have been, only said, 'that so, father,' staring at the timid little creature so critically, that her pale face flushed rosy red under my raw gaze. I helped her out (light as a bird she was), and showed her into the house, where mother took her right to her heart on the spot. From that on she melted into the home life as if she had always been part of it, a quiet patient helper that made mother's life a very easy one. God knows it had been hard enough. Many little attentions and comforts unknown before, grew to be a part of our daily routine, but if I noticed them at all (and I hardly think I did then), I took them as a matter of course, nor ever gave sign that I appreciated the thoughtful care that provided them. So the years slithered past uneventfully till I was twenty-one, when dad fell sick. Within a week he was dead. It was a terrible stroke to mother and Cicely, but neither of them were given to much show of feeling (I reckon there was scant encouragement), and things went on much as usual. I didn't seem to feel it very much—didn't seem to feel anything much in those days, except mad with my folks when everything wasn't just as I wanted it. Dad's affairs were all shipshape. He left mother fairly well off, and Cicely just enough to live on in case of necessity, while I came in for everything else, which meant an income of 1500 dollars a year if I chose to realize and not work any more. Being now, however, fairly wound up like any other machine, and warranted to go right on in the same jog, I had no thought of change. Don't suppose I ever should have had; but— Excuse me, boys, I'm a bit husky, and there's something in my eye. All right now.

"That summer we had boarders from Boston, well-to-do city folks pining for a change of air and scene, who offered a big price for such accommodation as we could give them for a couple of months.

"I drove down to the village to meet them with the best waggon, and found them waiting for me at Squire Pickering's house—two elderly ladies and a young one. Boys, I can't begin to describe that young lady to you; all I know is, that the first time our eyes met, I felt kinder as I guess Eve must have done when she eat the apple, only more so. All my old life that I had been well contented with came up before me and looked just unbearable. I felt awkward, and rough, and ugly; my new store clothes felt as if they'd been hewn out of deals, my head burned like a furnace, and my hands and feet were numb cold. When, in answer to some trifling question put to me by one of the old ladies, I said a few words, they sounded 'way off down a long tunnel, and as if I had nothing to do with them. Worst of all, I couldn't keep my foolish eyes off that young lady, do what I would. How I drove the waggon home I don't know. I suppose the machine was geared up so well, it ran of its own accord—didn't want any thinking done. For I was thinking of anything in the wide world but my duty. I was a soldier, a statesman, a millionaire by turns, but only that I might win for my own that wonderful creature that had come like an unpredicted comet into my quiet sky.

"Now, don't you think I'm going to trouble you with my love-making. I'd had no experience, so I dare say it was pretty original, but the only thing I can remember about it is that I had neither eyes nor ears for anything or anybody else but Agatha Deerham (that was her name), and that I neglected everything for her. She took my worship as a matter of course, calmly, royally, unconsciously; but if she smiled on me, I was crazy with gladness.

"Meanwhile my behaviour put mother and Cicely about no end. But for their industry and forethought, things would have been in a pretty muddle, for I was worse than useless to them; spent most of my time mooning about like the brainsick fool I was, building castles in Spain, or trying to invent something that would please the woman I worshipped. Oh, but I was blind; a poor blind fool. Looking back now, I know I must have been mad as well as blind. Agatha saw immediately upon coming into my home what I had never seen in all those long years—that Cicely—quiet, patient little Cicely—loved me with her whole heart, and would have died to serve me. So, with that refinement of cruelty that some women can show, she deliberately set herself, not to infatuate me more—that was impossible—but to show Cicely that she, the new-comer, while not valuing my love at a pin, could play with it, prove it, trifle with it as she listed.

"Sometimes her treatment nearly drove me frantic with rage, but a tender glance from her wonderful eyes brought me fawning to her feet again directly. Great heaven, how she made me suffer! I wonder I didn't go really mad, I was in such a tumult of conflicting passions continually.

"The time drew near for them to return to their city home. Now, although Agatha had tacitly accepted all my attentions, nothing definite had yet passed between us, but the announcement of her imminent departure brought matters to a climax. Seizing the first opportunity of being alone with her, I declared my passion in a frenzy of wild words, offered her my hand, and swore that if she refused me I would do—I hardly remember what; but, among other things, certainly kill her, and then myself. She smiled pityingly upon me, and quietly said, 'What about Cicely?' Bewildered at her question, so little had any thought of Cicely in connection with love entered my head, I stared for a few moments blankly at the beautiful and maliciously smiling face before me, muttering at last, 'Whatever do you mean?'

"With a ringing laugh, she said, 'Can it be possible that you are unaware how your cousin worships you?' Black shame upon me, I was not content with scornfully repudiating the possibility of such a thing, but poured all the bitter contempt I could give utterance to upon the poor girl, whose only fault was love of me. While thus basely engaged, I saw Agatha change colour, and turning, found Cicely behind me, trembling and livid as one who had received a mortal wound. Shame, anger, and passion for Agatha kept me speechless as she recovered herself and silently glided away.

"But I must hurry up if I'm not going to be tedious. Encouraged by Agatha, I sold the farm, sending mother and Cicely adrift to live upon their little means, and, gathering all together, took my departure for Boston. Arrangements for our marriage were hurried on at my request, not so swiftly, however, but that news reached me on my wedding morning of mother's death. For a moment I was staggered, even the peculiar thing which served me for a heart felt a pang, but only in passing. What had become of Cicely I never troubled enough to think, much less to inquire.

"Some weeks of delirious gaiety followed, during which I drank to the full from the cup of my desires. Our lives were a whirl of what, for want of a better word, I suppose I must call enjoyment; at any rate, we did and had whatever we had a mind to, nor ever stopped to think of the sequel. We had no home, never waited to provide one, but lived at a smart hotel at a rate that would have killed my father to think of.

"One night at the theatre I slipped on the marble staircase, fell to the bottom a tangle of limbs, and was taken up with a broken leg, right arm, and collar bone. At some one's suggestion I was removed to hospital. There, but for the ministrations of the nurses and surgeons, I was left alone, not a single one of my acquaintances coming near me. But what worried me was my wife's neglect. What could have become of her? Where was she? These ceaselessly repeated and unanswered questions, coupled with my utter helplessness, drove me into a brain fever, in which I lost touch with the world for six weeks.

"I awoke one morning, a wan shade of my old

self, but able to think again (would to God I never had). I was informed that no one had been to inquire after me during my long delirium, and this sombre fact stood up before me like a barrier never to be passed, reared between me and any hope in life. But, in spite of the drawbacks, I got better, got well, came out into the world again. I was homeless, friendless, penniless. The proprietor of the hotel where I had stayed with my wife informed me that she had left in company with a gentleman, with whom she seemed so intimate that he thought it must be some relative, but as he spoke, I read the truth in his eyes. He took pity on my forlorn condition and gave me a little money, enough to keep me alive for a week or two, but strongly advised me to go back to my native village and stay there. I was too broken to resent the idea, but in my own mind there was a formless plan of operations insisting upon being carried out.

"Husbanding my little stock of money with the utmost care, and barely spending sufficient to support life, I began a search for my wife. Little by little I learnt the ghastly sordid truth. Virtue, honour, or probity, had never been known to her, and my accident only gave her an opportunity that she had been longing for. Why she had married me was a mystery. Perhaps she sought a new sensation, and didn't find it.

"Well, I tracked her and her various companions, until after about three months I lost all traces in New York. Do what I would, no more news of her could be obtained. But I had grown very patient in my search, though hardly knowing why I sought. My purpose was as hazy as my plan had been. So, from day to day I plodded through such small jobs as I could find, never losing sight for an hour of my one object in life.

"I must have been in New York quite six months, when I was one day trudging along Bleecker Street on an errand for somebody, and there met me face to face my cousin Cicely. I did not know her, but she recognized me instantly, and I saw in her sweet face such a look of sympathy and loving compassion that, broken-hearted, I covered my face and cried like a child. 'Hush,' she said, 'you will be molested,' and, putting her arm through mine, she led me some distance to a dilapidated house, the door of which she opened with a key. Showing me into a tidy little room, she bade me sit down while she got me a cup of coffee, refusing to enter into conversation until I was a bit refreshed. Then, bit by bit, I learned that she had heard of my desertion by Agatha, and had formed a resolution to find her and bring her back to me if possible. She did find her, but was repulsed by her with a perfect fury of scorn, and told to go and find me and keep me, since such a worthless article as I was not likely to be useful to any other person on earth. Such a reception would have daunted most women; but I think Cicely was more than woman, or else how could she do as she did.

"Driven from my wife's presence, she never lost sight of her, feeling sure that her opportunity would soon come. It came very suddenly. In the midst of her flaunting, vicious round of gaiety small-pox seized her, and as she had left me, so she was left, but not even in an hospital. Cicely found her alone, raving, tearing at her flesh in agony, with no one to help or pity. It was the opportunity she had sought, and hour by hour she wrestled with death and hell for that miserable woman. It was a long fight, but she was victorious, and although a sorrowful gap was made in her small stock of money, she was grateful and content.

"Agatha was a wreck. Utterly hideous to look upon, with memory like a tiger tearing at her heart, she yet had not the courage to die, or, doubtless, she would quickly have ended all her woes. Quietly, unobtrusively, constantly, Cicely waited on her, worked for her, and at last had succeeded in bringing us together. The knowledge that she whom I had sought so long was in the same house took away my breath. As soon as I recovered myself a bit, Cicely went to prepare her for meeting me. Unknown to Cicely, I followed, and almost immediately after she entered the room where my wife lay, I presented myself at the door. Looking past the woman who had preserved her miserable life, she saw my face. Then, with a horrible cry, unlike anything human, she sprang at my poor cousin like a jaguar, tearing, shrieking. If I dwell any longer on that nightmare I shall go mad myself. I did what I could, and bear the marks of that encounter for life, but I could not save Cicely's life.

"The room filled with people, and the maniac was secured. After I had given my evidence on the inquiry, I slunk away, too mean to live, afraid to die. A recruiter secured me for this ship, and here I am, but I know that my useless life is nearly over. The world will be well rid of me."

When he stopped talking, there was a dead silence for a few minutes. Such a yarn was unusual among whalemen, and they hardly knew how to take it. But the oldest veteran of the party dispelled the uneasy feeling by calling for a song, and volunteering one himself, just to keep things going. In the queerest nasal twang imaginable he thundered out some twenty verses of doggerel concerning the deeds of Admiral Semmes of the Alabama, with a different tune to each verse. It was uproariously received, but story-telling held the field, and another yarn was demanded.

LOST AND FOUND

A Sea Amendment

He stood alone on the little pier, a pathetic figure in his loneliness—a boy without a home or a friend in the world. There was only one thought dominating his mind, the purely animal desire for sustenance, for his bodily needs lay heavily upon him. Yet it never occurred to him to ask for food—employment for which he should be paid such scanty wages as would supply his bare needs was all he thought of; for, in spite of years of semi-starvation, he had never yet eaten bread that he had not worked for—the thought of doing so had never shaped itself in his mind. But he was now very hungry, and as he watched the vigorous preparation for departure in full swing on board the smart rakish-looking fishing schooner near him, he felt an intense longing to be one of the toilers on her decks, with a right to obey the call presently to a well-earned meal. Whether by any strange thought-transference his craving became known to the bronzed skipper of the Rufus B. or not, who shall say? Sufficient to record that on a sudden that stalwart man lifted his head, and looking steadily at the lonely lad, he said, "Wantin' a berth, sonny?" Although, if his thoughts could have been formulated, such a question was the one of all others he would have desired to hear, the lad was so taken aback by the realization of his most fervent hopes that for several seconds he could return no answer, but sat endeavouring to moisten his lips and vainly seeking in his bewildered mind for words with which to reply. Another sharp query, " Air ye deef?" brought his wits to a focus, and he replied humbly—

" Yes, sir!"

" Well, whar's yer traps, then?" queried the skipper; " 'kaze we're boun' ter git away this tide, so it's naow er never, ef you're comin'."

Before answering, the boy suddenly gathered himself up, and sprang in two bounds from his position on the quay to the side of the skipper. As soon as he reached him, he said, in rapid disjointed sentences—

" I've got no close. Ner no boardin' house. Ner yet a cent in the world. But I ben to sea for nearly three year, an' ther ain't much to a ship thet I don' know. I never ben in a schooner afore, but ef you'll take me, Cap'n, I'll show you I'm wuth a boy's wages, anyhow."

As he spoke the skipper looked down indulgently at him, chewing meditatively the while, but as soon as he had finished, the " old man " jerked out—

" All right. Hook on ter onct, then;" and almost in the same breath, but with an astonishing increase of sound, " Naow, then, caest off thet guess warp forrard there, 'n run the jib up. Come, git a move on ye—anybody'd think you didn't calk'late on leavin' Gloster never no more."

Cheery " Ay, ay, cap's," resounded from the willing crowd as they obeyed, and in ten minutes the Rufus B. was gliding away seawards to the musical rattle of the patent blocks and the harmonious cries of the men as they hoisted the sails to the small breeze that was stealing off the land.

. The grey mist of early morning was slowly melting off the picturesque outline of the Massachusetts shore as they departed, and over the smooth sea before them fantastic wreaths and curls of fog hung about like the reek of some vast invisible fire far away. It was cold, too, with a clammy chill that struck through the threadbare suit of jeans worn by the new lad, and made him exert himself vigorously to keep his blood in circulation. So hearty were his efforts that the mixed company of men by whom he was surrounded noted them approvingly; and although to a novice their occasional remarks would have sounded harsh and brutal, he felt mightily cheered by them, for his experienced ear immediately recognized the welcome fact that his abilities were being appreciated at their full value. And when, in answer to the skipper's order of " Loose thet gaff taupsle," addressed to no one in particular, he sprang up the main rigging like a monkey and cast off the gaskets, sending down the tack on the right side, and shaking out the sail in a seamanlike fashion, he distinctly heard the skipper remark to the chap at the wheel, " Looks 'sif we'd struck a useful nipper at last, Jake," the words were heady as a drink of whisky. Disdaining the ratlines, he slid down the weather backstays like a flash and dropped lightly on deck, his cheek flushed and his eye sparkling, all his woeful loneliness forgotten in his present joy of finding his services appreciated. But the grinning darky cook just then put his head outside his caboose door and shouted "Brekfuss." With old habit strong upon him, the boy bounded forrard to fetch the food into the fo'c'sle, but to his bewilderment, and the darky's boisterous delight, he found that in his new craft quite a different order of things prevailed. Here all hands messed like Christians at one common table in the cabin, waited upon by the cook, and eating the same food; and though they looked rough and piratical enough, all behaved themselves decently—in strong contrast to the foul behaviour our hero had so often witnessed in the grimy fo'c'sles of merchant ships. All this touched him, even though he was so ravenously hungry that his senses seemed merged in the purely physical satisfaction of getting filled with good food. At last, during a lull in the conversation, which, as might be expected, was mostly upon their prospects of striking a good run of cod at an early date, the skipper suddenly looked straight at the boy, and said—

"Wut djer say yer name wuz, young feller?"

"Tom Burt, sir," he answered promptly, although he was tempted to say that he hadn't yet been asked his name at all.

"Wall, then, Tom Burt," replied the skipper, "yew shape 's well 's yew've begun, and I'm dog-goned ef yew won't have no eend of a blame good time. Th' only kind er critter we kain't find no sort er use fer in a Banker 's a loafer. We do all our bummin' w'en we git ashore, 'n in bad weather; other times everybody's got ter git up an' hustle fer all they're wuth."

Tom looked up with a pleasant smile, feeling quite at his ease among men who could talk to him as if he, too, were a human being and not a homeless cur. He didn't make any resolves to do his level best—he would do that anyhow—but his heart beat high with satisfaction at his treatment, and he would have kept his end up with any man on board to the utmost ounce of his strength. But meanwhile they had drawn clear of the land, and behind them dropped a curtain of fog hiding it completely from view. To a fresh easterly breeze which had sprung up, the graceful vessel was heading north-east for the Grand Banks, gliding through the long, sullen swell like some great, lithe greyhound, and yet looking up almost in the wind's eye. In spite of the breeze, the towering banks of fog gradually drew closer and closer around them until they were entirely enveloped therein, as if wrapped in an impenetrable veil which shut out all the world beside. The ancient tin horn emitted its harsh discords, which seemed to rebound from the white wall round about them, and in very deed could only have been heard a ship's length or so away. And presently, out of the encircling mantle of vapour, there came a roar as of some unimaginable monster wrathfully seeking its prey, the strident sounds tearing their way through the dense whiteness with a truly terrific clamour. All hands stood peering anxiously out over the waste for the first sight of the oncoming terror, until, with a rush that made the schooner leap and stagger, a huge, indefinite blackness sped past, its grim mass towering high above the tiny craft. The danger over, muttered comments passed from mouth to mouth as to the careless, reckless fashion in which these leviathans were driven through the thick gloom of those crowded waters in utter disregard of the helpless toilers of the sea. Then, to the intense relief of all hands, the fog began to melt away, and by nightfall all trace of it was gone. In its stead the great blue dome of the heavens, besprinkled with a myriad glittering stars, shut them in; while the keen, eager breeze sent the dancing schooner northward at a great rate to her destined fishing-ground, the huge plateau in the Atlantic, off Newfoundland, that the codfish loves.

But it was written that they should never reach the Virgin. The bright, clear weather gave way to a greasy, filmy sky, accompanied by a mournful, sighing wail in the wind that sent a feeling of despondency through the least experienced of the fishermen, and told the more seasoned hands that a day of wrath was fast approaching, better than the most delicately adjusted barometer would have done. When about sixty miles from the Banks the gale burst upon the staunch little craft in all its fury, testing her powers to the utmost as, under a tiny square of canvas in the main rigging, she met and coquetted with the gather-

A huge sailing-ship crushed her into matchwood.

ing immensities of the Atlantic waves. No doubt she would have easily weathered that gale, as she had done so many others, but that at midnight, during its fiercest fury, there came blundering along a huge four-masted sailing-ship running under topsails and foresail that, like some blind and drunken giant staggered out of the gloom and fell upon the gallant little schooner, crushing her into matchwood beneath that ruthless iron stem, and passing on unheeding the awful destruction she had dealt out to the brave little company of men. It was all so sudden that the agony of suspense was mercifully spared them, but out of the weltering vortex which swallowed up the Rufus B. only two persons emerged alive—Tom Burt and Jem the cook. By a miracle they both clung to the same piece of flotsam—one of the "dorys" or flat little boats used by the Bankers to lay out their long lines when on the Banks. Of course she was bottom up, and, but for the lifeline which the forethought of the poor skipper had caused to be secured to the gunwale of every one of his dorys, they could not have kept hold of her for an hour. As it was, before they were able to get her righted in that tumultuous sea, they were almost at their last gasp. But they did succeed in getting her right way up at last, and, crouching low in her flat bottom, they dumbly awaited whatever Fate had in store for them.

A mere fragment in the wide waste, they clung desperately to life through the slowly creeping hours while the storm passed away, the sky cleared, and the sea went down. The friendly sun came out in his strength and warmed their thin blood. But his beams did more: they revealed at no great distance the shape of a ship that to the benumbed fancies of the two waifs seemed to behave in most erratic fashion. For now she would head toward them, again she would slowly turn as if upon an axis until she presented her stern in their direction, but never for five minutes did she keep the same course. Dimly they wondered what manner of ship she might be, with a sort of impartial curiosity, since they were past the period of struggle. Well for them that it was so, for otherwise their agonies must have been trebled by the sight of rescue apparently so near and yet impossible of attainment. So they just sat listlessly in their empty shell gazing with incurious eyes upon the strange evolutions of the ship. Yet, by that peculiar affinity which freely floating bodies have at sea, the ship and boat were surely drawing nearer each other, until Tom suddenly awoke as if from a trance to find that they were so close to the ship that a strong swimmer might easily gain her side. The discovery gave him the needed shock to arouse his small store of vital energy, and, turning to his companion, he said—his voice sounding strange and far away—" Doc, rouse up! Here's the ship! Right on top of us, man!" But for some minutes the negro seemed past all effort, beyond hearing, only known to be living by his position. Desperate now, Tom scrambled towards him, and in a sudden fever of excitement shook, beat, and pinched him. No response. Then, as if maddened by the failure of his efforts, the boy seized one of the big black hands that lay so nervelessly, and, snatching it to his mouth, bit a finger to the bone. A long dry groan came from the cook as he feebly pulled his hand away, and mechanically thrust the injured finger into his mouth. The trickling blood revived him, his dull eyes brightened, and looking up he saw the ship close alongside. Without a word he stooped and plunged his hands into the water on either side the dory, paddling fiercely in the direction of the ship, while Tom immediately followed his example. Soon they bumped her side, and as she rolled slowly towards them, Tom seized the chain-plates and clung limpet-like for an instant, then, with one supreme effort, hauled himself on board and fell, fainting but safe, on her deck.

When he returned to life again, his first thought was of his chum, and great was his peace to find that the cook had also gained safety. He lay near, stretched out listlessly upon the timber, with which the vessel's deck was completely filled, rail-high, fore and aft. Feebly, like some decrepit old man, Tom rose to his knees and shuffled towards the cook, finding that he was indeed still alive, but sleeping so soundly that it seemed doubtful whether waking would be possible. Reassured by finding the cook living, the boy dragged himself aft, wondering feebly how it was that he saw no member of this large vessel's crew. He gained the cabin and crawled below, finding everything in disorder, as if she had been boarded by pirates and ravaged for anything of value that might be concealed. She seemed a staunch, stout, frigate-built ship, of some eleven or twelve hundred tons register, English built, but Norwegian owned; and to a seaman's eye there was absolutely no reason why she should thus be tumbling unguided about the Atlantic—there was no visible cause to account for her abandonment. Aloft she was in a parlous condition. The braces having been left unbelayed, her great yards had long been swinging to and fro with every thrust of the wind and roll of the ship, until it was a marvel how they still hung in their places at all. Most of the sails were in rags, the unceasing grind and wrench of the swinging masses of timber to which they were secured having been too much for their endurance, and their destruction once commenced, the wind had speedily completed it.

All this, requiring so long to tell, was taken in by the lad in a few seconds, but his first thought was for food and drink wherewith to revive his comrade. He was much disappointed, however, to find that not only was the supply of eatables very scanty, but the quality was vile beyond comment—worse than even that of some poverty-stricken old British tub provisioned at an auction sale of condemned naval stores. The best he could do for Jem was to soak some of the almost black biscuit in water until soft, and then, hastening to his side, he roused the almost moribund man, and gently coaxed him to eat, a morsel at a time, until, to his joy, he found the poor darky beginning to take a returning interest in life. Fortunately for them, the weather held fine all that day and night, relieving them from anxiety about handling the big vessel, and by morning they were both sufficiently themselves again to set about the task of getting her under control. A little at a time they reduced the chaotic web of gear aloft to something like its original systematic arrangement, and under such sail as was still capable of being set they began to steer to the south-westward. In this, as in everything else now, the boy took the lead, for Jem had never set foot upon a square-rigged ship before, and even his schooner experience had been confined to the galley. But Tom had spent his three years at sea entirely in large square-rigged ships, and, being a bright observant lad, already knew more about them and their manipulation than many sailor-men learn all their lives. He it was who set the course, having carefully watched the direction steered from Gloster by the hapless Rufus B., and now he judged that a reversal of it would certainly bring them within hail of the American seaboard again, if they could hold on it long enough. So all day long the two toiled like beavers to make things aloft more shipshape, letting the vessel steer herself as much as possible, content if she would only keep within four points of her course. With all their labours they could not prevent her looking like some huge floating scarecrow that had somehow got adrift from its native garden and wandered out to sea. Her appearance simply clamoured for interference by any passing ship in trumpet tones had one entered the same horizon, but much to the youngster's wonder, and presently to his secret delight, not a sail hove in sight day after day.

Thus a fortnight passed away satisfactorily enough but for the wretched food and the baffling winds, that would not permit them to make more than a meagre handful of miles per day towards the land, and worried Tom not a little with the idea that perhaps the Gulf Stream might be sweeping them steadily eastward at a much greater rate than they were able to sail west. But he did not whisper a syllable of his fears to his shipmate in case of disheartening that docile darky, whom even now he often caught wistfully looking towards him, as if for some further comfort. He himself was full of high hopes, building a fantastic mental edifice upon the prospect of being able to make the land unaided, and therefore becoming entitled not only to the glory of a great exploit in ship-handling but also to the possession of a fortune, as he knew full well his share of the salvage of this ship would be. For although she contained but a cheap cargo of lumber, yet from her size and seaworthiness she was worth a very large sum could she be brought into port without further injury, her hull being, as sailors say, "as tight as a bottle"—that is, she leaked not at all. But both the shipmates were puzzled almost to distraction to account for a vessel in her condition being abandoned. Nearly every spare moment in which they could be together was devoted to the discussion of this mystery, and dark Jem showed a most fertile inventiveness in bringing out new theories, none of which, however, could throw the slightest glimmer of explanation upon the subject. Except that from the disorder of the cabin and fo'c'sle, and the absence of the boats, with their lashings left just as they had been hacked adrift, there was no other clue to the going of her crew; and, if, as was probable, the deserters had afterwards been lost by the swamping of their frail craft, this mystery was but another item in the long list of unravelled sea-puzzles.

But one evening the sun set in a lowering red haze, which, though dull like a dying fire, stained the oily-looking sea as if with stale blood. The feeble uncertain wind sank into fitful breaths, and at last died completely away. Gigantic masses of gloomy cloud came into being, apparently without motion of any kind, marshalling their vast formlessness around the shrinking horizon. As the last lurid streaks faded out of the sky, and utter darkness enfolded them, the two lonely wanderers clung together, as if by the touch of each other's living bodies to counteract the benumbing effect of the terrible quiet. Deeper, denser grew the darkness, heavier grew the burden of silence, until at the thin cry of a petrel out of the black depths their hearts felt most grateful. It was like a tiny message telling them that the world was not yet dead. A sudden, hissing spiral of blue flame rent the clouds asunder, and immediately, as if it leaped upon them through the jagged cleft in that grim barrier, the gale burst. Wind, lightning, thunder, rain; all joined in that elemental orchestra, with ever-increasing fury of sound as they smote upon the amazed sea, as if in angry scorn of its smoothness. In the midst of that tremendous tumult the two chums were powerless—they dared not move from the helm, even though, with yards untrimmed, their presence there was useless. But, in some curious freak of the neglected vessel, she flung her head off the wind farther and farther until the boy suddenly snatched at hope again, and spun the wheel round to assist her. Off she went before the wind like a hunted thing, and knowing it was their only chance for life, the two friends laboured to keep her so. It was so dark that they could not see anything aloft, so that they did not know how far the small amount of sail on her when the gale burst still remained; but that mattered little, since they were powerless in any case. But they stuck to their steering, caring nothing for the course made as long as she could be kept before the gale. And in the bitter grey of the morning they saw a graceful shape, dim and indefinite, yet near, that reminded them painfully of their late vessel and her hapless crew. The shadowy stranger drew nearer, until, with thumping hearts, they recognized one of the schooners belonging to that daring, hardy service, the New York Pilots. Rushing to the side, Tom waved his arms, for they were now so close together that he could see the figures grouped aft. With consummate seamanship, the schooner was manœuvred towards the ship until so close that three men sprang from her rail into the ship's mizzen rigging. Few words passed, but leaving one of their number at the wheel, the other two worked like giants to get a little sail set, while the schooner, shaking out a reef, bounded ahead to bespeak steam aid.

With such assistance, the troubles of the two wanderers were now at an end, and in less than thirty hours they were snugly anchored in New York harbour, with a blazing fire in the galley and a Christian meal before them. At the Salvage Court, held soon after, their share came to $7,000, equally divided between the two of them, the pilot crew receiving $3,000 for their two days' work. Feeling like millionaires, they hurried back to Gloster, fully agreed to do what they could for the benefit of their late shipmates' bereaved ones, and handing over to the authorities for that purpose on their arrival half of their gains. Then Jem, declaring that he had seen all he wanted of fishing, opened a small oyster saloon in Gloster, while Tom, aided by the advice of a gentleman who was greatly interested in the whole story, entered himself at Columbia College. He will be heard of again.

THE END